A DARK GOTHIC

Firethorne

NIKKI J SUMMERS

Copyright Material
Firethorne
This book is a work of fiction. Names, characters, businesses, places, events, and incidents are either the product of the author's imagination or used in a fictitious manner. Any resemblance to actual events or persons, living or dead, is purely coincidental.

Any trademarks, product names, or names featured are assumed to be the property of their respective owners and are used for reference only. No AI has been used in the writing or cover art for this book.

Copyright 2024 by Nikki J Summers.
All rights reserved. No part of this work may be reproduced, scanned, or distributed in any print or electronic form without the express written consent of the author. A CIP record of this book is available from the British Library.

Edited by: Lindsey Powell & Caroline Stainburn
Interior designed and formatted by: Designs By Charly
Cover Designer: Designs By Charly

Blurb

They told me Firethorne would be my salvation, but all I found were sinners hiding inside those walls.

Firethorne is a place best viewed from afar. Strangers aren't welcome in the dark, gothic mansion. A mansion steeped in twisted myths and urban legends. No one really knows the truth about Firethorne or its elusive family. If they did, they'd realise the reality is far worse than any of the secrets they've heard whispered in the town.

When Maya Cole's father falls on hard times, everything seems hopeless, until the day he's given a lifeline.
A live-in post at the Firethorne estate...
For him and his daughter.

He thinks all their prayers have been answered.
But Maya is no fool.
She knows to be careful what you wish for.
And after meeting the Firethornes, she learns that wishes sometimes turn into nightmares.

Devilishly beguiling and wickedly corrupt, they try to pull her into their games of lies and deceit.
But with Maya, they soon learn, what they can't have, they can't resist.
Which only makes the chase even sweeter.

But they're not the only ones chasing her.

Someone else is lurking in the shadows.
Watching...
Waiting...
Biding their time...
Ready to show her that the devil you know isn't always the one you should trust.

Firethorne is a dark, gothic, standalone romance. It is intended for readers 18 years and over. Please take note of the trigger warning at the beginning of the book before starting this journey.

Playlist

Available to download on Spotify
https://open.spotify.com/playlist/5kPcOuZONd7uHNa3uX3nFy?si=DdXzuAtyQRChGJJ8SOPLmg&pi=e-1pW2HQ6FTJuE

Waiting for the Night – Depeche Mode
The Killing Moon – Echo & the Bunnymen
Only Happy When It Rains – Garbage
How Soon Is Now? (2011 Remaster) – The Smiths
Connection – Elastica
Halo – Depeche Mode
Devil Inside – INXS
Setting Sun (Radio Edit) – The Chemical Brothers
6 Underground – Sneaker Pimps
Kool-Aid – Bring Me The Horizon
Hit – The Sugarcubes
Lullaby (Remastered) – The Cure
Going Under – Evanescence
Take Me Back To Eden – Sleep Token
She's A Star – James
Never Tear Us Apart – INXS
The Scientist – Coldplay
Tattoo – Loreen
you should see me in a crown – Billie Eilish
Dusk Till Dawn (feat. Sia – Radio Edit) – ZAYN, Sia
Wings - Birdy

Trigger Warning

Firethorne contains dark and disturbing situations and references that some readers may find triggering. Please see the list below for details, and feel free to reach out to the author for further clarification.

It is also written in British English; therefore, the spelling and grammar will differ from American English.

- Stalking
- Sexual harassment
- Guilt and gaslighting from a parent
- Discussion of suicide
- Seeing a body hung (following a hanging that isn't described on page)
- Group sex
- Double penetration
- Use of date rape drugs
- Non-consensual sex but not with the FMC
- Voyeurism
- Abduction
- Drugging
- Kidnapping
- Captivity
- Trafficking
- Non-consensual sexual medical examination
- Graphic violence and torture
- Non-consensual oral sex
- Biting
- Consensual sex scenes
- Cum kink
- Anal play
- Knife play (Not the pointy end)
- Interesting ways to use yoghurt
- Death
- Shooting

For all the readers who love red flags and invisible strings.
This one's for you
x

One
MAYA

"I know we made the right decision," my father said, smiling absent-mindedly as we sat in the dimly lit carriage of the night train. "Leaving that town and taking this job, it's the best thing that could've happened to us. It'll be a fresh start. Just what we need."

I let the steady beat of the track beneath us and the gentle sway of the train lull me into a false sense of security. But my mind echoed troubling words that refused to be silenced.

Where are we going?
Why is my stomach in knots?
What will we find at the end of this journey?

Firethorne

That inner voice, changing from a whisper to a roar, became more persistent as it tried to drown out the other noises around me.

Like a mantra on repeat that mimicked the rhythm of the train.

A chant that became a warning the longer it went on.

This feels wrong.
This feels wrong.
This feels wrong.

But I'd never say the words out loud. I couldn't, despite them clinging to the tip of my tongue. I didn't want to rain on my father's parade.

There'd been enough rain clouds darkening our lives.

Clouds he didn't deserve.

Neither of us did.

Instead, I closed my eyes for a moment and tried to block out the taunting voices in my head, smiling as I replied, "It'll be great. You're right. It'll be just what we need," faking sunshine as I envisioned those clouds drifting away.

Admitting that I was devastated to say goodbye to the town I'd grown up in, and the only life I'd known seemed selfish.

My father had hit rock bottom.

If this move brought him out of his pit of despair, then it was a small price to pay.

And I couldn't bear to lose him, not after everything we'd been through.

My mother had died when I was eight years old. To say my father took it badly was an understatement. He'd started drinking, his mental health plummeted, and for him, life held no meaning without her. I was devastated about her death too, but watching my remaining parent decline in front of my eyes, knowing I could lose him as well, totally shattered me.

One of my most vivid childhood memories was the time I stayed home from school because my father was so drunk he'd passed out on the bathroom floor.

I missed the school bus to stay at home and watch him. To make sure he didn't stop breathing as he lay on the tiles curled up in a ball.

When he was sick, I cleaned it up. I knew he couldn't do it himself.

When he woke and started to cry, I held him and told him it'd be okay.

And when school rang, asking where I was, I pretended to be the grandmother I'd never met and told them I was sick.

He doesn't remember any of it, and I'd never want him to, but it's scorched into my mind.

I'll never forget it.

I lost both parents on the day my mother died, but I fought to get one of them back.

Back then, after hitting rock bottom, my father managed to build himself back up. He sought counselling and started working, and life became steadier, more manageable. He'd found purpose in living, and slowly, so did I.

Until the day it all came crashing down.

So, where did it all go wrong?

My father's problem was he'd always listened to the wrong people. He was a financial advisor who took the worst advice. And after a few misguided business dealings, placing trust where it shouldn't have been placed and thinking he was savvier than he was, my father lost it all. Our money, his clients' money, his job, our home, and our standing in a community that was fickle and fierce in their revulsion of how far we'd fallen. They couldn't turn their backs on us fast enough. We were discarded like last week's newspaper. Left on the rubbish heap of life. Learning the hard way that the people we'd had in our lives only wanted us around if it benefited them.

Because after everything fell apart, they didn't want to know us.

Firethorne

They crossed the street to avoid us. If bad luck was catching, like a virus, we were riddled with it, and they avoided us like the plague. Nobody wanted to help, but that was okay, we were used to the hard knocks of life. In my opinion, it'd always been the two of us against the world.

I was the only one who knew what'd happened to him in the years after Mum died.

But I had to admit, I was scared out of my mind, that after this latest catastrophe, he'd turn to the bottle. I couldn't bear the thought of losing him again to drink.

Creditors had turned up on our doorstep. They took everything we owned, leaving us with a few worthless belongings and the clothes on our backs.

The dire reality of our situation also meant I couldn't continue with my studies. I needed to go out and earn money too. I couldn't let my father face this alone.

So, I told my professors at the university that I wouldn't be returning the following term. It broke my heart to leave, but what else could I do? I couldn't afford to be there. I needed to be with my father and help him through this. I wanted to make sure he didn't fall victim to his demons again.

"We have a hardship fund set up to help students just like yourself, Maya," my English Literature tutor had stated, hope flickering in his eyes. "The Earnshaw Scholarship was created especially for cases like yours," he went on, but I didn't listen. I switched off as he explained the ins and outs of the fund, begging me to apply.

But there was no hope, and I didn't want false promises.

When he'd finished, I thanked him and took the necessary forms. But the minute I left his office, I put them straight in the bin. Hardship funds might cover the cost of tuition fees, maybe housing. But what about food and basic needs?

I wasn't going to beg anyone.

I would make my own way in this life.

And I might be leaving my studies behind now, but it wouldn't be forever. I'd find my way back one day.

And then, last week, everything changed.

The dark clouds that were circling, suffocating the life from us, lifted when my father announced that all our prayers had been answered.

He'd been offered a job.

A live-in post on an estate owned by a wealthy family.

My father would become the estate manager in exchange for board and lodgings. I'd never heard of the family, and when I questioned him, trying to find out more about his new, infamous—according to him—employees, his answers were vague and non-committal.

Google was no better. Their names were listed on a few business websites, but no photographs, no social media. Nothing. They were ghosts in an age where nothing and no one could hide from the world.

It made me wary.

I wasn't stupid. And I struggled not to doubt my father's judgment after everything that'd happened with his bankruptcy. But I couldn't deny the news that someone wanted him after all he'd been through had put a smile on his face, and that was worth more than anything to me, because it gave him hope. It had restored his pride.

Maybe, in a few years, when we'd gotten ourselves into a better position, I'd go back to university and have the life I'd always dreamed of. But for now, I had to accept the life we were living. I had to try and make the best of it. I had to be there for him.

I continued questioning him, though, because that was my job as his meddling, well-meaning daughter. And he just kept on reiterating that I should be praying to every God there was because they hadn't just offered my father a position, they'd agreed to take me on, too. To do what, I had no idea. But it can't have been much, seeing as I hadn't even met the family or done any form of interview. But apparently, they were happy to take us as we were.

Yes.

There were red flags flying everywhere.

Who employs someone they've never met?

But when all was said and done, what choice did I have? I had to go with him. I couldn't let him go alone, he meant too much to me, and he was adamant about taking the job.

I stared blankly at the dark fields and stormy night skies that rolled past as we sat on the train. Rain hammered against the window, rivulets racing across the glass that broke into smaller branches, crawling and spiking like roots of a watery plant that eventually withered and died in front of my eyes. I placed my fingertip on the cold glass and began to trace the fractured lines, all the while wondering why, with everything we'd been through lately, I hadn't shed a single tear.

Not one.

Had I really become hardened to this life?

"I'm sorry you had to leave home and university," my father said quietly, probably picking up on my seemingly well-hidden reluctance. Or at least, I'd thought it was well-hidden. "But I know, in time, we'll come to see it was for the best. I'm your father and I need to take care of you. Opportunities like this don't come along every day. We have to grab them with both hands. Seize the day."

My father went on about how lucky we were to get a second chance at life. He didn't see the irony in his words. I hadn't even had a first chance. But I let him speak as I stared blindly out of the window, watching the spidery, watery veins as the train carriage swayed us back and forth like it was trying to rock some sense into this crazy situation we found ourselves in.

"They're well respected, you know," he continued. "They'll

make excellent employers. We're lucky to get a foot in. Just think about all the doors this could open for you, Maya."

I hummed in response, but I was reserving judgement until I'd actually met these people, even though my father seemed to think they were the best thing since sliced bread.

"Apparently," my father went on, drumming his fingers on the table to try and expel some of his nervous energy. "The estate is the largest in the county. It dates back to the Victorian era. It was originally built in eighteen thirty-four. And it's a grade-two listed building."

"Really?" I replied, my voice flat, emotionless, but responding all the same. "That sounds exciting."

"There's eighteen bedrooms," he added proudly.

Slowly, I turned to face him. The lights from the carriage gave his ragged, hope-filled face a gentle, ethereal glow, and I smiled wryly. "Great. I'll enjoy cleaning those every day."

He blanched at my cutting remark.

"It might start out as cleaning, but who knows where it'll lead? The Firethorne family have a lot of businesses in their portfolio. A lot of influence. Firethorne could be the stepping stone to something much greater for you, Maya."

Firethorne.

The name of the house that my father and I were going to live and work at for the foreseeable future.

It was also the name of the family who owned it.

A name that I was starting to realise held significance for people around here, and maybe not in a positive way.

The train we were on was practically empty. Only one other man was sitting in our carriage on the opposite side to us, just a little way down, with his head stuck in a newspaper. A stranger dressed in a black suit and tie, looking weary, like he was on his way home after a gruelling day at the office. But when my father mentioned the name Firethorne, I noticed how he reacted.

Firethorne

Startled.

Then apprehension.

Followed by revulsion.

He turned his nose up like the carriage had suddenly been filled with a bad smell, and he furrowed his brow, shaking the newspaper in his hands as he cleared his throat, doing a terrible job of looking unaffected.

Then, slowly, he lifted his gaze from his paper and pinned me with a stare that sent chills of ice darting through my veins. A warning stare, like he'd gut me right here, right now for being associated with that family. I held his gaze, refusing to show an ounce of fear, and eventually, he relented, dipping his head to refocus on his reading. But he kept the scowl on his face.

His throat bobbed as he swallowed, and I half expected him to mutter something under his breath, but he didn't. He just buried his head in his paper, pretending he wasn't eavesdropping on what my father was saying.

But he was.

And that didn't sit right with me, because I didn't trust this man. His presence set me on edge. He pretended to read, but his jaw was clenched, and his demeanour was guarded and hostile as he sat upright in his seat, noting every word my father said. He obviously knew a lot more about the Firethornes than we did, judging by the visceral effect their name had on him.

"Mr Firethorne is one of the most respected and accomplished men in the county," my father announced, oblivious to the man across the aisle from us, and I found myself blocking him out, focusing on our fellow passenger; beads of sweat glistened on his brow as his jaw ticked with irritation. He began folding his newspaper and fidgeting in his seat impatiently as my father went on with his diatribe of praise.

Then the man stood up, his eyes fixed straight ahead as he

focused on the exit, grabbing the handrails to steady himself because the train was still moving, and we were miles away from the next stop.

I could hear my father's voice ringing in my ears, but I ignored him, watching the passenger make his way down the aisle of the carriage towards us, but refusing to make eye contact. The train veered to the left, and he lost his footing close to where we were, bumping into my seat before he muttered, "I'm so sorry," and awkwardly stumbled past.

I turned, peering over my shoulder as he walked through the door at the end of the aisle, heading into the neighbouring carriage to ours. Then, I faced forward again, and that's when I noticed a scrap of paper lying in my lap.

Paper that the stranger had dropped.

Discreetly, I picked it up, cupping it in the palm of my hand so my father wouldn't see it, and slowly, I opened it to find three words that'd been hastily scribbled down.

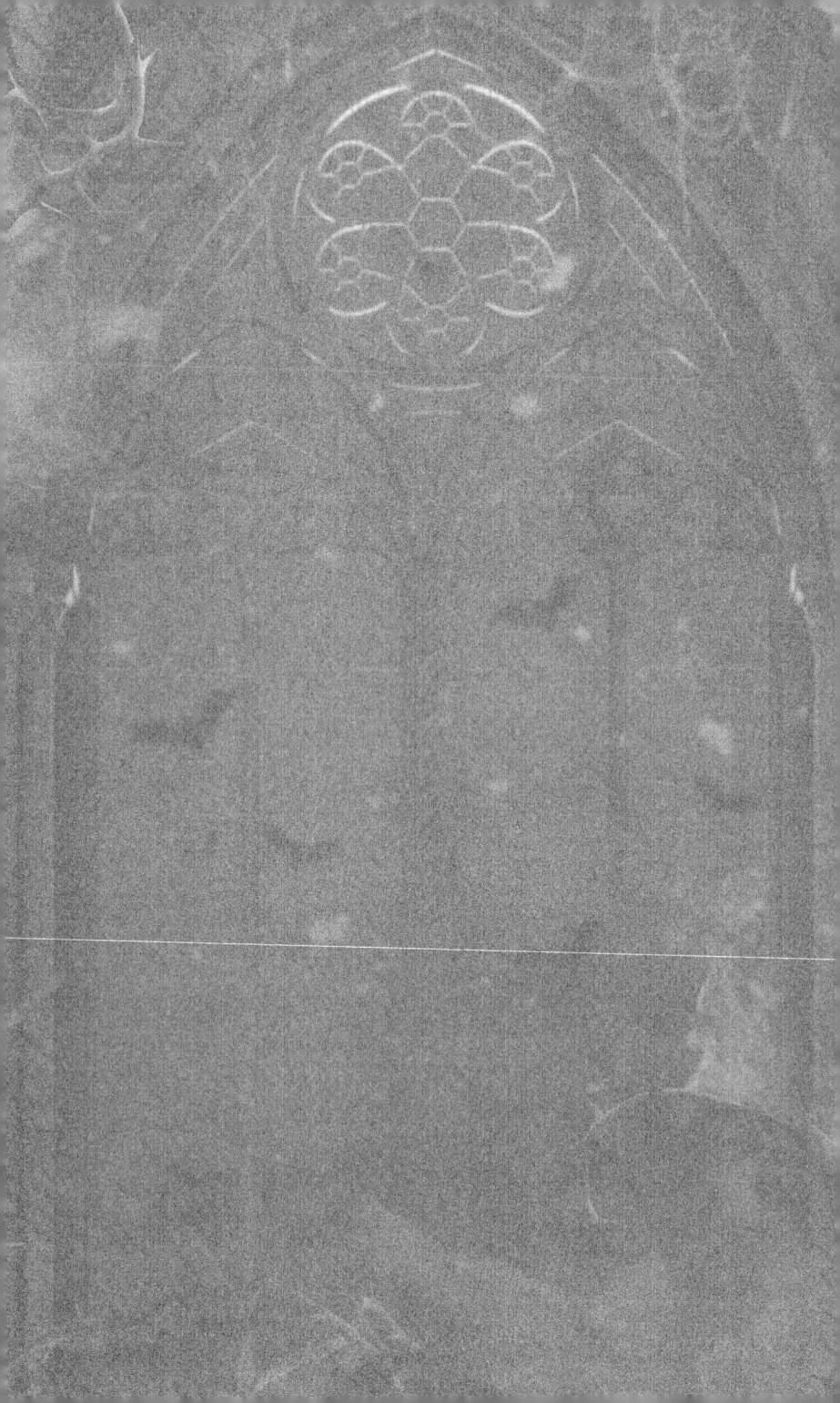

Two

MAYA

Trust no one.

That's what the note said.

Fear and dread flooded my system, my already chilled veins froze as my stomach rolled, and instantly, I screwed the message up. But I didn't want to throw it away. Something deep inside told me to hold onto it. So, I slid it into my jacket pocket, and stood up, telling my father, "I'll be right back," as I strode forward, following the passenger as he headed into the next carriage, intent on finding him and asking him what he meant, what he knew.

Why was he hellbent on giving me that note?

Firethorne

I opened the carriage door and walked into the next part of the train, but I couldn't see him anywhere. He wasn't here. He'd moved on.

I stalked the length of the train to try and find him, but he was nowhere to be seen. It was as if he'd evaporated into thin air.

If it wasn't for the scrap of paper sitting safely in my pocket, I might've questioned what I saw or whether he'd even existed. But he had, and his note, that he'd haphazardly dropped into my lap, had been a warning. A warning that made all the red flags I'd been seeing fly higher. But at this point, I knew trying to talk my father out of this was pointless. It was too late. We were already on the train, and his heart was set on this move. I didn't want to be the one to break it.

So, I kept that note in my pocket. Kept the words at the forefront of my mind, and I swore I would protect us from a fall this time.

I would be on my guard.

Always.

After what we'd been through, I didn't trust anyone. Only my father. And that's why I was standing by him now.

"Are you okay?" my father asked as I approached our seats and sat back down, trying not to show any hint of fear on my face.

"I needed to stretch my legs," I replied, smiling, and then I turned to look out of the window, trying not to show that I was feeling any sort of way. And he nodded, happy with my explanation.

I wasn't happy though, and after a breath, I couldn't stop myself from asking, "Are you sure this is the right thing? I mean, we know nothing about this family. How do we know we can trust them? What if we're walking into some kind of trap?"

My father scoffed. "What trap? I've told you everything you

need to know about the Firethornes. This is going to be good for us. You need to trust me, Maya."

There it was again.

Trust.

That word was starting to haunt me.

I'd asked him about the family multiple times.

I'd questioned him until I was blue in the face.

But the response was always the same.

They were a family with a proud reputation. A private family. One that was revered and respected. A family that my father knew very little about, judging from the sweeping statements of their standing and wealth. I tried to dig below the surface, but it was pointless. I knew I'd have to wait and see for myself. And sitting on the train, I still stood by that decision, paper warnings or not. My father was adamant he was going to do this, so I would support him. He was vulnerable and he needed me.

"I do trust you," I told him. "It's other people I don't trust."

My father smiled sadly and patted my knee. "It's been a tough time. I know that. But it's all going to be okay now." Then he moved his hands to his lap, wringing them nervously as he stared straight ahead. "The estate sounds perfect. The main house backs on to a beautiful lake. Just think about taking a morning stroll around there." He sighed wistfully, staring blindly into space, like he was marvelling at an ethereal image of the grand estate he'd already fallen in love with but never seen in real life. "Or a run." He turned to smile at me again, warmth radiating from his face. "I know how much you love your morning runs."

"Let's hope it's not a run for our lives then, hey?" I remarked, but he ignored me, still lost to his dreams as he added, "I'll need to read up on the different wildlife, the vegetation, all of the trees and flowers. I need to get this right."

I let out a slow breath and let my head fall back against the headrest, closing my eyes as I replied, "I'm sure you'll be fine. You always do a good job; whatever it is you're doing."

Only, he hadn't, had he? He hadn't done the best job as a financial advisor. He'd lost everything.

A good reputation is the easiest thing to lose and the hardest thing to rebuild. We were learning that the hard way.

"You should always take pride in your work," he responded, but I was too bone tired, too weary to reply. Pride in your work meant honour, too. Honesty. Things he'd sometimes managed to forget along the way.

Trust no one.

Those words echoed, resounding in my head, but I ignored them, for now, and reached out my hand to take his.

"It's going to be okay," I said. "This *will* be a new beginning for us."

They were the words he wanted to hear. Saying anything else at this moment in time was pointless, even I knew that. We were about to embark on something, and what that was I had no idea.

He squeezed my hand and gave me a warm smile that was too jovial, too elated for the unknown we were heading into.

"You're right. We have employment, food to eat, a roof over our heads. What more could we possibly need?"

Three

MAYA

It was dark by the time the train pulled into the station. Wearily, we stepped off the train, both of us carrying our own well-worn suitcases. The wind whistled down the station, cutting right through my coat, jeans, and black T-shirt, making me shiver as my teeth chattered. But at least the rain had subsided. Thank heavens for small mercies.

My father buttoned up his old suit jacket, but I could tell it did nothing to ward off the chill of the night air as he breathed warm breath into his cupped hand. So, we walked a little faster to counteract the cold.

Waiting ahead on the empty platform, we noticed a dark-haired man in a black suit, overcoat, and black leather gloves holding up a card with my father's name on it. With confident strides, we walked over to him, and he glared back at us, his gaze sweeping up and down as his lip curled ever so slightly to show he was less than impressed with who he was faced with. And then he announced plainly, "Arthur Cole, I presume," and without waiting for a response, he barked, "Follow me."

His clipped and condescending tone only amplified the warnings blaring in my ears. But we followed him all the same.

He led us into a dark car park to a black Bentley parked in a quiet corner. The boot of the car opened, and we placed our suitcases in as he looked on with a bite of irritation. Then he got into the driver's side as we let ourselves into the back seat. There were no airs and graces here. He wasn't going to open the doors for us.

"It's so kind of Mr Firethorne to send a car for us," my father said, by way of a thank you and to break the tense atmosphere.

"Mr Firethorne's generosity knows no bounds," the driver replied drolly and with a hint of sarcasm. And when I peered up at the driver's rearview mirror, I could see his pointed stare glaring right back at me. Dark eyes that were narrowed, harsh and judgemental. Dipped, furrowed eyebrows as he frowned, like he was trying to figure out why *I* was here in this car. That he didn't think I belonged.

"That's what I've heard," my father replied, and I shifted in my seat, trying to ignore the butterflies fluttering wildly in my stomach.

Trust no one.

We left the car park and drove in an awkward silence for about twenty minutes through narrow country lanes. In the darkness, we could see the trees lining the roads, hanging low, closing in on us, like the spindly fingers of death looming down, ready to clutch us in their grasp and drag us to hell.

The reflection of the moon and the car headlights were the

only things lighting our way, and with each twist and turn of the road, I felt my insides buckle and contort as we headed further into the abyss. It felt like the journey to hell, and we all know what they say about the road to hell. Yes, my father had good intentions, but where exactly *were* they leading us?

Eventually, the car slowed as we turned into a driveway, stopping in front of tall, black, wrought-iron gates that looked precocious, austere, and wholly uninviting. And at the top, welded ornately into the swirls of the gate, was the name 'Firethorne'.

The driver, who still hadn't given us his name, pressed a button on the dashboard, and the gates began to move. Once fully open, he drove on, heading down the driveway that was lined with old Victorian streetlamps. I peered out of the window, surprised to find the land was relatively sparse and barren. Granted, it was nighttime, so my ability to fully assess the situation was limited, but they weren't the well-tended gardens I'd expected from what my father had told me. There were trees and wild bushes, but nothing that stood out. Nothing grand like I'd expected.

As the house came into view, I craned my neck, peering through the window to see it.

Firethorne was an imposing, gothic mansion that stood two stories high and was easily the length of a football field, probably longer. The windows and doors had pointed archways above them, and spires along the roof that gave it an old church feel. Even though it was dark, only a few windows were lit up from inside. It barely looked lived in, there seemed to be no life in the place. It was sinister, eerie, and altogether disturbing.

The driver swung the car around the circular driveway, past a fountain that appeared to have fallen angels or some kind of winged demons inside, and headed for the main steps to the house. Steps that were flanked at the bottom by two gargoyles that looked like horned little goblins, sneering at visitors like us as we pulled up in front of the building.

Most houses of this scale had something grand at the entrance, like lions, to signify power, but not this family. Seems they were more interested in warding off evil spirits, seeing as that was the purpose of a gargoyle. Although, why they had them on the ground puzzled me. Usually, gargoyles were carved into a building, acting as a clear warning for anyone approaching from a distance. Perhaps this family expected their threats to be walking straight through the front door.

Maybe we weren't going to get the warm welcome my father had hoped for.

The welcome that I knew was probably wishful thinking on his part.

Trust no one.

The driver cut the engine, removed his gloves, draped them over the steering wheel, and then opened his door. We opened ours too, and I stepped out, following the driver to the rear of the car, watching as he went to lift out our cases from the boot. I made a grab for mine at the same time as him, and his cold, callused hand pushed mine away as he scowled at me.

"I can carry my own stuff in," I griped, expecting him to let it go, but he didn't.

Instead, he snapped, "It's my job," before lifting the two pitiful suitcases we had with us out of the boot. All the time, he stared down at me with a stony expression that showed he wasn't all that impressed with the newly hired help he'd brought to Firethorne tonight.

I spun on my heels as he pushed past me and walked up the steps. One deep breath in and another out, and then I followed him, my eyes boring into his back, hoping he'd trip over as my father kept in step beside me, huffing and puffing his way up the steps.

The driver pushed open the doors of the mansion and a

waft of warm air hit us.

I was surprised.

I'd expected the interior to be as cold and foreboding as it was on the outside.

But as we stepped into the grand entrance, with its sweeping staircase, wood-panelled walls, and huge stained-glass windows, I gave an involuntary shiver. Despite the initial comforting warmth, I felt a chill when I saw the tall, menacing figure that waited for us at the foot of the stairs.

Four

THE FIRETHORNES
DAMIEN, LYSANDER, AND MIRIAM

"It looks like your new pets are here," Miriam purred as she stood in front of the drawing room window in her cream, tightly fitted, designer pantsuit.

Her long blonde hair flowed down her back, glistening as it reflected the light from the fireplace. There wasn't a hair out of place because that was who Miriam was, what she wanted the world to see... outward perfection. The inside, however, was a different matter entirely.

She leaned forward, bracing her hands on the windowsill and gave a quiet gasp of anticipation as the car headlights shone in the distance, lighting up the dark grounds of the estate. Then, she tilted her hips seductively and cocked her head to the side as she hummed in approval, watching those headlights creep closer.

Miriam was easy to please.

Just like a cat when you give it a ball of wool to keep it amused. She couldn't wait to start batting and clawing away at the new playthings making their way to the front door.

"I wonder how long these ones will last?" she remarked, and then whipped her head around with a look of disgust as she heard a resounding snort. "What?" she chided. "Like you're any good at keeping staff. Apart from your father's lacky, Beresford, who's driving that car, and Mrs Richardson, who cooks your meals every day, you haven't managed to hold onto a single member of staff for longer than a month." She turned back to focus on the impending arrival. "Maybe you're both losing your touch."

"Or maybe we just don't give a shit and prefer to keep our staff numbers small. Exclusive. Like that club you got thrown out of last weekend," Damien remarked, his demeanour as dark as his jet-black hair, his attitude as cutting as the sour look he always had on his face. He didn't even glance up from the book he was reading as he spoke.

Miriam decided to ignore his cutting remark and barked back, "Or, *Damien dear*, your father is a tight-ass who doesn't pay well enough."

"That too." He shrugged nonchalantly.

She spun around, turning her back to the window so she could face the room head-on with her killer smirk as she said, "Knowing how fussy my two darling cousins are, how everything has to be just right, I'd have thought you'd have pestered daddy dearest to dig a little deeper into his pockets to pay for decent staff. It's not fair to expect Mrs Richardson to pander to your every whim, Damien. Or to clean up all your shit, Lysander. Not to mention the complete mess that seems to follow you both around."

Her narrowed, accusatory stare flickered from her dark, brooding cousin, Damien, to the one who lived his life with sunshine smiles as bright as the blond hair on his head.

Lysander.

The eldest son of Nicholas Firethorne. The one she was always drawn to. But they were both hers, despite what Damien might say to the contrary. Her dark and light angels... or should that be demons?

She took a few steps forward and reached out a hand to stroke Lysander's cheek. "For such pretty boys, I'd have expected you to pile on the charm and make them stay. All those pretty girls right under your roof, ready to do whatever you want." She dropped her arm dramatically and sighed. "But no." She paused, then gave a low chuckle and grinned wickedly. "Scrap that, I'm not surprised at all that they left. In fact, it's a wonder they lasted as long as they did with you scowling at them from the shadows, Damien, using your sharp tongue to nick them every chance you got. And you, Lysander, with your constant demands and over-inflated—"

"I don't have *demands*," Lysander butted in, trying to argue back. "We all have standards here, and mine are no different to both of yours. Don't drag me into your arguments, Miriam."

"Who's arguing?" she replied with a sickly-sweet grin. "All I'm saying is, everyone has their price, but being in your company for any length of time was obviously too high a price for them to pay. My dark and dirty princes of Firethorne." She winked as Lysander scoffed and glowered at her.

Damien flipped the page of his book as he carried on reading, showing he didn't care and wasn't listening at all.

But Miriam ignored them both and stepped back, turning to stare out of the window again.

"Dark and dirty in all the best ways," she hummed to herself. "But they didn't stick around long enough to find out... Lucky for me."

"And you stick around too long," Damien announced drily, his nonchalant act cracking as he bit back.

Miriam flicked her hair from her shoulder, and revelling in the insult and attention, she laughed. "You love having me here. Admit it. I make things... interesting."

"I'll admit, sometimes you make things... mildly amusing. Distracting. As cousins go, you're in our top five," Damien said, but he didn't react or look up from his book as Lysander threw his head back and laughed loudly.

"I'm your *only* cousin," Miriam huffed, totally missing the subtlety of the comment. "Anyway," she went on. "You're both distracting me right now. Look"—she gestured to the car that'd stopped outside beside the steps leading to the front door—"they're about to get out. I love this part."

"They're servants. You're getting way too excited about this," Damien remarked, but she didn't care.

Miriam stayed focused on the driveway, riveted by what was going on outside. "They're an opportunity, is what they are," she mused, her reflection in the dark window showing the glow of her eyes as she contemplated every wicked thing she intended to do while they were here.

"What are you cooking up in that evil, pretty head of yours, Miriam?" Lysander questioned; his eyes boring into her back with a twisted curiosity.

Her responding hum of approval spoke volumes. This one was going to be particularly wicked.

"I'm thinking..." She tapped her finger on her chin in thought. "Something that you're both going to lose your shit over." She glanced over her shoulder and added, "And pretty, yes, but evil? I don't think so." She refocused on the new arrivals outside. "I prefer to think of myself as a puppet master. It isn't my fault evil deeds seem to follow. All I do is... facilitate."

"And what is it you plan on facilitating this time, exactly?"

Damien asked.

Miriam took a moment, and as the sound of car doors opening from below echoed in the room, she gave a little squeal. "Damien, she's just your type."

A cruel chuckle filled the room.

"How do you know, Miriam? Is she mute? Or deaf? Blind, even? Maybe all three," Lysander said, laughing at his own cruel remark.

But his laughter wasn't reciprocated.

"How would you know by looking out of the window if they're deaf, mute, or blind, *brother*?" Damien rolled his eyes, and under his breath, he added, "She'll be your type, too... if she's breathing."

"Pretty girls are always my type," Lysander added.

"And she'll probably still be your type even if she's not breathing," Damien muttered to himself, but loud enough for them to hear.

"I know someone closer to home who might not be breathing soon if he carries on being a complete and utter asshole tonight," Lysander added, growing irritable as he clenched his jaw and moved closer to the window to get a better look.

Miriam ignored the brothers as they started their usual bickering, merely stating, "Damien, you'd see that she's your type if you closed that damn book and got your bloody ass off that chair by the fire to come and look at her."

"But that would require effort on Damien's part, and you know how he struggles to conform," Lysander bit back.

But Miriam wasn't listening.

She didn't care.

All she was bothered about was what was going on outside, as she added, "Long, dark hair. A pale complexion. The type of face that looks... innocent. Ripe for corruption."

Then she gave a slight gasp, and announced, "Would you

look at that, she tried to pick up her own suitcase from the car to carry it inside herself. And look…" She pointed, growing more animated by the second. "I think she's arguing with Beresford about it. The hired help is so brainwashed into serving, they can't switch it off. That's so…" Her voice, that'd been light and airy, changed in an instant. "Pathetic," she sneered.

"Maybe not Damien's type after all," Lysander retorted.

"Oh look." Miriam chuckled. "The old man beside her can barely climb the stairs." She laughed as she turned to stare at her cousins. "What's his position in the house? Because I can tell you now, after a few days of climbing the stairs here, you'll be burying him out the back after his heart gives way." She grinned wickedly and shook her head. "Such a terrible shame."

"I neither know nor care," Damien stated. "They won't be here long."

"But they're here now," Miriam hissed, her eyes growing hazy as her voice became seductive. "And I think we should have a little fun."

Damien snapped his book shut, placed it on the side table and pushed himself out of his chair. With long strides he walked over to the window, and Lysander joined him. Curiosity had gotten the better of them… eventually, and they wanted to see what was going on below, without being detected.

"What kind of fun were you thinking?" Lysander asked as he watched Miriam's new pets walk through the front doors into Firethorne.

Miriam took a step back, as her wicked smile grew wider. And she stared at each of them in turn as she purred seductively, "I might've lied earlier."

"You? Lie?" Damien quirked his brow as he stared back at her. "Now, there's a surprise."

She traced her fingertip along the corners of her mouth like a cat that'd got the cream, devoured it, and would claw the whole world to shreds to find more. "A little bird told me that girl coming to work for you is... special."

Lysander narrowed his eyes in question. "Special how? And what *little bird?*"

"A lady never reveals her sources," Miriam replied. "A little bird is all you need to know. But there's been talk in the village." She stared out the window again, even though there was no one out there now. "Her name's Maya. She's twenty years old. And from what I've heard..." She peered over her shoulder, staring provocatively through her lashes. "She's never been touched."

Both cousins scoffed.

"How would you know that? How would anyone in the village know that?" Lysander replied.

"Like I said," Miriam replied snippily, strolling farther into the room. "I have my sources. Which brings me to the fun I was talking about."

"Go on," Lysander urged, as Damien stayed suspiciously quiet, standing in the shadows of the room, watching and waiting.

Miriam paused, biting the inside of her cheek before she spoke again. "I think we should play a game, have a little bet."

"I think I know where this is going." Damien rolled his eyes and went to walk away, but Miriam put her arm out to stop him.

Damien peered down at where her hand touched him, a hint of disgust on his face, but he stayed still to let Miriam say her piece.

"I'm sure you do, Damien, but at least let me finish. I think you might like my terms."

He waited for her to elaborate, folding his arms over his chest, an air of disinterest emanating from him.

Lysander, on the other hand, stared intently at her, hanging onto her every word.

"I want to see which one of you can trick her into your bed,"

Miriam said, a fire burning within her as she spoke. "Take her virginity. Take whatever you want. You know how much fun it is to play with pets like her."

"Who said we'd need a bed?" Lysander replied. "Give me a wall or a surface and I'm good to go."

Miriam huffed a laugh. "I know exactly how you operate, Lysander, but let's give the girl something pleasant to remember you by. I doubt she's ever felt anything as luxurious as the silk sheets on your bed... or Damien's for that matter."

"You want us to fuck the hired help? And why should we do that?" Damien replied, his clipped, bored tone highlighting how unimpressed he was by the prospect she was presenting to him.

"Because, Damien dear, you thrive under pressure, you love a challenge, and you always have to win. Don't you want to beat your brother? Prove who the best Firethorne is once and for all."

"He won't beat me," Lysander announced, standing a little taller, as if that'd fortify his statement further.

"Won't he, Lysander?" Miriam shot back, playful wickedness twinkling in her eyes. "Why's that, cousin dear?"

"Because once she sees my face, and gets hit with the Lysander Firethorne charm, it'll be game over. She'll be putty in my hands."

"So confident, brother. And yet, so, so wrong," Damien replied.

"Am I?"

Miriam watched the brothers glare at each other, like two lions ready to rip each other's throats out to claim the pride. Then she shrugged, ready to throw her grenade into the mix. "Maybe she's one of those girls that likes the dark-haired, brooding in the shadows, scowling at the world, ready to burn it all to the ground, bad-boy type. Who knows? Maybe she's not into boys at all." She winked, but Lysander ignored the last part.

"She'll be into us. Why wouldn't she? But when she sees me standing behind him, all bets will be off. Remember, I bring the fire; he brings the thorns. I know which one women prefer."

Miriam let out a low chuckle. "Oh, Lysander. Always so confident, so self-assured." And she moved to stand in front of the roaring fire, warming her hands as she said, "The fire in Firethorne. I like it. I don't know how much I believe it, but I like it."

"Seeing is believing, cousin, and when I win this bet, you'll do more than like it."

The flames from the fire reflected a luminous glow on Miriam's conniving, evil grin. A grin that showed she was more than ready for the wicked games that were about to begin.

But not all of them were as excited as she was.

Damien frowned, a dark, brooding glare painted on his face as he said, "If I wanted to fuck the hired help, I would. But I don't want to. You can count me out of this one."

Miriam cocked her eyebrow in surprise. "Throwing in the towel so easily, Damien? What happened to your legendary fighting spirit?"

"I'm saving it for a fight that's actually worth winning."

Miriam huffed, but her eyes glowed with wicked intent. "And being crowned the best Firethorne isn't worth it? Well, if you change your mind, let us know."

"I already have that crown, and I won't change my mind."

"He will," Lysander butted in. "I give him a day."

"Whatever," Miriam purred, dismissing them as she flicked her hand and sauntered across the room. "I say the bet stands for both of you. For all of us, in fact." As she reached the door, she called out, "Come on... let's go out there and meet our new guests. The sooner we start this, the sooner I can prove who's the best."

Firethorne

"Which is me," Lysander replied, making his way across the room to join her.

"In your dreams." Miriam cackled, then added, "Wouldn't it be something, if I managed to beat you both?" She lifted her chin in defiance, and strolled through the door to head out, calling over her shoulder, "May the best man win... or should I say... the best woman."

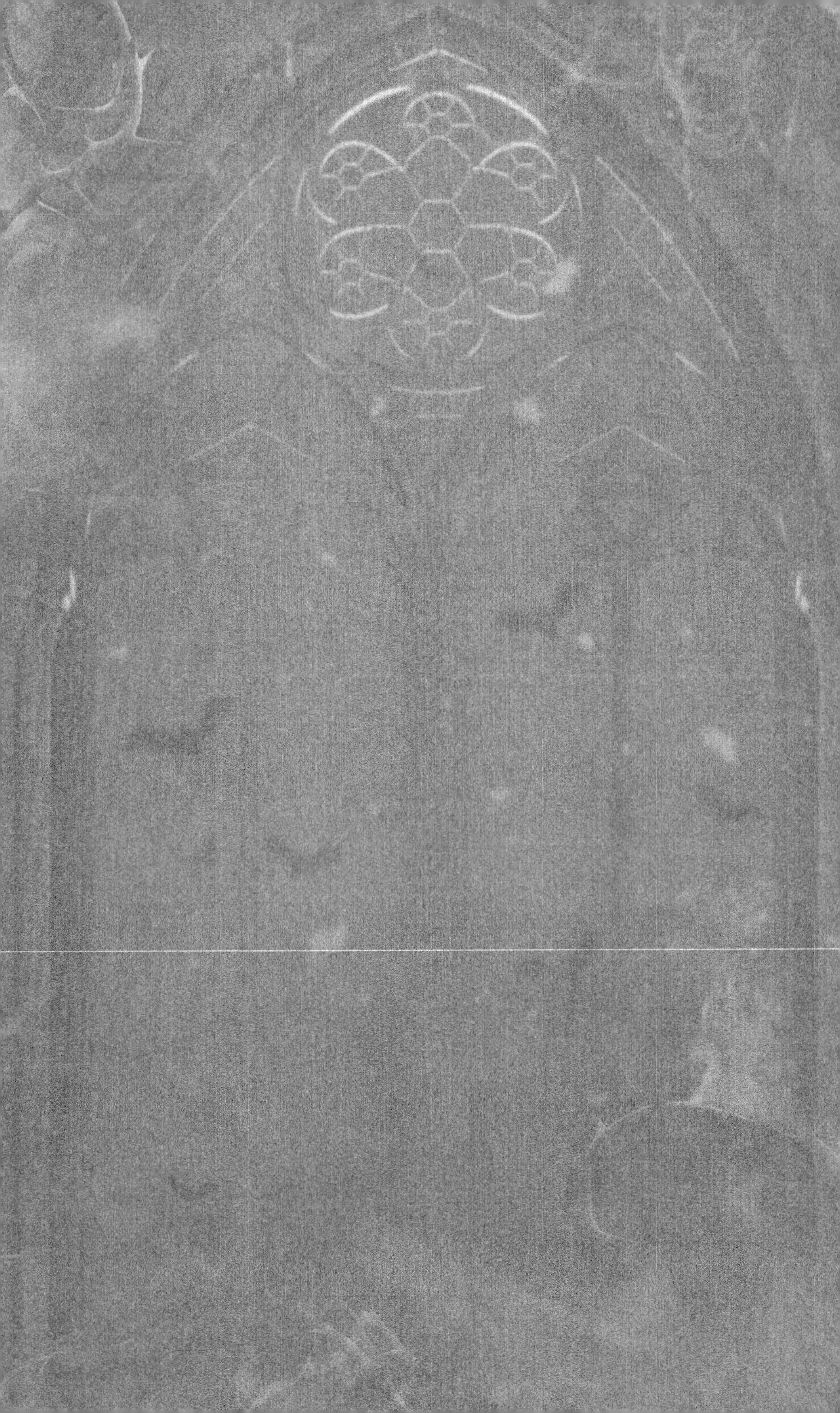

Five

MAYA

"I trust you had a pleasant journey."

The man standing at the foot of the dark, sweeping staircase in the foyer didn't make any effort to come to us, or give us any kind of warm or heartfelt greeting. All he offered were blandly spoken words as he watched us with an unapproving eye. He stood tall. Eerily menacing, some might say. Quietly studying us like we were curiosities. He was keeping his distance, observing everything as we walked into the centre of the foyer.

He was an older man, probably in his late forties, or early fifties. His blond hair was thinning in places, but you could tell from his chiselled, strong jawline and pronounced cheekbones that he'd been attractive once upon a time. He wore a black suit, his face stony and expressionless as the driver placed our cases on the floor beside us and took a step back.

"Thank you, Beresford," the man said, and I turned to see the driver, who'd regarded us with such disdain, bow in acknowledgment.

I could feel the nervous energy radiating from my father beside me, and he stepped forward, offering his hand to this stranger in a jovial manner that was in stark contrast to the chilly reception and dark, gothic surroundings where we stood.

"It's a pleasure to meet you again, Sir," my father gushed. But the *'Sir'* in question, Mr Firethorne, I presumed, just stared at my father's hand, like taking it was the last thing he intended to do, and he couldn't quite believe the audacity of my father in offering it to him in the first place.

"Yes, quite," he replied abruptly, and left my father to drop his hand when he realised a handshake wasn't going to materialise.

I wasn't all that thrilled to be here, a fact I was struggling to keep from the world around me as my brow furrowed and my jaw ticked despite myself. I wanted to be supportive, but I couldn't deny that my father had made a rash decision in coming here, taking up this position in an effort to claw his way back to the polite society he loved so much. A society I wasn't all that keen to rejoin, if I was being completely honest. But right then, I was beyond furious at the audacity of this stuck-up asshole for being so bloody rude to him. Mansion or not, who the fuck did he think he was?

I was about to make a cutting, snide remark about his lack of manners when my father, no doubt guessing what'd happen next, blurted out, "I can't thank you enough, Sir, for giving me... I mean us... this opportunity." My father turned to look at me, a pleading promise whispering in his eyes as he added, "Isn't that right, Maya?"

My mouth opened and closed as I tried to conjure up the words to express what I felt in that moment, without upsetting my father or getting us kicked out of the house before we'd even started.

But I didn't have to worry.

Mr Firethorne beat me to it.

"Ah, yes. The *daughter*," he replied, his voice dripping with condescension.

His dark, piercing eyes fell on me, and I began to retreat into myself, feeling a little smaller. So, I straightened my back in an effort to counteract the effect. I wasn't going to be belittled. Not by anyone.

"She's exactly as you said she would be," he added, and an icy chill sliced through me as he looked me up and down.

A prickle of irritation soon followed, and I glared back at him.

What the hell did that mean?

What had they discussed about me?

And why was he looking at me like I was here for reasons that made my insides crawl?

At that moment, I heard footsteps echoing down the hallway, high heels clicking, and other muted steps from the highly polished wooden floors. I watched as three figures emerged from the dark corridor to the left of the staircase, and Mr Firethorne turned his head to acknowledge their presence, but his demeanour remained as cold as ever.

"And here they are," he announced apathetically. "My beloved family." Then, addressing them, he remarked, "I'm so glad you could tear yourselves away from whatever mindless pursuits you young people do these days to come and greet our new employees."

The three of them stepped into the light—two men dressed

in dark suits, and a girl around my age in a smart cream pantsuit that fitted her like a second skin.

"This"—Mr Firethorne gestured to the man standing directly beside him—"is my eldest son, Lysander." His face softened a little as he said his name, but not much. It clearly took a lot to impress the elder Firethorne. "He's very knowledgeable about the estate, and very sociable. So, if you need any help settling in, I'm sure he'll happily oblige." He patted his son's back as he said the last part, and I noticed a proud grin creep across Lysander's face as he discreetly peered at the man who stood on the opposite side of Mr Firethorne.

As he revelled in the brief attention his father was giving him, I studied Lysander Firethorne.

He was beautiful.

I couldn't deny that.

Like a Greek God.

He had thick, golden hair that fell in waves to his shoulders. His skin was tanned, and his face was warm and friendly. He had the kind of ethereal perfection you rarely saw in real life. Even standing here in front of him made me feel a certain way, and when he turned and bowed his head to my father, then let his eyes land on me, a wave of something hit me.

Was it nerves?

I wasn't sure, but I felt a little exposed and out of sorts. It was a feeling I hadn't felt before, and I could sense the heat in my cheeks as I tried not to blush.

Lysander began to speak, "It's nice to—"

But Mr Firethorne cut him off, dismissing him completely as he turned his back on him. And it made me feel sorry for Lysander, that his father would embarrass him in front of other people like that.

"And this is my youngest son, Damien." He gestured to the man standing at his other side. I saw Lysander's jaw tick as he tried to remain unaffected, but even I, a stranger, could tell he was hurt.

The other son, Damien, had his hands stuffed into his trouser pockets and a bored, vacant expression on his face. He clearly didn't want to be here and didn't care who knew it. His whole aura screamed rich, privileged, spoilt asshole.

"Damien has... many qualities," Mr Firethorne went on. "How useful they are to this family is yet to be determined."

Lysander stifled a snort, but Damien didn't react. He just stared straight ahead, not really focusing on any of us.

He wasn't golden like Lysander.

No.

Damien had a darkness about him.

Dark hair, shorter than Lysander's, that fell over his forehead, almost touching the lashes of his eyes.

Dark eyes that seemed hollow and emotionless.

And a dark mood that seemed to hang over him like a storm cloud.

If Lysander was a God, then Damien was the devil. Or that's how it appeared at first glance.

The girl standing beside Lysander cleared her throat to get our attention. A sunny, pleasant, and altogether fake smile was painted on her pretty face. Then she flicked her beautiful, long, blonde hair over her shoulder and stepped forward. Mr Firethorne's gaze fell on her with a look of irritation that she'd interrupted his introductions, but it didn't deter her. She didn't seem to care, and her smile grew wider as she focused solely on me.

"And this," Mr Firethorne stated plainly as he regarded us. "Is my niece, Miriam." He turned his head slowly to glare at her. "Who should have something better to do with her time than be here wasting ours."

Miriam giggled provocatively like it was an inside joke. "Oh, Uncle. I do love your dry sense of humour," she remarked. But judging from the look on the rest of the Firethorne's faces, it was no joke.

She moved forward, heading closer towards us, like she was floating across the floor. Her eyes were bright as they stayed focused on me, but my stomach recoiled as I glanced over her shoulder and saw the elder Firethorne watching her in a way that made me uncomfortable.

"It's so lovely to meet you," Miriam said, holding her hand out to take mine. I hesitated, then frowning, I took her hand and gave it a light shake. Her hands were warm and fragile, but I doubted very much that the girl standing in front of me was either of those things. "I think we're about the same age," she went on. "We should spend some time together, get to know each other."

I heard someone scoff behind us and Miriam glanced over her shoulder, then focused back on me, smiling brightly.

"Us girls have to stick together. Especially in a house like this," she stated, and then leaning close to my ear, she whispered, "You can't trust anyone in this house. But you can trust me. Always." As she leaned back, she winked at me. But all that flashed through my mind was images of snakes, the sound of hissing, and warnings of deadly poison. Much like the words I'm sure she'd like to pour into my ears, given half a chance.

I didn't trust her.

I didn't trust any of them.

The note from the train had only highlighted the importance of that.

But I nodded politely and gave her a smile to placate her.

I might be in a nest of vipers, with Miriam's fake promises of friendships and Damien's dark scowls, but I wasn't about to become their prey.

Miriam returned my nod, then glanced over her shoulder and said, "I'll see you boys tomorrow. Be good. Don't do anything I wouldn't do." And then she left, breezing past us and out of the front door, leaving behind a cloud of expensive perfume to linger in the air where she'd stood, like a heady memory that felt like it was trying to choke me.

My father leaned to the side and whispered, "See, you're making friends already. I knew this was going to be the making of us."

I guessed the old saying, 'keep your friends close and your enemies closer', was going to be useful to me in this house, but I just smiled and nodded in acknowledgment.

"Come," Mr Firethorne snapped sharply, pulling our attention back to him. "My son can show you to your lodgings, and then tomorrow, we can discuss"—he paused, his gaze solely on my father—"terms."

Terms?

What terms?

We'd just travelled hours to get here, to take the jobs that he'd offered us. What possible terms could they have to discuss? Surely that'd all been finalised when the contracts had been signed.

In my gut, something felt off, but again, I stayed quiet, reminding myself to quiz my father about it later.

"Tomorrow," my father repeated back to him, bowing his head as if Mr Firethorne were royalty.

I watched as Mr Firethorne glanced between his two sons. Sons that couldn't look or act more different. If they hadn't been introduced as siblings, I'd never have guessed that they were. Apart from them both being over six feet tall, they were nothing alike. From the moment he'd walked into the foyer, Lysander had been smiling, his eyes twinkling, mischievous but kind. A stark contrast to everything else that was going on around him.

The polar opposite to his brother, Damien.

Where Lysander stood confidently, open and friendly, Damien was closed off, disinterested, like he was bored with life, people... everything. I almost expected him to turn on his heel and storm off, unimpressed with what he saw here. Unable to spend another precious second of his time on something that was clearly unworthy of him.

I could see myself warming to Lysander.

I did *not* like Damien.

"Lysander." Their father spoke with authority. "Show them to the cabin. Mrs Richardson has sent some supper down. Then I need you to report to me in my office."

"Yes, Father," Lysander answered subserviently, bowing his head.

The tightness in my stomach eased up a little, knowing Lysander would be taking us to wherever we were going. I don't think I'd have been able to hold my tongue if the other one had been chosen, and he'd used it as an excuse to look down his nose at us like his father.

"Can I just say, once again, how grateful we are for this opportunity," my father said, but he needn't have bothered. Mr Firethorne was already striding out of the foyer without giving us a second glance. Leaving my father's words to hang in the air like a bad smell.

"Save your breath," Damien sneered at us, condescension dripping from each word that spilled from his tongue. Then, as he too turned to leave, he called over his shoulder, "You were lucky to get that much out of him."

And I couldn't stop myself from scowling at him as he sauntered out of the foyer like we were nothing, not even shit on his shoe, because even that would have made him stop to look. We weren't worth a glance. Not even worth a proper introduction. Because for all the time we'd stood here, Mr Firethorne hadn't used our names once to introduce us. And they hadn't bothered to ask.

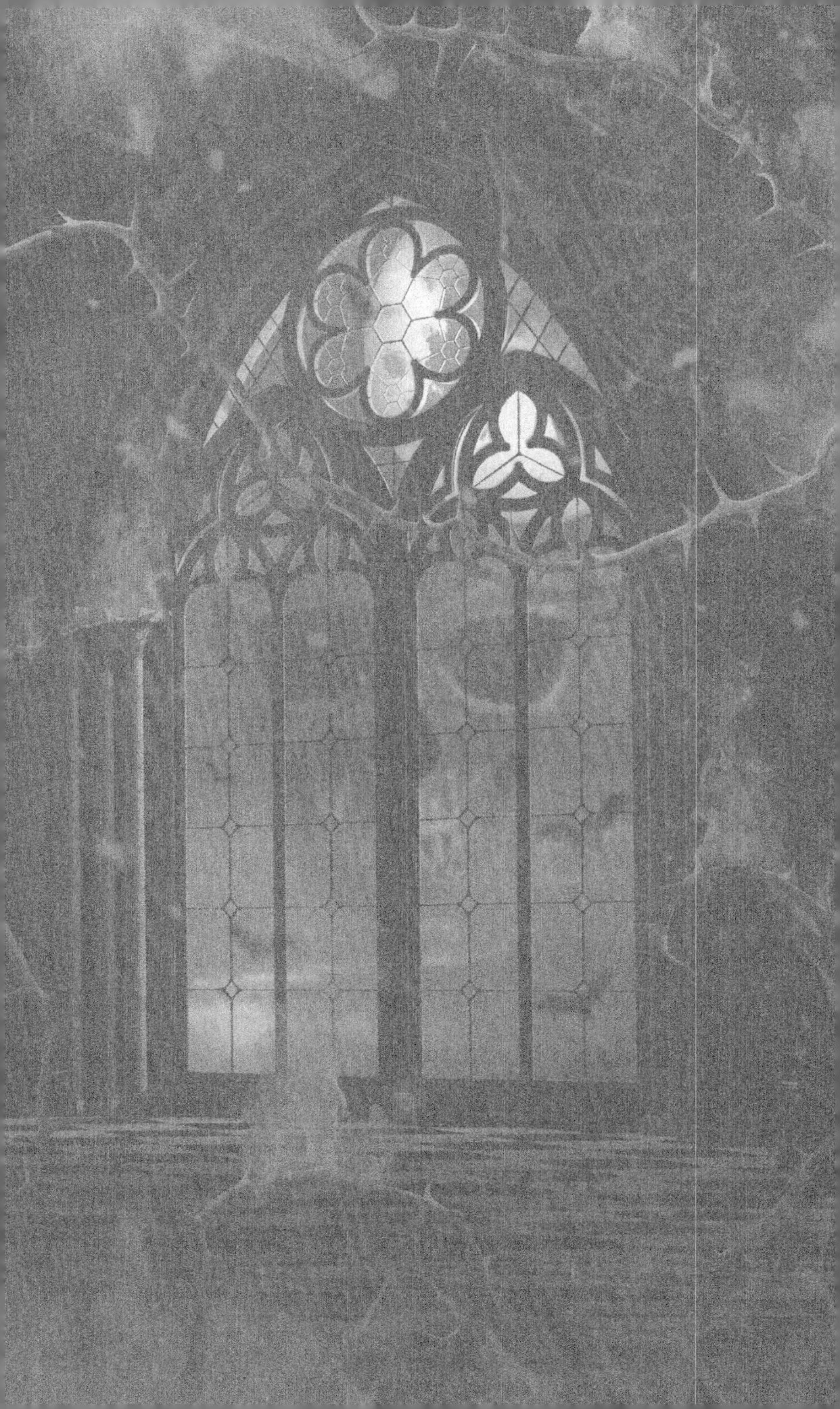

Six

MAYA

"I'm so sorry about my father, and... *my brother*," Lysander said apologetically, saying the last part a little quieter and rolling his eyes as he glanced over his shoulder. Then he turned back around, dazzling us with his smile and a kindness that shone from within. "And I'm so sorry, but I didn't catch your names." He stuck his arm out for my father to shake his hand.

"I'm Arthur. Arthur Cole," my father said, gripping Lysander's hand firmly to give the handshake he'd wanted to give and been denied only moments ago. "And this is my daughter, Maya."

Firethorne

Lysander's gaze moved to me.

"Maya Cole." He said my name like he was testing how it sounded on his tongue, and the way he said it made the blush I'd stifled earlier start to bloom on my cheeks.

What the hell was wrong with me?

"The pleasure is all mine," he said as he picked up my outstretched hand and dipped his head to kiss the back of it.

I didn't know how to react to his old school charm, but I smiled back at him sweetly. He was making an effort—effort that'd been lacking from the other Firethorne men.

He stared at me for a few seconds longer than I expected, his eyes twinkling with forbidden promises as he held my hand in his. The warmth of his palm sent sparks of electricity into mine, and I tried not to show he was affecting me as I kept my breathing regular and my smile neutral and friendly. Then he shook his head as if he were waking himself from a daze, gently let go of my hand, and gestured to the door behind us.

"Shall we?" he asked, then he winked, and a flutter erupted inside me.

I really needed to get a grip.

There was a boyish charm on his face as he strode past us and headed out of the house with a spring in his step.

"It's not far, just across the park," he announced, and then turned and peered down at my black boots, and his smile widened. "You wore the perfect shoes for this estate, Maya Cole. Miriam is always complaining about her heels whenever she has to venture outside. I can already tell you're a wise woman."

I didn't own a pair of high heels. These were the only boots I had, the only shoes I owned. But I smiled back at him and nodded in response. I liked being called wise, and they *were* the perfect boots. They'd lasted longer than my last pair.

"Can I take your luggage?" Lysander asked, ever the gallant gentleman, but he didn't try to grab it like the driver had.

"No, it's fine," I replied.

"We can manage," my father chipped in.

I didn't want us to appear ungrateful, so I quickly added, "Thank you, though," as I tried to keep up with Lysander's long, confident strides on the pebbled path.

"I feel a little awkward, walking you to your cabin while you both carry suitcases. It's not very gentlemanly of me, is it?" He glanced back at us, slowing his steps when he saw we were struggling to keep up. "But you're an independent woman. I like that. I won't insult you by forcing the subject."

The way his eyes stayed locked on mine, and the playful warmth that burned in his gaze made me feel like he was flirting with me. It wasn't something I was used to, and I was a little unnerved about how to react. So, I pushed the thought away, concentrating instead on keeping in step with him and my father, and taking in our surroundings, despite the darkness around us. The grounds had an eerie presence, mist and fog looming in the distance as the gravel crunched under our feet.

"How long has your family lived at the manor?" my father asked, making small talk and asking a question I was sure he already knew the answer to.

"Our family have owned this estate since it was originally built back in eighteen thirty-four," Lysander stated proudly, and proceeded to tell my father the history of the building, pointing out recent renovations and restoration work that'd been carried out. Lysander was attentive, answering my father's questions and taking an interest in everything he said.

I couldn't help but zone out, leaving them to chatter as I glanced around, wondering how far away the closest neighbours were. The only lights I could see came from the main house and the streetlamps leading up the drive. But we were heading away from those, and in front of us lay nothing but darkness. The irony wasn't lost on me. We were heading into the unknown. But with Lysander leading us, I felt a little less wary.

After a while, as the glow from the house faded behind us, Lysander remarked, "It's so dark out here. I need to talk to my father about installing more lights in this part of the grounds. We can't have you wandering out here alone in the night like this. God knows what could happen. You could fall and hurt yourselves. It's a liability."

He seemed genuinely concerned, but I frowned. Surely, they'd had other live-in employees? Ones that had used this cabin that we were heading to. Why was the lack of lighting suddenly a surprise to him?

But before I could question it, Lysander turned to me and asked, "Are you excited to start work tomorrow, Maya?"

"I would be…" I shrugged my shoulders, huffing as plumes of cold air clouded in front of me. "If I knew what I was doing."

Lysander threw his head back and laughed.

But I hadn't meant it as a joke. I really was struggling to get my head around all of this. But I was keeping it together, for my father's sake.

Lysander tilted his head, moving it closer to mine as we walked, and whispered, "Didn't they tell you?" He paused, his eyes narrowing, questioning, waiting to see if I'd take the bait.

I didn't.

I just stared back at him and waited.

"They hired you to come to the main house and look pretty." He winked, and his eyes moved subtly up and down my body, but not so subtle that I didn't notice.

"Nice to see misogyny is still thriving in this county," I shot back without a second thought, as Lysander hung his head and laughed quietly.

"Maya!" my father snapped, but Lysander butted in.

"It's okay, Arthur. If telling a lady she's beautiful is misogyny, then yes"—he held his hands up—"I'm guilty. But I am sorry if I've caused any offence. I'd hate to get off on the wrong foot. I speak before I think sometimes. It's my greatest downfall. I will try harder and do better, though. I don't want to make anyone feel uncomfortable."

I began to feel guilty for biting back, but before I could speak, my father spoke first.

"I apologise for my daughter," he said, sounding ashamed, but Lysander cut him off.

"Not at all. A woman needs to stand up for herself in this world. Never criticise her for that. It's a good thing."

"Thank you," I replied.

I liked that he was defending me.

I was warming to Lysander with every minute I spent in his company.

"All joking aside," Lysander went on sincerely. "If you do happen to find yourself in the main house at any time, come and find me. I'd love to paint you."

Instantly, he had my attention.

"You paint?" I asked, curiosity brimming as I pictured him standing in a bohemian artist's studio, probably in an attic or a conservatory with the perfect lighting, painting whatever his current muse was. Passion rolling off him as he created a masterpiece.

I peered at him out of the corner of my eye as he walked beside me, a Greek God with hidden depths. First impressions could be misleading sometimes. He was beautiful, but he was so much more than that. And then I realised, my first impressions were no better than the misogynistic comments he'd made earlier, and I bit my lip, inwardly cursing. I had to learn to do better, too.

He had a candid yet proud smile on his face as he lowered his head. His hair fell in soft waves, covering his eyes, and he reached up to push it behind his ear.

"Painting is what I live for." He lifted his head then, and glanced up at the starry night sky as he added, "I specialise in landscapes, but I'm trying to improve my portrait skills. Dad wants me to paint something he can feel proud to hang in his study." He tilted his head towards me, and with a smirk, he added, "A portrait of himself."

I gave a low chuckle and felt myself warming to him even more. He was easy to talk to and easy to be around. I could tell it'd be effortless to be friends with Lysander because he was so laid back and amiable.

He started to talk about the landscapes he'd painted on the estate and in the area. We nodded, responding with impressive sounds, even though we didn't know what those landscapes looked like. But Lysander was drawing us in, lulling us, casting his spell as we headed closer to the cabin.

"I'm not sure I could do you justice in a painting," he declared. "The ebony of your hair. The way the light catches the different shades of darkness, almost inky blue and black. Pure perfection," he said, swirling his hands in front of him like he was trying to capture the night sky.

"I'm sure you have some black paint stored away somewhere," I replied, then snapped my mouth shut at how rude that sounded. My mouth seemed to have a habit of running away before my brain could engage. I guess Lysander and I were alike in that respect.

"And your eyes," he went on, not reacting to what I'd said. "The hazel with delicate flecks of gold." He sighed. "I could paint them a thousand times and they would never be right. Never be... perfectly stunning... like the real thing."

"My eyes are blue," I stated plainly, and my father hissed, "Maya," chiding me for my rudeness once again.

"Are you sure?" Lysander spoke with a hint of humour, and he narrowed his eyes as he peered down at me, even though he couldn't see the colour in the dimness of the grounds we were walking through. "I could've sworn they were hazel when I looked into them back at the house."

"They're definitely blue," I replied, bowing my head. My cheeks were bright red, but I wouldn't disclose that fact any time soon.

He'd looked into my eyes.

"Blue eyes, black hair. The perfect combination," he stated. "And that smile." He pointed at me, at the smile that seemed to appear of its own accord whenever he was speaking. "The way it tilts up at the corner, and the shine in your eyes. That would be the crowning glory for my portrait."

Some might say he could be a little cringey, but I had to admit, I liked it. I'd never met anyone like Lysander Firethorne before. I found him to be refreshing.

Just then, the delicate glow of a lamp lighting up the porch of a small wooden lodge came into view, and I couldn't deny I was glad to see it.

"Ah! Here we are," Lysander announced jovially, and he strode ahead as we both stayed back to take in our new home.

It was a single-story cabin. Small but cosy, with three small steps leading onto the porch area.

We took each step slowly as Lysander opened the door and turned the inside lights on, getting everything ready for us to see.

"Mrs Richardson made sure it was heated for you. And as my father said, she's left some supper here, too."

He stepped back to let us walk through the door.

The interior was simple and plainly decorated, with blue gingham curtains at the windows and well-worn woven rugs on the wooden floors. It was open-plan, with a small galley kitchen against one wall, a table with two chairs against another, and a small, blue sofa with a matching armchair in front of the fireplace. It was a little shabby, but it was clean, and I walked across the room to explore further.

There was a tiny hallway at the back of the room with three doors leading off it. Opening each one, I found two single

Firethorne

bedrooms and a small, sparse bathroom. Adequate, that's what it was. Quaint, even. Not at all like the main house we'd left, because unlike that cold, soulless building, this cabin had the potential to be... *a home.*

"It's perfect," my father remarked, and I agreed.

"Well, if there's anything you need." Lysander's eyes met mine. "Anything at all, just dial zero and we'll have you sorted out right away." He tapped his finger on an old landline phone on a side table by the door. "That's your hot line." He winked.

"Thank you," I told him. "But I think we need to settle in and get some rest now. It's been a long day."

"Of course." He bowed his head, and then he stepped towards the door. "I'll see you both tomorrow," he said before he shut the door.

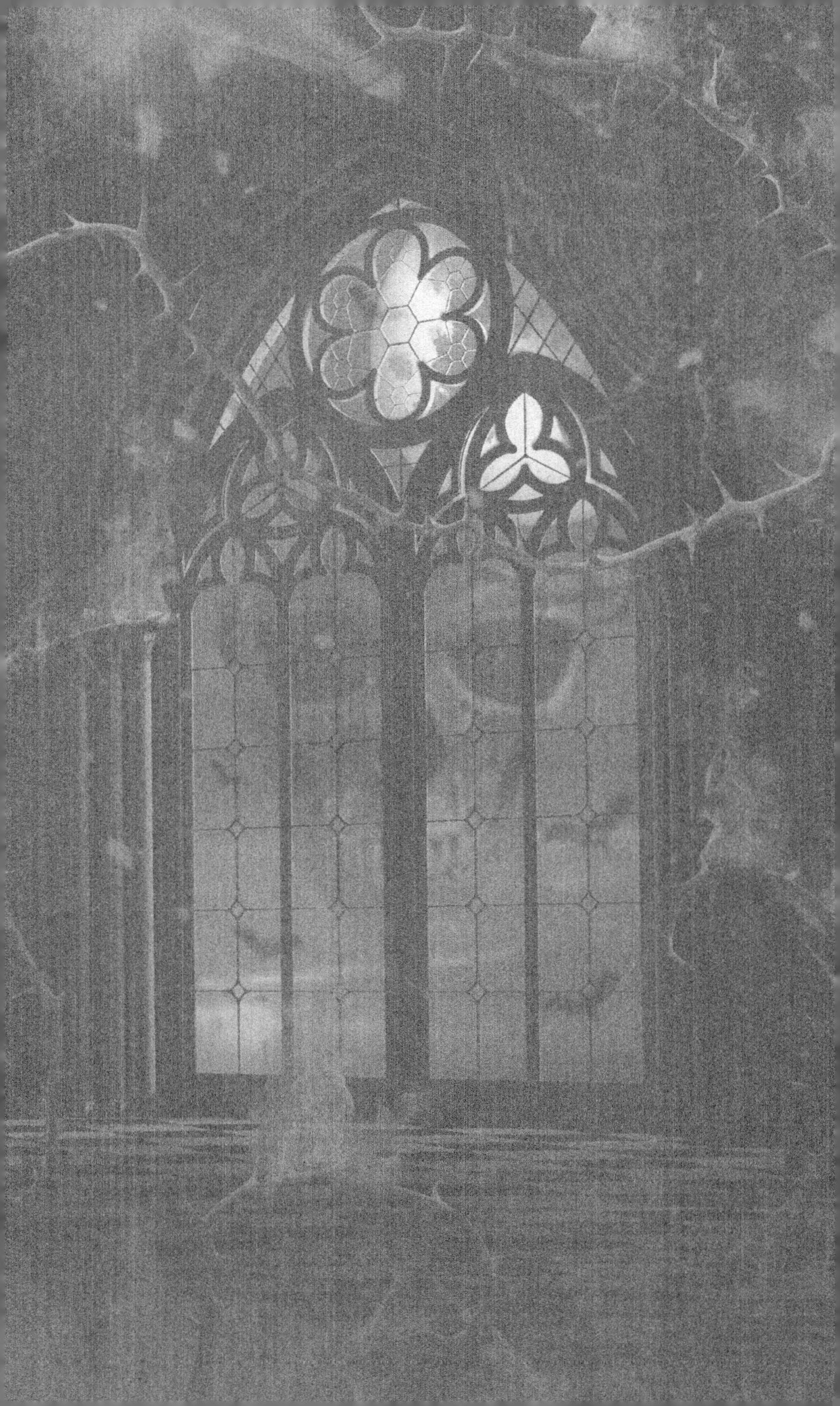

Seven

MAYA

I sat with my father at the breakfast table the next morning, chewing my toast as I mulled over the events of the night before.

"What did you mean yesterday, when you said you needed to discuss terms for this job?" I asked.

"Exactly that," he replied. "Mr Firethorne wants to discuss a few little issues. It's nothing to worry about. Just that there are terms we need to agree on in addition to what was in the contract."

As usual, his answer wasn't really an answer.

"Why haven't I seen this contract? Or better yet, why

haven't I signed one?"

My father sighed, dropped his toast onto his plate and brushed the crumbs off his hands.

"Because this is on me. You're free to work here, live here, but if you want to leave at any time, you can."

"That's not how employment works," I reminded him, niggling doubts burrowing away in my brain.

"And that's why we need to iron some small specifics out this morning," he replied, and I could feel a headache coming on. His inability to be transparent made my head hurt.

"What specifics exactly?" I asked, my jaw locking as my exasperation grew. "And how can they be small and specific?"

"It's nothing for you to worry about."

"But I do worry."

"Well don't."

My tension multiplied as I retorted, "That's really helpful. Thanks."

Why was I going along with this?

Why was I letting him get away with sweeping statements and sweeping shit under the metaphorical carpet?

Why was I like this?

But I didn't have the energy to argue with him, so we finished our breakfast in silence before I asked, "Where do I go this morning? Who do I report to?"

"Mrs Richardson is taking you under her wing. She's the housekeeper. But don't worry so much, Maya. Everything will be fine. Today is the start of a new life for us."

I ignored him, standing from the table and walking over to the kitchen area to rinse my plate and put it in the sink, ready to wash. Then, I told my father, "I'm just gonna get some fresh air before starting this new life of ours."

"A new chapter," he announced, smiling as I headed for the door.

I stepped out onto the porch and closed the door behind

me. Breathing deeply, I closed my eyes and savoured the cool morning air. I loved how the crispness of it sparked in my lungs, making me feel alive. The mellow breeze grazed my skin, kissing my face and gently fanning my hair. A calmness washed over me, and slowly, I opened my eyes. But as I glanced down, something caught my eye on the step of the porch.

I took a few steps forward to get a closer look, and then... the calmness that I'd been revelling in only moments ago was ripped away in an instant when I saw what lay there. I gasped, covering my mouth with my hand in shock.

A rat.

A dead rat in a trap.

What the actual fuck?

I stared at it for a few seconds, feeling utter revulsion at the dead rodent lying at my feet, wondering whether to call my father to come out. But then, I noticed something white peeking out from underneath. Feeling sick, I kicked the trap lightly with my foot, grimacing at how the rat's tail quivered as the trap moved. Then, I bent down, and trying to ignore what lay in the trap, trying to block it from my mind, I picked it up between my thumb and finger. My face screwed up as I lifted the trap in front of me and stood back up.

Tucked in the trap, beneath the dead rat, was a piece of paper. Tentatively, wincing in disgust, I pulled it out and unfolded it. It was a handwritten note and the black ink on the paper looked eerily familiar.

They're all liars here.

I read the words over and over again.

They're all liars here.

They're all liars here.

My eyes scanned the text as if the words might change any minute and give me another clue, tell me who it was that was sending these warnings.

I swallowed, even though my throat had gone dry, the

sensation like razor blades scoring into my skin. This was the same handwriting as the other note. The flecks and curls of the letters were exactly the same. This wasn't a coincidence. Someone was following us. And I had to know who they were.

I pushed the note into the pocket of my black work trousers, and that's when I felt it. The sensation of someone watching me. My head snapped up, eyes darting around the wooded area where our cabin was.

"Hello. Is anybody there?" I called out, but there was no response.

I waited, watching the trees like a hawk, expecting to see movement, and then I heard the crack of a branch. Without a second thought, I ran down the steps of the cabin, racing over to where I'd heard the sound.

"Who is that?" I cried a little louder, but again, there was no reply.

Then, I heard footsteps retreating, and my fear spiked, my heart beating out of my chest as I lurched forward, ready to follow them, chase them, catch them and find out what the fuck was going on.

"Who's there? Do you think this is fucking funny?" I hollered as I charged through the woods, chasing after those footsteps, my anger rising as I tried to hunt them down.

I picked up speed, running and focusing on the crunching leaves and the clicking branches ahead.

I'll catch you.
I'll find you.
I'll never give up.

I chanted in my mind as I ran and ran. My breaths were pants now as I pounded through the woods. The uneven ground beneath my feet made me stumble a few times, but I didn't fall. I couldn't. I was so determined to catch them.

And then, I emerged from the trees as the woodland turned to open land, and I stopped. My breaths were icy clouds as

I breathed heavily and stared at the foreboding image of Firethorne Manor that stood before me in all its gothic glory.

But that wasn't all.

Damien Firethorne stood on the edge of the woodland too, smoking a cigarette as he stared at me. His eyes were narrowed, his brows knitted, but he had a devilish smirk on his face. Like I'd just stumbled unwittingly into his trap, and he was ready to devour me.

"I heard you were a runner." He glanced down at my feet and sneered. "Nice to see you came prepared for it."

I glanced at my feet and grimaced at the tatty slippers I was wearing.

"I wasn't expecting to run this morning." I held my head high. I wouldn't let him intimidate me. "Not until I heard you skulking around, stalking us."

At first, he didn't react, just took a slow, long drag of his cigarette, and then he flicked it to the floor, and in a bored tone, he replied, "I don't know why I'm even bothering to entertain this conversation, but I'll humour you. What the *fuck* are you on about?"

"This," I hissed, throwing the rat in its trap onto the ground at his feet.

He snarled, staring down at the rat, then he peered up at me, grinning like a devil as he said, "A rat? What exactly do you expect me to do with this?"

"You tell me. You were the one who left it on our porch."

He threw his head back and laughed. Actually, it was more like a cackle, and hearing it irritated me. But I stood my ground and waited to hear his response.

He let his head fall forward, the black, silky threads of his hair grazing his lashes as the cool, couldn't care less aura radiated from him.

"Why would I leave *that* for *you*? Do you think I've got nothing better to do than leave dead rodents around the estate for the hired help to find?" His grin widened, and he tilted his head. "What makes *you* so special?"

"I don't know. You tell me," I shot back, bristling with anger in response to his disdain.

"You keep repeating yourself. You do know that, right? Which tells me you have absolutely no idea what you're on about. But for the record, I'd be careful if I were you." He took a step closer to me. "You never know who might be lurking around the woods at this hour."

At that moment, Lysander appeared to the side of us, and Damien muttered under his breath, "And to prove my point, here he comes."

Then, standing taller and painting a fake smile on his face, he turned towards Lysander and announced, "Brother. Do tell me..." Damien frowned, folding his arms over his chest. "What source of witchcraft pulled you out of bed before midday?"

"I always take a morning stroll," Lysander replied brightly, but then he peered at the ground and screwed his face up. "What the hell is that?"

"A little gift from our new employee here." Damien pretended to whisper as he mocked me. "I think these city girls have a warped sense of humour."

"I think whoever left that on my doorstep has a warped sense of humour," I spat back.

"Maybe they were giving you a message," Damien said, turning to pin me with a wicked stare. I held my breath, waiting for him to say something that would incriminate him. Anything that might give him away. But then he said, "They say a dead rat symbolises a warning, like an omen."

"An omen that we need to employ pest control today," Lysander butted in, his nose wrinkling as he stared at the dead rodent.

"Indeed." Damien took a step back. "Or the pests we need to control are closer than we think." He glared daggers at me, making it painfully clear he thought of me as the pest. Then he turned on his heel and strode away from us, leaving Lysander to stare at the carcass and me to stare at Damien's retreating form, willing his body to self-combust like my mind currently was from how bloody rude he was.

"I'm sorry you had to see this," Lysander said, apologising. "I'll get Beresford to come and dispose of... *that*." He pointed at the rat, and then, with a kindness on his face, he stepped closer to me and asked, "Are you okay, Maya?"

I nodded, and when the breeze blew strands of my hair out of place and he reached up to tuck them behind my ear, I froze, not sure how to react.

"You've still got your slippers on. Do you want me to walk you back to your cabin?" he asked, but I shook my head.

"No. It's fine. Honestly. I'll be okay."

He didn't seem happy, and he bit his lip as if to stop himself from arguing his case. Then he nodded, staring at the floor as he said, "I'll let Mrs Richardson know you're running a little late this morning. Why don't you go back home. Take a moment to get yourself together."

"I don't have a home," I blurted out, and I felt tears well in my eyes.

"Yes, you do. Your home is with us," he said. "Firethorne is where you belong now."

I didn't feel that way, but I smiled nonetheless. Lysander did make things slightly better. He was kind.

"Thank you. That's nice of you to say," I told him, edging away from him, back into the thick of the woods behind me, suddenly feeling embarrassed that I was standing out here in ratty, old slippers.

"My pleasure. I'm just speaking the truth." He bowed. "I hope your day gets better." Then he smiled and turned to walk away, heading in the same direction as Damien. "And ignore my brother," he called over his shoulder. "He lives for making others feel uncomfortable. But I think even he draws the line at torturing small animals. I don't think he'd have it in him to torment you to that extent. My guess is Beresford set some traps and you got unlucky this morning, stumbling upon that one."

"Very unlucky," I whispered in response, but he didn't hear me. He was already out of earshot.

Damien *fucking* Firethorne.

I'd bet there were no limits that a man like Damien Firethorne *wouldn't* go to so he could torment someone like me.

I'd had two messages now, warning me about this family. I needed to place more bricks on that wall around myself and my father.

Trust no one.

They're all liars here.

But despite everything, I had to admit, Lysander was starting to grow on me. He'd offered to walk me back to the cabin. Told me he'd get rid of the rat, and he'd speak to Mrs Richardson to explain why I might be a little late. All Damien had done was blow smoke in my face and smirk at me like a fucking devil.

If I had to trust anyone in this godforsaken place, I know which one I'd choose.

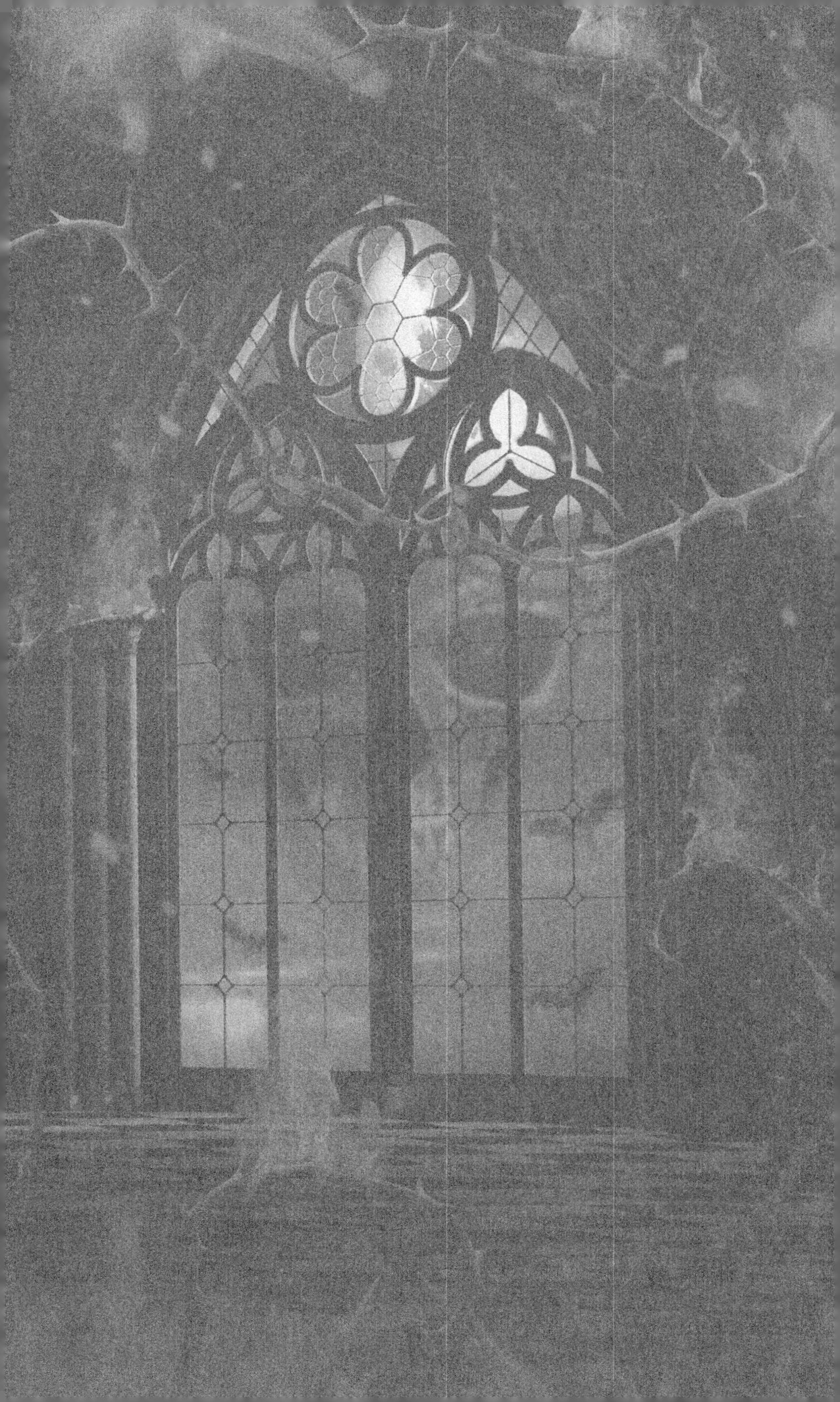

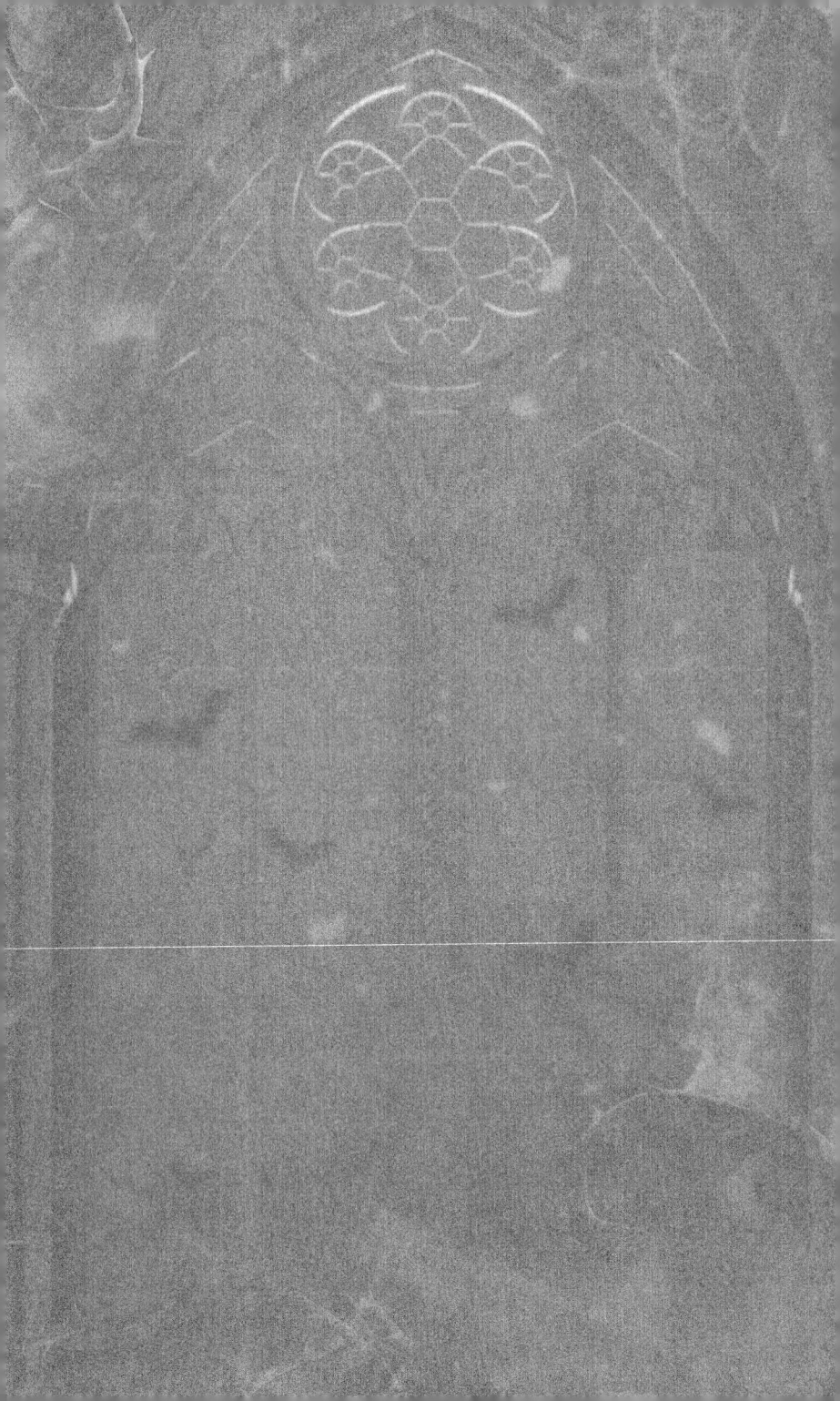

Eight

MAYA

I ran back to the cabin, quickly changed and put on my boots, ready to face my first day. And what a first day it was shaping up to be.

As I sprinted on the gravel path that ran around the perimeter of the manor house, heading towards the front doors, I saw Beresford, the driver from the night before, standing in front of me. His face was screwed up, and his sneer grew deeper and more pronounced the faster I approached.

"And where are you going?" he snapped, holding up his hand to stop me in my tracks.

I halted, the gravel sliding under my boots as I did, and my

Firethorne

face flushed as I replied, "It's my first day. I'm here to work." I gestured to the house, but he just tutted in response.

"Not through the front door you're not. The service entrance is around the back. That's where staff like you are permitted to enter." And he circled his finger in a patronising way in front of me, to tell me to turn around and go.

I spun around, stomping away from him as I muttered under my breath, "You're staff too, mate. No need to act like your shit don't stink."

I was sure I'd been quiet enough, but when he shouted, "And you'll find language like that is best used in the privacy of your lodgings. We have standards to uphold at Firethorne," I couldn't help it; my middle finger shot up of its own accord, standing proud in the air as I faced forward and strode off. I'd probably get into trouble for it later, but in the heat of the moment, I didn't care. I'd had more than enough encounters with rats this morning. I didn't need another one.

I walked to the other side of the manor house, stopping when I came to a small wooden door. It was open, and I could hear the sound of pots and pans clanking around inside. The smell of freshly brewed coffee wafted through the air, and I knew this was the service entrance he wanted me to use. I took a deep breath, nerves kicking in a little as my stomach rolled. But I straightened my shoulders, standing taller as I stepped over the threshold and took the small staircase to where all the noise was coming from.

At the top of the staircase was another open door, and I crept through it, into a large kitchen where a woman with her back to me was bending over, rifling through a cupboard and humming to herself.

"Hello," I said quietly, not wanting to startle her. "I'm Maya. I'm here to start work today."

Hearing my voice made her shoot upright and then spin around to face me. She smiled so wide that I couldn't help but smile back at her.

"Maya!" she exclaimed excitedly. "I've heard so much about you. I'm so glad you'll be working down here with me."

Her eyes sparkled as she spoke, and the nerves that'd swarmed and stung my belly eased a little at how warm she was. She put the saucepan she was holding down onto the counter and walked over to me, her arm outstretched to shake my hand; then she thought better of it and grabbed me into a hug I wasn't expecting. When she pulled away from me, she kept a hold of the tops of my arms and said, "I'm Mrs Richardson, but you can call me Cora." She rubbed my arms, then let hers drop to her sides as she stood still, smiling and watching me.

"Thank you. I'm Maya," I repeated, my nerves making me a little tongue-tied.

"You'll be fine here. Please don't be nervous," she said, reading me like a book.

Cora Richardson came across as a homely woman. Late forties, maybe early fifties, with short dark hair, a round, ruddy, but utterly charming and friendly face, and her aura felt good, positive. Like no one I'd met here at Firethorne since I'd arrived, apart from Lysander, perhaps. He always had the same sunshine following him around. But with Cora, there was an honesty and truth about her. She was the kind of woman you warmed to instantly, and that's what she was doing right now, making me feel warm and welcome.

"Take a seat." She gestured to a stool near the island in the middle of the kitchen. "Can I get you a coffee? It's always a good idea to start your working day with a decent cup of coffee." She began arranging cups with milk and sugar onto a silver tray, but I shook my head.

"That's really kind of you, but no. Honestly, I'm fine. But thank you." I glanced around the kitchen, then hopped off my stool and headed over to the hob, where a frying pan of bacon was sizzling. I picked up a spatula nearby and went to turn them over so they wouldn't burn, but Cora stalked over to me and took the spatula out of my hand.

"I'll sort that. Lysander is very particular about his bacon."

"Lysander is particular about everything," a deep voice drawled from behind me, and I turned to see Damien strolling into the kitchen with that cocky swagger he always seemed to have. He grabbed an apple from the fruit bowl on the counter, and then, as he stared at me, he took a huge bite.

"That's the Firethorne men for you," Cora replied, as if Damien wasn't one of them. "Impossible to satisfy." And I found myself cringing inwardly, waiting for him to bite back.

But he didn't.

Instead, he sauntered over to where she stood, leant down, and placed a kiss on her cheek that made her blush as he said, "But you manage to do it every day. And you do it so well. Where would we be without you?"

Cora scoffed, batting Damien away as she grinned to herself and replied, "Always the charmer. Just like your father."

And I had to stop myself from blurting out, "Really? Him?" Because the last word I'd use to describe Damien or Mr Firethorne was 'charmer'.

"Is there anything I can help you with?" I asked Cora, trying to ignore the Damien-shaped elephant in the room that seemed more than happy to linger in here and make me feel uncomfortable, glaring at me as he ate his apple. His countenance towards me was in stark contrast to the one he presented to Cora. She got the charmer; I got the snake.

Why was he in here?

Was it to find me and taunt me some more after what'd happened first thing this morning?

The darkness of his presence made the hairs on the back of my neck stand on end. But I knew he didn't care. He revelled in it.

He stared at me with his piercing eyes, like he had the ability to make me burst into flames with one glance. The muscles of his neck flexed as he swallowed. And then he stopped. And I realised I was staring a little too intently, so I looked away.

So much for ignoring him.

Now I looked like the stalker.

I focused all my energy on Cora, or tried to, and watched as she turned the heat on the hob down then wandered over to the tray of hot drinks she'd just laid out.

"Maya, for your first job this morning, you can take this tray to Mr Firethorne's office for me," she said. "He's in a meeting at the moment, but he requested that coffee be brought up to him and his client."

"Out of the question," Damien snapped, butting in, and we both whipped our heads around to glare at him.

"Why do you say that?" Cora questioned as I furrowed my brow and stepped a little closer to her, ready to take the tray. I was here to do a job, after all.

"It's her first day." Damien strutted slowly to stand on the opposite side of the island, and he threw his apple into a bin to the side, before bracing his arms on the countertop and leaning forward, glaring across the kitchen at me. "And you're going to send her into my father's study to serve drinks at an important meeting, when she clearly isn't up for that kind of responsibility yet?"

He spoke with such disdain, so much condescension, that I didn't care if he was the boss's son. I didn't hold back as I snapped, "If pouring a cup of coffee is your idea of responsibility, you really need to aim higher in your aspirations in life."

"Says the *girl* employed to wipe my father's ass if he asks her to," he spat back, emphasising the word 'girl' to try and put me down. He wanted to get a rise out of me, and he was succeeding.

"Better his ass than yours," I retorted, and he snorted, a half-smile curling his lip like a fucking devil. He was loving this.

Firethorne

"Now, now," Cora interrupted. "There's no need for any of this. I'm sure Maya is quite capable of serving a few drinks. And you, Damien"—she lowered her gaze at him, peering through her lashes as if she were scolding him—"you must have better things to do with your time than be in here, intimidating my staff. Leave us alone and get on with your own work."

I held my breath, waiting for Damien's response, but he just huffed and then gave a wry smile. Cora had obviously worked here for a long time to have the courage to speak to Damien the way she did. I'd seen how he interacted with his brother, with me, with everyone else here. But in this kitchen, he seemed different. He didn't go on the defensive or try to attack Cora. Instead, he just turned around and stalked towards the door, calling over his shoulder, "I take my coffee black. Let's see if she has the mental capacity to remember that."

I wanted to flip him off. I wanted to react so badly, but I reached out to take the tray, to give my hands something to do. A distraction. Because if I had my way, I'd be showing Damien Firethorne exactly how far my mental capacity could provoke him.

Cora breathed deeply, then smiled at me.

"Take the stairs to the second floor. Turn right, and head to the end of the corridor. Mr Firethorne's office is the last door on the right. Don't forget to knock before you enter."

I nodded, smiled back, and then, keeping hold of the tray, I headed towards the door with my head held high.

"Second floor, go right, and the last door on the right," I called out to show I knew what I was doing.

"And don't forget to knock first," Cora replied in a sing-song tone, humour evident in her voice.

"I think my mental capacity can cope with that," I joked, and I heard her laugh quietly as I made my way out of the kitchen and down the hall.

Despite it being early in the morning, the house was dark

and foreboding. The corridor I walked down was dimly lit with mahogany wood panels on the walls, and dark, ornate ceilings. Large windows let in light, but even they seemed to dim in the shadowed grandeur of this gothic mansion.

I reached the staircase, and with each step I took on my way to the second floor, I heard a sinister creak, as if it was groaning with age. I kept a tight grip on the tray as I made my ascent, navigating my way to the floor I needed.

Once there, I turned right, walking past the elegant sconces set in the walls either side of me, with dimly lit lamps. My heart was beating out of my chest, even though it was such a simple task. Take the tray in, ask Mr Firethorne if he wanted me to serve the drinks, then leave. It wasn't rocket science. But still, I felt my nerves spike as I approached the end of the corridor.

Once I reached the door to his office, I stopped, balancing the tray on one hand as I knocked on the door. I could hear deep, muffled voices coming from inside, but upon hearing my knock, a loud voice called out for me to enter.

I turned the door handle, and let myself into the room, faltering a little when I saw who sat there.

Mr Firethorne was behind a large mahogany desk, smoking a cigar. His eyes fixed on the man sitting opposite him as they exchanged small talk. That man was middle-aged and balding. He was someone I'd never seen before. But to the left of them, sitting with his feet stretched out and looking as smug as anything, was Damien.

I took a breath, trying to keep my nerves in check.

I didn't want him to know he was getting to me, so I ignored him, walking forward as the door closed behind me. I placed the tray on a side table against the wall and started to arrange the cups, ready to pour the coffee.

"Thank you, Maya," Mr Firethorne announced.

I turned to face him, but he didn't break eye contact with

his guest to look at me.

"Would you like me to serve the coffee?" I asked, my voice steady and confident.

I felt the bald man shift in his seat to face me, and the heat of his stare made the hairs on the back of my neck stand on end.

"You can service me if you like," he said, lounging in his seat with his legs spread wide in that way that some men do to make themselves feel important. And even though ripples of revulsion pulsed through me, I kept my cool and smiled sweetly.

"What would you like, Sir?"

He huffed, smirking at some inner joke he'd amused himself with, then tapped the desk in front of him and said, "Coffee. Cream, two sugars."

I poured the coffee into a cup, added the cream and sugar and carried the cup and saucer over to the desk, placing it down gently in front of him. I was just about to ask Mr Firethorne what he'd like when I felt a rough, calloused hand touch my leg and run slowly up my thigh. A spike of dread, nausea and repulsion coursed through me, and I froze. Part of me wanted to vomit, and the other half wanted to smack him for touching me. I decided to opt for the latter and I spun around, ready to slap the man's face.

But I was too late.

Another hand had beaten me to it.

I peered down in disbelief at where Damien's fist was wrapped tightly around the man's wrist, and I watched dumbfounded as he yanked his hand away from my leg with a viciousness that he then injected into his voice as he spoke.

"We don't behave like that here," Damien hissed through his teeth. "We're not fucking animals. You need to learn some fucking manners."

Damien was seething, his face growing red as he clenched

his jaw angrily. But across the desk, the elder Mr Firethorne let out a long and weary sigh. And he tapped his fingers on the desk as if what he was witnessing was a tedious waste of time for him. Mr Firethorne obviously didn't think his client was an animal, like Damien suggested.

I stood for a moment, unsure what to do or say. I didn't know how to play this. I just wanted to leave.

I took a step back, and Mr Firethorne huffed again. Then, in a low, almost bored tone, he said, "You can let him go now, Damien. I'm sure Edward will behave himself. It was just a touch. A mistake. Isn't that right, Edward?"

I watched as Damien glared at Edward, his nostrils flaring as he breathed deeply, and part of me thought he might ignore his father. But after a beat, he released his wrist, then sat back in his chair. But his eyes pierced through Edward like he wanted him to drop down dead.

Edward, on the other hand, sneered back at Damien. "I don't make mistakes," he hissed. Then he turned his attention to me, looking me up and down like he had every intention of touching me again, and no one was going to stop him. "But I'd make all the mistakes in the world if she was who I was making them with."

He made me feel sick.

And I had no doubt he meant every word he said.

I wanted to get out of here.

I cleared my throat, standing taller, ready to ask Mr Firethorne if he wanted me to pour him a drink, even though I wanted to tip the contents of the coffee pot into Edward's vile lap. But for some reason, I failed miserably at finding my voice.

Mr Firethorne waved his hand and announced, "That'll be all, Maya. I'm sure we'll manage to pour our own drinks. You can go back down to the kitchen now."

I nodded, said a quiet, "Yes, Sir," and turned to leave. But not before I heard, "I haven't seen your kitchen, Nicholas.

Firethorne

Maybe I need to make a detour before I leave today. After all, as we were just discussing, I may need to sample the merchandise myself before I sign on the dotted line."

Edward's voice made me shudder. Goosebumps prickled over my body. I think I'd reached a new low this morning. I'd found someone even worse than the Firethornes.

Leaving that office and closing the door behind me felt like I'd stepped out of the lion's den into blissful refuge and safety. The invisible insects that'd been crawling over my body were slowly scuttling away. I stood for a moment, fisting my hands as I closed my eyes, threw my head back and took a few deep breaths to right myself.

"Maya, are you all right?" I heard a familiar voice ask from down the hallway.

I opened my eyes and saw Lysander stalking towards me, genuine concern etched onto his face. Then, at that moment, I felt the door behind me open and close, and a dark presence loomed over me.

"What the fuck have you done to her?" Lysander hissed as Damien came to stand beside me, his hands stuffed casually into his trouser pockets as he puffed his chest out and rocked back on his heels.

"Nothing that you can't fix with your dazzling wit and knockout charm," Damien replied, not even trying to defend himself.

"He didn't do anything," I added, glancing at Damien's profile. His face was stoic, but I could see a faint tick of his jaw as he stared straight ahead.

"Well, something happened in there," Lysander said, coming to a standstill in front of us. "Maya, you look upset. What happened?"

"I wasn't upset," I replied defensively.

"She was just pissed off," Damien cut in, and I whipped my head around to stare up at him.

"I can speak for myself."

"Clearly," he replied, turning slowly to look down at me. "God forbid I should ever step in."

I swallowed, trying to formulate a response to what he was implying, as he turned back to face Lysander. Then he stepped forward and took his hand out of his pocket and placed it on Lysander's shoulder. "It's all okay now, though, right? Her knight with shining hair products is here to save the day." He patted his shoulder one more time, then strolled off down the corridor saying, "She's all yours, brother."

Lysander rolled his eyes then silently stared at me for a moment as Damien disappeared down the hallway, and then, with empathy in his voice, he asked, "Are you sure you're okay?"

"I'm fine. Honestly."

He cocked his head, narrowed his eyes at me to show he didn't quite believe me, and the boyish way he looked made me dip my head and give a quiet chuckle.

"I am. Really," I reiterated, staring back up at him.

He sighed, evidence that he might push further flickered in his eyes, and then it disappeared, replaced with a softer, more mischievous glow. "Well, now you're up here, would you like to see my studio?"

I faltered in my response. It was my first day here. I didn't want to piss Cora off by shirking my duties.

"I should get back to work. Mrs Richardson will wonder where I am," I told him, stepping past him to head down the hallway. But he grabbed my arm to stop me.

"She'll be fine. If she asks, I'll tell her you were doing a job for me." His eyes crinkled at the corners as he smiled, then he gave me a subtle little wink. A look I'm sure he'd used on Mrs Richardson more than once to get what he wanted. That he'd probably used on a lot of people. I was starting to learn that Lysander had a certain way about him. A way that made you

Firethorne

want to soak in the sunshine of his smile.

And I was a girl who'd lived through too many rainy days.

"I have something to show you," he went on, boyishly pleading with his puppy dog eyes. "Something special."

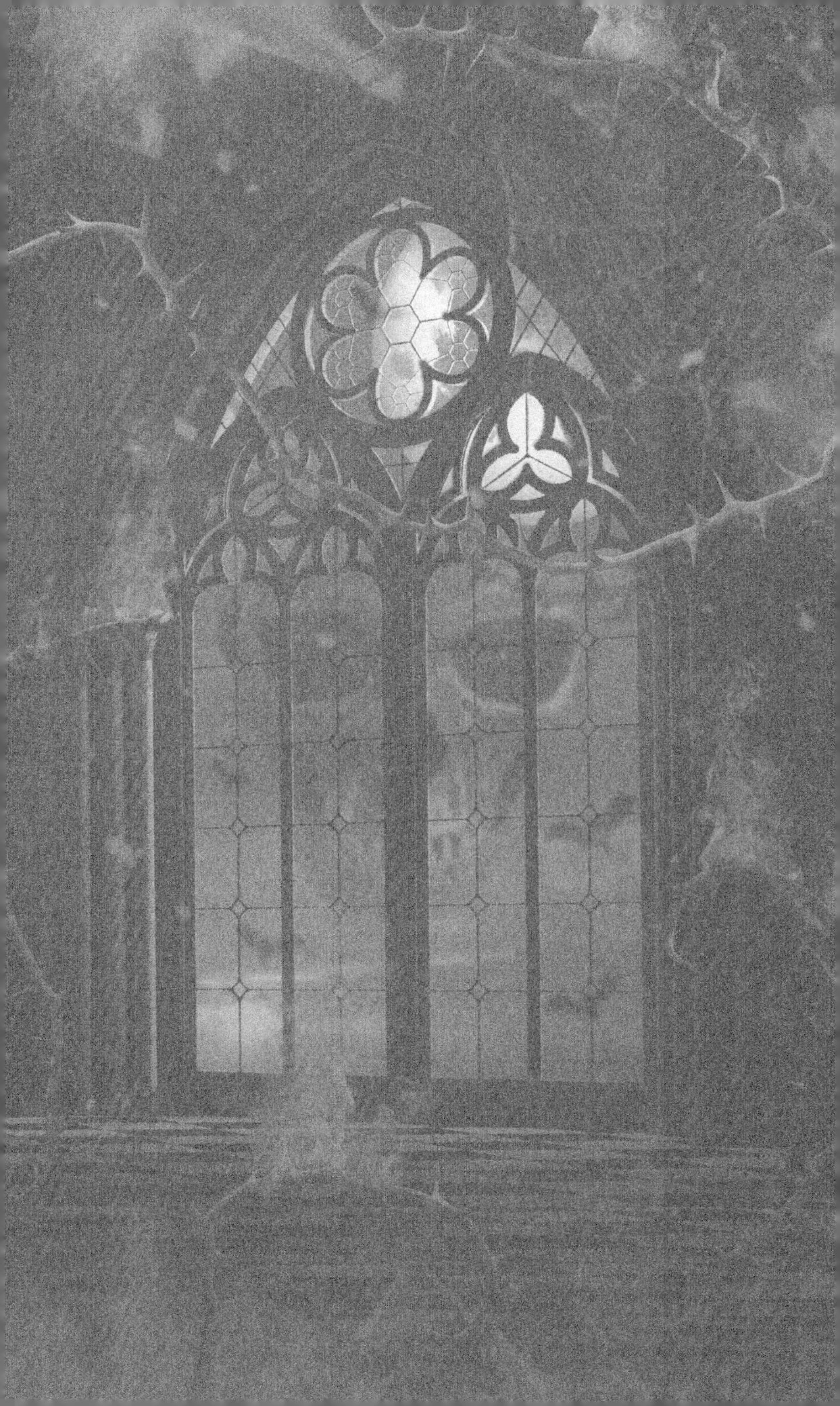

Nine

MAYA

Lysander led me to the opposite side of the mansion, to the wing farthest away from his father's office. And as we walked, he said, "I spoke to Beresford this morning. He said he won't set anymore traps on the estate where people might stumble across them. I'm so sorry again for what happened to you."

I smiled and thanked him. It was sweet that he was looking out for me. But at the same time, I was pretty sure it wasn't Beresford that'd left that note. Beresford probably had no idea what Lysander was talking about. But I left the matter there... for now.

Firethorne

When he reached the door to his studio, he stood still for a moment, pausing dramatically before announcing excitedly, "Are you ready to see where the magic happens?"

"It depends what kind of magic you're talking about," I replied.

His comment was innuendo, I knew that, and I couldn't help getting sucked in as I stifled a grin.

"The best kind." He winked, then pushed the door open and stepped back to allow me to enter first.

As I stepped forward, I was surprised at how much light flooded into the room, warming the air and beckoning me in. It was a stunning space. It took my breath away. Truly.

Lysander's studio was on the corner of the building, with a semi-circle of floor-to-ceiling windows on the far side of the room, overlooking the Firethorne estate. I was instantly drawn to those windows, and as I walked towards them, I gasped at the breath-taking panoramic view. The fields and green hills rolled on for miles, trees as old as time standing tall and proud, leaves and branches swaying in the autumn breeze. The sky was cool and grey, so cool it was almost white, cotton clouds rolling across slowly, creating the perfect accompaniment to this quintessential English day. It was perfect. Even I felt the urge to paint the scene. The room really did have a magical aura.

"Wow," I marvelled, my eyes sweeping across the landscape, taking it all in. "It really *is* magical. Everything looks so beautiful from up here." I felt the warmth of his presence as he came to stand behind me, the heat of his breath as it fanned across the back of my neck. "It's just so... beautiful." I'd used that word twice, but I was speechless, fumbling over my words. This was a room I could stay in forever.

"Yes, it is," he hummed seductively, making me think he was talking about more than the view. His voice was close, so close, and I turned around to find him staring right at me, his eyes penetrating through me.

"Are those your paintings?" I asked, feeling a little nervous.

I already knew the answer as I moved to the far side of the studio. But I needed to give myself some space, to clear my head of the improper thoughts that were running through it.

Painted canvases were propped up against the wall, each one capturing a different aspect of the estate; the fields, the forest, and the lake that I'd yet to discover for myself. Each painting was so atmospheric, so consuming, that it made me want to reach out and touch them, run my fingers over the swirls and flicks of the paint. They made me yearn for the real thing. To experience the natural beauty of this place in all its forms.

"You're so talented," I said, taking time to study each painting as I went.

"It's my passion," he replied, moving to walk in step beside me. "I like to convey how I see the world, what it makes me feel. And hopefully, pull you into it too. Make you... *feel*."

I turned to look at him, and he smiled.

"I meant, as a lover of art. I want anyone who sees my paintings to be pulled into that world. To experience the moods and emotions that a place like Firethorne can give you."

"I think you do that," I told him. "It certainly makes me want to go outside and explore."

"Maybe stay a little longer here and see a few more of my paintings first, before you bail on me," he replied, and I laughed lightly.

I glanced down at a painting of the lake, the image of a sinister, shadowy figure standing in the thick of the forest in the background, leaning against a tree trunk, almost hidden amongst the beauty of the scene made the hairs on the back of my neck stand on end.

"Who's that?" I asked.

Lysander sighed, and I wasn't sure he'd answer me as he

stood still and hummed to himself. Then on a whisper, as if he was scared someone would overhear him, he said, "That's Damien. But don't tell anyone. I hide him in most of my paintings."

He moved to stand next to a painting of the sweeping driveway of the Firethorne estate. The same driveway we'd driven down last night, with its Victorian lamps lining the way. Then he pointed at one of those lamps, showing me the silhouette of a man hidden behind.

"There he is in this one," Lysander said, then he moved to point to a painting of the fields, with a cluster of rocks in the bottom left-hand corner. He indicated where a shadow was cast on the ground, as if someone was hiding behind those rocks. "And here he is again."

I found it strange that he felt the need to put dark, shadowy images of his brother in his paintings, like he was placing easter eggs that only he knew about.

"Why do you put Damien in all your paintings?" I asked, wanting to know what went on in his mind at those points in his artistic process.

"Because I like to put him outside, where he belongs."

Lysander was speaking candidly now. Lost in his thoughts as he stared at his work.

"Why does he belong outside?" I asked, hoping he'd keep spilling his truths to me, because I wanted to know them all. I wanted to know everything I could about the Firethorne family.

"Because he might have the Firethorne name, but he's not a real Firethorne. Not like me."

Interesting.

"Why isn't he a real Firethorne?" I pressed, my focus on him now, the canvases merely spectators to the reality he was now painting for me.

"Because..." Lysander tensed his jaw, and then, with his

eyes fixed on his paintings, he said, "We might have the same father, but my mother didn't give birth to him. He's a bastard. A living reminder of my father's indiscretions. He isn't a true-born Firethorne."

They were half-brothers. I'd had no idea, but it certainly answered a few questions and explained why they were so different.

"I thought you were the eldest?" I asked, and Lysander nodded.

"I am. My father brought him to live with us when he was born. I was four at the time."

"That must've been tough. Was your mother still around when that happened?" I asked and watched him swallow. His voice broke a little as he started to speak.

"She died when we were young. She'd been ill for most of our lives, but I know, when he brought Damien to live here, it didn't help matters. That broke her."

I wanted to ask how she'd died, what illness she'd had, but I found myself saying, "I'm so sorry to hear that." And then, "What about Damien's mother? Where is she?"

"I have no idea, and I don't want to know." I felt him snap back to reality, shaking his head slightly as he stepped away from the canvases against the wall and reached out to touch my arm. "Talking about my bastard brother was the last thing I wanted to do when I brought you in here." His eyes softened as he added, "Come over here. I want to show you something."

I took one more glance at the paintings laid out in front of me, my eyes searching each one for the darkly hidden figure. The brother that didn't belong here. Then, I lifted my gaze to look at Lysander. Kind, honest Lysander.

"I'm sorry you lost your mother. I know how that feels. I lost mine, too," I said, giving him a little bit of myself in return for his openness.

Lysander stepped closer to me.

Firethorne

"Let's not lose ourselves to the ghosts of our past," he replied, ignoring my confession like it was nothing. As if they were words he hadn't heard me speak. The sunshine he always exuded was glowing brightly now as he walked towards a large mahogany desk on the opposite side of the room. "I find living for the moment far more rewarding. And the future is much more exhilarating than the past."

I knew he was deflecting. Avoiding the pain he didn't want to feel. Who was I to challenge him on that? I did the same, too, most days.

I followed him to the desk, watching as he rooted through papers, trying to find whatever it was he wanted to show me. The desk was a clutter of artwork, pencils, brushes and paint tubes.

"Ah, here it is," he announced, pulling out a piece of paper from the pile. "I did this last night. It's not perfect, but it's a start."

He handed the paper to me, and I took it, glancing down at the pencil sketched there, almost losing my breath as I did.

"Is this me?" I asked, struggling to find my voice.

"Yes. I sketched it from memory last night, after I'd dropped you off at the cabin. It's only a rough, first draft, but once I've convinced you to sit for me, I can work on it. I can create that portrait we talked about."

He'd gone home, sat and thought about me, and drawn this sketch from memory. No one had ever done anything like that for me before. I was speechless. Again.

"That's just so.... so..." I didn't know if I could find the words to describe how I was feeling. But I went with, "Thoughtful."

It wasn't the right word.

It wasn't nearly enough to describe the buzz of electricity currently flowing through me. The warmth in me that realising he'd taken time to do that elicited.

That he thought I was in some way special.

Trust no one.

They're all liars here.

But maybe I could trust Lysander. He was giving me every reason to.

In this moment, all my apprehension and mistrust evaporated for a split second, like a break in the clouds, giving me a glimpse of what could be. This sketch was a selfless gesture. A kindness. He really did want to paint me. Capture whatever it was he saw that made him feel something. And maybe it'd make me feel something, too.

"Do you really like it?" Lysander asked, and the fact he seemed unsure made my heart swell a little more.

"Of course I do. I love it." I went to pass the sketch back to him, but he shook his head.

"That's yours. You can keep it."

"Don't you need it for reference? To work from?" I asked.

"No. I have the real thing I can use for that." He reached forward and cupped my cheek with his warm hand, and I leaned into it, closing my eyes briefly as I got lost in the haze he was creating. He was the flame, and like a moth, I was flying blindly into the brightness he was promising me. Burning in the sunshine of his presence.

"Do you want to pose for me now?" he asked, his voice low, his lips a whisper away from mine.

My heart fluttered, anticipating what might come next, but my head broke through the haze, reminding me I was at work. I was here for a reason. I couldn't let myself get carried away. Not now.

"I'm flattered that you want to paint me," I said, enjoying his warmth for a second longer. Then taking a step back, I added, "But I have to get back to work. I can't pose for you today. I'm so sorry." I walked back over to the windows to try and break the spell he'd put me under. "Maybe you could get lost in another landscape today. After all, you said yourself you love painting those the most."

Lysander began to reply, but suddenly, the air around me cooled, and my ears rang as I noticed my father through the window, walking outside. Lysander's voice was nothing but background noise that I couldn't comprehend as I watched my father stride up the driveway towards the house. He wasn't dressed in his work attire like he had been this morning when I left. No. He was wearing a tailored suit. One he used to wear when he worked in finance. His best suit.

Lysander's voice went on, just a distant hum as I witnessed my father heading towards the main steps, and I watched open-mouthed as Beresford tipped his hat to greet my father, a greeting he'd give to any visitor to the estate. A visitor of importance. But not a worker. He didn't tell *him* to go to the service entrance like he'd told me. Oh no. He let my father walk right past him and up the steps, towards the front door.

I knew Mr Firethorne had spoken about discussing some terms of the contract with my father, but from how he was dressed, and the way he'd carried himself as he'd walked inside just now, it looked to be a lot more than that.

Through the buzz in my ears, I heard Lysander mention a schedule for sitting for him, and I spun around, suddenly unable to think clearly.

"I need to get back to the kitchen," I announced abruptly, wondering whether I'd bump into my father on the stairs if I left this studio now. Or would he be kept waiting in the foyer or in some side room while Firethorne continued to entertain his client? Another display to my father, to show him how unimportant the elder Firethorne thought he was.

I didn't know. But I didn't feel comfortable being here anymore, and I wanted to leave. To get back to the security of the kitchen, and Cora.

"Shall I come and find you later, book in a few sessions for us?" Lysander asked, his brow furrowed in confusion as I headed for the door.

"Not yet," I replied. Then feeling a little ungrateful, I added, "Let me settle in first, then we can sort something out. I want to make a good impression."

"You've already made a good impression," Lysander said in that velvety-smooth tone of his.

But I wasn't deterred.

"I have to go back to work. Thank you for showing me all this. And thank you for my picture." I held the sketch tightly in my hand and glanced over my shoulder to where Lysander stood in the middle of his studio, looking forlorn, as if I'd abandoned him when he needed me the most. But I gave him an apologetic smile, pulled the door open and walked away.

As I headed down the hallway, I heard the faint sound of floorboards creaking behind me, and I stopped, turning to see who it was, expecting to find Lysander following me. But I couldn't see anyone, and the door to Lysander's studio remained closed.

A few more steps forward and I heard those creaks again.

I whipped my head around and called out, "Who's there?" But no one answered.

I slid the sketch into the pocket of my apron and charged forward with more purpose now, my heart beating faster as I moved through the house, feeling like the walls were watching me, the ceilings tracking my every move. Even the house felt like it was judging me. The mansion was a living, breathing entity ready to encase me in its dark halls and never let me go.

I came to the top of the staircase and expected to see my father ascending as I made my way down, but he wasn't there.

I didn't see anyone.

But as I made my way downstairs, I heard movement from above.

I stopped, my heart beating faster now, and I held my breath as I peered up, straining to hear every little sound, expecting to see someone on the stairs. But no one was there.

Shaking my head, convincing myself that it was just an old house that made those sorts of noises, I carried on walking down the hallway, aiming for the kitchen. But the creaking started up again, and I lost my shit.

"Whoever you are, stop fucking following me," I bellowed as I spun around. And there, standing in the hallway with a smirk that told me she'd gotten the reaction she was hoping for, stood Miriam.

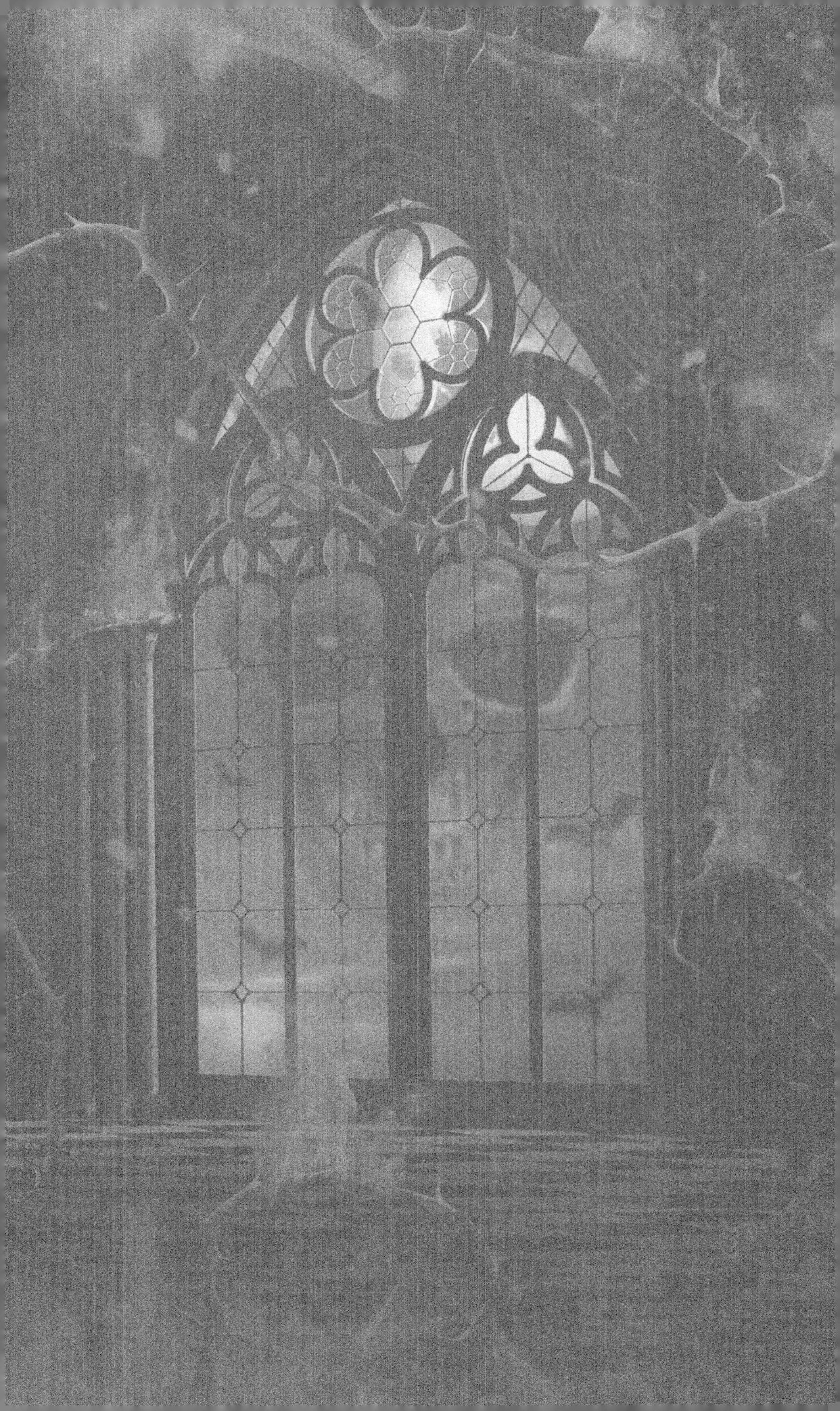

Ten

MAYA

Miriam kept her smirk in place and quirked her brow in a questioning manner, as if she was wondering why I was bawling down the corridor at her, asking her what she was doing following me. She belonged here, and I didn't. I knew that. I felt it with every step I took, every breath, every awkward and creepy encounter.

Miriam stepped towards me and started to speak, her earlier smug expression replaced with concern as her face softened and her eyes grew warmer. Concern that looked so perfect, and yet... too perfect. Like she'd practised in front of a mirror to get it just right. Maybe she had.

Firethorne

"Maya, are you okay? I was worried about you. I saw you heading out of Lysander's studio, and you seemed out of sorts. I came down here to check you were all right and you started shouting at me. I didn't mean to scare you."

"I wasn't scared," I replied. "I just don't like people creeping up on me, is all."

Miriam's brows hit her hairline. "*Creeping?*" She sneered, and then she righted herself, as she smiled and said, "I wasn't creeping. I saw you head into Uncle Nicholas's office first, and then you darted out of Lysander's studio, and I assumed something awful had happened. I don't creep around here, Maya, I just... see things. More than the others do." She took a step closer and put her arm out, resting it on mine in a comforting, friendly gesture. "I'm your friend, Maya. You don't have to be defensive with me. Maybe with Damien and Lysander, but never with me."

"Lysander is always lovely to me," I replied, choosing to stay quiet about Damien. He might've stopped Edward from assaulting me earlier, but the jury was out and deliberating pretty quickly on him.

"Lysander's lovely to everyone," Miriam said dismissively, shrugging her shoulders, and I didn't like the way that made me feel. Like his kindness wasn't genuine. As if it was something he bestowed on everyone. Like I wasn't anything special.

I wanted to argue back, but that, in itself, would only prove her point, that I was being defensive. So, I smiled, trying to ignore how the heat of her hand on my arm made me feel a little uncomfortable. As if I was being coaxed into a trap like the rat I'd found on my step this morning. I tried to subtly edge away from her, but she grabbed my hands and held onto me.

"Anyway, I'm so glad I bumped into you today," Miriam went on. "I wanted to give you something."

She reached into her pocket and pulled out a silver chain. Then she held the locket that was attached to it and announced,

"I want you to have this."

She thrust the locket and chain towards me, but I didn't take it, I just stared at it in disbelief.

I didn't even know this woman.

Why was she giving me jewellery like we were lifelong friends?

"I can't take that," I told her, and she frowned in confusion.

"Why not? It's just a necklace. A gift from a friend."

"But I work here," I stated, watching the subtle twitch of her jaw as her smile stayed frozen in place. "I'm an employee. It wouldn't be right to take gifts."

She popped her hip, her head tilting as she gave me a sorrowful sigh. "Don't put yourself down, Maya. You're worthy of a gift. And hopefully, one day soon, we'll be more than acquaintances. We'll be friends. Best friends. But this..." She thrust the chain forward again, almost touching my chest as she held it out expectantly. "Is more than that. Remember what I said yesterday? Us girls have to stick together. You can't trust the boys here." Another breath as she waited for me to take it, then, when I didn't, she added, "It's to keep you safe."

The way her demeanour changed as she said the last part had me questioning everything.

"How will a locket keep me safe?" I asked, reluctantly taking the oval-shaped pendant from her and holding it up. I marvelled at the ornate patterns and swirls on the silver casing, running my fingertips over the smooth, cold metal.

"Because it has my number engraved on the other side, see?" She reached forward and turned the pendant over to show me, her fingers grazing my palm oh-so-gently as she did. Lingering a little longer than I'd have expected, and I stared at her, a million questions swirling in my brain.

"Am I in danger here?" I asked in a low voice, expecting her to tell me something.

Maybe she knew about the notes.

Firethorne

Maybe she was the one behind them, making sure I was forewarned and guarded. She had told me I shouldn't trust anyone in this house except her when we first met.

She leaned forward, her face a breath away from mine as she whispered, "You *are* in danger. Grave danger. And any moment you may fall victim to..." A beat, and then she pressed her lips so close to my ear I almost shivered. "Lysander's terrible jokes or Damien's sour moods and salty put-downs."

She giggled to herself as I stepped back. After the morning I'd had, I wasn't in the mood for her teasing.

"Why would I need to ring you?" I snapped, growing irritated. "I don't even have a phone. There's one in the cabin, but I don't have my own."

Miriam's eyes widened as she scoffed. "You don't have a phone? But everyone has a phone."

"Not me," I replied, and the silence that hung between us was deafening. "And this is really pretty," I went on, peering down at the pendant in my hand. Then, thrusting it forward to give it back to her, I added, "But I don't wear jewellery."

"Maya," Miriam stated firmly, ready to chastise me. "It's a gift. Take it. Stop finding excuses not to." I went to argue, but she interrupted me, holding her hand up and saying, "And maybe my next gift should be a phone." Then, under her breath she muttered, "How anyone can survive in this day and age without a phone is beyond me." She rolled her eyes then spun around and stalked away, giving me no choice but to keep a hold of the necklace. A necklace I had no intention of wearing.

I stood for a moment, watching her disappear down the hallway. I thought about leaving the necklace on the side table next to me, but I didn't. Instead, I stuffed it into my pocket, where Lysander's sketch was safely tucked away, and I turned to head for the kitchen.

My head was beginning to hurt from how much I was frowning. The people in this house were strange, aggravating, perplexing, walking contradictions, and yet I seemed to keep getting dragged further and further into their tangled web. I wanted to know more. I wanted to be a fly on the wall, learning secrets. Secrets I knew were embedded in this house as dark and eerie as the mansion itself.

And I needed to know who was sending me the notes.

"Did you manage okay, love?" Cora asked as I walked through into the kitchen.

"I think so." I was still frowning, and Cora noticed.

"Why do you look like you have a thousand questions you need answered?" she said, as she kneaded dough, flour dusted all over her hands and up her arms.

"Probably because I do," I replied. "But maybe I need to start with the most important one."

"Which is?"

"Why am I here?"

Cora laughed, but it wasn't in a mocking way. No. It was in a kind and motherly way.

"Isn't that the question we all ask ourselves?" she said as she continued to knead the dough.

I went to the island and sat on one of the stools, my eyes fixed on the way her hands twisted and moulded the dough as she hummed to herself. She seemed happy here, content with her life. She even spoke back to Damien, which I guessed not many people did, especially not staff. She fitted in, and yet she appeared normal, like me. Not like them.

"Everyone here is..." I took a moment to think of the right word. A word that wouldn't insult Cora, seeing as she seemed so attached to the Firethornes. "Different." Not the best word, but it got my point across.

Cora stopped what she was doing, took a cloth from the counter to wipe her hands, and sat on a stool opposite me.

"Different doesn't always mean bad. I've worked for the Firethorne family for thirty years, and yes, they can be difficult, but there's so much more beneath the surface."

"Lysander seems nice," I said, starting with the positive.

"Lysander has always been the golden child. He was so placid as a baby. The apple of his mother's eye growing up. But he has his problems, just like the rest of us. He can be vulnerable at times, but he doesn't show it. He likes to make people happy."

"I can't believe they're brothers," I said on a whisper, my eyes pinned to the counter in a daze as the words came out before I could stop them. I knew they were half-brothers, but I wasn't going to disclose that I knew that.

"They're more alike than you think," Cora replied. "But Damien is guarded. He doesn't trust many people. Life hasn't been kind or fair to him, so he acts accordingly. But I will say, if you are one of the lucky ones, the ones he trusts and accepts into his inner circle, he'll do anything for you. He's the kind of man you want on your side."

Because having him against you is lethal, I wanted to reply, but I kept my thoughts to myself and asked, "And Miriam?"

Cora chuckled.

"Miriam can be a little minx. But I know she has a heart of gold."

"I know she's their cousin," I went on. "And she spends a lot of time here, but where does she live?"

"She lives in the village. Her mother is Mr Firethorne's sister. But she spent most of her childhood here at the estate. Mr Firethorne practically raised her as his own."

"And Mr Firethorne? He's quite... foreboding."

"He's firm but fair. He's always been a good employer to me." She stared into her lap, smoothing her apron as she spoke. "They're not like you and me. I know that. They're aristocrats. The life they've lived is a far cry from what we know. But it doesn't make them bad." She looked up at me with a pleading yet pleasant smile.

"Just different," I added with a wry smile.

"Perhaps." Cora nodded in agreement. "I guess you're right. But you'll get used to them soon enough."

But I wouldn't.

I wouldn't get used to secret messages being left for me. Or necklaces with emergency phone numbers on. Or having visitors treat me like I was an object for them to abuse.

I wouldn't get used to men skulking around the woods like Damien did this morning, or snide comments from the other staff like Beresford.

I wouldn't get used to any of it. But I was here now. Here for my father. And the minute I'd saved enough money to leave, we'd be out of here.

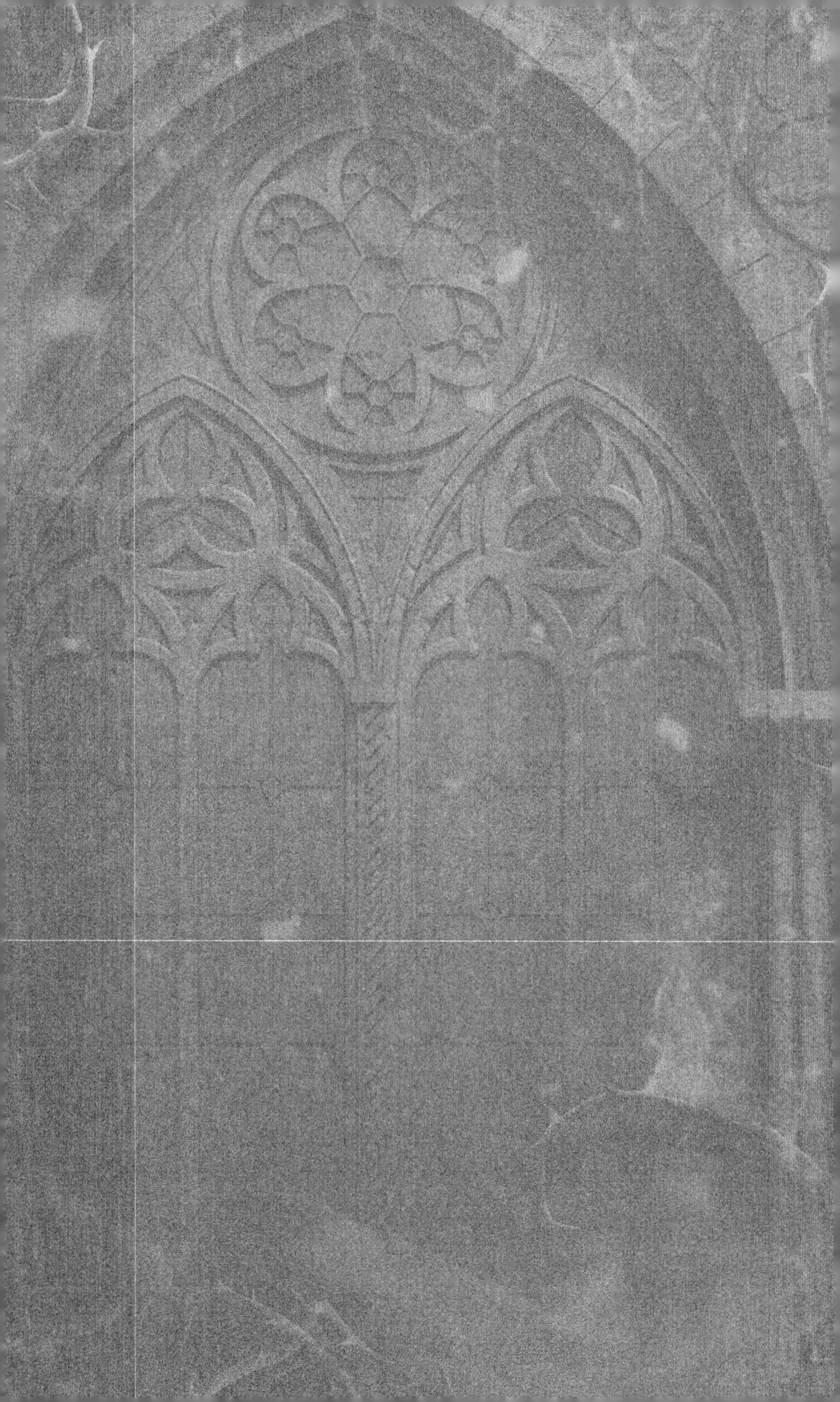

Eleven

THE FIRETHORNES

"Here you are," Miriam purred as she found Damien sitting in a high wingback chair, well hidden in the recesses of the Firethorne library. He'd chosen the space to avoid a meeting such as this, but luck wasn't on his side today. The universe really was testing his patience. A fact he didn't hide from his sour-looking face.

"Here I am, indeed. How lucky for me that you found me," he replied, his tone jaded and laced with sarcasm, not once looking up from the book he was reading as Miriam glared at him expectantly.

"Why have you always got your head stuck in a book?" she

fired back, sauntering over to sit in a chair opposite him, her high heels clicking on the polished wooden floor as she went.

"Because life is boring. And as for the people..." He deigned to glance up now, a blank, vacant look in his eyes as he observed her, then he went back to reading, as if to reinforce how tedious he found their exchange. "I find fictional characters far more complex and much more pleasing."

"Having no luck with the new *challenge* then?" Miriam was gleeful as she tried to tease him, but Damien had to care in order to actually be teased.

"There is no challenge," he replied drolly. "I already told you. I don't fuck the hired help."

"He's right," Lysander announced confidently as he strode around the corner towards them. "There is no challenge. I've got this one in the bag."

"You're at the body bag stage already?" Damien cocked his brow and then sarcastically whispered to himself, "Like I said, breathing or not, you're not fussy. You'll take whatever you can get."

"And I get what I want," Lysander shot back. "The Firethorne charm never fails to win them over. Some of us have it by the bucket load, and some of us..." He pinned his stare on Damien, unable to hide the hatred in his gaze. "Only have half."

The fact that Lysander despised his half-brother wasn't a secret. But Damien didn't care.

"The Firethorne charm," Damien mused. "Something our father has always used to his full advantage. His bucket overflows." He rested his arm on the side of his chair, his hand gripping his chin in thought. "Do you ever think there might be more clones of me out there, just biding their time, waiting for the opportunity to claim the Firethorne name?"

Lysander clenched his jaw, but Miriam interjected, "God forbid. We struggle to cope with one of you."

Damien whipped his head around to stare at her.

"Why are you still here?" Damien snapped; his gaze full of fire. "Don't you have some other poor sod to torture?"

"It's your turn today," she quipped, flicking her long blonde hair over her shoulder. "You're the lucky one."

"Your definition of lucky is somewhat distorted, cousin dearest," Damien sneered.

"Then it'll align with your whole world, Damien darling. Distorted is your middle name, after all." Miriam smirked, feeling content that, in her mind, she'd won. Then she sighed dramatically. "I saw you in Uncle's office, scaring the girl half to death. Whatever you did, Damien, it didn't help your cause."

"I already told you, I'm not competing in your petty games," he replied plainly, his tone clipped and bored.

"Whatever," Miriam replied with a flick of her hand. "And you, Lysander. I had such high hopes for you, inviting her up to your studio to show her your etchings."

"She was upset, and I took care of her," Lysander replied. "I fail to see how that was a loss in your eyes."

Miriam gave a sly smirk. "Because she bailed on you, walking away like you'd shown her a dead corpse."

"Sounds like an oxymoron to me," Damien shot back. "Can a corpse be anything other than dead?"

"You two are the only morons around here," Miriam hissed, clearly agitated. "But me? I've well and truly locked that shit down, and I think it's time to move to phase two."

"First, how exactly do you think you've locked anything down?" Lysander questioned as he leaned against a bookcase, folding his arms nonchalantly. "I was with her hours ago, and I think if anyone is winning at the moment, it's me."

"Oh, really?" Miriam questioned.

"Yes, really." Lysander pushed himself off the bookcase to stand taller.

"That's funny." Miriam tapped her manicured nail on her chin in thought. "Because I've already given her my number and gained her trust. I'm the first one she'll come running to when either one of you fucks up, which you will."

"You gave her your number?" Lysander repeated, frowning.

"Yes, dummy. Engraved on a locket that I insisted she wears, even though the little weirdo said she doesn't wear jewellery."

"Don't call her a weirdo," Lysander snapped, his muscles tensing as a darkness fell over him.

"Why? Have you seen a side to her that the rest of us haven't?" she scoffed.

"Maybe," Lysander replied, but Miriam dismissed him and carried on belittling the girl she saw as her newest project.

"I mean, what kind of girl doesn't wear jewellery?"

"God forbid." Damien rolled his eyes dramatically as he repeated Miriam's earlier remark back to her.

"And don't even get me started on the fact that she doesn't own a phone," Miriam went on. "What is up with that? Maybe one of you can gift her one. Drag her into the twenty-first century, although it'll probably be kicking and screaming."

The dark veil that'd shrouded Lysander suddenly fell away. He never wore it for long, not in company, anyway.

"Kicking *and* screaming?" Lysander laughed. "Sounds like a job for Damien." Lysander was proud of his quick retort.

"And phase two?" Damien asked, lifting his chin to show he was ignoring his brother.

"Phase two." Miriam's eyes sparkled, her face lighting up as she spoke. "We show her who we really are. Enough tiptoeing around."

"She's only just got here," Damien replied. "Do you really think she's ready to find out who we really are?"

"She already knows who some of us are," Lysander muttered.

"Or rather, who you want her to believe you are," Damien mumbled to himself.

"Of course she's ready to experience the full Firethorne effect," Miriam replied, talking over the mumblings of her cousins. "I think we need to throw one of our parties."

Lysander's grin grew wide. "That's the most sense you've spoken all day, Miriam. I totally agree." Then as his eyes grew wide, he announced, "I have an idea."

"Thanks for the warning," Damien retorted as Miriam stifled a laugh from her corner of the library.

But Lysander ignored him, his enthusiasm at full throttle as he said, "Angels and demons. That should be our theme."

"And let me guess, you'll be God, overseeing it all." Damien slammed his book shut and let it rest in his lap as he let out a long sigh.

"Let's face it..." Miriam shrugged. "You'll be the devil, so it's only fair someone is God. But why does God have to be a man? We all know God is a woman." She winked.

"God or devil, I'm sure you'll kill the role, whatever it is you choose to go as." Damien stood up. "But you can count me out."

"Why?" Miriam's voice came out shrill as she stood up, too, staring at Damien as he turned and strolled away from her. "You never miss a party."

"Oh, I won't miss the party," he replied, spinning around to face her but backing away towards the door as he did. "I just won't be a part of your circus. I'm not your puppet."

He turned one last time and left the room, just as Miriam muttered, "That's funny. I always seem to be able to pull your strings, cousin dear."

Twelve

MAYA

I walked through the door of the cabin to find my father sitting in the living room in his work clothes, a proud but tired smile on his face.

He turned his head as I shut the door and headed into the living area.

"How did it go today?" he asked, reaching down to take his boots off and then sitting back into the armchair and letting out a weary breath, wriggling his toes in his well-worn socks as he lazed there.

"It was good," I told him. "Mrs Richardson... Cora... she was lovely." Then I decided to address the elephant that wasn't quite in the room, more like stomping around in my head. "I saw you today."

"Did you? Was I weeding, or pruning bushes? Or let me guess, knee deep in filth, trying to clean the dirty duck pond?"

"Neither. You were in your suit. I saw you come in through the front door of the main house."

He swallowed. Maybe it was a nervous swallow, but he kept his smile in place and replied lightly, "I had a meeting with Mr Firethorne to discuss the terms of the contract." Then, seeing my frown, he added, "It's nothing to worry about. Just routine stuff. It's all fine. Don't look so worried."

"I'm not worried," I replied. "Just make sure you keep me in the loop if it's anything I need to know."

"It's my job to take care of everything," he stated. "You don't need to worry yourself about anything."

I was too tired to venture into the minefield that statement evoked, so I gave a weak hum in response and headed for the fridge. I took out a can of Coke, and after taking a long swig, I told him, "I'm heading into the shower. It's been a long day."

I walked to my room, closed the door behind me, and then took out the sketch Lysander had drawn and held it in my hands, studying it. Carefully, I reached over and pulled a pin that was already stuck in the wall out, and putting the sketch on the wall, I pinned it above my bed. Then I opened the drawer of my small bedside table and took the necklace out of my pocket, placed it in the drawer, and then shut it. I wanted to admire the sketch. The pendant felt wrong. I preferred to keep it hidden.

I took a breath, struggling to comprehend the events of the day. Then I pushed myself off the bed, grabbed a towel from my drawers, and headed to the bathroom.

As I stood under the steaming hot shower, I took a moment to think about everything that had happened. I thought about Lysander and his sweet, beguiling ways. His bright smile, his air of sunshine, and the dark figure he painted into every single one of his pieces that he hid in his studio. I thought about Miriam and her hand of friendship, that on the surface seemed to be considerate, like she was an ally. And yet, I feared it carried with it a lethal sting in the tail.

And then there was Damien.

Darkly, brooding Damien. With his glacial stares, sharp tongue, and hands that protected me at a time when I least expected it.

What was this place?
And who were these people?

As I stepped out of the shower into the misty bathroom, grabbing my towel from the rack where I'd left it by the door, I caught sight of the mirror above the sink and my heart leapt from my chest as my pulse hammered. Sirens blared in my ears as I tried to hold onto my sanity—sanity that was rapidly draining away.

On the glass, written for me to find when the room was steamy, like it was right now after my shower, were the words, 'He's the devil'.

I stood staring at the words, panting out my breaths as condensation trickled down the glass, not quite believing what I was seeing. My stomach was tied in knots, my throat dry, and all I could think was, who the fuck has been in our home?

And who was the devil?

I wanted to dart from the bathroom, get my father, and leave this cabin. Get as far away from this place as I could. Anger surged through me as I wiped my hand over the words to erase them, my body trembling as I tried to block out every message that'd been left for me. Messages that were replaying in my head like a twisted mantra.

Trust no one.
They're all liars here.
He's the devil.

Firethorne

He's the devil.
He's the devil.

Panic raced through me as I flung the door open, and standing on the other side, looking at me with grave concern, stood my father.

"What on earth has happened? Are you okay, Maya? I thought I heard you scream."

"We need to get out of here," I snapped, clinging to the towel wrapped around me as I pushed past him, focused on getting to my room to repack the suitcase I'd unpacked the night before.

"What are you talking about?" my father asked, following me the short distance to my room. "Why do we have to leave?"

I spun around to face him, wet strands of hair whipping in my face as I glared with urgency to let him know I wasn't kidding this time. "Someone has been in here, while we were working. Someone broke in." I wanted to say they'd threatened us, but I didn't. Instead, I barked, "We. Need. To leave. Now."

My father stood his ground in my doorway, folding his arms over his chest as a deep crease lined his brow. "What do you mean, broke in?" He looked confused, and added, "Cora came here earlier to leave some food for us for supper. I gave Beresford my key earlier so he could drop off some extra work uniforms for me." Then as his nostrils flared and he met my angry glare with one of his own, he said, "I'm not going anywhere, Maya. These people have been good to me. This might be my only chance to rebuild a life for myself."

It wasn't lost on me that he said *I* and *me* instead of *we*.

"These people..." I tried to regulate my breathing as I spoke. "This house..." I gritted my teeth. "All of it." One last breath, and then I lifted my chin. "It doesn't feel right. We don't belong here. *I* don't belong here."

My father's lip curled up, almost like he was snarling, and he replied in a bitter tone, "You don't belong... *with your father?*" He shook his head in disgust. "How do you think that makes me feel?"

"I don't think we're safe here," I replied, my shoulders sagging as I tried to get through to him. "These people... they aren't what we think they are."

His snarl was more pronounced now, and his brows almost touched as he sneered back at me. "What? Polite, helpful, considerate, kind... I could go on listing more adjectives, but I don't think I need to. You think that's something we can turn away from? Us? In our position? I have nothing, Maya. And that means, neither do you. This is my lifeline. *Our* lifeline."

He didn't have a clue what he was talking about. He didn't know what he was dealing with.

"Someone's been leaving me messages," I blurted out, expecting his expression to change. For empathy to seep in where revulsion currently radiated from him, but it didn't.

"What messages?" he replied.

"On the train here, and this morning, on the porch." I gestured to the bathroom. "And just now, in there."

I don't know what I'd expected, but I honestly thought he'd believe me.

What I didn't expect was for him to widen his eyes, almost like he was mocking me.

"This is crazy talk," he said. "It's probably just kids messing about. The messages might not even be for you."

He didn't bother to ask me what the messages said, and from the way he was reacting, I didn't want to tell him.

"If you want to go, I can't stop you," he added. "But if you leave, you'll be leaving me with a broken heart. Don't you think there's been enough heart break in our lives recently?"

Guilt, like a ten-tonne weight, fell heavy onto my shoulders.

Duty that had been instilled in me from birth, like an invisible thread, wound its way around my heart.

The thirst to please and the hunger for pride thrummed

through me, despite the blaring warning signals firing in my brain.

"I won't be targeted. I won't let anyone scare me," I stated firmly. "But... But I... I don't want to leave you here."

"Then stay." My father stepped closer to me, and with his hand, he cupped my face. "I promise, no one here wants to scare you. I think it's all just a misunderstanding."

I nodded, my eyes dropping to the floor, but I didn't believe him.

There *was* someone targeting us. The messages *were* meant for me. Someone had broken into our fucking home and scrawled one on the fucking bathroom mirror, for Christ's sake. This was serious shit, and when I found out who was sending these messages, they'd live to regret ever crossing my path.

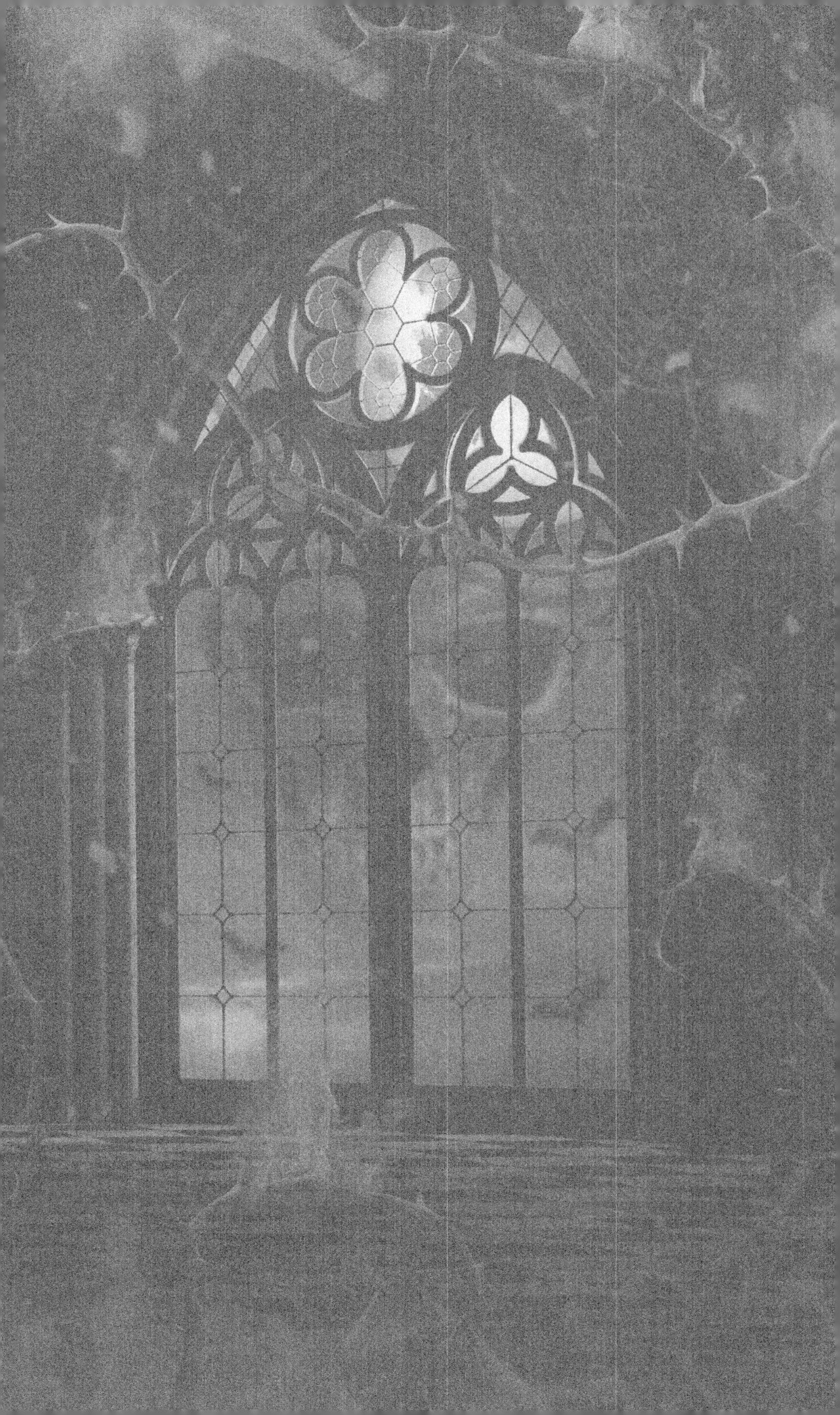

Thirteen

MAYA

I didn't belong here, and I didn't want to be here, but I had to bide my time. It was the only way I could survive, knowing I'd find the culprit of the sick little notes, and eventually, I'd get out of here. Those were the thoughts running through my head as I put my trainers on, after deciding to go for a morning run around the estate. I let my father sleep for those last few minutes before his alarm went off and I crept out of the cabin.

As I emerged into the crisp morning air, I breathed deeply, the coolness refreshing my lungs despite the knot of anxiety in my stomach. I scanned the porch for anything nefarious that might've been left there overnight, but there was nothing.

I was hoping a good run would distract my racing thoughts, so I took off, running through the woods first, my feet pounding the uneven woodland floor. Then I emerged into the open, heading for the lake. I did a few laps around it, then made my way into the woods on the opposite side to where I'd started.

The muscles in my legs burned, as did my lungs, but I wanted to push myself. Running meant all the other crap in my head quietened a little, because all I could focus on was the pounding of my feet, the rasps of my breaths, and the urge to keep going. To never stop.

And then I saw it.

My feet faltered as I came to a stop, bracing my hands on my thighs as I bent forward, panting, but my eyes didn't waver from the sight in front of me. I peered up, squinting, then grimacing as I tried to make sense of what I saw.

The woods were much denser around here, it felt dark, spine-chilling even. A fact that was magnified by what was in front of me. High up in one of the trees, swinging gently in the breeze, was a rope. A noose, to be more precise.

"What the fuck?" I whispered to myself as I stood up, stretching my back, rolling my neck, and shaking my aching limbs. "What the fuck is this shit?"

I took a step closer, the whistle of the light wind and the creak of the branches adding to the creepiness of it, and I shuddered. "This is so fucked up."

"Ah. You found it," a deep voice echoed from behind me.

I spun around to see Lysander strolling towards me, his hands shoved into the pockets of his sweats as he meandered without care, like what I'd found was the most regular, unremarkable thing ever. He stopped a few feet away from me and his gaze shifted from my wide-eyed, horror-struck face to the rope dangling above us.

"What the hell is that?" I pointed to the noose but kept my eyes on him.

"That," Lysander said, his lips in a thin line as he squinted up at the tree through the brightness of the morning sun that was blazing through the gaps in the branches. "Is one of Firethorne's many, and more unusual heirlooms."

I screwed my face up, giving him an incredulous look as I replied, "An heirloom? A fucking heirloom? Are you serious? It's a bloody noose." I was surprised he was talking about it so calmly, like it was the most natural thing in the world. Lysander was sunshine, and this... was so far removed from sunshine. It was pitch black. "Why would you keep it up there? That's fucked up."

"Fucked up is our middle name." His responding half grin and slight shrug of his shoulders only made me screw my face up harder. "Well, for some of us it is."

Damien and his father.

"Please tell me no one used that." I swallowed, waiting for him to respond.

He took a few steps closer to me, then folded his arms over his broad chest and stared wistfully at the noose.

"You know, when we were kids, we never really thought anything of it, hanging up there, swinging away. Damien once asked our father if he could make a swing out of it to play, but we weren't allowed to touch it."

"Why?" I asked, turning to face him.

"You know Damien. He always wants things. He was always the most demanding when we were kids."

"No. I mean, why wouldn't he take it down? Why were you allowed to see that? What sort of sick parent lets their kids play when something like that is up there above their heads?" I stabbed my finger in the air towards the offending ligature.

"The kind that wants to teach them a lesson," Lysander replied without missing a beat. "To teach everyone a lesson."

Firethorne

"Which is?" My eyes bugged as I recoiled, waiting... no... urging him to elaborate. Lysander always told me the truth, and this was one truth I wanted to hear.

Lysander watched the noose as he sighed.

"That rope has been up there for years. No one's ever dared to take it down. My father said it was cursed, and anyone who touched it would bring downfall to the Firethorne name, which is ironic, seeing as the noose was put there by someone who almost destroyed the Firethorne name."

"Go on," I urged.

"It's left there as a reminder," he said. "That no one fucks with the Firethornes and lives to tell the tale."

"Now I really need to know more."

Lysander's eyes didn't stray from that noose as he told his story.

"When my great grandfather left here to go to war, my great grandmother was left on her own to oversee the estate. She had to employ extra staff to help her manage the day-to-day running of the place. But a lot of the men in the town had gone away to war, too. Well, almost all of them.

"A local man, Jeremiah Cramner, came to work here. He wasn't fit for military service, some medical issue, I don't know what, but what I do know is he was fit enough to come here and start an affair with my great grandmother." He paused momentarily to catch his breath, maybe gather his thoughts, and then he went on.

"They were together for some time. Eventually, they became blatant about it; they flaunted it. Everyone knew. There was talk in the town that she was going to leave my great grandfather and run away with Jeremiah. And then, one night, my great grandfather came home unexpectedly and caught them together.

"From what I heard, Cramner thought she'd leave right there and then. But when my great grandfather gave her a glimpse of what her alternate reality would be like, made her see what she was giving up by leaving him for a guy who had nothing, she ghosted him. Cramner, I mean." Lysander put his arms out and shrugged. "The guy couldn't handle it. He loved her. He was obsessed. Cramner lost everything when he lost her. He couldn't come back from that, so one night, he put that rope up there and hung himself."

I took a step back, my gaze falling to the woodland floor to avoid looking at the rope.

"Why there?" I asked.

"Because he wanted to be where she was. He gave his life for her. And legend says, my great grandfather refused to have him cut down until my great grandmother and most of the workers had seen him. I've heard he even invited townsfolk to the estate, so they'd see him too. He was a warning. You don't fuck with the Firethornes. And so, when it got too much to have his decomposing body hanging up there, he was taken down and buried in an unmarked grave. But my great grandfather insisted the noose stayed where it was. He wanted everyone to know, even his wife."

"What? That he had no humanity?"

"That he took no prisoners. That there were consequences to actions when you messed with him."

"And your father thought this was a symbol worth keeping... in the twenty-first century?" I mocked, but Lysander didn't react. "How old were you when he told you that story?"

Lysander frowned as he pondered my question.

"Five, maybe six."

"Jesus, it just gets better and better." I couldn't believe this family were so fucked up that they'd terrorise their own kids like that. And part of me knew I was only scratching the surface of their fuckery. I knew there'd be more below the surface if I dug deeper.

And I would.

Firethorne

"My father would do anything to preserve the family name," Lysander announced proudly, lifting his chin defiantly.

"Yeah, anything..." I shot back. "But refrain from cheating on your mum." Instantly, I felt like shit. The words had come out before I could engage my brain. "I'm sorry," I added, remorse burning in the growing redness on my face. "I shouldn't have said that."

"Why not? It's true," Lysander replied sadly, bowing his head as if he felt the shame of what his father had done. "Damien is the byproduct of my father's sexual gratification. You may as well say it like it is."

"It's not Damien's fault, though, is it? Or yours."

Lysander took a moment to think, then shifted to face me, peering down at me as he spoke.

"We keep our family issues where they belong; in the family. But to the world, father likes to remind everyone that we're a force to be reckoned with. I guess that's why it's still up there."

"And when you take over the estate?" I asked.

"It comes down and I'll burn it," he replied without missing a beat.

I turned my back on the tree that held so much tragedy. A sick reminder that Mr Firethorne felt he needed to put out to the world.

"I don't want us to dwell on something so depressing, though," Lysander said, an easy smile gracing his beautiful face as he stared at me.

The morning sun peeking through the trees made his golden hair shine like silk. He was captivating to look at, but the more I got to know him, the more his true character shone through. The darker side he hid so well in everyday life. And the brightness he exuded that infected everyone around him, a brightness he used to mask the truth.

"I'm so glad I caught you out here this morning," he went on. "I have something exciting to ask you."

I guessed he was going to ask me to sit for him for the painting he wanted to do. But he didn't.

"We're having a party at Firethorne next week. And I'd love you to come, as my guest." He cocked his head, excitement growing with every word he spoke. His face beaming as he waited for me to respond with the word he wanted to hear. Yes.

But I faltered, and he stared at me, waiting expectantly like an excitable child.

I hadn't been to many parties. But a niggling voice in my head told me a party at Firethorne would be like no other. Something I'd never forget. Or perhaps something I'd want to forget.

"I don't think I should," I replied, and Lysander's face dropped. "I work here. You're my employers. I don't think it'd be right for me to socialise—"

"Nonsense," Lysander butted in, and then he reached forward, a gentle finger stroking my cheek as he smiled. "Our parties are legendary. You'll have the best time." And from the way he beamed at me, I wanted to say yes to this man who'd known such sadness but still lived every day in the light, being positive, being kind.

Then a darkness fell over him as he cupped my jaw and brushed his thumb along my bottom lip, his touch morphing from innocence to something else entirely.

"If you don't come, I'll call the whole thing off," he threatened with an insistence I'd never seen before. An urgency to get his own way. His gaze stayed fixed on my lips as his hand kept a hold of my jaw. "And besides," he said suddenly, using a breezier tone, snapping from mysterious devil back to bright angel in a nanosecond. "You'll get to dress up. It's an angels and demons theme. And I can't wait to see you dressed as the angel you are." His eyes twinkled as he spoke, and I wasn't surprised by what he said. Angels and Demons seemed to fit the people of Firethorne Manor pretty well.

I knew the word 'no' wasn't going to cut it. Lysander wouldn't take no for an answer. So, I moved my head back slightly to peer up at him, and he dropped his hand from my face.

"I'll think about it," I said, giving him a thin-lipped smile.

Lysander gave a silent celebration as he pumped his fist and whispered, "Yes."

"I can't promise anything. I only said I'll think about it," I reiterated, not wanting him to get his hopes up.

"It wasn't a no, and that's enough for me," he replied.

It wasn't a no, but it wasn't a yes. It was an 'I don't know what to say'.

I backed up, then told him I had to get to work, sprinting out of the woods, away from the tragic rope in the tree, the ghosts that danced around it, and the man who smiled like everything was right with the world, despite what he was standing under. Maybe that was who Lysander was, an oasis of calm serenity in a world where death and destruction reigned.

Could Lysander be the devil from the mirror message?

I doubted it.

But I couldn't rule him out just yet. After all, wasn't the devil himself a fallen angel?

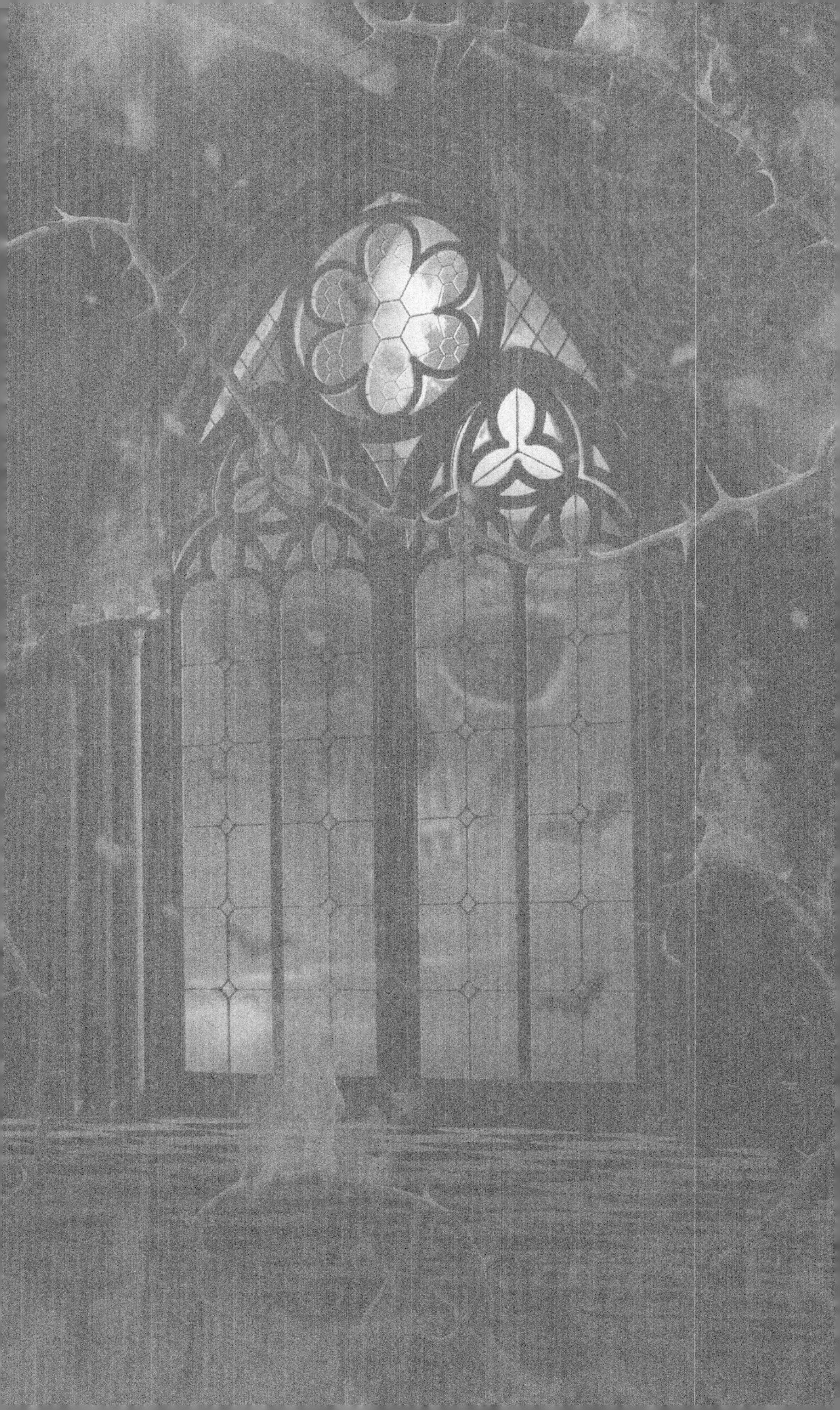

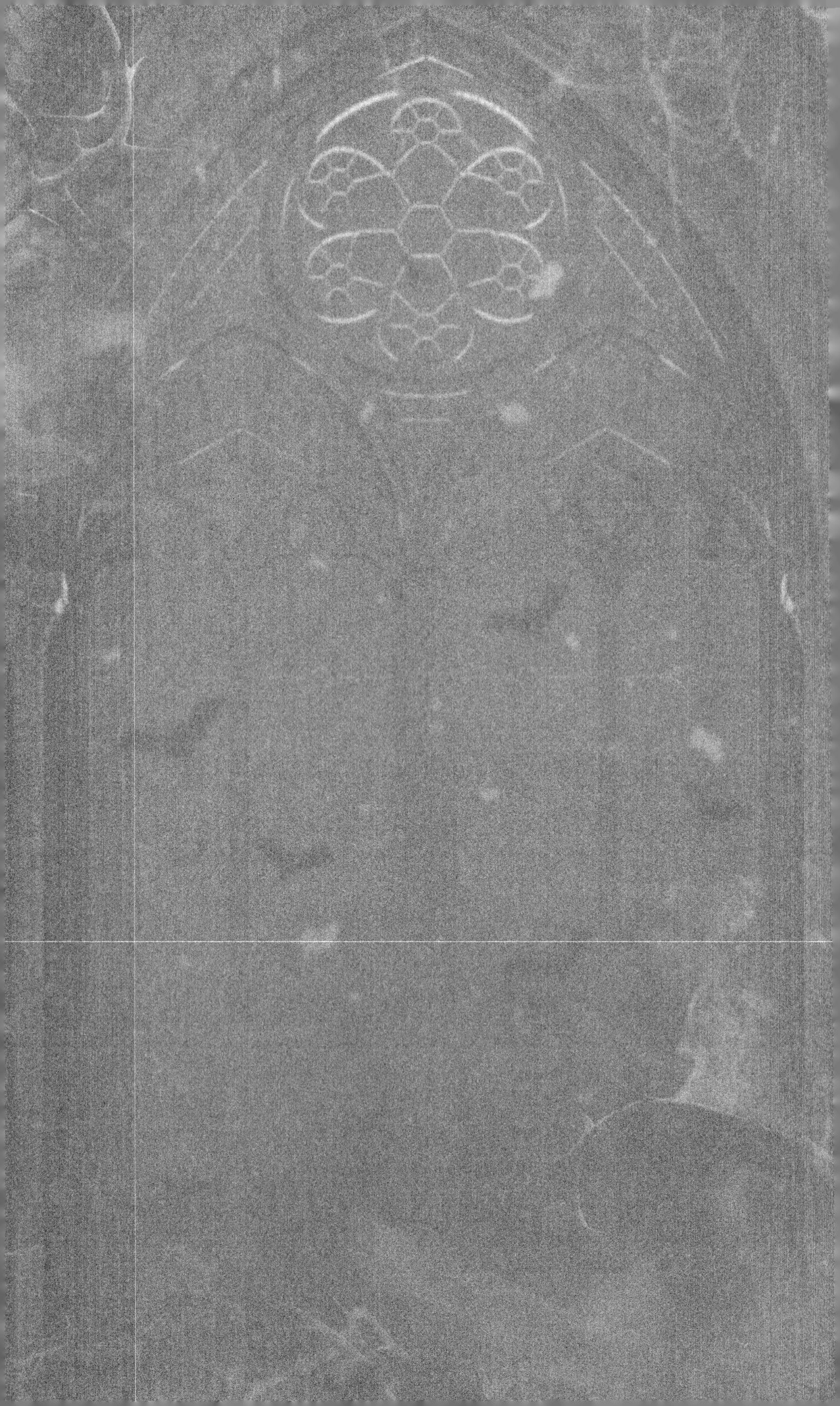

Fourteen

MAYA

I'd been cleaning the second floor all afternoon. Thoughts of the creepy noose in the woods plaguing me.

It'd been a few days since I'd seen it, but I couldn't get the images out of my mind.

This place grew more sinister by the day.

Apart from Cora, I hadn't seen a soul today, and in a way, I was grateful. I could do my job and be with my thoughts. I also found it gave me the opportunity to really explore the house and take it all in.

I wandered down the wood-panelled corridor, heading towards the next room on my schedule. I'd been told to clean and dust every room up here, and I could see the door for the next room was open. Light streamed out from the open doorway, casting a welcome ray of light across the dark wood floor. Like a sign that I was welcome there. And when I reached the doorway and saw what room it was, I knew that I was.

The library.

I didn't even bother to push my cart into the room. I was too taken aback by the floor-to-ceiling shelves that held a mountain of books that I could see clearly as I stood on the threshold. This house held some secrets that appealed to me, after all. Lysander's studio, and now this place. I took a step into the hidden oasis, noticing a rolling ladder in the corner, and I had the overwhelming urge to climb it and study all the titles on the shelves. I felt drawn to this room, like the promise of escaping to another world was beckoning me on. There was nothing I loved more than reading.

I breathed deep, the smell of wisdom and adventure that came from the pages around me made a calmness settle in my body and mind. A calm I hadn't felt in a long time. And then I walked further into the library, heading to the far side so I could take a look at some of the titles, touch them, and imagine this was all mine. That this was a place I belonged.

Once I reached the furthest shelf, I scanned the spines, lifting my hand to gently stroke the leather-bound books like they were priceless jewels. To me, they were. When I saw a copy of one of my favourites, *Sons and Lovers by D. H. Lawrence*, I pulled the edition off the shelf and opened it, reading the first lines with the kind of excitement I always felt when I was starting a new book.

And then...

A cough from behind startled me, and I jumped, almost dropping the book as I spun around to face where that cough had come from.

Right behind me, sitting in a leather armchair in the corner, with a book open on his lap was Damien.

"Do you make a habit of sneaking into rooms and touching other people's belongings?" Damien asked, wearing an expression that showed he loved torturing me. His grin was wicked, his one eyebrow raised, and his eyes glowed like a deadly furnace ready to burn me alive.

"No," I spat back. "Do you?"

I waited for something, anything in his expression that might give him away as my mystery note writer, but he just widened his demonic smile and huffed a laugh. Then he closed his book and placed it on the table beside his chair, and the image of his hand on Edward's as he stopped him touching me in his father's office appeared in my mind, a reminder that maybe he wasn't the devil I imagined.

Or was he?

I stayed rooted to the spot as he stood up, and with slow, measured steps, he sauntered over to me.

"What caught your eye?" he asked, then he snatched the book out of my hand so fast I didn't even see it coming, and he snapped it shut to look at the title. "Sons and Lovers. Interesting choice. Very... telling." He nodded to himself as he stared at the book.

It was my turn to cock my head and frown as I asked, "Why?"

He tilted his head and studied me as he replied, "I think it's funny that of all the books in here, you chose the one that tells the story of a man with an Oedipus complex that struggles to form long lasting relationships with women following the death of his mother. Change the character's name to Lysander and you've got a Firethorne history right there."

If I needed another reason to hate Damien Firethorne, he had just given me one, gift wrapped and branded with the acid from his tongue.

The urge to defend Lysander burned within me, and I

couldn't stop myself from snatching the book back off him, a move which seemed to amuse him even more.

"You might interpret it like that," I snapped. "But I don't. Everyone has a different experience when they read a book. Everyone has their own opinion."

"Oh, this'll be interesting," he mocked. "And your opinion is?"

"Not like yours, *thank God*." I muttered the last part, but he still laughed. I ignored him as best I could and carried on, the English Literature student part of my brain taking over. "There are theories that it's an oedipal novel, that the story was influenced by Sigmund Freud, but for me it's the themes of suffocation and the duty to a parent that strike harder. It's something I can relate to."

"Oh yes," he announced, superiority bristling as he stared me down. "Because you have to suffer in silence and work here to please your own parent that suffocates your every waking moment?"

I wasn't in the mood for my relationship with my father to be psycho-analysed by the likes of Damien Firethorne. He was in no position to judge my family. His own was more fucked up than any I'd known. So, I shoved the book back onto the shelf and gestured to where he was sitting.

"What are you reading?" I lifted my chin, trying to exert my confidence.

"Orwell. Animal Farm," he announced proudly, rocking back on his heels.

I quirked a brow. "Trying to decide which animal you represent?" I was mocking him, but it didn't work.

"I already know which animal I am, and it's not the one you think." He took a step closer, leaning forward to whisper in my ear. "The mask we wear for the world, and the reality we keep hidden inside can be two very different things." Then moving back and spreading his arms out, he said, "But I guess you already know that. As they say, don't judge a book by its cover. I'd hate for you to do that, Maya. Because if you did, that'd make you just like every other lame asshole I've ever met, and I'd hate for you to be so... disappointing." I swallowed, and he went on. "Disappointing is the last thing I'd expect... from *you*."

I didn't like the way he glared at me after saying that last part, and I took a step back.

"You don't know me." I gritted my teeth as his intense glare unnerved me. Like he was stripping me bare with the condescension of his gaze.

"I think I know you well enough," he replied flippantly, walking back to his chair and then sitting down, resting his legs out in front of him, one ankle crossed over the other, like he didn't have a care in the world. "You're the dutiful daughter, throwing her life into the trash so she can make daddy dearest happy. A promising honours student who now cleans the shit off our toilets for a living. But one who does it like it's the most important job she'll ever do. One that comes to this house every day, even though the warnings blare in her head telling her that she shouldn't be here, but she comes here anyway, and she does it with conviction. Eager to please Mrs Richardson, my father, Lysander, anyone who she thinks she needs to. But not me. Or Edward, for that matter. No. She'd probably cut his hand off with a blunt, rusty knife for touching her if she had the chance." He tilted his head in thought. "Or would that be too much? Too showy?"

"I'll leave the torture and maiming to you," I shot back. "Something tells me you'd enjoy it more than I would."

"I do love the debased honesty of the human spirit when it comes out to play," he replied, his words crafted in hell by the devil himself. "But we have to make it worthwhile, don't you agree?"

"I'm not sure I'd agree with anything that passes through your mind."

Firethorne

"That's a bold statement, Miss Cole, seeing as you'll never truly know what I'm thinking."

"But I can guess."

He smiled to himself and waited a moment before he asked, "And what is your guess right now?"

I glared back at him, our eyes locked in some kind of silent battle, and then I replied, "You don't want the hired help in your precious space, touching your things, tainting it."

"On the contrary," he retorted. "I have no problem with you being here. In fact, I'm happy for you to come in here whenever you want." And in a quieter voice, he said, "No one else comes in here. It's the perfect place to be if you need to... *hide*." He narrowed his eyes at me, unspoken accusations lying within.

I wasn't sure what he was implying, but I didn't like it, and I didn't want to stay here for a moment longer, so I told him, "Don't worry, I won't disturb you again. In future, I'll make sure the room is empty before I come in to clean." And I stalked out before he could give me a snarky, venomous response.

My breaths were ragged, my heart beating out of my chest as I stalked down the corridor, pushing my cart. My mind willing me to put distance between myself and Damien Firethorne, my body shaking with anger and the spike of adrenaline I always seemed to experience when I was around him.

I was hoping luck would be on my side as I escaped down the corridor, but as I turned a corner, I realised that was wishful thinking. At the end of the hallway stood Mr Firethorne, with his head bowed, in deep conversation with Miriam.

When he saw me, his head snapped up, and he took what appeared to be a guilty step backwards, before whispering something to Miriam. Then he moved to open a door close to where they stood, stepped through it and shut the door, leaving Miriam to turn and face me. Her cheeks were pink, like she had something to hide, but as a feline smirk spread across her face, I knew that wasn't the case. Miriam didn't hide anything. She didn't care enough to go to all that trouble.

"Maya!" she said in that over-excited tone of hers. "I was just looking for you. Uncle said you were cleaning up here." As she moved closer, she put her arms out, ready to envelope me in one of her heavily perfumed hugs.

I let her, my arms staying limp by my sides as she wrapped hers around me. Then, I froze and recoiled as I heard her breathe deeply, like she was breathing me in.

"I love that scent in your hair." She grinned as she pulled away from me. "What products do you use?"

I'd been cleaning all day. I knew I didn't smell my best. I didn't smell bad, but she was making out I was some scented princess floating down the hall. It was just plain weird.

"Cheap shampoo," I replied, my voice flat, and I'm sure my puzzlement was playing out on my face too, but she didn't react.

"We need to have a girls' night," she stated, and by the way her eyes darted about, I could tell she was already mentally planning it, whether I agreed to it or not. "I could come over, we could do face masks, share make-up tips, do all the stuff sisters do. I never had a sister. I always wanted one, though. I've had to settle for two morose male cousins, but Lysander is pretty. Maybe we should rope him in, too? Get him to be our model. With his cheekbones..." She was laughing as she spoke, and I had to stop her. I didn't have time for this.

"Why were you looking for me?" I didn't want to be rude, but the sooner I cleaned this level, the sooner I could get away from this place and go back home.

"Oh that, yes." She peered over her shoulder then moved a step closer to me and said, "We're having a party next week, and you *have* to come."

"Lysander already invited me," I replied, and instantly, her face dropped. A look of utter defeat and disappointment shone back at me, and in that moment, I felt a little guilty for bursting her bubble of excitement. "I'm not gonna be able to make it, though," I added. "I don't think it's right for me to attend a party thrown by my employers."

"Oh, Maya, will you stop! That's nonsense," she said, determination burning in her eyes now. "You're my friend. And if you don't come, then... then... I'll call the whole thing off."

"That's what Lysander said," I couldn't help blurting out, and she narrowed her eyes at me.

"And Damien?" she asked.

"Hasn't said a thing," I replied honestly.

But from the way she maintained her glare, I don't think she believed me.

"Well... anyway..." she went on. "I want you there as my plus one. I need you there. It's hard being the only girl in this house."

"I don't have anything to wear, and I can't afford to buy anything new, so—"

"I'll lend you something," she announced. "I have too many clothes. Honestly, Maya, you're not getting out of this that easily."

That was becoming painfully clear.

"I'll think about it," I told her, and she folded her arms, popped her hip and gave a little huff like a spoilt child.

"Is that the best you can do? Think about it?"

I nodded and she gave another huff.

"Fine. But I will get you there." Then a little brighter, she added, "Maybe we could get ready for the party together? I could do your make-up for you."

"Maybe." I kept my smile in place and stepped towards my cart to push it down the hallway. But as I went to walk past, Miriam put her arm out to stop me.

I gasped, standing still, and she reached up and stroked her finger down a stray whisp of hair that'd fallen from my messy bun, and then, gently, she tucked it behind my ear, a move that felt way too intimate.

"I have the perfect white dress for you," she said on a whisper, as if she was imagining me in it. "You'll be the prettiest angel."

I wanted to tell her that Lysander had said that, too, but I didn't. I swallowed, nodded politely, and walked away, trying to ignore the boulder of dread that hit my stomach in reaction to how she was acting. I had no intention of going to their party, or being the angel they thought I was, of being anything for them.

The sooner I got out of here, the better.

After a long day, I trudged back through the grounds on weary legs, heading towards our cabin. When I got to the clearing and saw something sitting on the door mat, I stopped dead. I peered around me, listening for any noises, but all I heard were the tweets of the birds overhead and the rustling of the leaves in the trees blowing in the breeze. I couldn't sense anyone watching, but I still took slow, careful steps as I made my way to the porch.

Once closer, I saw the brown cardboard box that was sitting on the mat had no name or address on it, and a cautionary shiver ran down my spine. I took the last few steps up to the porch, stood over the package and then crouched down.

Cautiously, I pulled the parcel tape off the top, and with bated breath and my heart pounding in my ears, I slowly opened the box. What lay inside was the last thing I'd expected to find.

Firethorne

Books.

Leather bound books that made me quietly gasp as I reached in to pick the first one out.

I opened the cover to see it was a first edition of The Mayor of Casterbridge by Thomas Hardy. Underneath that, was a copy of Wuthering Heights, and then, at the very bottom, sat the edition of Sons and Lovers that I'd picked out in the library earlier today. No note. No message, but it wasn't necessary. I knew who'd sent this.

But the question I had to ask myself was, why?

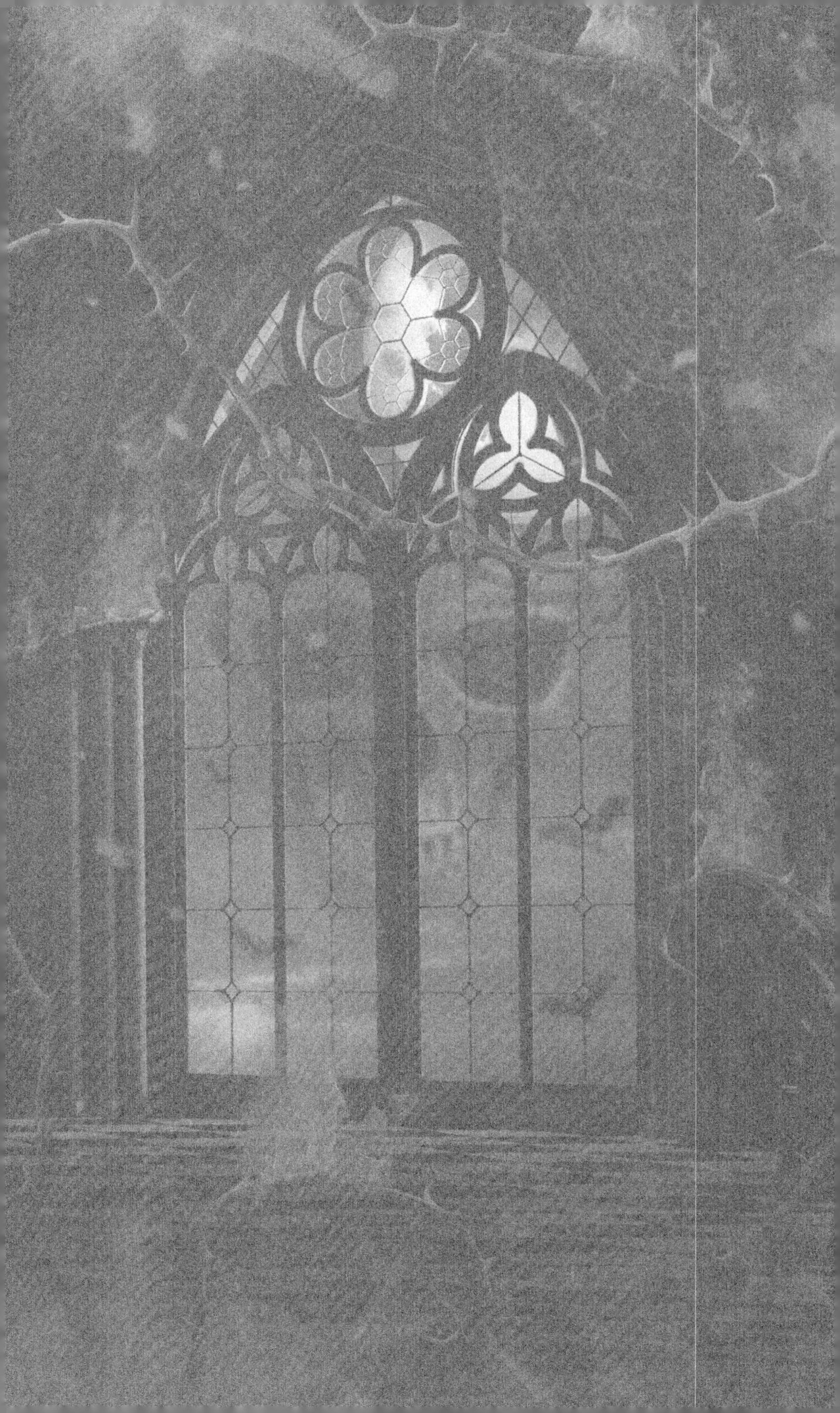

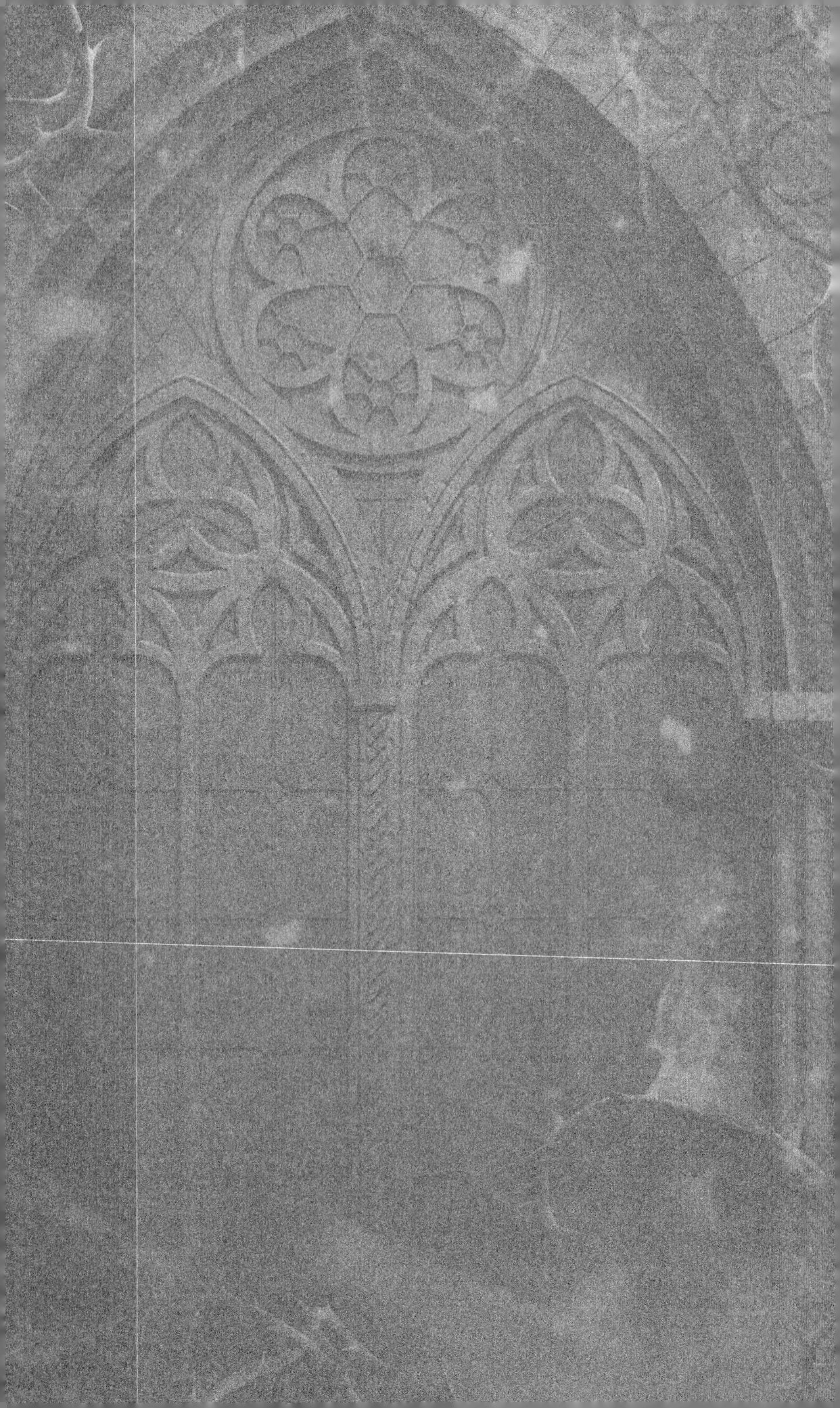

Fifteen
THE FIRETHORNES

"I do love our little catch ups," Miriam remarked as she sat with Damien and Lysander in the dining room, having breakfast. "Although, I'm surprised to see you here, Damien. I thought you only came out at night, you know, with the rest of the vampires."

"If I'm a vampire, then you'll be safe. After the stories I've heard about last night, your veins are filled with ninety percent alcohol, and you haven't been a virgin in a very long time." Damien lifted his coffee cup and took a sip.

And Miriam ignored him, her eyes narrowing as she said, "Our little project might not be safe from you, though." Her

Firethorne

lip curled in a smug smile. "Don't vampires lust after young, beautiful virgins, seducing and manipulating them for sport?"

"Speaking from experience?" Damien sneered. "You do have manipulation down to a fine art, after all, *cousin dear.*"

Miriam huffed in response, but from the way she grinned to herself, she agreed with him.

"And what about you?" Miriam turned in her seat to face Lysander. "What's happening with you?" she asked, poking him playfully in the side as she grinned at him. "I know I'm ahead of you in our little game, but have you managed to make any headway? Did you impress her with more of your little drawings?"

Lysander sat back in his chair, and with a contemplative quirk of his brow, he said, "You make it sound like you're winning, which we both know you're not. Maya has more intelligence than to fall for your tricks. Has she even worn that necklace you gave her?" He smirked back at her, and Miriam's lips thinned as she replied, "No, but that's not the point. She never gave it back."

"I'd check the bins if I were you," Damien piped up from across the room. "It'll probably be in there, along with the sketch Lysander gave her."

"How do you know about that?" Lysander glared at his half-brother.

"Because you told us, the last time Miriam accosted us in the library, remember?"

Lysander furrowed his brow in thought, trying to recall exactly what he'd said at that meeting, but Miriam interrupted.

"Tell me what's happened since. Do you have anything to report?"

"I told her the Jeremiah Cramner story," Lysander said.

"For fuck's sake." Damien sat forward; deep lines set in his brow as he glowered at his half-brother from across the table. "You're supposed to be seducing the girl, not scaring her half to death. Why did you take her there? Did you want to give her a glimpse of her own future or something?"

"I didn't *take* her there. I met her there, when she was on her morning run."

"So you're stalking her," Miriam said. "Memorising her schedule."

"Aren't you?" Lysander retorted, and by the way Miriam grinned to herself, it was obvious she was doing the same.

Damien just rolled his eyes.

"I didn't choose that location, it just happened," Lysander went on, trying to defend himself. "And anyway, I sweetened the story with an invite to the party."

"And?" Miriam leaned forward, placing her chin on her clenched fist as if waiting with bated breath for Lysander to finish the story.

"She said she'd think about it."

Miriam couldn't keep the relief and the smugness off her face as she sat back and sighed wistfully.

"And what about you?" Damien asked her, his head cocked as he rested his elbows on the table and steepled his fingers together, studying her closely. "Have you locked her down yet?"

"We're gonna get ready for the party together. She's borrowing one of my outfits," Miriam announced proudly, but it didn't go unnoticed that she wouldn't look either of them in the eye and instead chose to stir her cup of tea with her spoon, even though it had already gone cold.

"So, she's not thinking about it anymore?" Damien's dark gaze scrutinized his cousin, and then, as he peered over at Lysander, he could see jealousy creeping over his half-brother as his clenched jaw ticked and his eyes narrowed on Miriam.

"She'll be there," Miriam replied.

"But she hasn't said yes." Damien was fanning the flames, shaking his head as his own smug grin spread over his face.

"Not exactly." Miriam didn't like to be interrogated,

especially not by Damien. He had a way of knowing exactly how to get under her skin, and it vexed her more than she'd ever let on. "Anyway, what have *you* managed to do to win the bet?"

Lysander's gaze jumped from Miriam to Damien, like he was watching a tennis match.

"I'm not a part of your ridiculous bet, remember?"

Miriam rolled her eyes.

"Let's not kid ourselves. If you had the chance, you would. She's exactly your type."

"You've said that before, and I've already told you, I'm not interested."

At that moment, the elder Firethorne strolled into the dining room, bringing with him a wickedly dark air of hostility that reverberated around the room, making everyone sit up a little taller and become a little more guarded.

Everyone except Damien.

The elder Firethorne sat at the head of the table and poured himself a cup of coffee, took a sip, then stared around the table at his family.

"I have to go away for a few days for an important business meeting," he announced plainly. "I trust I can leave you all to hold the fort while I'm gone."

"I could come with you," Lysander said, hope ringing in his voice.

"Out of the question," Firethorne shot back. "If I was going to take anyone to an important business meeting, it'd be Damien. He has a good head for business. Better than yours."

Their father was doing what he did best, playing the sons off against each other. Choosing who he'd bestow his sparse and meagre compliments on. Today it was Damien. That wouldn't be the case tomorrow. He liked to keep them where he wanted them, below him and begging for any scraps of attention.

"But I don't have time to babysit your brother and hold

his hand through this meeting. It's too important," he added, knocking Damien down after building him up. "Do you think you can manage to keep things ticking over here? I refuse to come home to total mayhem."

"I'll keep them in check," Miriam snipped.

But he didn't even look at her as he said, "You're the one I'd worry about the most."

Miriam wasn't immune from his snide comments, but she had armour just as sturdy as any man.

"Maybe I'll prove you wrong," she replied, but Firethorne ignored her.

The four of them sat in silence as Mrs Richardson walked in and placed a plate of food in front of Mr Firethorne. Crippling tension hung in the air, but it was Lysander who attempted to break it.

"Who are you meeting with?"

Firethorne dropped his cutlery onto his plate, the noise jarring as it clattered and he braced himself in his chair, anger burning from being questioned by his eldest son.

"It's none of your fucking business. And for once, could I eat my breakfast in peace?"

Miriam and Lysander stood up, and as they headed for the door, Miriam whispered, "At least we'll be able to party without having to think of an excuse to get rid of him."

Damien stayed sitting where he was. He wouldn't let his father's disdain force him out of the room before he was ready to leave. He wouldn't let anyone tell him what he had to do. Lysander might say he was only half a Firethorne, but in truth, Damien was more Firethorne than any of them. And as the elder Firethorne grinned to himself as he sliced through his bacon and eggs, it was obvious he knew that too.

Sixteen

MAYA

It'd been a while since I'd seen anyone other than my father and Cora. For days now, Cora had me working in the extensive cellars and storerooms below the estate, taking inventory of stock, rearranging shelves and tidying. At times, I thought she was making extra work for me, telling me to rearrange things a certain way one day, then revert to the old way the next. But I did it, and I did it like Damien had said I would, with a smile on my face.

I hadn't worn the necklace Miriam had given me. I hadn't even taken it out of the drawer in my room. I'd read the books Damien left for me, though. The fact that it was him who'd lent

𝔉𝔦𝔯𝔢𝔱𝔥𝔬𝔯𝔫𝔢

them was something I tried to ignore. They were classics, after all. It would be a crime not to enjoy them. I had no intention of returning to the library any time soon, though.

I was moving boxes of spare cutlery and kitchenware, ready to wipe the surfaces down for the third time this week, when I heard the faint hum of voices coming from a vent. There was a gap in the shelving, so I shimmied through it to get closer to the wall and stood on my tiptoes, pressing my ear as close to the vent as I could to hear what was being said.

"But if I'm not there, if I don't learn these things, how am I supposed to take over when you're gone?"

Lysander's voice was firm and insistent, but there was a vulnerability to it that I wasn't used to hearing. Like he was pleading but didn't want to upset the person he was talking to.

"I've already told you; this doesn't concern you. I won't discuss this any further."

Firethorne's stern tone always made me recoil, even when I wasn't in the room when I heard it.

"But you trust *Damien*," Lysander shot back, and the sound of glass smashing made me flinch. When I heard the next words, I knew exactly who had caused that smash.

"Speak to me like that again and my aim will be better."

Firethorne.

It was silent for a moment, and I thought maybe Lysander had left and the conversation was over. Then, a murmur echoed through the vent.

"All I want to do is please you. All I've ever wanted to do was make you proud."

Lysander's vulnerability was palpable now, and I held my breath, closing my eyes as I listened intently.

"If you want to please me, then shut the hell up and stay out of my way," Firethorne hissed. "And as for proud, I think that ship sailed a long time ago."

"What's that supposed to mean?"

"It means I couldn't give a rat's ass what you do. You're nothing. And you'll never be anything. You're a nobody. Stick to your fucking paintings of trees and let the real men do the important jobs."

My heart ached for Lysander. When God was appointing fathers, he really was at the end of the queue. Firethorne didn't even deserve the title. He spoke to his son like shit and kept a sick reminder of how fucked up their family was with that vile rope he kept in his woods. I had no words to describe how much I hated Mr Firethorne.

"I'm not a nobody," Lysander fought back, and I could clearly see him in my mind's eye, lifting his chin defiantly, standing taller to counteract his father's disdain. "I am somebody. I have talent. Other people can see it."

"Who?" His father laughed, a laugh that made my skin crawl.

"People," Lysander responded weakly.

"What, Beresford? Or Mrs Richardson? Miriam, maybe? Or that new little slut that creeps around the corridors pretending to clean? I know for damn sure it's not Damien."

"Don't call her that," Lysander growled, and Firethorne laughed again.

"What, the slut?"

"She's not a slut. And she works damn hard for you. Her name. Is. Maya," he barked.

I could barely breathe as I waited for Firethorne's response. My heart was pounding, my body shaking, but I didn't dare move in case I missed anything.

"Her name is whatever the fuck I want it to be," Firethorne snapped back. "And she'll do whatever the fuck I want."

I heard movement, maybe a door slamming, chairs scraping on the hardwood floor from the room they were in, then Damien's voice as he said, "Did I hear my name mentioned? You know it's rude to talk about people behind their back."

Firethorne

"We didn't talk about you," Lysander replied haughtily. "You barely register on our radar."

But Firethorne's response was more telling. "I have some contracts I want to go over with you, Damien. I would appreciate your advice." And I could tell those words would be like a knife through Lysander's heart. That his father could be so dismissive of his importance and his self-worth. Making Lysander feel like he was second best to his half-brother, Damien. Pitting Damien against Lysander as the superior son. It made me sick.

"I'm free now, shall we go to your office?" Damien replied, and I heard Firethorne agree and the sound of a door opening and closing.

In that moment, I wanted to go and find Lysander, tell him he was somebody, that he was talented. But in doing that, I'd have to admit that I'd been eavesdropping and heard his private conversation.

And then it hit me.

There was something I could do.

I squeezed myself out of the space against the shelving and brushed the dust off my hands onto my apron, then untied it and left it on the shelf.

I took the stairs back up to the kitchen, and when I entered, I told Cora, "I just need to pop out for a second. I won't be long."

Cheerfully, she answered, "Okay, love." But, when she realised I was heading for the door to the main house, and not the one that'd lead me outside, she tried to call out to me to wait, but I didn't listen. I carried on walking, heading out into the hallway towards the room that I guessed they'd been in when I'd overheard them talking.

As I came to the doorway, I lifted my hand to knock, but the door swung open, and I was left holding my clenched fist in the air like an idiot. My mouth hung open as I stood staring at Lysander, beautiful, wholesome Lysander with sunshine in his eyes and warmth in his heart.

"Maya?" He frowned, no doubt questioning what I was doing standing in front of the door to the room he was in, looking like a creeper. "Are you okay?" He cocked his head, empathy and concern swimming in his eyes.

"I'm fine. I'm okay. It's just..." I was nervous and rambling.

"Do you need help with something?" he asked and stepped aside to let me in, but I didn't move. I just stood there, wringing my hands.

"I wanted to say... I mean... I wanted to tell you... Yes."

"Yes?" His brow remained furrowed as he stared, waiting.

"Yes, I'll go. To the party. With you."

He closed his mouth, and I watched his neck constrict as he swallowed. And then a massive smile appeared, and I knew I'd done the right thing. I'd made him happy after all the shit his father had dumped on him. I was showing him he was somebody. He was worthy.

"Really?" he asked, his eyes wide like a child. "You'll come?"

I nodded. "Yes."

"That's just... wow... that's—" He was cut off when a curt voice behind jumped in.

"That's so exciting!" Miriam squealed. She stalked over to stand beside me and threaded her arm through mine. "I won't be able to do your make-up because I'll be running a little late that day, but I can totally lend you a dress. You're going to look amazing." She squeezed my arm. "It's going to be so much fun!" She waggled her eyebrows at us both, then dropped my arm and sauntered off, leaving us both staring at her as she floated down the hallway and out of sight.

"You do know she thinks you're her plus one," Lysander remarked quietly.

"She can think what she likes," I replied before engaging my brain, and then I backtracked, saying, "I didn't mean that to sound rude. I just meant..."

"You don't have to explain." Lysander smiled kindly. "You never have to explain anything to me."

Later that afternoon, as I was setting up the dining room ready for their evening meal, I opened the cupboard where the plates and bowls were kept. And there, placed on top of the plates was another drawing. A sketch.

I picked it up and took it out of the cupboard, holding it like it was something precious, as delicate as snowflakes that might disappear at any moment.

It was another portrait of me, only the lines were cleaner, the likeness near perfect, and he'd used colour this time, capturing the blue of my eyes perfectly. But that wasn't what stole my breath away. It was the words written at the bottom.

Not all of us are lying to you.

I read the words over and over, the reality of what they meant sinking in as clarity hit me.

It was him.

Lysander.

He was the one warning me.

Why hadn't I realised it before?

I couldn't work out how he was linked to the man on the train, but he'd been there, when I found the note under the rat trap and I'd run through the woods, chasing the sound of trodden leaves and the feel of prying eyes. He could've put those words on our mirror in the bathroom. He had the opportunity. It had to be him. He'd shown me the rope to warn me to be careful. He'd shown me kindness to protect me. To let me know I wasn't alone. Lysander was sending me messages, and I had to let him know that I knew.

I placed the sketch in my apron pocket and made my way out of the dining room, taking the stairs to the second floor and heading towards Lysander's studio. Once there, I knocked and waited. I could hear him behind the door, paintbrushes clinking against glass, the shuffle of paper, and then the sound of his footsteps as he came to open the door.

"Maya," he exclaimed. "What a nice surprise."

"I just wanted to say thank you," I replied, nerves sparking as I stared at his beautiful face. Butterflies invaded my stomach as I tried not to become tongue-tied.

"Thank you for what?" he asked.

"For..." I swallowed. "For being there. For letting me know I'm not alone. It's been tough, coming here, but knowing I have you, it helps... so... thank you."

"It's my pleasure," he replied. "I'll always be here."

"I know." I smiled, feeling a strange sort of relief wash over me. Then I took a deep breath and added, "I know everything, and I'm grateful. But you don't need to worry about me. The messages were a little... unique, but I know you were just looking out for me."

He frowned and opened his mouth like he was going to say something, then he closed it and took a moment, tilting his head as if he was deep in thought before he replied, "I'm happy to be of service."

We stood staring at each other, getting lost in a world that was slowly erecting around us, a world we were creating, one delicate moment, one stolen glance, one kindness at a time. Then Lysander cleared his throat, and I remembered myself and where I was.

"I have to go and finish setting up for dinner," I told him, but I reached forward and took his hand in mine, the warmth of his palm sending a spark of electricity right through me.

Firethorne

"I'm glad I met you, Lysander Firethorne," I said as I tried to hide the emotions that threatened to break free as my voice began to crack.

"I'm honoured to have met you, too, Maya Cole," he replied, and reluctantly, I dropped his hand. But his warmth stayed with me, like it was branded on my palm as a reminder that he was here. That I'd found him. That something special was blossoming.

As I walked away from his studio, heading back to the dining room, the hairs on the back of my neck stood to attention, my heart fluttering as I felt his gaze searing into my soul.

Not all of us are lying to you.

No, he wasn't.

He was telling me his family couldn't be trusted. Warning me to be on my guard. But with him, I could feel myself soften in a way I never had before. A way I'd always been afraid to, but maybe I needed to be more daring. Let my guard down with the right person.

Once my shift had finished, I made my way back to our cabin and went straight to my room, taking the sketch out and pinning it on my wall, right next to the other one he'd given me when he'd first shown me his studio. Then I sat back, comparing the two sketches, marvelling at how improved this latest sketch was compared to the one he'd given me days ago. The colours and shading were stunning, making my eyes sparkle and my hair shine. He'd captured features of my face perfectly, the fullness of my lips, the blush of my cheeks, the lines of my nose, my face, all of me. This sketch was a million times better than his first draft. It proved to me that he really saw me, the real me. Proud, curious, fragile, vulnerable at times, but ultimately, strong. He knew me, and he was showing me through his art.

Maybe I should've been pissed off that he'd messed with my head by sending the messages, leaving writing on my mirror, toying with my emotions and my sanity, but I wasn't. Like Cora said, they didn't function like we did.

The Firethornes were different.

Lysander was different.

And he was doing his best, considering his father and the upbringing he'd endured, the daily venom Damien spat at him, and the battering to his self-esteem. He was trying his best to make sense of it all.

And so was I.

Maybe it'd be better if we tried to make sense of it together.

Maybe this party would be the answer to everything.

Maybe.

Just maybe.

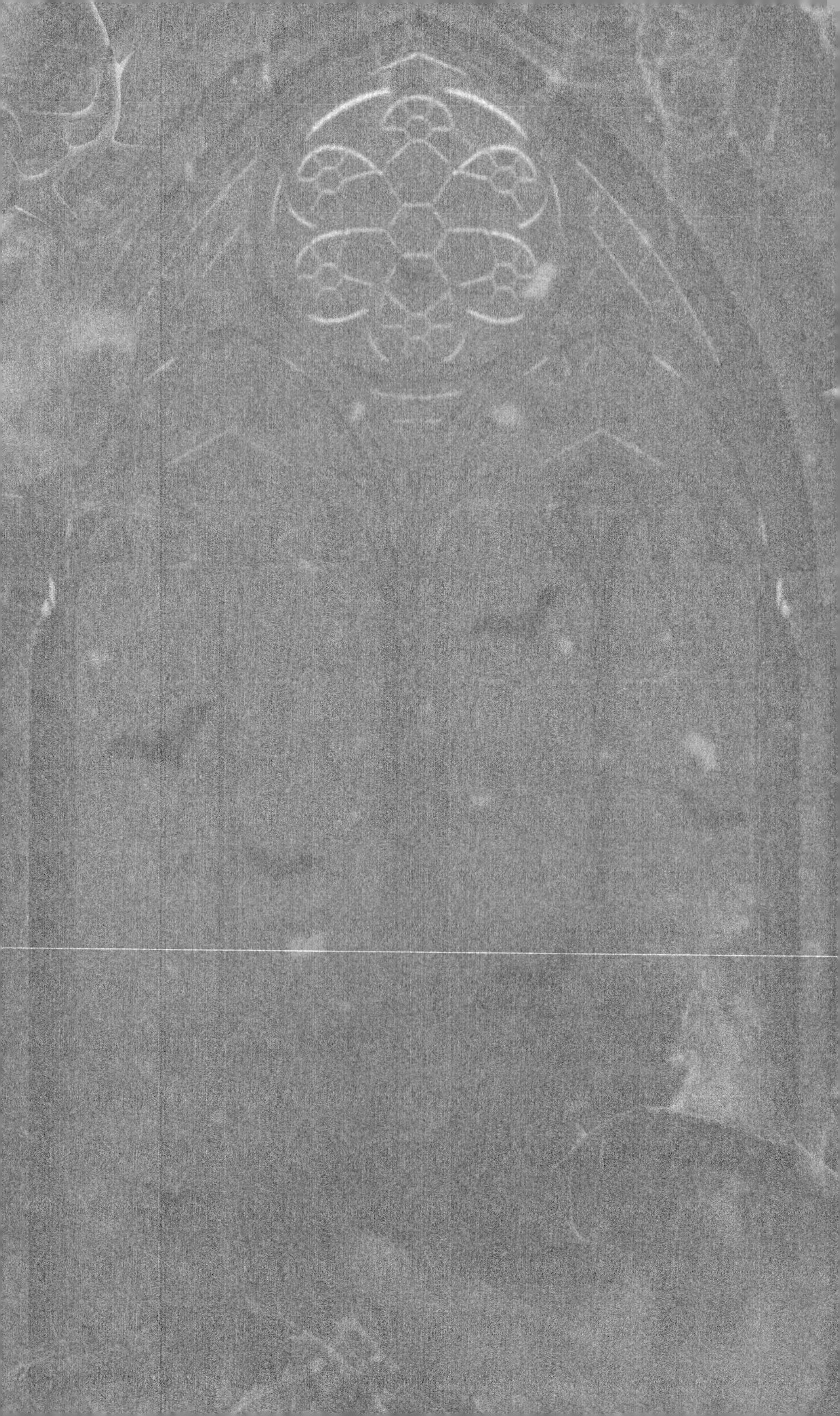

Seventeen

MAYA

It was the night of the party, and in a way, I was relieved my father had gone on a weekend business trip with Mr Firethorne. He told me it was something to do with future building work on the estate, and I was glad he was being included in important decisions, but I'd zoned out when he was explaining it all. And now, as I stepped out of the shower and headed to my room, I was grateful of the time alone so I could get ready and psyche myself up for what lay ahead.

A large box had arrived on my doorstep an hour ago, which I assumed was my outfit from Miriam. I hadn't opened it yet, I'd just placed it on my bed, leaving it for later. But now, I eyed it with curiosity as I sat on the end of the bed and dried my hair, wondering what she'd chosen, hoping it would fit, praying it was okay. The longer I stared, the more nervous and apprehensive I got. So, as soon as my hair was dry, I shut my hairdryer off, dropped it onto my bed and stood up.

I loomed over the box like it held an explosive device, and as the nerves tickled my stomach, I reminded myself that it was just a dress, an angel outfit, nothing to worry about, and I lifted the lid.

Inside there was red tissue paper. Carefully, I folded it back, confused when I saw black leather underneath. This sure as hell wasn't an angel outfit.

What the fuck had she sent me?

I picked up the short, black leather dress—so short I wasn't even sure it'd fit. Holding it up, I noticed it was strapless and there was a tail on the back. It was more risqué than anything I'd ever worn before and on the front, the numbers six, six, six were embroidered in red.

The sign of the devil.

I placed it on the bed and went back to the box, pulling out a pair of thigh-high black leather boots, a hairband of black devil horns, and a black pitchfork.

I smiled to myself. Miriam was obviously pissed off that I was going with Lysander, and this was her way of getting back at me. But it wouldn't work.

So, I wouldn't be an angel. It was no big deal. If she thought she could embarrass me, I'd prove her wrong. I'd wear the damn devil dress. I'd wear the fuck out of it and show her that her little prank had backfired. If she wanted me to be the devil, I'd be the best devil at the party.

I applied my make-up, giving myself smoky eyes to complement the outfit, and then I shimmied into the dress, surprised that it fitted me so well. Okay, it was a little short, shorter than I'd have liked, but as I stood in front of the mirror,

I had to admit that I looked good. Damn good.

I sat on the bed and pulled each of the thigh-high boots on, zipping them up, then standing again. I admired how much taller and leaner they made my legs look. Last, it was the horns. I brushed my long black hair and then slid the hairband on, the horns sitting perfectly on the top of my head. I hadn't been to many parties. I hadn't been to any costume parties. But I knew, as outfits went, this one was kick-ass.

"Not bad at all, Cole," I whispered to myself, picking up the pitchfork and giving a wicked chuckle. "Who wants to be an angel, anyway?"

Walking up the front steps of Firethorne Manor, I could hear the music thumping from inside, the bass pounding in beat with my heart. I felt so nervous, but I didn't want to show it.

Heading to the open door, I could see a crowd of people already gathered in the reception area; red devils, horned demons, and angels all mingling, holding glasses of champagne as they chatted easily with one another. I took a moment to stand in the doorway and take it all in.

I didn't know anyone here, and scanning the room, I couldn't see Lysander or Miriam anywhere. It was blatantly clear I was an outsider, and suddenly, I had an attack of nerves and had to fight the urge to turn around and walk away. But then, I heard a familiar voice call to me from across the crowd.

"Maya! Oh my God, Maya. You look amazing."

Lysander pushed his way through the crowd, and I caught my breath as I stared at him, looking absolutely breathtaking.

His chest was bare and covered with shimmering golden paint. Every perfect pec and ab, every muscle shining as he flexed while walking over to me. He wore a gold loin cloth, had huge golden wings on his back, and above his head sat a golden halo. Lysander, the God of angels, looked stunning. I was speechless.

"Wow," I managed to say as he came to stand in front of me and leant down to place a tender kiss on my cheek.

"Maya the devil. Who knew?" He winked, and I blushed. I know I blushed because I could feel the heat rising in my cheeks, and I dipped my head, but he put his finger under my chin, and I lifted my eyes to look at him. "You look gorgeous," he said quietly in my ear. "I think being a devil suits you."

"I think being an angel suits you," I said, feeling clumsy with my words and then stupid that I'd mirrored his words back to him. "I love the wings."

Oh jeez, I really was losing it.

I love the wings?

I needed to get a grip.

But being around Lysander, when he looked the way he did tonight, turned me into a tongue-tied fool.

And with perfect timing, as if to bear witness to my inability to successfully communicate like a sane adult, Miriam sauntered through the crowd. Her outfit was an exact replica of Lysander's, only she wore a gold bodysuit with crystals that sparkled as they caught the light. Her long blonde hair shone perfectly, and her halo was exactly the same as his. She kept her smile fixed firmly on her face as she came to stand next to us, and then she looked me up and down as she said, "You changed your mind then?"

I frowned back at her. "What do you mean?"

She gestured to my outfit with her hand, sweeping it up and down as she said, "I thought you were coming as an angel. I thought we agreed. I even picked out my favourite full-length white silk dress for you to wear and a halo just like mine.

But I guess Givenchy is too good for you tonight. Why wear designer when you can wear... *this*." She turned her nose up at the last part, but I was still stuck on, 'I picked out my favourite dress'.

"You sent me a dress?" I asked, and she recoiled.

"Yes, I sent you a dress, but I guess you didn't like it, so—"

"I didn't get a dress delivered. Not a white one. All that came was this." I was so confused, my brow furrowing as I tried to work out what was going on.

Had there been another box delivered that I hadn't noticed?

Did I do something wrong here?

Was I going mad?

And then, as the murmur from the crowd turned to gasps and ripples of excitement, and people turned to look towards the staircase, I wasn't confused anymore.

Walking slowly down the stairs, taking each step with precision, like he was walking a runway, was Damien.

The devil, Damien.

He was dressed in a crisp black suit, with the same black horns as mine sprouting from his black hair, and an eerie skull painted on his face to add to his menacing look. He held the same pitchfork that I was carrying, and on the pocket of his jacket were the numbers six, six, six, embroidered in red, exactly the same as my dress.

Miriam hadn't done this.

He had.

I'd been tricked by the devil himself, and knowing that made my stomach roll.

As he reached the bottom of the staircase, every greedy eye in the room was on him. It was as if everyone here were his subjects, all pawns in his game, and he was the master.

He stood for a moment, like a model posing at the end of a runway. Then he dipped his head, but his eyes shot up, staring right at me with a dark, predatory stare that pinned me in place, making it difficult to breathe, move, to do anything.

I noticed people around us begin to turn and glare at me. Women looked me up and down, most with a vicious disdain that they couldn't conceal. The men stared with appreciation they weren't afraid to hide, until Damien strode across the room to stand in front of me, and then, they turned away. They appeared to be afraid of him, like he really was the devil he'd come dressed as, or maybe they were just in awe. But I gritted my teeth, my jaw clenched as I prepared myself for what was coming next.

"Nice outfit." Damien grinned wickedly, pointing to the six, six, six on my dress with the pitchfork in his hand.

Miriam folded her arms across her chest, unable to mask her fury as she faced Damien.

"And there I was thinking you were a man of your word and you wouldn't play these games with us," Miriam hissed. "I thought you weren't going to be a part of... *all this.*"

His eyes stayed on me the whole time she spoke, an evil glint twinkling back at me. Then, slowly, he turned to stare down at Miriam and he grinned wider.

"And miss out on all the fun?" He cocked his head. "Now why would I agree to that?"

"You switched the outfits," Miriam hissed, her eyes narrowing on him.

"She didn't have to wear it, though, did she?" Damien retorted, and I couldn't stop myself from snapping through gritted teeth, "I had nothing else to wear."

"And it suits you," he replied plainly. Then leaning closer, his eyes flickering from Lysander to the left of me, and Miriam to my right, he added, "You wouldn't want to come dressed as a bland, dreary angel like they wanted you to, anyway. Why blend in when you can stand out?"

"She always stands out," Lysander bit back.

Damien lifted his chin in the air. "For once, I agree with

you, brother," he replied, taking me aback. Damien didn't do compliments, and I was sure he'd said it just to annoy Lysander. "But don't we all look the part," he went on. "You and Miriam in your matching halos." He gestured to me. "And us, the devils, not giving a fuck what anyone else here thinks. We're playing by our own rules."

"Playing dirty rules," Miriam sneered.

"I thought that's what you preferred?"

Miriam ignored him, and turning to me, she said, "I'm sorry for my asshole cousin."

"You can't help who your family are," I replied.

And Damien snorted. "No, you can't, can you."

I could feel Lysander growing tense beside me, and he took my hand and announced, "I think we've heard enough." Then he turned to ask me, "Shall we go for a wander?"

I nodded.

Damien huffed, then barked back, "Taking her for another tour of the gardens, *brother*? What is it tonight? The scenic route to see the noose again, or how about the haunted lake? Maybe a bit of midnight skinny dipping with the ghosts in the water?"

"Fuck you," Lysander hissed. Then, losing his cool, he got into Damien's face as he sneered, "Maybe we'll stop off at the wooden hut your mother used to lure my father to so she could fuck him."

Damien's jaw locked, a tell-tale muscle twitching to show Lysander had gotten under his skin.

"Be careful with those accusations." Damien's voice was low and threatening as he spoke. "Throwing out insults like that could get you into trouble."

"Not if it's true," Lysander snarled back.

"Ah, yes. Truth." Damien stepped back, plastering that killer smile he'd perfected so well onto his face again like nothing had vexed him. "That's something we're renowned for in this family, isn't it," he proclaimed with sarcasm dripping off his tongue. "We're all about truth."

"Whatever," Lysander replied, his voice dull and lifeless, showing he'd had enough of sparring with Damien for one night. "The truth is, you're boring me now. Come on, Maya, let's go and get a drink."

Damien chuckled to himself.

"Be careful, Maya," he warned. "Even salt looks like sugar at first glance. And remember the saying... sometimes it's better the devil you know."

"I know who's the devil in this scenario," I replied. "Don't worry about that." And we walked away, but as we walked, I could feel the heat of his stare boring into my back. I didn't think I would shake the devil as easily as that tonight.

He was out to play.

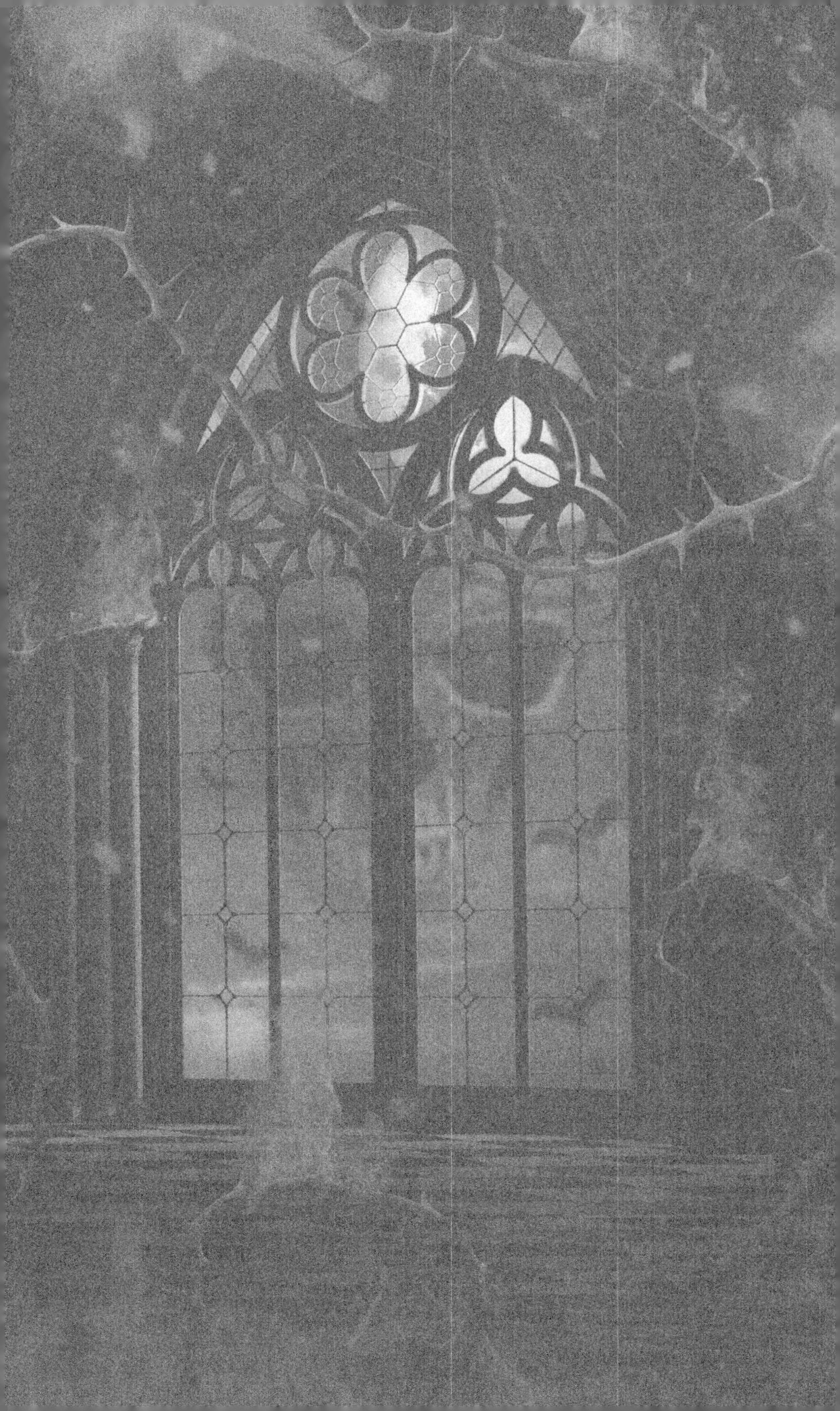

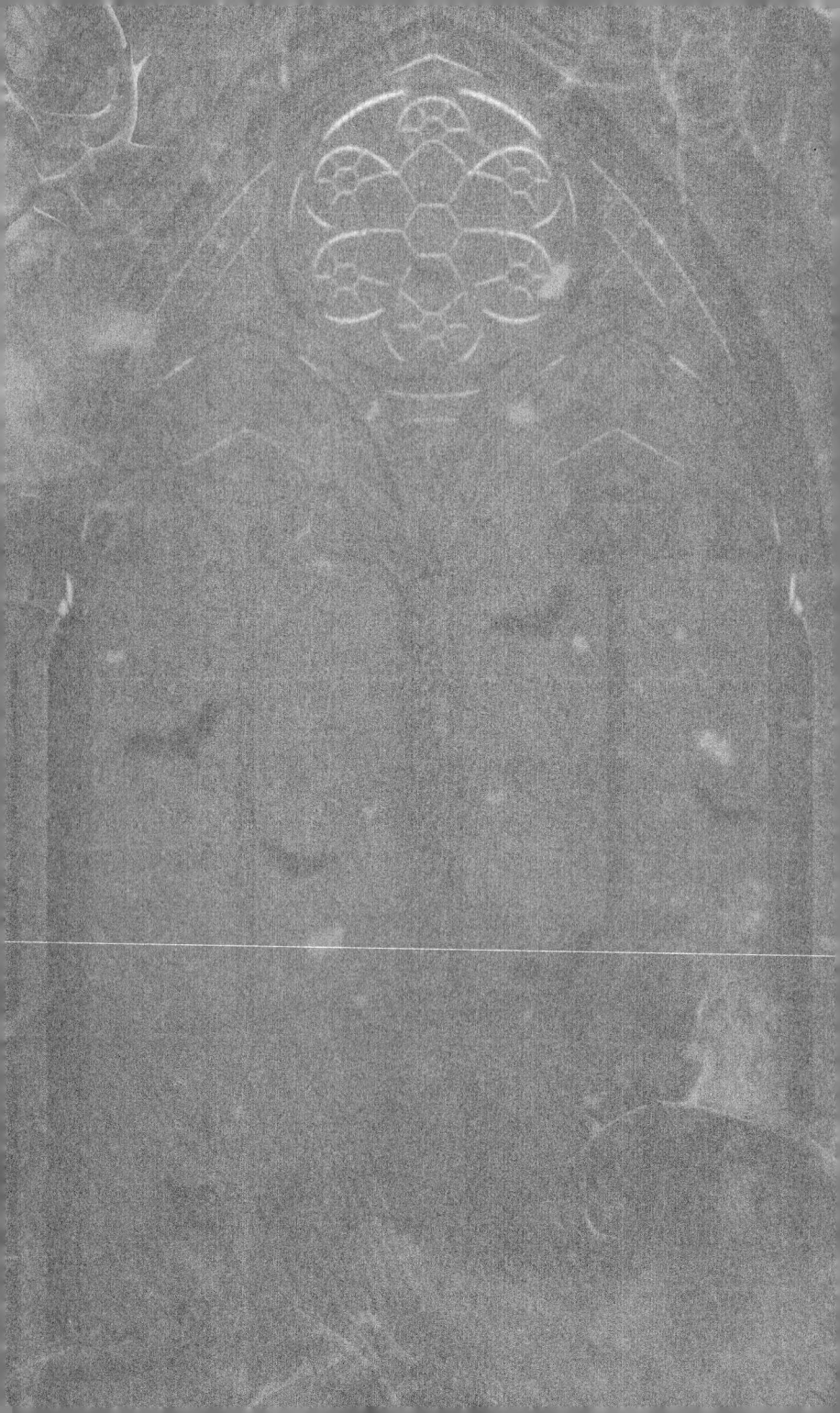

Eighteen

MAYA

"You shouldn't let him get to you," I told Lysander as he led me through the crowd. "You're better than that."

"I'm better than him," Lysander replied, his head high to prove it. "I know it, and so does he. That's why he goads me."

I thought he'd take me somewhere private, a place where we could talk away from all the partygoers. But Lysander loved the spotlight, and he dropped my hand and stood on a chair to shout out, "Hey everyone! Let's move onto the terrace and get this party started!"

Everyone cheered and began to move away from the

reception area and down the hallway. I stood still, not really wanting to follow them, but Lysander jumped down, gave me a boyish grin and said, "Come on. I need to introduce you to a few people."

I took his hand and let him lead me away, even though every fibre of my being was protesting. But I had to push myself outside of my comfort zone. Just because I preferred a quieter life didn't mean I couldn't enjoy a different pace and style of living every now and again.

As we walked through the double doors to the terrace, I took a moment to appreciate the lake in the distance, shimmering in the moonlight, and the dark woods that bordered it. The terrace was beautifully lit with fairy lights, like a twinkling, sparkling haven. Somewhere magical, that was whispering promises for what the night might hold. There was a bar set up along one side and a DJ along the other, and waiters wandered around with trays of champagne.

"I'll get us a drink. Wait here," Lysander said, and I tried to stop him.

"A drink from this tray is fine," I replied, putting my arm out to take a glass from a passing waiter.

But Lysander didn't hear me.

He was already striding away without a second glance, heading to the bar, waving and greeting every person he walked past as he did, planting air kisses and patting others on the back.

The waiter stood still, waiting for me to take one of the glasses from his tray, but I shook my head.

"It's okay. I'm fine," I told him, and he walked away with a hint of disgust on his face.

That reaction only heightened my nerves. I felt self-conscious, standing on the terrace on my own, dressed in an outfit that was shorter than anything I'd ever worn and wishing I didn't feel so awkward. I didn't know anyone. I wanted the ground to open up and swallow me. Or for Lysander to come back, so I didn't look like a nervous outsider standing in a sea of people who all seemed to know each other.

I spotted a group of girls about my age, that Lysander had greeted with hugs and kisses after he'd walked away from me. They were doing a terrible job of pretending to ignore me, but I could tell they were talking about me. I smiled at them, but they didn't return the gesture, and then I heard one of them say a little too loudly, "You know what he's like. He plays games. He'll never change. This one won't last as long as you did, though, Tabitha."

I tried not to let my emotions show. I held myself with dignity, and I took a deep breath. But inside, I felt like I was crumbling. I wanted my legs to work, to walk me away from this disaster, but I was stuck like a fucking statue enduring it all. I had no idea who Tabitha was, and I didn't want to know.

"Are you going to let them get away with talking about you like that?" a voice whispered in my ear, and I spun around to find Damien leering over me.

"I don't know what you mean," I replied, playing dumb.

"Yes, you do. They said you wouldn't last long, and I saw the way your shoulders tensed. They're right, though." He sipped his drink before adding, "He does play games."

"And you don't?" I shot back. "You swapped my dress to make me look like an idiot."

"I made you look like someone *they* wouldn't dare to fuck with." He pointed to the group of girls, and as I looked over at them, they all turned their backs on me, embarrassment evident on most of their faces because they'd heard every single word Damien had said. "Grow a backbone, Maya," Damien hissed. "If you want to survive here, you'll need one, and right now, you've got about as much backbone as a fucking slug."

I fucking hated him.

"At least I don't have the charm of one, *unlike you*," I snarled, feeling angry and wishing he'd fuck off and leave me alone.

"That's better." He smirked, nodding to himself. "You're not a total write-off. I can work with that."

I was just about to tell him exactly what I thought about him working anywhere near me, when I spotted Lysander holding two drinks and heading towards us, and relief washed over me.

"You just can't stay away, can you?" Lysander seethed at Damien as he handed me my drink. "You're always hanging around like a bad smell."

"I think you'll find that's your aftershave," Damien replied. "Eau de desperation."

"I'm not the desperate one around here," Lysander hissed, sipping his drink and glaring at his brother.

"Are you sure about that?" Damien replied.

I lifted my glass to take a sip, but Damien suddenly barrelled into me, knocking me sideways and making me stumble. I didn't fall, Lysander caught me just in time, but the glass I was holding smashed on the floor before I could drink any of it.

"What the hell?" I snapped, staring first at the shattered glass, then at Damien, who was staring around him at no one in particular.

"People can be so rude at these events," he moaned. "Pushing and shoving." He was trying to blame whoever had knocked into him first, but I hadn't seen anyone. No one had been there.

Damien clicked his fingers at a waiter, and they came rushing over with a dustpan and brush to tidy away the broken glass.

"You need to watch yourself," Lysander hissed, but Damien just grinned back at him.

"Here," Damien said, taking a flute of champagne from a passing waiter. "Have this instead, Maya. It might taste less... *bitter*." And with that, he turned and walked away.

After the debacle with Damien on the terrace, things began to settle down. I started to enjoy myself, sort of. Lysander was a social butterfly, there was no denying that, and he did try to include me in all his conversations as he flittered around the party, gracing everyone with his smiles and gentle wit.

But I was so far from a social butterfly it was a joke.

I tried my best to match his enthusiasm, but after a while, I found myself needing space, wanting to be alone. So, when he was deep in conversation with one of his old school friends, I excused myself, saying I was going to the bathroom. But once I stepped away from the crowds, my legs moved of their own accord, leading me to the staircase.

Once I was on the second floor, I breathed a sigh of relief. No one was up here, and it was quieter. I felt like I could finally relax.

I walked down the corridor, feeling as though the room I was heading towards was calling out to me.

The library.

I pushed the door open and felt a blanket of serenity wrap itself around me. The subtle lighting created the perfect ambience in this room. Rows and rows of books were sitting, waiting for someone like me to come along and choose them, to pick them from the shelf and open them, then get lost in a world that'd never be perceived in the same way by anyone else ever. That was the magic of stories, everyone's experience was different. I felt at home here, far more than in the crowd downstairs.

I crept across the library, my heels clicking softly on the hardwood floor, and then I stopped and stood in front of a bookcase at the far end of the room, scanning the shelves. I found a copy of *Jane Austen's 'Emma'*, and I opened it and started to read, not even bothering to find a chair to sit in.

I don't know how long I stood there; it was a lot longer than I'd expected to be away from the party. But when I looked at my watch and saw that it was almost midnight, I exclaimed, "Jeez, the party is probably finished now."

"I doubt it," a deep voice answered from behind, making me jump, gasp, and drop the book I was holding.

I spun around, my hand clasped to my chest, and I saw Damien sitting in a dark corner, staring at me.

"What the fuck are you doing, creeping around?" I snapped.

He raised his brow in response.

"Creeping? Really? Can it be described as creeping when I was in here before you?"

"It's creepy as fuck that you've been sitting there for however long, watching me without letting me know you were in here," I shot back, bending to pick up the book and put it back on the shelf, all while keeping my eyes on Damien. I didn't trust him.

"But then I'd have missed out on listening to your little sighs as you read and watching your facial expressions in the reflection of the window over there. You're a very expressive reader."

I glanced at the window as he spoke, the darkness outside making the glass mirror-like. And then I snapped.

"And you're a fucking stalker. What kind of man sits in the dark watching a woman?"

"I'm not going to justify my actions," Damien announced, pushing himself out of his seat. "You'll paint me as the villain no matter what I say or do." He took a few slow steps towards me and then asked, "Did you read the books I sent you?"

"Yes," I snapped.

"And what did you think?"

I wasn't in the mood to chat with him or discuss my

thoughts. I felt violated by him invading a quiet moment I'd taken for myself.

"I think it's time I get back to the party," I said to cut the conversation dead, but he was having none of it.

"Have you read much of Hardy?"

"No." Again my answer was sharp and curt, an indication that I didn't want to interact with him.

"You should," he responded. "You could really learn something from his style, plots, and character driven stories."

"I'll bear that in mind," I replied, stepping past him to head out of the library.

"Why do you think he invited you here, tonight?" he asked out of the blue, and I stopped in my tracks and turned to face him. "Why did *she* invite you?" he went on. "Don't you think it's strange that they're both so eager to befriend you?"

I tilted my head and glared back at him.

"Do you know what I find strange? That you would send me books, this outfit, and stalk me in this library to freak me out."

He took a step closer.

"If you're freaked out by that, then I may just blow your fucking mind if I show you what lies behind the curtain."

"You know what..." I folded my arms over my chest and lifted my chin defiantly. "I don't think anything behind your curtain would shock me. I believe you dressed perfectly for tonight. The devil. Out to play."

He gave a sinister chuckle.

"Oh, it's not me hiding behind the curtain. But if you want to see for yourself, I'll show you."

It was my turn to take a step forward now, and with my jaw clenched, I hissed, "Do your worst, Damien."

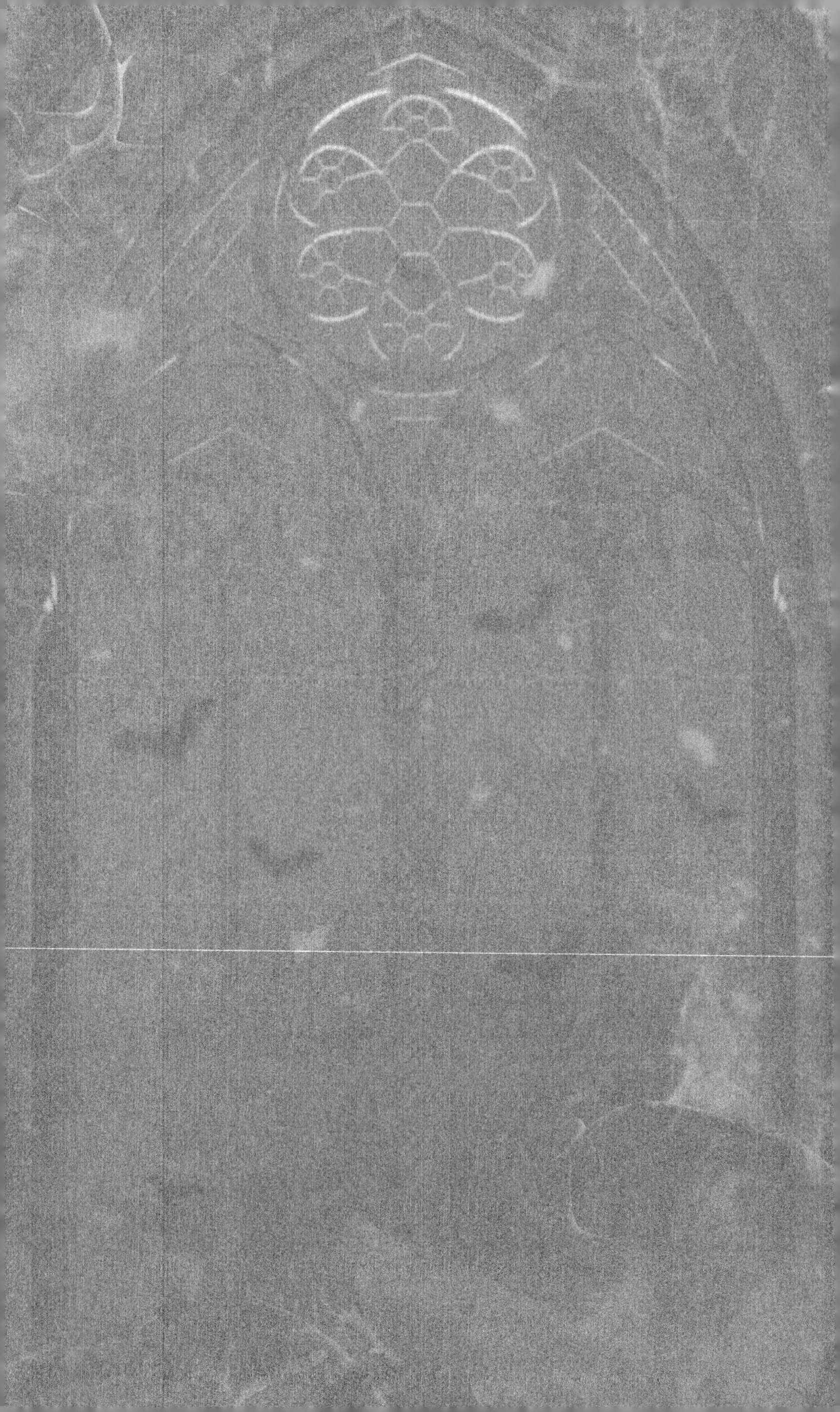

Nineteen

MAYA

There was no doubt in my mind that Damien was revelling in the prospect of 'doing his worst' to shock me, as I followed him along the dimly lit corridor of the second floor, then down the stairs to the ground floor. I'd played right into his hands, walked freely into his trap, but there was no looking back now. I had to see this through to the end.

I went to walk towards the terrace, but he told me, "Not that way. They won't be there anymore."

"Won't they?" I questioned, frowning.

I could still hear music and laughter coming from the

direction of the terrace.

"No, they won't. They'll have stepped it up a gear by now."

I had no idea what he meant by that, but I knew I was about to find out.

Damien sauntered ahead with a cocky confidence in his step, and I knew he was getting a kick out of taunting me right now. A cruel, twisted pleasure from proving something to me. But I reminded myself to stay calm, to act cool-headed and remain unfazed. After the things I'd been through in my youth, not much shocked me anymore.

His footsteps slowed, then he stopped beside a closed door, the door leading to the drawing room, and he turned to face me. This was one of the smaller rooms in the house, used for entertaining in a more intimate setting, and inside, I could hear a gentle beat from the music playing.

"The next part is entirely up to you," Damien said, his head bowed slightly as he stared at me through his lashes. "Stay in blissful ignorance and continue living in a world where you're an observer, watching life play out through your rose-tinted glasses. Or open the door and find out the truth." He took a step back to allow me better access to the door. "What'll it be, Maya? Will you take the red pill or the blue?"

"You want me to jump down a rabbit hole?" I replied, keeping a stoic expression on my face as my stomach fluttered with nerves. "Then you'd better step back, Damien, and give me a little more room."

He did as I asked without saying a word, and slowly, I turned the door handle and creaked the door open just a touch. Not enough to announce my arrival, but enough to see what he wanted me to see.

And I was...

Speechless.

There were about a dozen people in the room. The lighting was subdued, dim, but just enough to show what was happening, and the music was a slow, rhythmic beat that matched the room to a tee.

Because every person in this room was naked.

Fucking.

Lost in a world of debauchery and totally oblivious to me standing, watching in the doorway.

I held my breath; afraid someone might notice me as my eyes slowly scanned the room. Standing beside the fireplace, that I'd cleaned on numerous occasions, was a couple. He was leaning against the wall with his head down, eyes hooded as he watched her. And she was on her knees, peering up at him with black mascara streaming down her face as she bobbed her head back and forth, sucking his cock.

She held the base of his cock in her hand, as she took him down her throat, and then she popped him out of her mouth, stroking his glistening cock in her hand. He reached down and grabbed a handful of her hair, twisting and pulling it as he forced her head back into the position he needed to penetrate her throat deeper. And even though the music masked any sounds she made, I could tell she'd moaned, cried out maybe, at how brutally he was taking her.

Another man approached them and knelt beside her, watching intently as she deep throated her partner. His eyes were dark with lust as he stared, like he couldn't wait to be next, and he stroked his cock in time with her partner's thrusts.

Then, he reached forward and put his hand between her legs, playing with her pussy as he continued to stroke himself. The woman pushed her legs open wider, giving him better access as she continued to suck her partner's cock. The new guy moved so that he was behind her, his fingers probing and thrusting into her as he rose to his knees and began stroking his cock against her ass.

Sensing that he wanted more, the woman lifted herself, so she was on all fours, and the man behind her used both hands to spread her ass cheeks wide and slide himself through her folds. Then, he slammed his cock inside her, gripping her hips tightly as he set a punishing pace.

Both men thrust into her, using her for their pleasure; one pounding into her from behind, the other fucking her mouth and gripping the back of her head tightly as he rocked his hips into her faster and faster. She held onto the hips of the man who was standing, her body jolting on every thrust.

I tried to swallow, suddenly conscious that my mouth was hanging open and my throat was dry.

I'd never seen anything like this.

I let my gaze wander to a group behind them. There was a woman lying on her back on the Persian rug in front of the fireplace, with her legs wide open. A man was leaning over her, with his head buried between her thighs, licking her pussy. And behind him was another woman, holding a riding crop and smacking his bare ass.

I watched as the woman on the floor writhed in pleasure and grabbed the man's head to push him further into her pussy, her silent cries begging him for more as her fingers fisted his hair. Then the woman with the riding crop got on her knees, and using the handle of the crop, she started to push it into the man's ass. He pushed his hips back in response, wanting more, and she obliged, thrusting it into him harder.

I couldn't look away, and yet, I was dumbstruck. Scanning the room, I could see sex toys, bottles of lube, whips, all sorts of equipment lying around on the floor and the tables, and then I caught a glimpse of familiar silky, blonde hair.

Miriam's hair.

She was across the room on one of the sofas, but she wasn't alone. There was a dark-haired guy lying beneath her, and she was sitting in his lap, riding his cock, hands splayed on his chest as she slammed up and down on him. Her head was thrown back in ecstasy, and then she peered down at him, and he reached up to pull her to his chest.

Another man climbed onto the sofa behind her, and she turned her head to smile at him and say something. The guy lying down nodded, and with his cock still impaled in her pussy, he reached down and pulled her ass cheeks open, beckoning the other man to join them.

The other guy leant over her and pushed his cock into her ass, and then he started to fuck her—they both did. Miriam clung onto the guys as they lay on the sofa either side of her, thrusting into her with the same gruelling pace. She was taking two men, she had two cocks inside her. I felt hot and sweaty, and I didn't know what to say or do.

And then, I saw him.

Lysander.

Naked, and standing behind a girl who was bent over the back of one of the other sofas.

From the way she was lying, with her hair hanging over her face, I couldn't tell if she was conscious or not.

I guessed not.

But Lysander knew exactly what he was doing.

He took his long, stiff cock in his hand and gave it a few strokes. Then he grabbed her ass, pulled her cheeks apart and rubbed himself through her pussy before pushing into her. The way his face contorted with pleasure with each inch he pushed inside made my stomach roll. Then, when he was fully inside her, he took hold of her hips and started to thrust into her, his eyes glued to where he was penetrating her.

Another man walked up to them and knelt behind Lysander. He reached up and took Lysander's ass in his hands and pushed his face forward, licking Lysander's asshole. Lysander stilled inside the girl and threw his head back. Then he altered his stance, tilting his ass and moving his legs to open wider for the man, and as he ate his ass, the guy kneeling pumped his cock fiercely. After a few thrusts in his hand, he came, spilling white hot spurts of cum over the back of Lysander's legs, but he kept his tongue buried firmly inside his ass, feasting on him.

Lysander pulled his cock out of the girl, and she didn't move or react. But Lysander instructed the guy to bend over the sofa right next to where she was, and when he did, Lysander moved behind him, took his cock in his hand and started to push inside the guy's ass. As he did, he reached to the side and began fingering the girl lying limply over the sofa.

Fucking one and finger-fucking the other.

I couldn't look away.

And yet, I felt dirty for watching this. Dirty, and something I hadn't ever expected as wetness pooled between my thighs.

"If I hadn't knocked your drink over earlier, you'd be bent over that sofa, too," Damien whispered in my ear.

My cheeks felt like they were on fire, and through my gritty, dry throat, I asked, "What are you on about?"

"The drink." Damien's voice was so close his hot breath tickled my neck, making goosebumps prickle as I tried to regulate my breathing. "He spiked it. I watched him do it. He wanted you to be relaxed tonight because this is what he had planned for you. This is what they both wanted. To play with you, even if you weren't conscious and able to consent. They don't care about technicalities like that."

I couldn't speak.

Was that really what was going to go down tonight?

Was he telling me the truth?

I didn't want to believe him, but why would he lie?

The evidence was clear for me to see.

But at the same time, I didn't feel the furious rage, the all-consuming anger I thought I would at seeing something like this.

Was there something wrong with me?

Eventually, I found my voice and asked, "Why did you show me this?"

"I'm building you up to the big stuff," Damien replied.

"Big stuff?" I frowned.

Did it get any bigger than this?

"This house isn't what you think it is," he said, his voice gruff, low, and so close to my ear it sent a shiver down my spine. "And the people here aren't either."

"I think I know exactly what you all are," I replied, my voice so breathy, I didn't recognise it as my own.

"Angels and demons." Damien sighed, the heat from his body warming my back as he stood close to me. "Heaven and hell. You had no idea what you were getting yourself into when you got onto that train to come here, did you?"

"And you had no idea who you invited into your home that night, did you?" I shot back, and Damien gave a low, gruff laugh.

"See, now I'm taking that as a challenge." And leaning so close his lips grazed my ear, he whispered, "Why should they have all the fun?"

I stood still, my heart a physical beat, thumping through my chest, my breath so shallow I was quietly gasping, but I didn't move as Damien's hand touched my thigh, delicate fingers tracing gentle strokes on my skin. I felt his fingers make a slow trail across the front of my thigh, then dip between my legs, slowly moving up, and my traitorous body responded to him, my legs opening a little wider to allow him better access.

"Do you like watching them?" he asked as his fingers went higher and higher, heading to a place where I wanted him to be, that I needed him to touch. It didn't matter that it was Damien, and this was all kinds of wrong; I wanted it. My pussy was soaked, aching, needing what he was promising.

I didn't answer his question; I couldn't speak, but he went on, asking me, "Do you wish that was you? Do want to be bent over like that and feel yourself being stretched, taking his cock like a good girl? Do you?"

I made a whimpering sound as I felt Damien's finger graze over the silk of my underwear, and he hissed, "Answer me, Maya. Do you want him?"

"No. Yes." I could barely formulate a thought, let alone a sentence.

"Which is it?" Damien demanded. "Yes, or no?"

"Yes." I stilled, waiting for him to touch me, willing him to.

"Yes, what?"

He didn't move.

His body stilled against mine, his front to my back.

His breath heated the skin on my neck and his hand lingered between my legs, fingers dancing so close—so, so fucking close.

"Yes, I want it. But no. I don't want him."

"Good answer," he growled, and he grabbed my underwear, yanking them down then ripping them off, exposing me. "I'll keep these for later," he said, stuffing the scraps of silk into his pocket, and then he reached between my legs, and I cried out as he stroked his fingers through my pussy.

"So wet, Maya," he groaned. "That's my girl." And I wanted to fight back, tell him I wasn't his girl. But right now, I wasn't in control of anything. He was. And for once, I wasn't arguing.

I closed my eyes as I savoured every stroke, the way he rolled his fingertips over where I felt most sensitive before slowly pushing his finger inside me and making me gasp.

"Do you like that?" he asked, as he stroked my inner walls, the palm of his hand rubbing my pussy as I began to move in time with him.

I made an appreciative noise to tell him I did, and he wrapped his other arm around my body, his free hand sliding up from my stomach, over my breasts and up to my neck. Then he wrapped his hand around my neck, holding me in place against him as he began to thrust his finger harder, applying more pressure, making my hips buck and roll, chasing something I didn't know I needed to chase.

"You fuck my hand so well," he moaned. "That's it, watch them and feel me. Feel what I can do to you."

But I wasn't watching them. My eyes were closed and all I could see, feel, hear, everything was him.

He pushed another finger inside, stretching me, and I groaned, my own hands reaching down to hold his in place to make sure he didn't stop.

I never wanted him to stop.

"You're so close," he sighed into my ear, and I nodded. "Are you ready to come for me, Maya?"

His voice was demanding, insistent that I do what he wanted, and I knew I had to. I wanted to. I wanted to lose myself to this feeling that he'd created. I'd never felt anything like this before. I had no idea my body was even capable of feeling like this, of pulsing the way it was, of clinging to something I had no comprehension of. But I wanted it. I was chasing that high.

"Yes," I gasped, and I ground myself on his hand, my brain swirling as my body turned to jelly in his arms. My pussy contracted in the most sublime way; sparks of electricity ran through my whole body. My clit pulsed a beat as I cried a silent prayer, my mouth open but no words coming out, just thankful breaths and pants.

Damien buried his face in my neck as I struggled to stand up or hold myself together. Without his arms around me, I was sure I'd have collapsed to the floor in a puddle.

"You're so fucking beautiful when you come," he whispered, his fingers still buried inside me, and then, as he said, "Was that your first—"

A voice boomed from down the hallway, "WHAT THE FUCKING HELL IS GOING ON?"

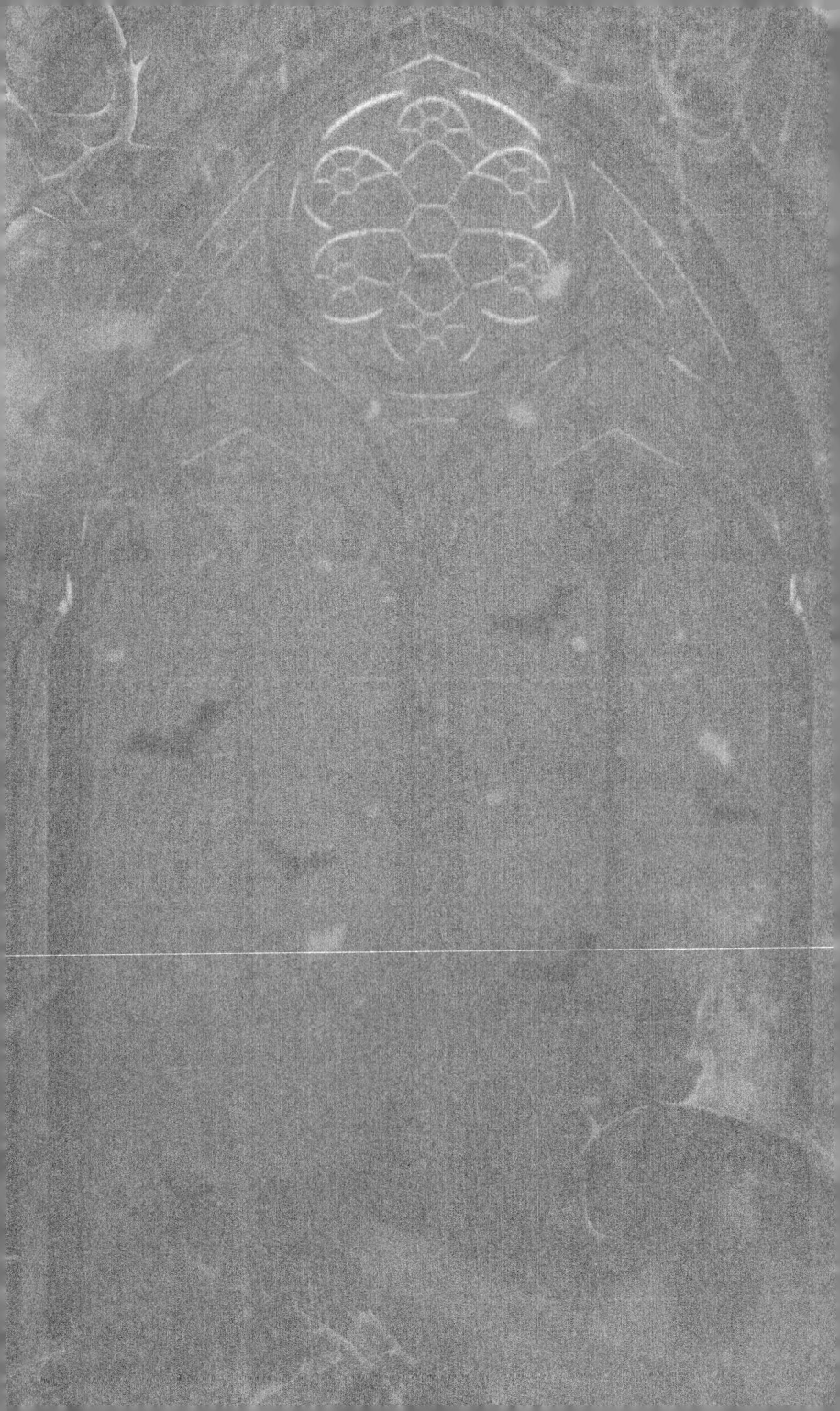

Twenty

MAYA

Instantly, Damien pulled his hand from between my legs, and my supple, soft body went cold and rigid when I heard that voice.

I turned to face Firethorne as Damien stepped away from me, the fire in my veins rushing to my cheeks as I panicked, hoping he hadn't seen what I thought he'd seen.

Firethorne was standing in the hallway, glaring at us, his hands fisted at his sides, his jaw clenched painfully tight, and a venomous glare in his eyes. Beresford was standing beside him with his nose wrinkled in disgust, and judging by the way his eyes were narrowed on me, I knew he'd seen everything.

Firethorne

"Answer me!" Firethorne barked, and Damien just cleared his throat and stepped forward, pushing his hands into his trousers like he didn't have a care in the world.

"Isn't it obvious?" Damien replied, and I didn't even need to look at his face to know he was smirking. "We're having a party."

"Then shut it down," Firethorne snapped, pointing his finger at Damien. "I want everyone out of here. Now. And that includes her." He snapped his finger at Beresford and said, "Take her home."

But I wasn't going to be walked home by Beresford or anyone else. I was already mortified about this night, and being found doing what we were doing in this hallway, I didn't need to prolong the agony.

"I'm fine. I can make my own way home," I said, stalking down the hallway, desperate to move past the two older men and get out of this house.

But I'd barely made it down the hallway when I heard Firethorne bark, "Follow her." And Beresford responded, "Yes, Sir."

I didn't want him to follow me, but when Damien announced, "I'll walk her back," I started to speed up. I didn't want either of them coming after me. I wanted to be alone.

"Not you," Firethorne bellowed down the halls. "You need to stay here and clean up the fucking mess you've made." He continued shouting obscenities at Damien, but I didn't stick around to hear any more.

I flung the front doors of the mansion open and ran down the steps onto the gravel drive. Then, without looking back, I marched forward, intent on heading straight home.

It was hard to walk with any speed or urgency in the ridiculous heels I was wearing, and as I stumbled, almost toppling to the floor, I heard Damien, call out, "Careful," and his warm hand reached out to grab my arm.

"I'm fine. You don't have to walk me home," I snapped, pulling my arm out of his grasp. "Your father doesn't want you following me, remember?"

"Like I give a fuck what my father wants," he hissed. "I don't take orders from him."

"Are you sure about that?" I goaded, huffing as I tried to walk faster and put some distance between us. But his strides were bigger than mine. I wasn't escaping him any time soon.

"Positive. I'm not his fucking lapdog. I leave that to my brother."

I didn't want to engage with him, I didn't even want to look at him. I was scared what might happen if I did. So, I kept striding forward, focusing on getting back to the cabin as quickly as possible. Back to normality, if that even existed for me now.

"You shouldn't be out here all alone," he went on. "It's dark. Anything could happen to you."

I hadn't even noticed that the lights Lysander had been so sure he'd get installed when we first came here had never materialised.

"It's not the dark I'm afraid of," I sneered, and he gave a low, gruff chuckle.

"I'm glad you think like that. The monsters in this place don't hide in the shadows. They're not afraid to stand right in front of you, smiling in broad daylight."

"Don't I know it," I spat back.

I carried on marching through the woodland, blocking him out as I got closer and closer to the cabin. But he was like a dog with a fucking bone. He wouldn't let me go.

"Do you really want to stay here, after everything you've seen tonight?" he questioned. "After everything that's happened?"

I stopped and spun around to face him.

"No. I don't want to fucking stay here," I seethed. "But I'm going nowhere without my father."

"Why? Is his hold on you that tight?"

I stepped towards him, pointing my finger in his face. The moonlight reflecting off his skull-painted face made him even more demon-like, but I stood my ground.

"My relationship with my father is none of your fucking business. And the minute I tell him what I saw tonight, and what you did, we'll be out of here."

"What *I* did?" Damien pushed his face close to mine, fury rolling off him as he clenched his jaw. "Don't you mean what *we* did. I don't remember you telling me to stop, Maya."

He was right.

"I don't have time for this," I huffed, and turned my back on him, stomping away. But he continued to follow me.

"If you wanna leave, I'll take you right now. Drive you off this fucking estate to the train station and buy you the goddamn ticket myself. I'll even walk you onto the damn train."

I ignored him. I'd already told him I wouldn't leave without my father. But he kept on.

"I mean it. You need to leave."

"And you need to leave me the fuck alone," I replied, as the dim lights of the cabin came into view.

Once I reached the porch, I called out to him, "Stay away from me and stay away from my father. I don't ever want to see you again." And then I ran up the steps and into the cabin, slamming the door behind me, and then leaning against it, letting out a breath, relieved that I was finally alone.

I managed to compose myself, then called out my father's name, expecting him to be here, now that Firethorne was back. But I was met with silence, so I raced across the living room, heading for my bedroom, and once inside, I closed the door.

I pulled the devil horn hairband off my head and threw it onto my dresser, then grabbed my oversized band T-shirt from my drawers. I sat on the bed and unzipped my boots, pulled them off with a feeling of relief and then stood up to slip the dress off, shimmying as it fell to the floor. I put my T-shirt on, turned the light off and lay on the bed, trying to focus on my breathing and not the pornographic film playing over and over in my head.

I stared at the ceiling as the moon cast shadows over it, reminding me that my curtains were open. I thought about getting up and closing them, but honestly, I didn't have the energy.

So, I lay there, thinking about what had happened. How Lysander had shown me parts of himself since I'd been here. Parts that made me warm to him, something I didn't do easily in life. And yet, tonight, I'd discovered another side to him. A side that was secret, forbidden, something he'd wanted to share with me, if Damien was to be believed. But would he really go so far as to drug my drink to do that?

Because that was a fucked-up way to bring me into his world.

It was all such a mindfuck.

They were a mindfuck.

And then, my thoughts turned to Damien. Darkly disturbing, and yet morbidly intriguing Damien. The man who made me want to tear my own hair out or throw all the books in the goddamn library at his head.

But...

I couldn't deny...

When he'd touched me...

He'd had me under his spell.

What was that about?

And why did I succumb to him so easily?

I lay in the dark and thought about everything he'd said, the warnings, the threats. And then I thought about what he'd done, and how he'd made me feel. I wasn't ashamed to say I'd never come before. I'd never been with anyone in that way. I was a virgin. Sure, I'd touched myself, but I'd never had that reaction. And maybe I should've felt shameful, but I didn't. I felt liberated. *He* had made me feel liberated, and I wanted more.

I glanced at the window at the end of the bed. The window overlooking the dark night and the woodlands. And I imagined he was still out there, standing amongst the trees, watching me, holding his breath, waiting to see what I'd do next.

I imagined him staring at the way I lay on my back on the bed, my T-shirt barely covering my ass, ready to show him everything.

And then, keeping my eyes on that window, I opened my legs, baring myself to the night, and to him. Tonight was a night for forbidden promises, for passion, and I was curious if I could recreate what he'd done, build on what he'd started.

I reached between my legs, and with my fingers, I started to stroke myself in the same way that he'd done, my fingertips grazing my swollen, wet pussy, igniting the flames he'd started, making them burn brighter. It didn't take long for that burn to grow stronger, that delicious pulse to pound harder, and I lifted my hips, edging myself as I stroked, circled and then pushed my fingers inside myself.

And all the time, I imagined him outside, watching me, touching himself because he was so fucking turned on by the show that I was putting on for him. I pictured him taking out his long, thick cock and stroking it as he groaned, imagining that his hand was my pussy. That my walls were wrapped tightly around his cock, gripping him, milking him, making him come and bringing him to his knees like a motherfucking queen. I arched my back, my legs trembling as I imagined him moving closer to the window, wanting to get to me, to claim me. My fingers rubbed faster, harder, as I fantasised.

Would he climb through the window?

Pin me to the bed and take what he wanted?

Would he make me his dirty slut?

Those thoughts ignited something powerful inside me, and I exploded, coming so hard I cried out as my body buckled. My legs shook, my pussy throbbed, and my clit pounded, making me press and hold my hand over myself, willing the feelings to never end, to go on and on and on. With my eyes closed, I savoured every spark, every ripple that ran through me. And then, as the sensation ebbed away, I sighed, feeling totally and utterly spent.

I needed to shower. I needed to move, but I couldn't. All I could do was lie still and thank God I was a woman. Because that was something I'd definitely be doing again.

My eyes shot open as I lay in the darkness of my room. I'd fallen asleep on top of the covers of my bed, but instantly, I knew something felt off. I didn't move as my eyes flittered around, watching the shadows as they danced on the walls, the moonlight casting spells over them, making my heart race and my mind play tricks.

Did something just move in the corner?

I listened carefully, expecting to hear the creak of a floorboard or silent footsteps, but all I heard was the eerie whistle of the wind outside as it passed through the cracks in the window, invading my room, curling around my already cold body. My skin prickled as goosebumps appeared, and I gasped as a shadowed branch from a tree outside appeared to scratch at the wall. Whistling winds and shadows. I was letting them play tricks on me like I did when I was a kid. There was nothing there. I needed to get up and close the curtains, maybe then I might feel a little more relaxed.

Firethorne

But as I turned to get up off the bed, those shadows moved faster. A dark figure from the corner of the room lunged towards me.

My racing heart became an eruption of fear, my mind struggling to comprehend what was happening, but the adrenaline in my body was way ahead of it, telling me I needed to run. Warning me that I was in danger.

I gasped, ready to shout out, but a hand slapped over my mouth. A strong, manly hand.

I clawed at it, kicking my legs, trying to get free, scratching the skin of his hand in an effort to get him off of me. But it was no use, because in his hand was a cotton handkerchief, a handkerchief doused in chemicals, and I couldn't breathe, couldn't fight hard enough. Lord knows I tried, but it was pointless.

And within seconds...

My world was lost to darkness.

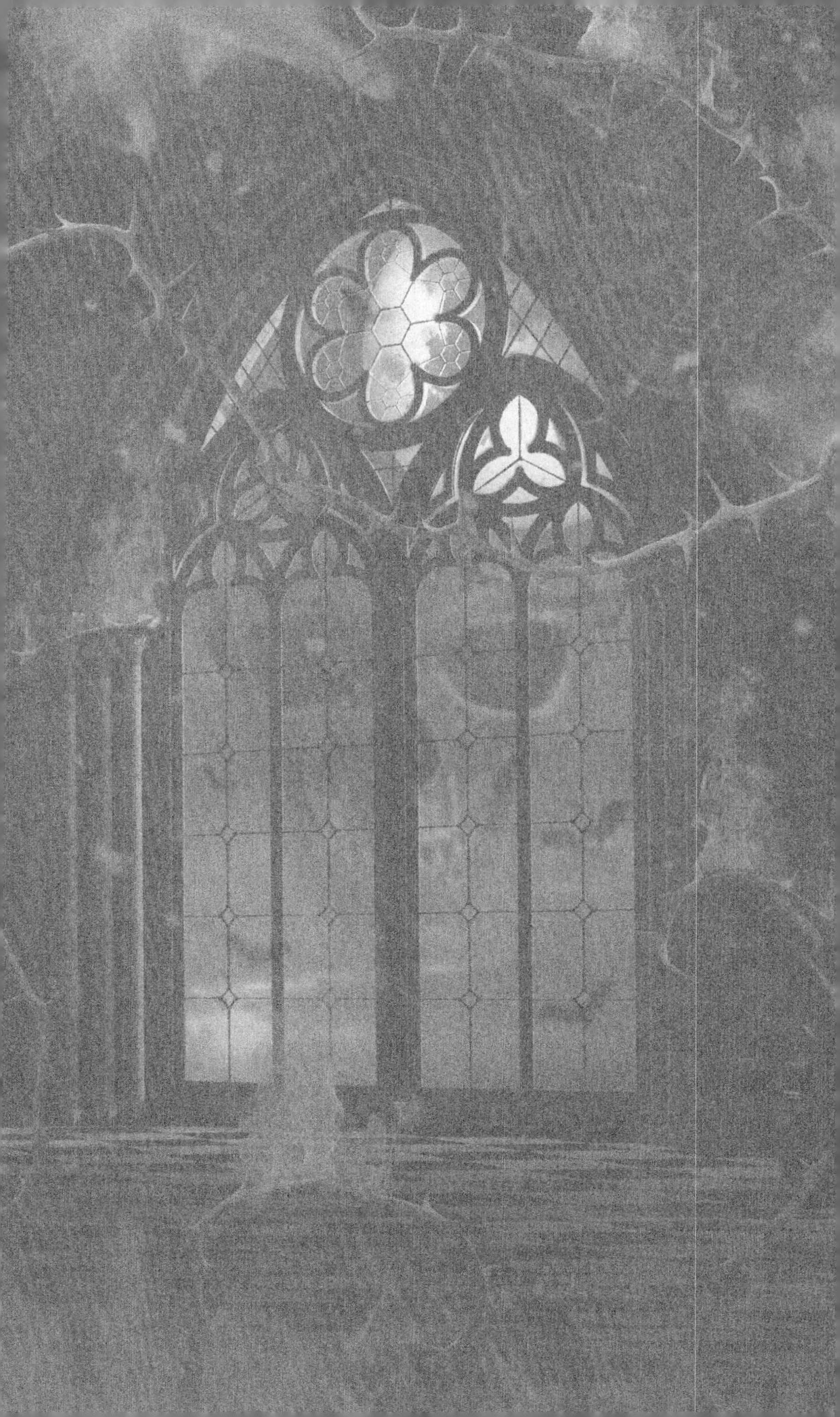

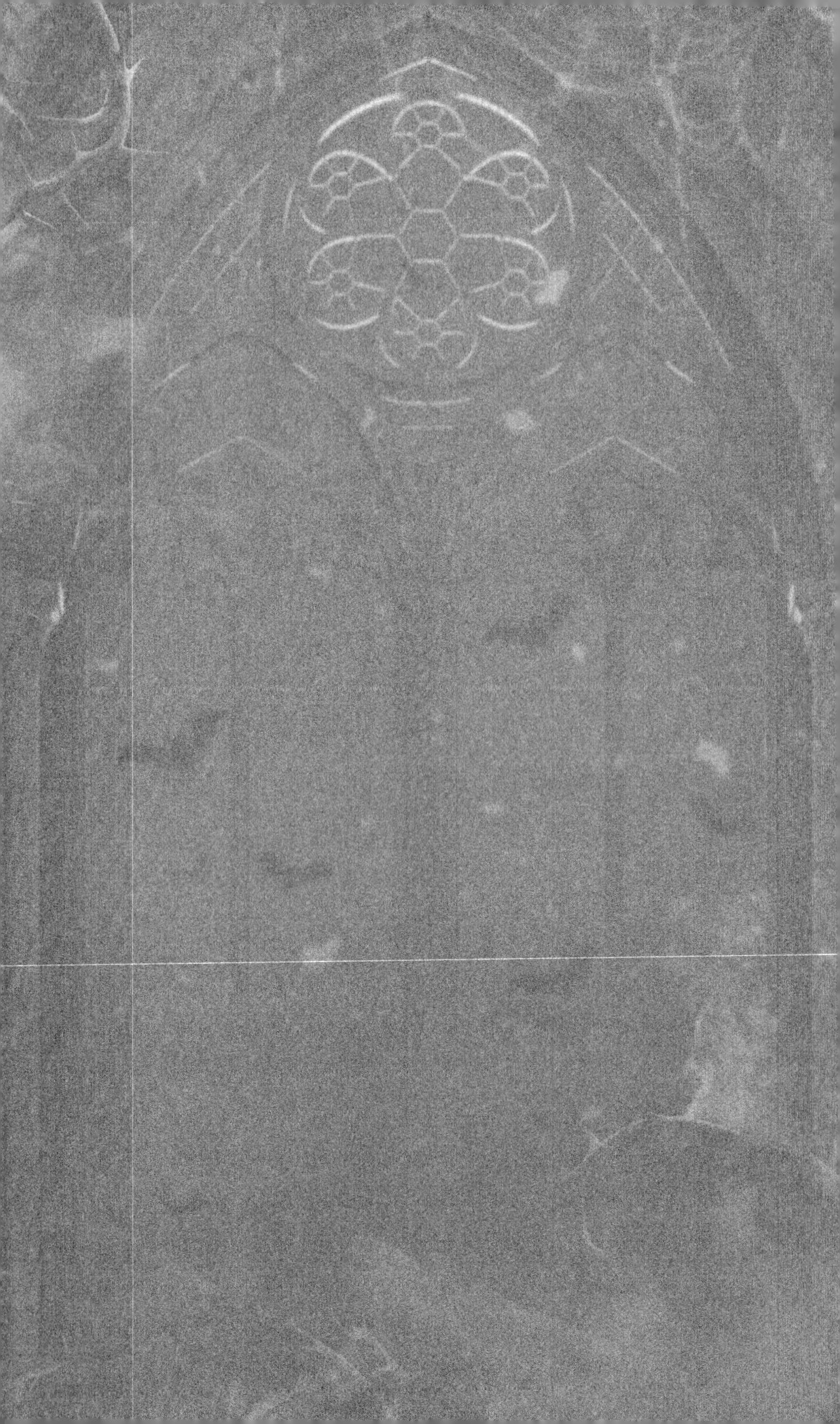

Twenty-One

MAYA

Thump.
Thump.
Thump.
My head pounded and swirled as I came around, noises were muffled, voices I didn't recognise echoed in my ears. Everything felt foreign.
Thump.
Thump.
Thump.
My body didn't feel like my own. It was as if I was stuck inside someone else's body. A body that didn't work.

Firethorne

I felt nauseous and achy.

I tried to swallow, but it was like swallowing sandpaper.

Everything felt wrong.

I prised my eyes open, and the room I was in seemed hazy and out of focus, like I was viewing it underwater, submerged in a sea and I couldn't breathe.

I was stuck in an eternal nightmare of pain.

Dots and stars danced in front of my eyes, and then slowly, so, so slowly, I began to gain focus.

I didn't recognise the face looming over me, and on instinct, I tried to move, but I couldn't. I was shackled, restrained on whatever surface I was lying on.

I went to speak, to cry for help, but all that came out were grunts, noises that didn't sound like they were being made by me. I was gagged, and my eyes bulged when I realised, pleading with the man who was looking down at me, begging him to help me.

"She's awake," I heard a familiar voice announce, and Firethorne appeared behind the strange man. "Just in time for the best part."

His eyes were glowing with a sadistic need, telling me the best part wouldn't be the best for me.

I thrashed on the bed or whatever it was I was tied to. Glancing to the side, I could see my wrists were secured by cuffs, there was a leather strap over my chest, but that wasn't the worst part. My legs were strapped to stirrups that were open wide, and all I had on was the old T-shirt I'd gone to bed in. Nothing else. I felt degraded, defiled, and there wasn't a damn thing I could do about it.

Mentally, I checked my body. I had no pain other than my pounding head and sore throat. I hadn't been raped. But was that about to happen? Was that why they had me strapped here?

The room was dark, but I knew I was still at Firethorne

Manor. I recognised this room. I'd cleaned it only days ago, and now, it'd be etched into my mind, my very soul, for the rest of my life. From the open fire that crackled at the end of the bed I was on, to the landscape painting of the estate that hung above it, the one with the shadow of *him* hiding amongst the reeds by the lake. The dark window to the side of me showed it was still nighttime, reflecting the horrors back to me that were about to ensue in this room. Taunting me. Reminding me that I was helpless.

"I'm going to get this on video," Firethorne announced, taking his phone from his pocket and pointing it in my direction. "I need to confirm this so my client doesn't pull out."

He was going to video whatever sick thing he was about to do to me.

I wanted to throw up.

I wanted to run as far away from this place as I could.

But another jolt on my restraints told me that was useless.

I was trapped.

"Sir, are you sure about this?" the stranger standing next to him asked, and a flutter of hope took flight in my belly.

He wasn't sure.

Maybe he'd save me.

"Of course I'm sure," Firethorne barked. "And you need to get on with it. This is why I keep you on a retainer, doctor, for issues like this."

He was a doctor.

A fucking doctor, who was going to do something to a helpless woman strapped to a bed.

He was no doctor.

Doctors swore an oath to heal and protect their patients.

This man was a monster, the same as Firethorne.

The man sighed, and I watched as he put a medical bag onto a table close by and opened it, taking out what looked like a fucking medieval torture device.

Firethorne

I screamed as loudly as my muffled voice would let me through the gag, and Firethorne rolled his eyes.

"For goodness sake, Maya, calm down. We just need to do a little examination and then this will all be over." And then his eyes became slits, throwing an evil glare my way. "This could've been avoided if you'd behaved yourself. But you couldn't help yourself, could you... and neither could my bastard child." And then he muttered, "If she thinks this is bad, she's not going to last five minutes when we do the handover."

Handover?

Behaved myself?

Bastard child?

What the hell was going on?

I didn't have time to process any of it as the doctor came to stand between my open legs. The stirrups clattered as I tried to move, tried to close them to protect myself, but I couldn't. Firethorne stood next to him, holding his phone up as he recorded what was happening, and I closed my eyes as he held up the long metal device, smearing it with gel, and then, as he pushed it inside me, I held my breath. Sweat trickled down my face and back. My body shook. And warnings blared loud in my ears, ringing as my heart felt like it was about to give out.

"The hymen is still intact," the doctor announced, and then he pulled the device free, and my eyes flew open as I gasped for breath.

"Good. I'll get this video sent to Edward right away. I want this deal finalised before noon tomorrow. And until then, she stays right here. There's a lot of money at stake, and I'm not fucking around anymore."

What the fuck?

He was selling me to Edward?

"She'll need food and water, she's very dehydrated," the doctor said, and then with a hint of remorse in his eyes, he added, "And she needs to be allowed to move her arms and legs. It's dangerous to keep her restrained like this."

"I employ you for your medical expertise," Firethorne snapped. "And you gave me that two minutes ago. I have no need or desire to hear anything else that you think I should or shouldn't do in my own home. And besides, she needs to get used to being restrained. It's not barbaric, it's training. She'll get a lot worse with her next owner."

Owner?

I started to thrash and scream again. I was no one's fucking property.

The doctor nodded, and as he walked towards the door, I hollered through the gag, begging him to come back, to do something. And then, I saw Beresford standing outside the door as the doctor opened it and walked away. And Beresford entered the room, taking the doctor's place.

"The father is asking to speak to you," he said to Firethorne, giving me a quick and shame-filled glance before refocusing on his boss. "I told him to wait next door."

"I've got nothing to say to him," Firethorne shot back. "Tell him the transaction has been completed and his role in all this has come to an end. I want him off my property."

"I told him that," Beresford replied. "But he's refusing to leave. Says he needs to see his daughter one last time."

"She isn't his daughter anymore," Firethorne hissed, then he clenched his jaw as he barked, "Deal with him. I don't have time for this. You know what to do."

Beresford nodded, and with his head hung low, he made his way out of the room, leaving the door ajar as if he was taunting me.

Firethorne huffed and came to stand over me.

"I'll give you ten minutes out of these restraints," he said. "But don't fucking try me."

I nodded as he unbuckled the straps on my legs, feeling relieved that I was able to move my legs back onto the bed.

Firethorne

Then he untied the strap on my body, and finally the ones around my wrists. But if he thought that in my weakened state, I would be docile and obedient, then he was wrong.

Instantly, I shot up, kicking my legs into action and jumping off the bed. He made a grab for me, but I was so desperate to escape I managed to evade his grasp and lunge for the open door.

As I sprinted past Beresford, who was struck dumb in the hallway, reacting too slowly to put his arms out and catch me, I heard Firethorne bellow, "Stop her."

My legs burned as I raced down the corridor, running a marathon for my life, aching to be free. And suddenly, in front of me, Lysander appeared, and I ran right into him, gasping as I stared up at him, begging him, "Please. Please help me. They're hurting me. They're going to send me away. You have to help me."

Lysander frowned. "What's going on?" he asked, as Firethorne hollered down the hallway, "Don't let her go. Hold her."

"You were right," I said through panted breaths. "I can't trust them. They lied to me. But I know... I know you weren't lying. Please."

"What are you talking about?" Lysander asked as he held me by the tops of my arms.

I didn't have time for this.

"The sketch. The warnings. You need to help me."

Even after everything I'd seen tonight, I still believed Lysander would help me.

I could feel danger hurtling towards me. Firethorne was right behind us. But when Lysander said, "What warnings?" the bottom fell out of my world.

"Hold her," Firethorne shouted.

"I've got her," Lysander replied, and his grasp tightened, painfully so.

"No," I begged, pleading as I stared at him, but he wasn't going to save me. He was holding me for his father.

So, I did what any sane person would do.

I kneed him hard in the balls, and when he let go of me to grab his crotch, I ran. I fucking ran down that hallway without looking back.

My bare feet pounded the wooden floor, my hands grabbing for the rail as I reached the stairs, and I flew down the steps, barrelling forward, praying the front door wouldn't be locked.

I could hear them coming after me as I raced across the foyer, heading for the door. When I reached it, I grabbed the handle, turned it, and to my relief, it opened and I shot out of the house, running down the sandstone steps in the cold night air.

My bare feet ached as I shot across the gravel drive, but I didn't care; I'd have raced over broken glass to get away from this house. I ran in the direction of the iron gates that I'd driven through a matter of weeks ago, figuring I could scale a wall, climb the gates, do anything to get myself off this estate to freedom. The Victorian lampposts that'd been lit when we'd arrived that night weren't lit up tonight. Instead, they stood like shadowed guards, watching my plight, bearing witness to my escape. I ducked to the side, running across the grass, willing my legs not to buckle as my feet screamed in pain, and then, I felt like I'd been hit by a truck as something charged into me, knocking me to the ground.

I face planted the grass as someone made a grab for me, trying to pin me down. But I fought them; I fought so fucking hard to break free, to crawl away from them. I kicked my legs and flailed my arms, but the weight of their body stopped me from gaining any traction.

Then a deep voice muttered in my ear, "You can stop running now. I've got you." And I felt a sharp prick in my neck before my world turned to darkness for the second time that night.

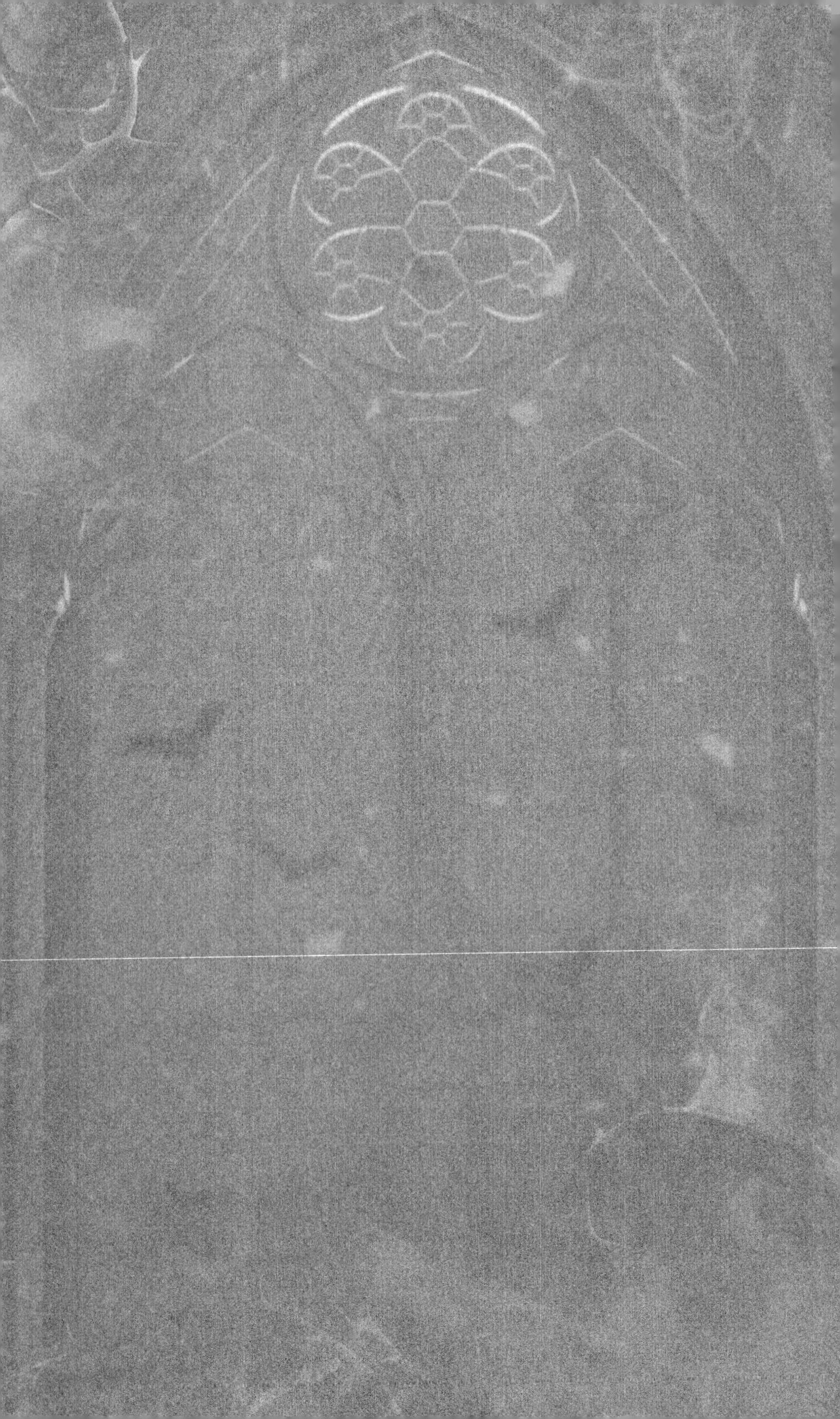

Twenty-Two

MAYA

My head was swimming.
I felt sick.
I was confused, disorientated, and I had no fucking idea where I was or what'd happened to me.

I lay still, taking stock of my surroundings before I dared to open my eyes. My head was on a soft pillow. The room smelt fresh, and the mattress I lay on was comfortable. There was a duvet over my body, but I was still wearing my T-shirt. Apart from a pounding head and a little soreness from escaping, I wasn't hurt. Not in the way I'd feared I would be.

Slowly, I opened my eyes, squinting slightly from the light, even though the blinds on the windows were closed. I'd never been in this room before, and thinking of the dangers that lay in wait for me here made my heart rate spike and fear flood my system. I needed to stay alert.

The room was all white, like a generic hotel room... or an asylum. The bed where I lay was covered in white cotton sheets, clinically crisp and foreign. There was a door opposite the bed, and another door to the right. As I peered around, I noticed a bottle of water on the bedside table. I couldn't hear anything, so I pushed myself to sit, wincing as my muscles groaned and my bones ached. I was thirsty, but I was wary of drinking anything here. But when I reached for the bottle and saw it wasn't tampered with, I twisted the cap off and drank like I'd just crawled out of the desert.

I wiped my mouth with the back of my hand and placed the bottle back down. Then, on shaky legs, I stood up, my feet sinking into the plush white carpet as I began to walk hesitantly over to the windows. I pushed the blinds to the side to peer through, but all I saw were fields. No other buildings, no people passing by below that might be able to help me. I was in the middle of nowhere.

I knew this wasn't Firethorne, but was I still somewhere on the estate?

I had no idea, but not knowing where I was made the undercurrent of panic and the ripple of fear grow inside me like a tsunami.

I checked to see if the window would open, I pushed the frame and banged on the glass, desperation growing with each second that passed, but it wouldn't open. It was as if I was sealed shut inside this room, a prisoner, and my only way of escape would be through one of the two doors behind me.

I turned to face the room, my prison cell, and I headed for the door opposite the bed.

Pushing it open, I found a simple white bathroom inside,

with a toilet, sink, and a basic shower. But no window. Just a vent that was so small I wouldn't stand a chance at breaking through it or climbing out to safety. I scanned the bathroom, then started scrambling around, looking under the sink, around the toilet, searching frantically to see if I could find anything I could use as a weapon, but there was nothing. Just like an asylum, this place had been secured and locked down. All I needed now was the straitjacket, and right now, I felt so trapped, so constricted, it was like I was already wearing one.

I stepped back into the room and took a deep breath, staring at the final door. Knowing that what lay behind it was going to be my downfall.

Firethorne's words echoed in my ears.

If she thinks this is bad, she's not going to last five minutes when we do the handover.

She's not going to last five minutes...

Not five minutes...

This had to be the handover he'd talked about.

I'd officially arrived in hell.

I swallowed. My body didn't feel like my own as my ears rang, and I struggled to breathe.

What kind of monster was waiting for me out there?

And how was I going to defeat it?

I could've waited for them to come in here, stayed in the room and tried to formulate a plan. Bought myself extra time. But I didn't. I wanted to know where I was and what was going on. I wanted to face whatever this was head-on. Show them I wasn't a pushover. I would fight back.

I approached the door with caution, turning the handle like it was a bomb ready to detonate, and I was responsible for diffusing it. And then, I pushed the door open, holding my already ragged breath, trying to listen out for anything over the pounding beat of my fearful heart.

I had to stay alert and ready.

Firethorne

There was a small, narrow corridor outside the room with white walls and carpet, just like in the bedroom. I crept down the corridor, each step harder to take than the last. Like a walk to the gallows, I knew I had to get there, but I wanted to prolong the inevitable. My stay of execution.

I stopped when I came to an open-plan living area.

Not what I'd expected at all.

There was a wide-screen TV on the wall, floor-to-ceiling windows that ran along one side of the room, looking out over the rolling fields below. The sun shone brightly through the windows, casting a beautiful glow on the room, like it was tricking me into thinking this was a safe space, not a torture chamber. A picture-perfect heaven to mask the depravity of hell that lurked beneath.

In one corner was a small dining table and chairs, with four placemats on it, ready for a meal. Another trick to fool me into thinking this was a home for civilised people.

A family.

A haven.

But it wasn't.

And the fear I was fighting began to choke me in its vice-like grip when I glanced down at the square set of sofas in the middle of the room... sofas with one person sitting on them. Feet up on the coffee table that sat in the middle, his back to me as he sat in silence, gazing out of the window.

"You were out for a lot longer than I expected," he said, taking his feet off the table and pushing himself slowly to stand.

Then he turned to face me, hands shoved into his trouser pockets like he didn't have a care in the world. Like this was fucking normal.

Damien.

I should have fucking known.

"You," I growled, balling my hands into fists and glaring daggers of fury at him as a hint of a smirk appeared on his face.

A smirk that made my blood boil. "Doing your father's work, I see. Or should that be the devil's work?"

He cocked his head and grinned back at me.

"What makes you think I'm working for anyone?" He lowered his gaze and glared at me through his lashes like the fucking devil I knew he was. "I can plan things on my own, you know?"

"And I can fight back. You can't keep me here." I glanced around, trying to find a door to escape, but he just tutted back at me.

"I know you're looking for a way out, Maya. But trust me when I say, this place is impenetrable. There is no way out for you. Every window, every door is locked, and I'm the only one that can open them."

"To keep me prisoner?" I goaded, knowing I'd spend every waking moment trying to find a way out of here.

"To keep you safe."

I huffed an ironic laugh.

"You're the one I need to be kept safe from. You and your sadistic father." I glanced around again and asked, "Is he here?"

"My father has no idea where you are, and I have no intention of telling him. As I said, Maya, I can work on my own sometimes." The way his eyes crackled with a glow of wicked intent didn't make me feel any better about that fact.

"Where am I?" I asked through gritted teeth.

"A safe place."

"It doesn't feel very safe... with you here."

He laughed.

I wasn't being funny.

"Didn't your father ever teach you that sometimes it's better to trust the devil you know?" He tapped his chin like he was thinking, then grinned to himself. "Ah, no. He didn't. Because your father is a spineless little shit. A waste of fucking oxygen."

"Fuck you," I snarled back. "Just let me go. Open the door

and let me fucking leave. You can't keep me here."

"I think all things considered, it's best you stay here," he retorted, and I flew across the living area, charging for him, ready to fight for my survival. But he was stronger than me, and he grabbed my arms as I tried to hit him. Then, pushing me onto the sofa, he leered over me. "I wouldn't do that if I were you."

"What? Fight for my life?" I glared back at him as anger rolled inside me.

"I'm not the one you should be fighting," Damien replied, standing back with so much ease I wanted to hurl myself out of the chair and launch myself at him again. "I'd save that fighting spirit for when you need it."

"And when exactly would that be then?" I cocked my head now, poisonous venom on my tongue ready to lash him. "When I'm tackled in my own bed in the middle of the night by a fucking mad man? Or when I'm shackled to a fucking torture chair and assaulted? Or maybe when I'm pinned down in the mud and someone sticks a fucking needle in my neck and drugs me?"

"I had no choice with the needle," he replied, his jaw suddenly clenching. "I had to get you out of there."

"You fucking drugged and kidnapped me," I hollered.

"I fucking saved you!" he shouted back.

And we were silent for a moment. Panting out our breaths. Him standing a small distance away from me, watching me, and me, sitting on the sofa, my rage a red mist clouding every rational thought.

Eventually, the silence became deafening. I had to speak.

"He'll find me, you know."

"Who?" Damien asked.

"My father."

His responding laugh made me even angrier, and he shook his head to tell me 'no', then added, "It's just us. Just you and me. Your father isn't coming. Your father doesn't care."

"Yes, he does," I hissed. "I won't listen to your poison. I know what you're trying to do."

"To save you?" he answered in his cocky manner.

"To brainwash me."

Another wicked laugh and then he said, "I don't need to brainwash you, Maya. Your father did a good enough job of that."

"Fuck you," I snapped.

"Yes, you already said that," he replied plainly. "But maybe you should start asking yourself why I brought you here."

I wasn't going to fall into his trap or play his mind games.

"Your father sexually assaulted me," I blurted out.

And his eyes widened, the muscles of his jaws twitching as he asked in a hushed tone, "He raped you?" The cockiness had gone now, replaced by seriousness and sincerity, or at least, that's what it seemed.

"No. But a doctor was in the room, and they examined me... there. He assaulted me to check that I was still a..." I didn't want to say the word, but as he nodded and looked at the floor, I knew he knew what I meant.

"That was my fault," he said, and I waited for him to elaborate. "If he hadn't seen us at the party... if he didn't think that I'd..." He couldn't speak the words either. "He wouldn't have done that if I hadn't touched you."

"It's a bit late to be remorseful," I snapped. "The damage has been done. By you."

He lifted his head defiantly, a fire burning in his eyes as he said, "I own my mistakes, Maya. At the party, I had a moment of weakness. But it doesn't change the fact that I saved you."

"Saved me?" I couldn't believe how he was trying to spin this. And I really wished he'd stop fucking lying. "How the fuck did you save me?"

He took a step closer to me.

"Well, I didn't see your father burning down the world to save you. Or Lysander. How much help was he when you needed him?" He took a moment, then said, "All this time you never stopped to ask yourself why you were there."

"I did," I argued back.

"No." He shook his head. "You really didn't. And now you're here, arguing with me, getting pissed at me. But I'm not the one you should be angry with, Maya."

"I'm angry with all of you," I barked.

"Then tell me why," he pushed. "What was going on? Why the fuck did I have to bring you here? Use your anger, Maya. Get the truth you need."

"Your father sold me," I hissed.

"Yes... go on," he urged.

"He took a video of the examination and said he was sending the proof to Edward. He sold me and then you drugged and kidnapped me."

He took another step, getting even closer.

"He needed to prove you were a virgin because he got more money for you if you were. I took you because time was fucking running out. But in all that time, tell me, Maya, did you never wonder what your father's role was in all this?"

"My father tried to talk to him. He tried to help me, but they kept him away."

Damien threw his head back in exasperation.

"For fuck's sake, Maya. Wake the fuck up. Do you really think your father is innocent? Are you really that fucking naïve?"

Maybe I was, but I didn't want to go down the thorny path he was trying to lead me. I knew that'd take me to somewhere so dark my mind wouldn't be able to cope.

"You know what," he snapped. "You're not ready for the truth. Not yet. And when you get your head out of the clouds and are ready to hear what's been going on, I'll tell you. But until then, there's food and drink in the kitchen, spare clothes in the bedroom. Make yourself at home and keep living in that bubble you seem so attached to. But when you're ready to burst it, I'll be here... ready... with the fucking needle."

He went to walk away, but I shot up from the sofa and yelled, "Running away again? You're pretty good at hiding, Damien, but it's usually in dark corners, ready to—"

"What the fuck do you want, Maya?" He spun around, holding his arms up.

"I want to leave. I've jumped from the frying pan into the fire."

He moved so quickly across the room to stand nose-to-nose with me that it'd barely registered before I felt his hot breath on my face, and he snarled, "Really? You think staying here with food and drink, in the warmth, with clean clothes, being safe is the *fucking fire*?" He tilted his head as he sneered, "No, it isn't the fire, Maya. Shall I tell you what is?"

I swallowed, preparing myself for his onslaught.

"It's being bundled into the back of a van with a sack on your head and cable ties around your wrists and ankles in the middle of the night. Being driven to an unknown location to be held in a fucking concrete basement with nothing to eat or drink. Left to soil yourself and wait for help to come. You scream, but no one answers. No one fucking cares. Then, after days of being locked in the dark, not seeing another soul, you meet the guy who actually bought you... and no, it isn't Edward. He's the facilitator. Your new master is known as The Butcher, and as he forces you down on your knees and starts raping you from behind, you suddenly realise how he got that name, The Butcher, when he takes out his knife and carves your flesh from your bones. He'll fuck you and slice you up until you either die or pass out from the pain. Hopefully death comes first, because if you wake up, he's doing it all again, only this time, he'll use the knife in place of his dick. Am I getting through to you now?"

I couldn't even bring myself to nod, let alone speak and say yes.

"And while we're at it," he added. "Getting some of these truths out into the open, maybe you should know what Lysander and Miriam had planned for you."

"What?" I managed to gasp.

Damien took a deep breath, his gaze moving to the ceiling before they landed back on me.

"They knew you were a virgin. And they had a bet going. They wanted to see who could fuck you first. They wanted me to join in, but I said no." His eyes narrowed. "I think their exact words were 'let's fuck her and leave her in the dirt where she belongs'. But then, I guess their twisted games pale into insignificance when you're still picturing what The Butcher was planning to do."

And without another word, he turned his back on me and walked towards the door.

"But why did he send me the warnings? Why did he leave me that sketch?" I found myself uttering.

Damien glanced over his shoulder and shook his head.

"When you finally wake up, let me know, because what I've just told you is only the tip of the iceberg."

Then he pushed the door open, walked through it, and the door clicked shut.

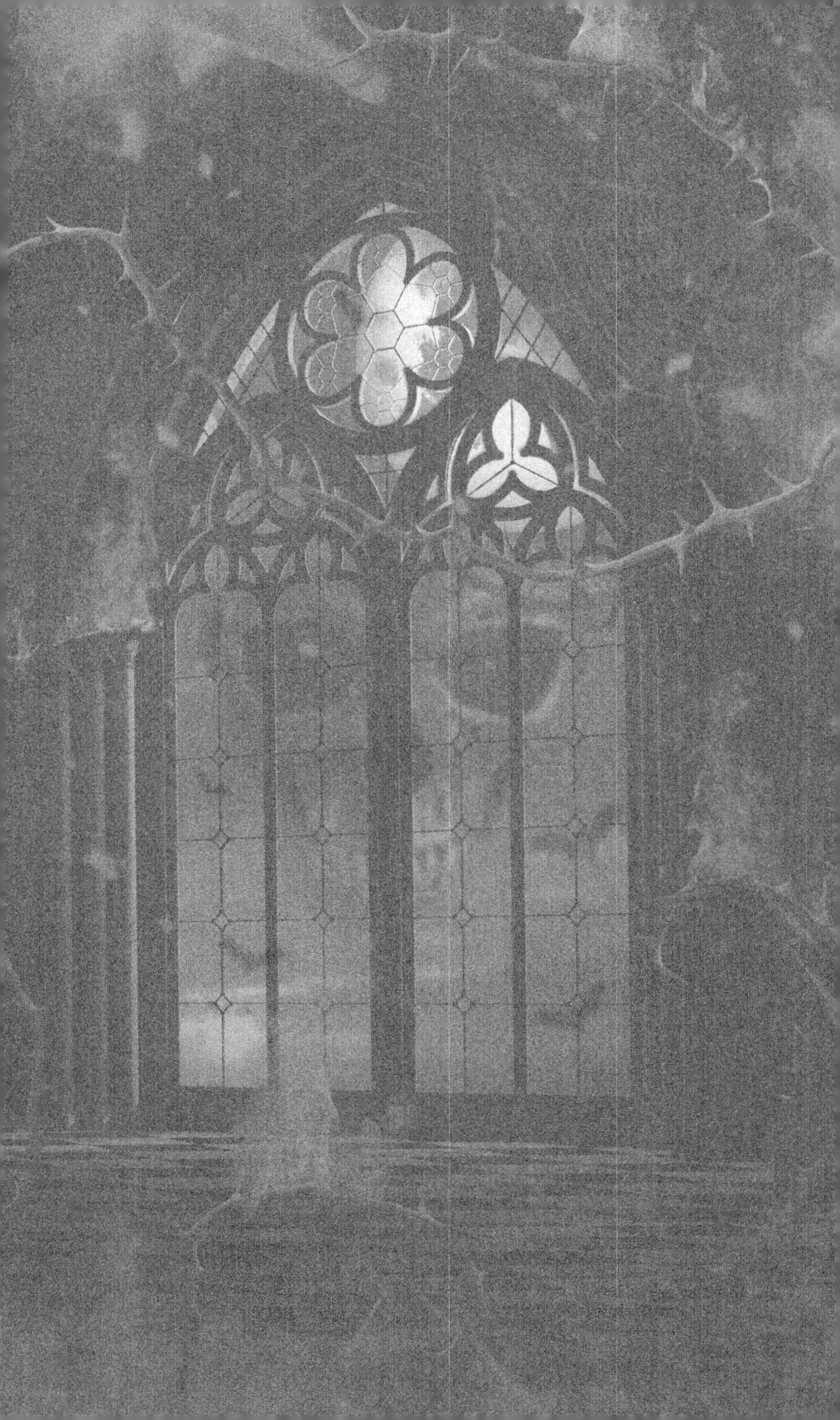

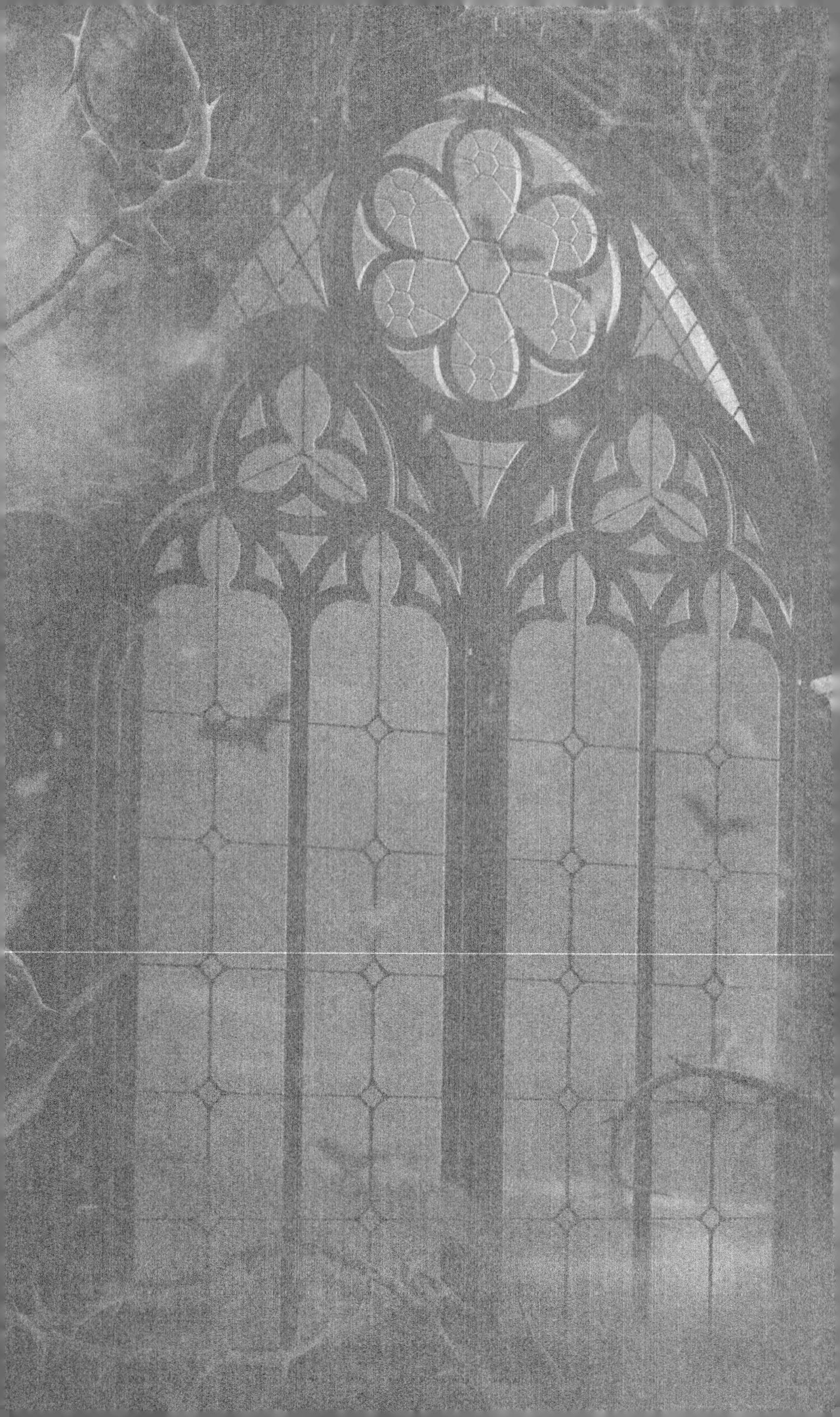

Twenty-Three

DAMIEN

I wanted to be as honest as I could with her. But she wasn't ready to face the utter annihilation of her whole life. Even though what she'd already been through was bad enough. She saw me as the villain, and I was okay with that. It was the role I was used to playing. If she still believed it, it meant I'd done my job even better than I could've hoped.

I had to admit, I felt a tinge of guilt, leaving her alone after everything I'd told her, but I had to get back to Firethorne. I couldn't risk being away for too long. I didn't want to raise suspicion.

I felt my phone buzz in my pocket and took it out, tapping

to answer the call.

"Is she okay?" Trent asked, cutting to the chase.

"Yeah, physically she's fine. Mentally? The jury is still out on that one."

"Give her time, man. It's a lot to process." He sighed, then asked, "Did you tell her everything?"

"No. Not everything. But I will."

There was silence on the line for a split second, then Trent said, "You did your best, mate. Under the circumstances, you did what you had to do, and in the end, it worked out okay. You got her out. She's still alive."

"For now."

"He won't find her," Trent assured me. "That safe house, the apartment, it's perfect. And she'll be gone in a few days. I have my contacts sorting out her new passport and papers. By this time next week, she'll have a new life."

"I hope you're right, Trent. I really fucking hope you're right."

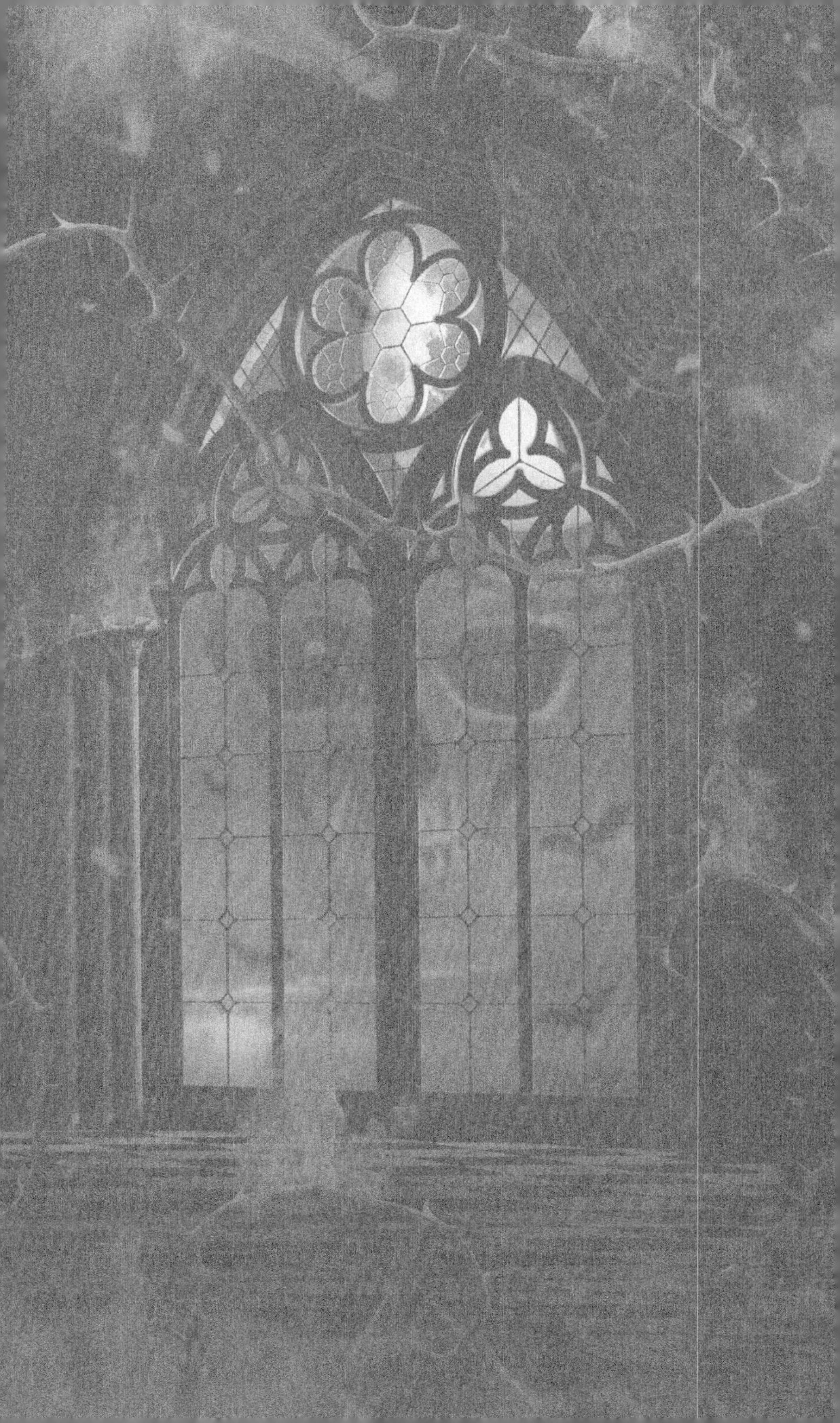

Twenty-Four

DAMIEN

I gave her twenty-four hours to cool down. I had cameras set up in every corner of the apartment, so I knew she was okay. I checked on her and watched her for most of the day as she paced the floor and scoured the apartment for a way out or for something she could use as a weapon. She wasn't successful, but I got a sick fascination from watching her squirm. My little captive had more fight for survival than I thought she would when I first met her. I admired her spirit. It'd help her in the long run.

As I pushed the door open and entered the apartment, she shot up from the sofa, charging over to me.

Firethorne

"Let me out," she snarled, like a rabid dog ready to rip me to shreds, and when the door closed and locked itself behind me, I grinned and said, "Oops," she threw her whole body at me, nails ready to gouge like claws, arms to fight, legs to kick. But she was tiny, and I was six-foot-two. She didn't stand a chance.

I caught her in my arms, twisted her and lifted her in the air, her back to my front, with her legs kicking as I whispered in her ear, "Calm down, little one. I'm not going to hurt you."

"Don't fucking patronise me," she growled, as she clawed and scratched at my arms, but I managed to put her back on the sofa, and as she huffed angrily and blew her hair from her face, I smiled.

"Sarcastic, yes... but patronising?" I shook my head. "Never."

"Why are you here?" she asked, sitting forward, her eyes beads of fury as she glared up at me.

"To check you're okay."

"Don't act like you care."

"I don't. Act, I mean. I leave that to Lysander." I shrugged, knowing that would piss her off, but I couldn't help it. I liked her feisty side.

"Fuck you," she barked.

And I smirked. "You really need to work on your putdowns. There's a whole lot of cuss words you could use instead of fuck. Mix it up a little. Call me a cunt, a bastard, a motherfucker, even." I cocked my head. "You like that f-word, don't you?" I laughed because I knew she was holding her tongue, trying not to tell me to go fuck myself.

"You told me you saved me," she said. "If that's the case, why are you keeping me here like a fucking prisoner? And why"—she gripped the edge of the sofa like she was holding herself back from launching at me again—"didn't you warn me back at Firethorne that I was in danger? Because you did know that, right? You said so yourself, yesterday." Then her eyes darkened as she lowered her gaze at me. "I'm guessing it was you that left the dead rat on my doorstep with the message, telling me, 'They're all liars here'. Did you really think that'd work? Did you think that was enough to drive me away? And the writing on my bathroom mirror..."

This wasn't going the way I wanted it to.

"I don't have to explain myself to you," I snapped.

"You didn't do enough though, did you?" she hissed through her teeth, and I took a breath, took a moment to calm the demons that were rising inside. Clawing their way out of the graves that I'd kept them buried in for a long time.

She shook her head as I stood there watching her, holding my tongue and waiting. "I can't believe I ever had a moment of weakness with you. I can't believe I let you touch me."

"We all have moments of weakness," I replied, smiling through the anger bubbling under the surface. "Don't beat yourself up about it."

"Oh, I don't," she replied. "I know you took advantage of me."

It was my turn to let the rage reign, and I balled my fists, wishing I could punch a fucking wall.

"I don't remember you using the word 'no', Maya. In fact, I seem to remember you telling me you wanted it, making all those little noises as you ground your soaking wet pussy on my hand."

Her cheeks blushed at my words, but her face glared as her eyes burned at me. If she could strike me dead right now, she would.

"I know the truth," she said. "My eyes are wide open to what you are."

"Which is?" I couldn't help but goad her.

"You're your father's little monster. His bastard." She grinned wickedly as she added, "You're right, it does feel good to use other words to describe you."

I'd been called a bastard more than my own name for most

of my life, so that insult rolled off me like water off a duck's back. But when she said, "Lysander has done more to save me than you ever could," I knew she was trying to poke the beast inside me.

"Lysander did fuck all to help you, and do you want to know why? Because he doesn't have a clue what our father does for a living. He has no idea what happens behind that fucked up curtain in Firethorne Manor. The curtain my father likes to hide behind. Lysander spends his days in his studio, pretending to be an artist, trying to fill the emotional void his daddy left him with when he told him he didn't love him and called him a failure. And when he's not painting his shitty landscapes, he's in the nearest town, fucking his way through every barmaid, shop girl, anything with a pulse, actually. He's not fussy."

"I don't believe you," she replied with scorn in her voice.

"I don't give a fuck whether you believe me or not, but I've got no reason to lie. He wasn't trusted with the family business like I was. I was fourteen when my father showed me what it was all about." Her eyes went wide. "That's right. He might be a failure, but he was still the golden boy. The one he wanted to protect. And me? I *was* the bastard. You're right about that part. I was the one he thought had the balls to take over from him when he died. The dark one, quiet, trustworthy, with an edge he could manipulate... or so he thought."

"And you took the reins so well," she snarled.

"I took fuck all. Those reins are ready to be cut, the chains broken. Not everything is black and white, Maya. And that's where I live, deep inside the murky grey shitstorm we call life. Being a shadow. Keeping secrets, twisting lies. He trusts me, and I've worked for over a decade to make that happen, to maintain it. You can't fuck up hell unless you take a trip there. I'm a trojan horse. Only, I don't need to enter my Troy, I play in the devil's lair every fucking day."

"If that's the case, why haven't you stopped him already?"

she asked, with a furrowed brow, judgment and condemnation clear on her face.

"I'm working on it."

"But it's not enough. And why haven't you stopped men like The Butcher? Because he's still out there, preying on innocent victims."

"Because Rome wasn't built in a day, Maya." I threw my head back, trying to calm myself. "Rome wasn't built in a fucking day, and neither was my organisation. I live in the real world, not some fucking Hollywood movie. You don't go in all guns blazing, take these people out and everything stops. It takes time. Work. Strategy. It takes patience. My father has bosses. The butcher has contacts, a network. If I take them out, I don't get any higher up the chain. The bosses, the really evil fuckers, they'll just move on and find others to run their business. And then what's the point of any of this? That won't stop them. Trust me when I say, I know what I'm doing."

"If you know what you're doing, why didn't you get me out sooner? I could've been taken at any minute."

"I told you, on the night of the party, after you ran away that I'd drive you to the fucking station. But you wouldn't listen, would you?"

"I didn't trust you. I still don't trust you. You think you're in control, but you're not."

"Do you want to know exactly what I did? Do you?" I knew I'd lost it now. But I couldn't help myself.

"Apart from send me shitty little messages? No, I don't know." She folded her arms over her chest. "So, go on. Tell me. What exactly did you do?"

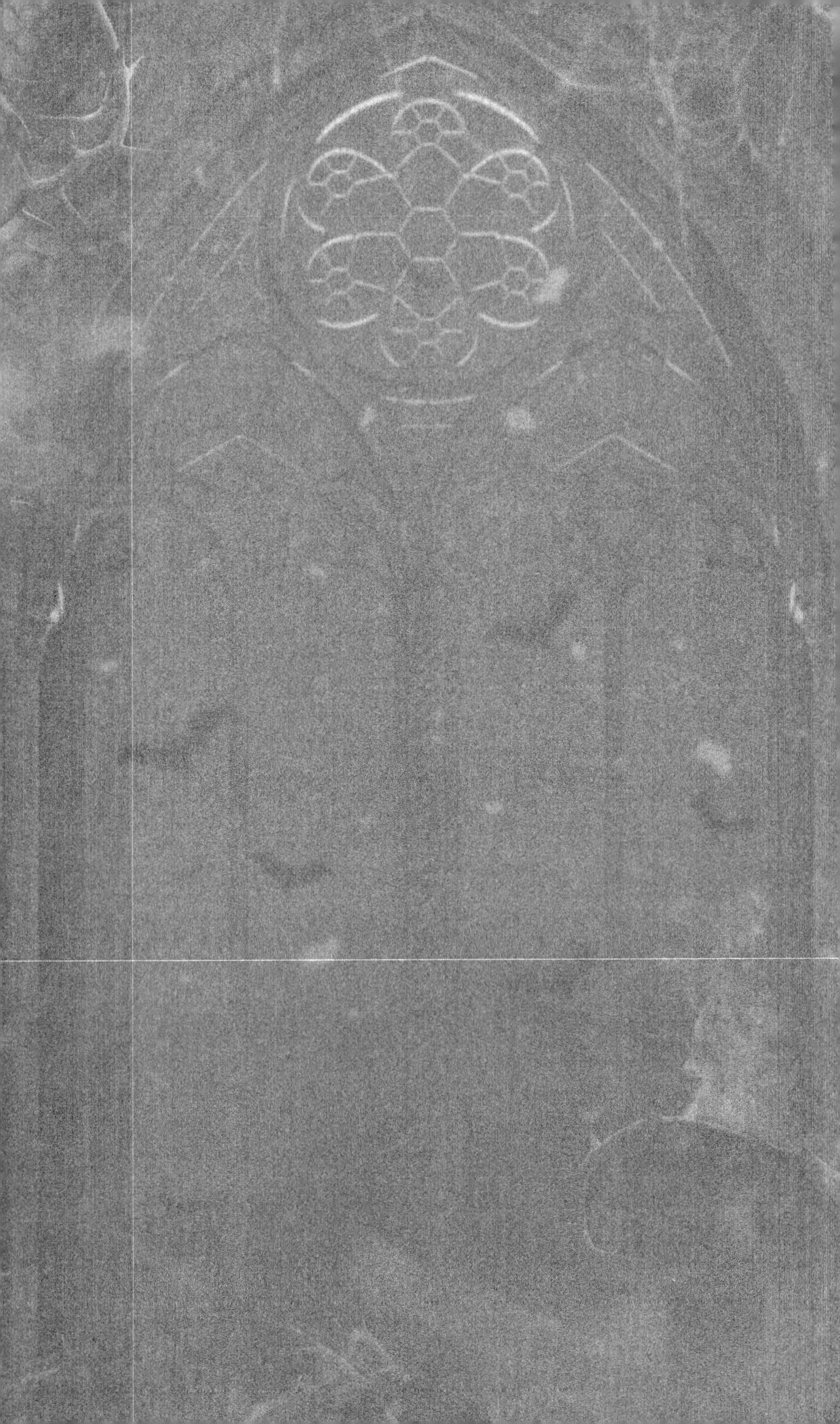

Twenty-Five

MAYA

His nostrils flared as he panted and stared back at me. I knew I was getting to him, challenging him like this. Proving him wrong. Tarnishing the saviour complex he seemed to think he had and exposing him for what he really was.

After a beat, he strode towards the kitchen, and I heard him open the fridge door. Then he strolled back out again, twisting the cap off a plastic water bottle and taking a swig. I think he'd have poured himself a large shot of whisky if he could, but there were no glass bottles in this apartment. There was no glass at all, not even to pour a drink into. Everything was plastic or shatterproof so it couldn't be used as a weapon or to cause harm. He said this place was to protect me, but it was set up to protect himself from me fighting back.

My eyes tracked him as he marched back over to the sofas and sat down opposite me. He placed the bottle on the table between us and leaned forward with his elbows resting on his knees, wringing his hands together. His black hair fell over his eyes, shielding him. But when he spoke, his deep voice felt like a knife cutting through my soul.

"I've been working to avoid this, to protect you from all this even when you were nothing but a rumour I heard whispered in the hallway. A name written on a contract. Just black ink staring right back at me. Maya Cole. The next victim."

I felt sick, and he glanced up at me, making me realise I must've made a sound to show this, despite myself.

"So, I did what I do with every girl that's passed through that house," he went on. "I researched you. Found out where you lived, where you studied."

"Do you have many girls coming through the house?"

"A few," he answered, without really answering.

I wanted numbers, but when I pushed him, asking, "Did you save all of them?" he shook his head regretfully.

"Most of them. Not all. But the ones we got out are living new lives now. Sometimes, things happen that are... out of our hands. We're working undercover, so it doesn't always go to plan. We try our best."

I wasn't sure if I believed everything he was saying, but at the same time, I dreaded to think of any other girls that'd been at that house. Girls that it hadn't worked out for. But I also picked up on one other thing he'd said.

"We?" I asked. "You said 'we try our best'. Who else is working with you?"

He took a moment, probably to think about how best to respond. Then he said, "I have a friend called Trent who works alongside me. Also a few contacts that I can trust, but I'll get back to that later. It's not important."

It was to me.

He reached for the water again, took a sip and put it back down. I waited, eager to hear what else he had to say.

"I made enquiries about you at your university. They told me you were a first-class honours student, that they had high hopes for you. You were a deep thinker, a hard worker. They had nothing but praise for you. So, I put a plan in place to try to get you to stay there. Does The Earnshaw Scholarship ring any bells by any chance?"

I cast my mind back, and with a hesitant shrug, I answered, "Maybe. I'm not sure."

It didn't.

"I set up a fund. That fund was called The Earnshaw Scholarship."

"You created a fund for the university?" I frowned, not understanding what he was saying.

"I created a fund... *for you*," he replied. And I had to catch my breath for a moment, as memories came flooding back to me. "The fund would've covered all your expenses for the remainder of your course. Tuition fees, too. You could have stayed there, and it wouldn't have cost you a penny. I'd have made sure you were safe there, Maya."

I remembered my tutor telling me about a scholarship, he even gave me the papers. And like a fool, I threw them in the bin, thinking it was pointless.

"But you left the university without even applying for a money pot that had your name on it. You left before anyone could stop you."

"I didn't know—" I spoke up, but he butted in.

"You didn't trust that something good could happen to you. I get it. Your father had fucked up his life, not yours. But you carried the burden of his betrayal. It wasn't your wrong to put right."

"He's the only family I have," I said by way of a feeble explanation, but he ignored me, carrying on with his story.

"So, I moved to my next plan. I had Trent follow you on the train down to Firethorne that night. He delivered the first message to warn you. We knew by this point you weren't going to back out of anything, so we figured we'd prepare you."

"Trust no one," I said, recounting the first message I'd gotten that was thrown into my lap by the man on the train. The man who disappeared into thin air.

"Exactly," Damien replied. "And you did well with that. You didn't trust anyone... *at first.*"

"And so, you decided to leave me a dead fucking rat," I added, spearing my gaze on him.

"I used the shock factor." He shrugged. "It got the message across. They were all liars. Lysander was pouring God knows what kind of shit in your ear, and Miriam had her claws out, ready to sink them into you. Beresford was an asshole, so there's no change there, and my father scared you. You tried to hide it, but I could tell. I think I did too, in a way. You held yourself well, but you were never going to win. Not against them. You're too kind, too thoughtful. You were the perfect candidate for them to walk all over."

"I'm not a fucking pushover," I snapped.

"I never said you were. I said you were kind and thoughtful. There's a difference."

"Not to me there isn't." I took a breath then hissed, "And then you broke into our cabin like a fucking stalker, writing on the bathroom mirror and scaring us both half to death."

He laughed at me then.

"Scaring you *both*? *Really*?" He shook his head like he was mocking me. "Do you even remember what that message said, Maya?"

"Of course I do," I barked. "It said 'he's the devil'."

"And did you never stop to think who the devil was?"

"Your father, obviously."

Damien's head shot up, eyes blazing with fury as he hissed, "No, Maya. Not *my* fucking father... YOURS!"

The adrenaline that hit me like a ten-tonne truck made my stomach swirl and my brain want to shut down.

I knew.

At the back of my mind, I knew things weren't as rosy as I wanted to believe they were.

But I'd always hoped in my heart that it wasn't true.

"He sold you, Maya. Without giving two shits about you, or what happened to you. He sold you to my father. The bonus being that you were a virgin, perfect for a fucker like The Butcher. And do you want to know what the real killer was for me?" I couldn't respond. I felt paralysed. "That he thought he was being noble, bringing you to the house himself. He thought it'd make the transition easier if he was there to see it all play out." He shook his head again in disbelief. "Like that was going to help. He was fucking clueless. He had no idea who he was messing with."

"I just... I can't... I don't believe..." I couldn't get my words out, so I settled for one. "Why?"

"Because he was broke and couldn't handle it. Because you were all he had. And my father is as evil as yours. They saw an opportunity."

"My father wouldn't do that," I said, feeling totally and utterly shell-shocked.

Damien rolled his eyes, and with exasperation he said, "Grow up, Maya. Of course he would. He did. You need to open your eyes and see this for what it is."

"If he knew you were going to send me to The Butcher, he wouldn't have agreed to it. Maybe he didn't really understand—"

"He knew exactly what he was getting you into," Damien interjected. "And he didn't care. All he thought about was the money. And it was *a lot* of fucking money. Don't let his last-ditch attempt at showing some sort of humanity cloud your judgment. He did what he did. End of."

"I need to speak to him," I proclaimed, but Damien shook his head again.

"You can't ever see him again, Maya. It'd be too risky. He can't be trusted, and the whole reason I brought you here was to get you to safety. If you saw him, that'd be compromised, big time. And besides, I have no idea where he is."

"What do you mean you don't know where he is?"

"I mean exactly that. Since the night we took you, he's been missing. He's probably off somewhere enjoying the cash he made off the back of your misery. Mind you, he didn't get the full settlement. Your leaving meant he forfeited any claim to that. That's the one thing my father is relieved about throughout this whole mess. He's desperate to find you, but he's glad he didn't transfer all the cash before your father disappeared."

"He wouldn't leave me," I whispered to myself.

"Your father would do anything for money," Damien said. "And I tried to tell you. I had to keep my cover, but I tried to let you know." He paused for a moment to gather his thoughts, running his hand over his mouth before he went on. "That day, when I found you in the library, I saw another opportunity to give you the truth. To show you what was going on. Did you even read those books I sent?"

"Of course I did," I answered truthfully, my mind still stuck on my father, wondering where he was, what was really going through his mind. Why would he do this to me? Did he really do this to me?

Damien quirked his brow and said, "And what happened at the beginning of *The Mayor of Casterbridge*, Maya?"

I swallowed, the sickness roiling inside me.

"The main character, Michael, was down on his luck, so he took his wife and daughter to the market, had too much to drink... and he sold them."

"He fucking sold them," he reiterated.

"But how was I supposed to see a parallel there? How was I supposed to know that was a message?"

"Because you read into everything, Maya. You're a thinker. And I was clutching at straws by this point, desperate to find anything to get through to you without showing my hand."

"You could've just told me."

"No. I couldn't. This operation is too delicate. Too important to risk anyone overhearing anything, especially from me. I'd risked too much already by telling you to leave and offering to drive you to the fucking station."

He was throwing so much information my way I could barely keep up.

As my mind whirled, I asked, "I get why you gave me the copy of Sons and Lovers. You knew it was my favourite. But why Wuthering Heights?"

"I thought you might make a link there, too, you know, Catherine Earnshaw. She's the main character; my scholarship fund was the Earnshaw Scholarship. Yeah, weak, maybe, but it was something." He smiled a regretful smile. "And anyway, everyone should own a copy of Wuthering Heights. It's fucking awesome."

His smile faded and he hung his head. I thought he'd told me everything, but there was still more to come. So much more. And I didn't know if I'd survive after this.

"Trent was monitoring communication, checking the dark web. We knew something was going to happen imminently. I asked Cora to keep you out of sight for as long as she could so we could devise a plan."

"Cora knew?"

"No. She had her suspicions that something wasn't right. She's seen enough girls come and go, sometimes in the dead of night, only staying for a matter of hours, others lingering for a day or two. You were the longest guest we had. But no, she didn't know. Or if she did, she never spoke about it."

"Guest," I huffed. "I wasn't a fucking guest." And then remembering the last message he sent me, I said, "I don't understand why you'd steal one of Lysander's sketches and leave it in the cupboard for me to find the way you did."

Damien smirked.

"What makes you think it was Lysander's sketch?"

I didn't respond. And he went on.

"I drew that. Didn't you notice the difference in style?" I'd noticed that it was better. I'd just thought he'd improved. "Lysander isn't the only artist in the family. But that wasn't the point. I knew you were beginning to trust him, so I wanted you to know you weren't alone. That there was someone good looking out for you. That we weren't all liars there." He paused. "And look at how that turned out. He proved once again what a spineless little shit he is."

"He held me, that night. He tried to stop me running off."

"I know," Damien replied. "He's bragged about how he tried to stop you every time my father mentions anything about that night. He's proud that he tried to help our father, which shows how utterly clueless he really is. But I'd thought, maybe, he might have a shred of humanity in him. I knew he was a fucker. I knew what he wanted to do to you at that party. That's why I fucked about with the outfits and then showed you who he really was. I couldn't help myself. But I never thought he'd give you up like he did. I thought he might've done something to help you. But, once again, he proved that he is nothing but a puppet for our father."

"You drew that sketch," I said, my mouth dry and my eyes watery with tears I didn't want to shed in front of him. Everything was hopeless. My life had become a desolate wasteland of nothingness. Like some kind of apocalyptic movie, a dystopian nightmare that I didn't know how to fix.

And yet, Damien grinned back at me as if this was all going to plan. His plan.

"It was a pretty good sketch, wasn't it?" he replied with a wicked glint in his eye.

"And you knocked the drink over at the party to save me."

"That was to save you from Lysander and Miriam. That night... it wasn't my finest hour."

I felt a ripple of shame wash over me.

"I meant," he went on, probably reading between the lines and seeing the flicker of shame, like a whisper on my face that I pushed away. "I shouldn't have let my moment of weakness be seen by my father. Once that happened, everything escalated."

"Why would you go to all that trouble?" I asked. "Why do all that... for me?"

"Because I won't stop until he does. I won't rest until I know women are safe from men like him. Mind you, Miriam has the Firethorne evil streak running through her, too. What did you do with that necklace she gave you? It had a tracker in, you know. I overheard her talking to my father about it."

"It's still in the bedside drawer back at the cabin," I replied in a daze.

My chest was heaving as I breathed deeply, my heart still pounding as I tried to make sense of it all.

We remained silent for a moment, not knowing what to say. There were no words.

And then Damien sat up, and with a wicked grin on his face, he said, "And now that I've told you all of that, there's only one more thing left for me to say."

"What?"

He steepled his fingers together, that grin growing wider.

"If you ever repeat anything you've heard here today, or let anyone know that in this worthless body, beneath these blackened, charred ribs, lies a heart that isn't totally pitch black... I'll have no choice but to cut out your tongue and boil the flesh from your bones, just for good measure."

I glared back at him, speechless. And after a beat, he threw his head back and laughed.

"I'm just kidding," he said, and then he stopped laughing and glared back at me like a psycho. "Or am I?"

This man was the definition of a mindfuck.

"I guess we'll never know," he went on. "Unless you talk. But you're not going to do that, are you, Maya?"

"No," I replied, and he nodded.

"Good. Because I'd hate for whatever friendship we're developing here to have its throat ripped out before its even had a chance to sing."

"What?" I frowned; my eyes narrowed on him.

"Bad analogy, I know," he replied flippantly. "I was just picturing throats being ripped out and the words just... kind of... fell out."

And with that, he stood up, strode over to the door, and left without another word.

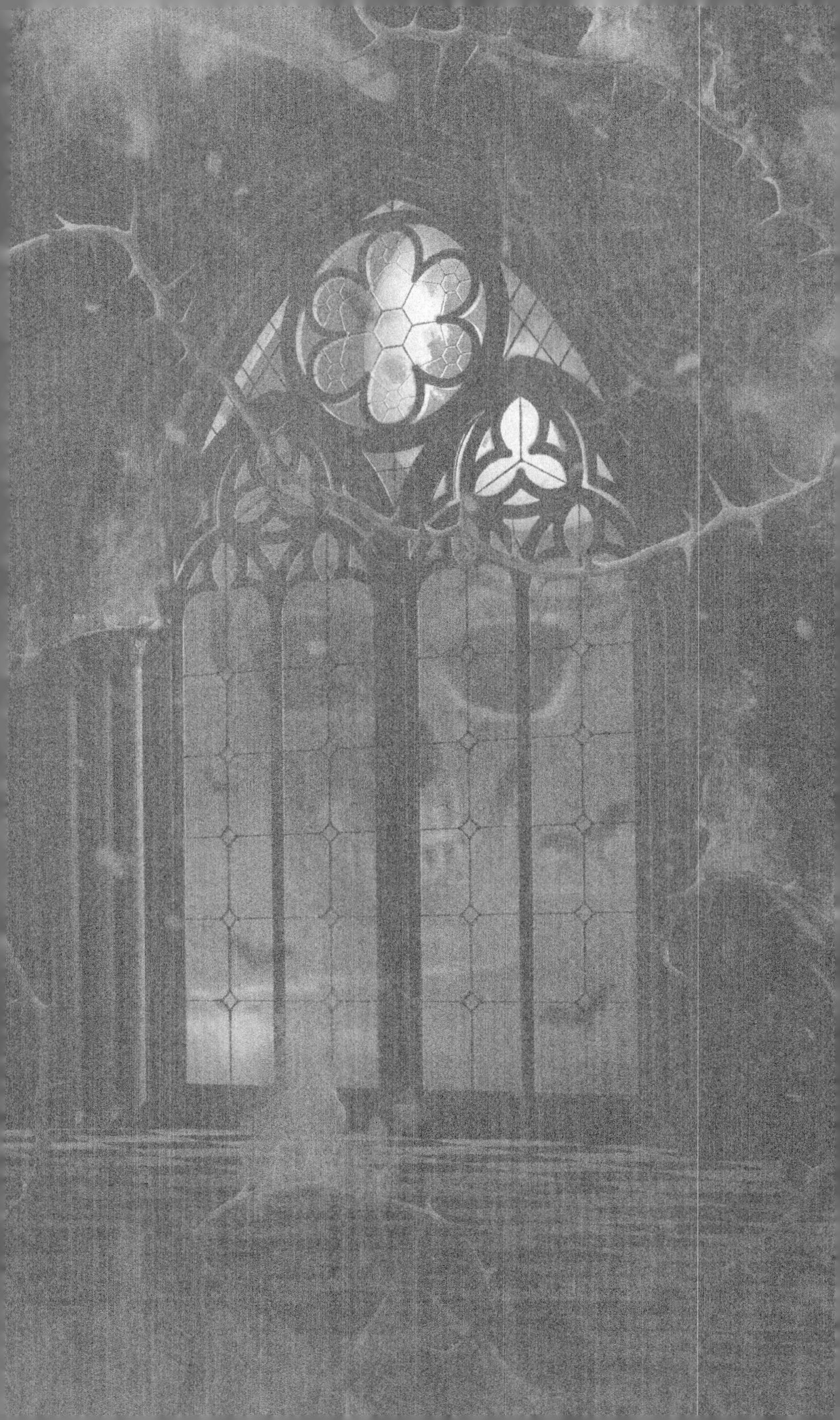

Twenty-Six

DAMIEN

"Where the hell have you been?" my father bellowed as I walked back into Firethorne an hour later. He was standing on the staircase, his phone clutched in his hand.

"Out," I replied. "I was looking at cars. I've been thinking about getting a new one."

"That can wait," he sneered. "I need you here. I've been ringing your mobile all morning."

"I noticed." I lifted my phone from my pocket.

"And you didn't think to call me back?" His jaw clenched. He was seriously pissed off. "When I call you, you fucking answer your phone. Do you hear me?" he hissed; every word spoken with venom.

"I was on my way back when I saw the missed calls. I figured it was quicker to just come back here and talk face-to-face." He was ready to argue, but I cut him off. "Anyway, what's up? What did you need me for?"

He took the last few steps down the staircase and came to stand in front of me in the foyer.

"Edward found something. It's grainy CCTV but he's working on cleaning it up. We think it's the van that took Maya that night. She must've managed to scale the walls and then they picked her up on the road outside. All we can make out so far is two men in the front seat. But if that camera caught them, there might be others. We might be able to get a registration number from one of them."

I wanted to swallow, but I didn't want him to notice that what he'd said had affected me, so I cleared my throat and asked, "And why do you need me? I can't do anything with CCTV."

"Because I've also heard things, on the dark web, more intel on that group that's targeting businesses like ours. There's a lot of money being offered to shut them down, and I want you to look into it. I want to know everything that's being said. I want to know what's happening before anyone else. Find them, Damien. This is why I paid your ridiculous school fees, so you could be educated enough to assist in times like these."

There was always someone offering money to take us out. What we did didn't come without its pitfalls. The worst being someone would put a bullet in our head if we made ourselves known and popped our head above the parapet.

Actually, that wasn't the worst thing. The worst would be shutting us down altogether, because for these women and children, women like Maya, we were a beacon. Hope in a world that was only filled with darkness. And yes, my father had paid an astronomical amount in private school fees to educate me. A private school that allowed me to escape the confines of this hellhole every term. That gave me the opportunity to think for myself.

What a shame Lysander and Miriam were home-schooled. They hadn't been afforded the same luxury, despite thinking that me being sent away was a punishment of sorts. It *was* a punishment, and that suited me just fine. While they wallowed in the spider's web that was Firethorne, I made plans and made a life for myself.

I made connections that I still benefitted from today.

"I'm on it," I told him. Because who better to go in search of me, than me. I'd make sure he never found us. I'd do whatever I could to shut down anyone who tried to track us down.

"Good. Because I plan to have her back here within the week, and when I do, we'll make sure she goes to Edward knowing exactly the kind of treatment she's going to get from her next owner. Maybe I'll let you or Lysander break her in, or better yet, I'll do it myself. But either way, we will get her back."

His words made me feel sick and stabby all at once.

"Why do you care about getting her back?" Lysander's voice chimed as he appeared from the hallway to the left of us. "She fucked us over and stole from us. Why go to all the bother of getting her back. Just let her go. Or report her to the police. I don't know why you're taking this all on yourself."

My father had spun a tale for Lysander, and he was so fucking gullible, he'd believed it. He said Maya had stolen from the family, that she was running away because she'd been caught out that night. But being the stand-up guy that my father claimed he was, he didn't want to involve the police. He wanted to deal with it himself.

"It's a matter of principle. She needs to know she can't get away with it. Not when it comes to our family."

Firethorne

Ah. Those twisted Firethorne morals. The ones that my father and his father before him had written on the back of every captive's broken back.

"I did what I could," Lysander went on, harping on about the heroic part he played in trying to avenge Maya's crimes. "But she was vicious."

"And you weren't made to outwit or outsmart anyone," our father stated plainly. "Damien is the cunning one. Best to leave the heavy work to him." Lysander gave me an evil glare. "That's why he's going to spend however long it takes locked in his study to help me find her. And you..." He turned to stare at Lysander. "Can use your painting skills to help Beresford with the fences tomorrow. Show us you can be of use in some capacity."

Lysander replied, "Yes, Father." Ever the dutiful son. But his eyes showed he wanted to say more, probably gouge our father's eyes out for being so fucking cruel, closely followed by mine for grinning back at him.

You'd think he'd be used to it by now, but Lysander lived for praise and adulation. He existed to try and reap the rewards from a father who would never give him any.

And me?

There was no love lost between Lysander and me. From day one, he'd hated me. I was the bastard who didn't belong. He thought I didn't know that he painted shadowed figures of me into every painting he'd ever made. But Lysander couldn't keep his mouth shut. And he'd told everyone else. Miriam, Beresford, Cora, they all knew. He was a damn fool for thinking it would never get back to me. Or maybe he simply didn't care. I know I didn't.

Lysander stomped away, and with a sly grin, my father followed him. But as he walked away, he called over his shoulder to me, "I want you on that dark web night and day. I want to find these people. Cut the head off the snake. They might think they can outsmart us, Damien, but we're always one step ahead. Remember that. Always one step ahead."

"I won't forget," I hissed under my breath. "I won't ever forget."

Twenty-Seven

MAYA

He'd dropped one hell of a bombshell or two on me and left me to wallow in my pit of despair. He'd left me questioning everything.

Was he telling the truth?

Was he really working against his father?

Or was this another trick, a ploy to ensnare me even deeper into their web of deceit?

I couldn't even think straight. I couldn't fathom any of it.

And then there was all the stuff he'd said about my father.

My father had sold me.

How could I ever come to terms with that?

Firethorne

How could I believe something so wicked and heinous?

As bombshells went, it was pretty atomic. A nuclear ball of what-the-fuck aimed right at my heart, intent on shattering my whole life.

Even thinking about it made my nerves spike and my heart race. I felt sick, and I didn't want to believe it. I couldn't. There had to be another explanation. My heart didn't want to grieve what my mind refused to believe, so I buried the hurt deep inside. Until I saw my father again, and he could tell me himself what had happened, I would wait. I wouldn't judge him. I'd hold my tears as best I could and try to get through all this. Take a step forward, even if it meant I took two steps back every day. I had to focus on the future, because I still had one, and I refused to contemplate what could've been.

I would survive this.

Regardless of whether Damien was on my side or not, the fact remained, they were a fucked-up family. And I had no doubt that what he'd said, about them trafficking girls, was all true. There were people out there who'd suffered something unimaginable at their hands, and I couldn't bear thinking about it

But at night, when I was fighting the demons trying to chip away at my brain and battle the sins of my father that clawed away at my heart, I thought about those girls. I thought about where they were now.

What they'd endured.

What they might continue to endure.

And what I could still endure in the days to come.

Damien claimed he was doing all he could to eradicate the evil in this world. The evil that'd invaded their lives. But clearly, he hadn't done enough, and there was a very large possibility that I was still in danger.

I didn't trust anyone, not really.

I was all alone.

And yet, Damien visited me every day. Checking up on me. Guarding me. Claiming he was keeping me here for my own safety.

At first, I'd resented him. I rued the day I'd ever met Damien Firethorne. I didn't want him here, invading my life, keeping me prisoner, haunting my every waking moment. But as the days went on, and his was the only face I saw, I began to feel a little less agitated. Less hateful. He was my only link to the outside world, and I never wanted to give that dream up, the dream that I'd eventually get out of here.

After he dropped the mother of all bombshells, Damien showed up at the apartment with a large cardboard box that he set down on the coffee table in the middle of the living room.

"Don't expect the VIP treatment every day," he said with his usual sarcasm. "But I thought you might like these."

I sat on the sofa and stared at the box as I replied, "Is there such a thing as VIP treatment when you're being held captive?"

"I can take these back if they're not wanted," he snapped, reaching for the box.

"Do whatever the fuck you want. I don't care." I sat back into the cushions of the sofa, avoiding his gaze as I huffed and folded my arms over my chest.

"Aren't you even a little bit curious about what's in here?" he asked.

"No."

"Fine." He tried to act like he didn't care, but within a few seconds he was sitting forward, ripping the parcel tape off the box he'd brought, with contents he already knew about. "I guess I'll open this fucking box myself then."

He opened the box, stared up at me, and when I didn't make any effort to look inside, he huffed, then pushed the box across the table towards me.

"At least take a look. It won't fucking bite."

"Are you sure about that?" I shot back. "You do have a history of giving me fucked up shit."

"That isn't all I've done for you," he lowered his head, and I could feel the heat of his stare burning into me, willing me to look his way. "But this might help."

"I can do without your kind of help," I hissed, but I made the mistake of turning my head and glaring back at him, and as I did, the contents of the box caught my eye. I stilled and then instinctively leaned forward. I couldn't help it. He'd found my Achilles heel.

Books.

He'd brought me books.

Despite how awful everything was, I couldn't deny that seeing them made me feel something. A flicker in my fractured, damaged heart. A glimmer of hope, maybe?

I held in my gasp as I saw copies of Jane Austen, The Brontes, Maya Angelou, Sylvia Plath, Margaret Atwood; the list went on and on.

I picked up a copy of Jane Eyre and quirked my brow.

"Are you trying to give me another subliminal message? Is there a mysterious wife hidden in your attic?"

He stood up and grinned back at me as his six-foot frame towered over me.

"No. There's no message."

But I knew there was. There had to be. There was always a message. He'd said so himself.

He'd given me books that were all written by women. Strong, powerful women telling strong, powerful stories. These were books to make a woman feel empowered. I couldn't lie. It was the nicest thing anyone had ever given me.

But I still hated him.

"Thank you," I said begrudgingly.

He shrugged, acting like it was nothing.

"I know you have the TV, but you're a reader, like me. I wanted to give you something to help you escape, just for a little while." He cleared his throat and added, "I wasn't sure what you'd already read. If there's anything specific you'd like, I can bring that with me tomorrow."

"These are perfect," I replied. "Even the ones I have read, I'll happily read again. It's so... thoughtful." I managed to give him a tight smile, despite everything. "Thank you."

We sat for a moment with an emotionally charged silence hanging between us. And then, my stomach dropped and my heart splintered in fear when I heard a knock at the front door.

Someone was here.

What the fuck was about to happen?

Was this Firethorne?

My head shot up, desperate eyes finding Damien to gauge his reaction.

He was chilled, and he gave me a wry smile as he stood up and strode over to the door, a door that only he could open.

When he greeted whoever was on the other side with a "Nice to see you. Couldn't this have waited till later?" my pounding chest eased up a little and I tried to get myself under control and stop shaking as I glanced at the door and ran my sweaty palms down my thighs. He'd never greet Firethorne that way.

Damien stood back to let whoever it was into the apartment, and they said, "I figured you'd want this sooner rather than later."

I twisted in my seat, craning my neck to see who it was, this man entering my safe space dressed all in black, with his suit and tie, and a manilla envelope in his hand. Then, as he turned to face me, my nerves spiked again. It was the man from the train. The one who'd dropped the first message into my lap.

"Maya, this is Trent," Damien said, introducing his colleague.

I swallowed, not sure how to act or what to say.

And then something inside took over.

"You could've helped us, that night. You could have done more to stop us on that train."

"Maya," Damien snapped back, admonishing me. "I've already told you; we couldn't do that. We're playing the long game here. We needed my father to believe he could trust me. And besides, we had to tread carefully around your father, too. It wasn't as simple as that."

"It seems pretty simple to me," I barked back.

"I'm sorry," Trent said, dipping his head with guilt.

"Don't apologise," Damien replied. "It's not black and white."

"It's not black and white, it's dark and fucked up," I spat venomously.

"We'll talk about this later," Damien said, turning his back on me, and then ushering Trent back through the door.

"It's all in there," I heard Trent say to Damien as he handed him the envelope and stepped back into the hallway. "There's also contact details, a burner phone, everything she'll—"

"Thanks," Damien snapped, interrupting him. "I'll look over it all later."

Trent frowned as he stared back at Damien for a beat, not saying a word. Then he glanced over Damien's shoulder at me, before focusing back on Damien again, a bewildered, puzzled look on his face. He shook his head, nodded to himself, then announced, "Okay. I get it. I'll talk to you later. Call me." And then a little louder, he shouted, "It was nice to meet you, Maya," just as Damien slammed the door in his face.

Damien stood facing the door for a moment, composing

himself. Then he turned and walked back over to the sofas to sit down.

I needed to know more about this Trent character. So, I started to quiz him.

"How long have you known Trent?"

Damien sat back, stretching his legs out as he answered, "I've known him for years. We met at boarding school."

"Is he married?"

Damien narrowed his eyes questioningly at me.

"What does that matter? No. He isn't. He lives alone."

"And lives where, exactly?"

He sat forward, his gaze full of suspicion.

"Not far from Firethorne. Why all the questions, Maya? You know you can trust us, right?"

"I don't trust anyone!"

I thought I saw something in his eyes when I said that. Disappointment, perhaps. But it disappeared as soon as it came, and he nodded. "I think that's wise, considering what's happened to you."

I sighed at the realisation that I might always have this neurotic, suspicion looming over me like a dark cloud.

"Does anyone else live here, in this building?" I went on, desperate for more information. Knowledge was power, after all.

"Not at the moment. There are other apartments here. Ones we use for the people we save, but you're the only one here right now. Sometimes Isaiah comes to the office we have set up in the basement to work, but he can't access this floor. You don't have to worry. You're completely safe here." And then, as if to distract me from my racing thoughts, Damien gestured to the box on the table between us and asked, "Which one are you going to read first?"

I didn't have to think, I knew my answer right away.

"Emma. Jane Austen. It's another one of my favourites." I

smiled as the shadows of my former life flickered in my mind. "I always wanted to write a book." I found myself saying, speaking before I could engage my brain, and inwardly cursing that I'd shared a private dream with him.

"You still can," Damien replied.

"Maybe." I shrugged, peering down at the books because I couldn't look at him right now.

We were quiet for a while, then Damien asked me, "If you wrote our story, what would you call it?"

"A disaster," I stated, and then I glanced up at him, watching me with what appeared to be quiet admiration. "A fucking disaster."

"Sounds like my kind of book." He nodded to himself. "Make sure you include me in the dedication. And it's Firethorne with an 'e'."

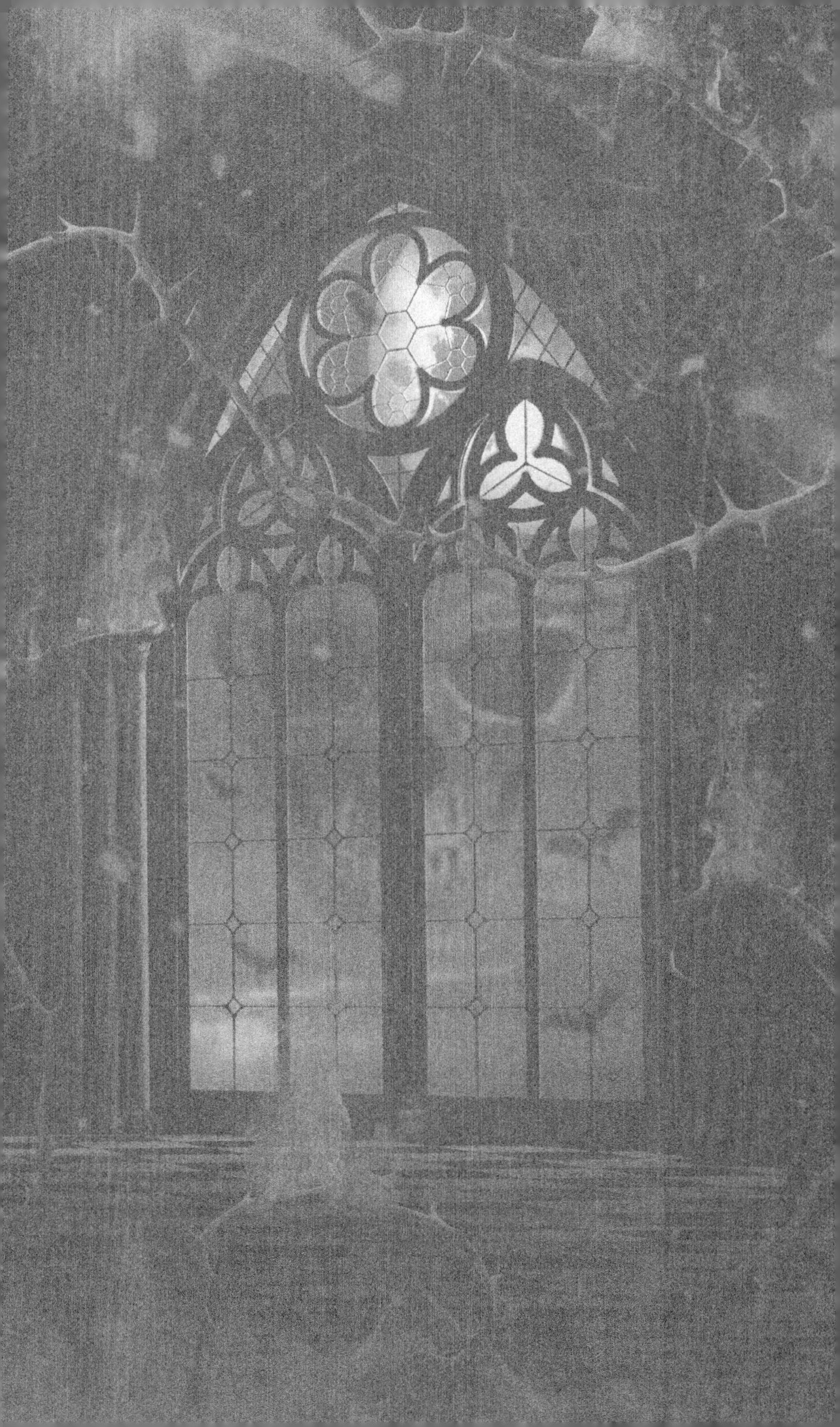

Twenty-Eight

DAMIEN

Once I left Maya in the apartment, I marched out of the building and found Trent leaning against his car in the small car park, at the back of the building, tapping away on his phone. As he saw me coming towards him, he pocketed his phone and pushed himself off the car to stand.

"Don't come here again," I snapped, pointing my finger at him. "Do you hear me? I don't want you here. She's been through enough."

"Enough of what?" He shrugged, not getting it at all. "Us saving her? Me showing up with her ticket out of here? Or didn't you tell her that's what I was delivering?" I stayed quiet for a moment, and he nodded to himself. "That's what I thought."

"You're a good friend, Trent, and I appreciate everything you do, honestly, I do," I said in earnest. "But she's vulnerable. Fragile. She isn't like the others. I'd prefer it if you just stayed away." I was trying the kinder approach, but in reality, I wanted to pick him up and throw him through the car windscreen for questioning me.

"They're all fragile and vulnerable. She's *exactly* like the others," he replied, but I disagreed. He had no idea what he was talking about. "So, are you going to give her the passport and the money?" he went on. "Are you going to explain what we've set in place for her?"

"No," I replied a little too quickly. "Not yet. It's too soon."

Trent sighed, folded his arms over his chest and speared me with a glare that made the prospect of me punching him more probable.

"The longer she stays here," he said. "The more dangerous it becomes, for her and us. The quicker we can get her out of here, the better. You know that. We've always done it this way. This time, it's no different."

"It *is* fucking different," I barked as he pinned me with his stare.

"Because you like her."

I wasn't going to answer that, but he went on, "You need to get your head in the game, mate. You can't let your personal feelings cloud your judgment."

I moved to stand toe-to-toe with him, my face close to his as I seethed, "My head *is* in the fucking game. It's so far in the game I can't see anything else but this. Don't fucking tell me what I need to do. I know what needs to be done and I'm doing it."

"Then let her go. Do the right thing, Damien, and let her start her new life."

"We do things my way," I stated, growing tired of his bullshit. "And that means you trust my judgment. And you don't ever fucking question it. For now, she stays here."

Trent shrugged noncommittally, and then he glanced across the fields as he said, "Whatever you say, boss. But just know there's been a lot of talk online, on the dark web. There's a new shipment coming in soon." He turned his head to stare at me again. "And you know what that means. We don't have time to stop and wait. We have to keep moving. Those apartments will be needed again soon enough... *if* we manage to get them out."

"We'll deal with whatever's coming our way when it gets here. But nothing is going to affect the way we deal with Maya, is that clear? She's going nowhere."

Trent nodded, turned to unlock his car and opened the door, ready to get in. "I hope you're right, my friend. And I hope you know what you're doing."

"I always do," I snapped and stood back, watching him drive away.

He meant well, I got that. He wanted the best outcome here, and so did I. But he'd picked the wrong time and place to question me about it. He'd made the wrong decision, coming here today. I wanted to keep Maya's space private, safe. I didn't want anyone barging in and destroying that.

Because everything was different with Maya.

I felt different.

I didn't want to admit it, but I didn't like the thought of letting her go. Of not seeing her again. Because when she left this apartment, that's what'd happen. Life would move on, and I wasn't ready for that to happen.

I couldn't explain it any more than I could explain why there were so many evil people in this world, like my father, who lived to cause immeasurable pain to others. I didn't know why this girl, who'd entered our world only weeks ago, seemed

Firethorne

to have such a hold on me. It didn't make sense. And yet, she did have a hold on me.

Maybe it was because she was a deep thinker, a reader like me. I found myself wanting to know what she'd read, what she was currently reading, and what she thought about it. I wanted to know all her thoughts and opinions.

I wanted to know what TV shows she liked to watch, what her favourite food was. I wanted to learn about the places she'd visited, what she thought about them, what dreams she had. I wanted it all. I was like a starving man. I craved it. Any shred of herself that she gave me, I soaked it up. Maya was a quiet, thoughtful girl. A private person. So, to gleam anything from her, to be gifted her thoughts or ideas was like catching lightning in a bottle.

In my youth, I'd read fantasy novels about fated mates and destiny. I'd never believed in it, but maybe that's what this was. Because what other explanation could there be for why this girl had come into my world and totally and utterly bewitched me?

I'd never admit it to anyone. I'd keep my mask firmly in place for the world around me.

I was Damien Firethorne.

Bastard son of Nicholas Firethorne.

Unscrupulous player, my father's right-hand man. The type of person you didn't dare cross.

But that wasn't all I was.

I was a thinker too, a reader, a philosopher. I loved poetry and art. I could get lost for hours sketching something I loved. I was a dreamer. And that's why I did what I did. I dreamed of a better world. I worked hard to achieve it. But there was always something missing. Like I was a puzzle missing a vital piece.

The longer I spent in Maya's company, the more I thought that maybe, she was that missing piece.

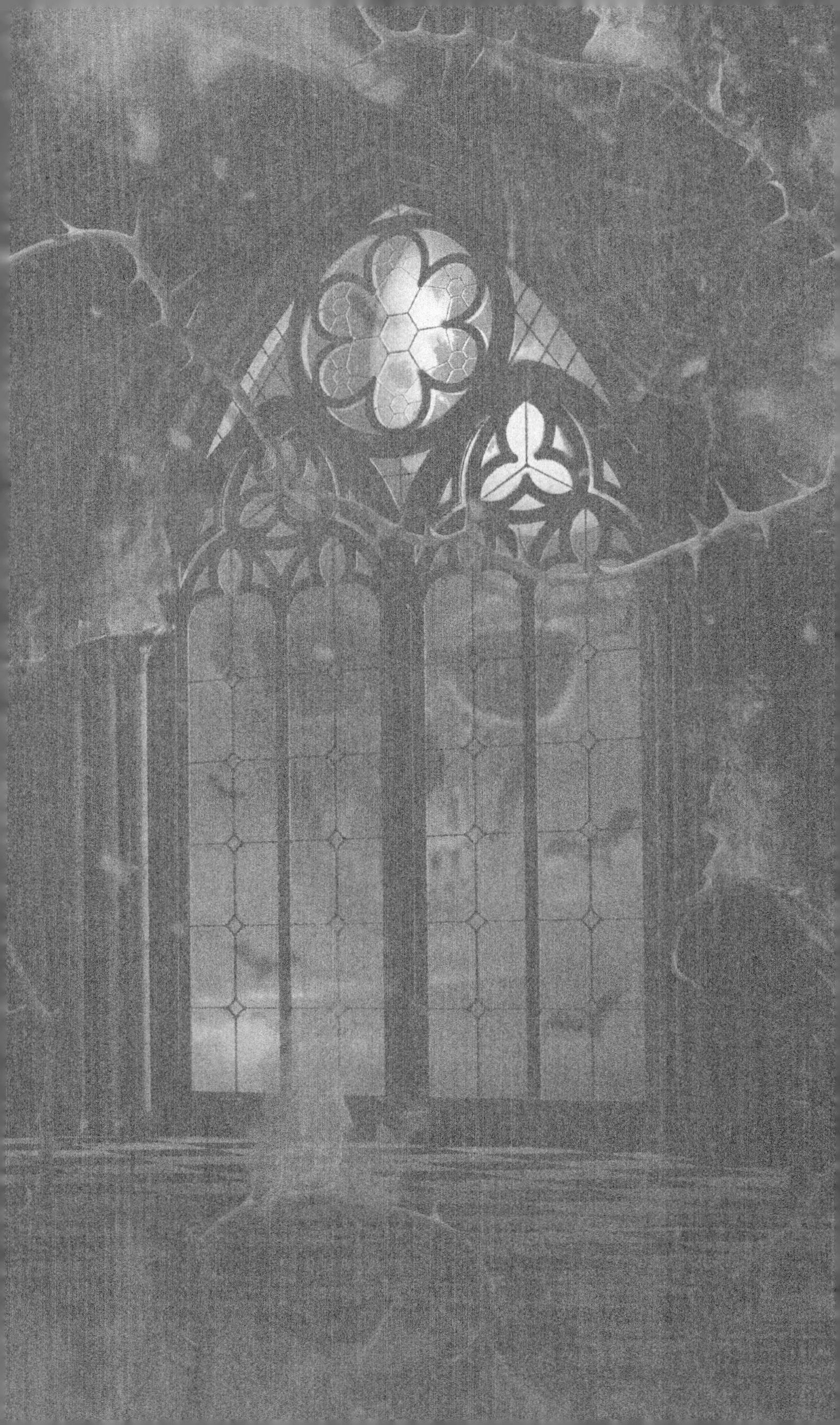

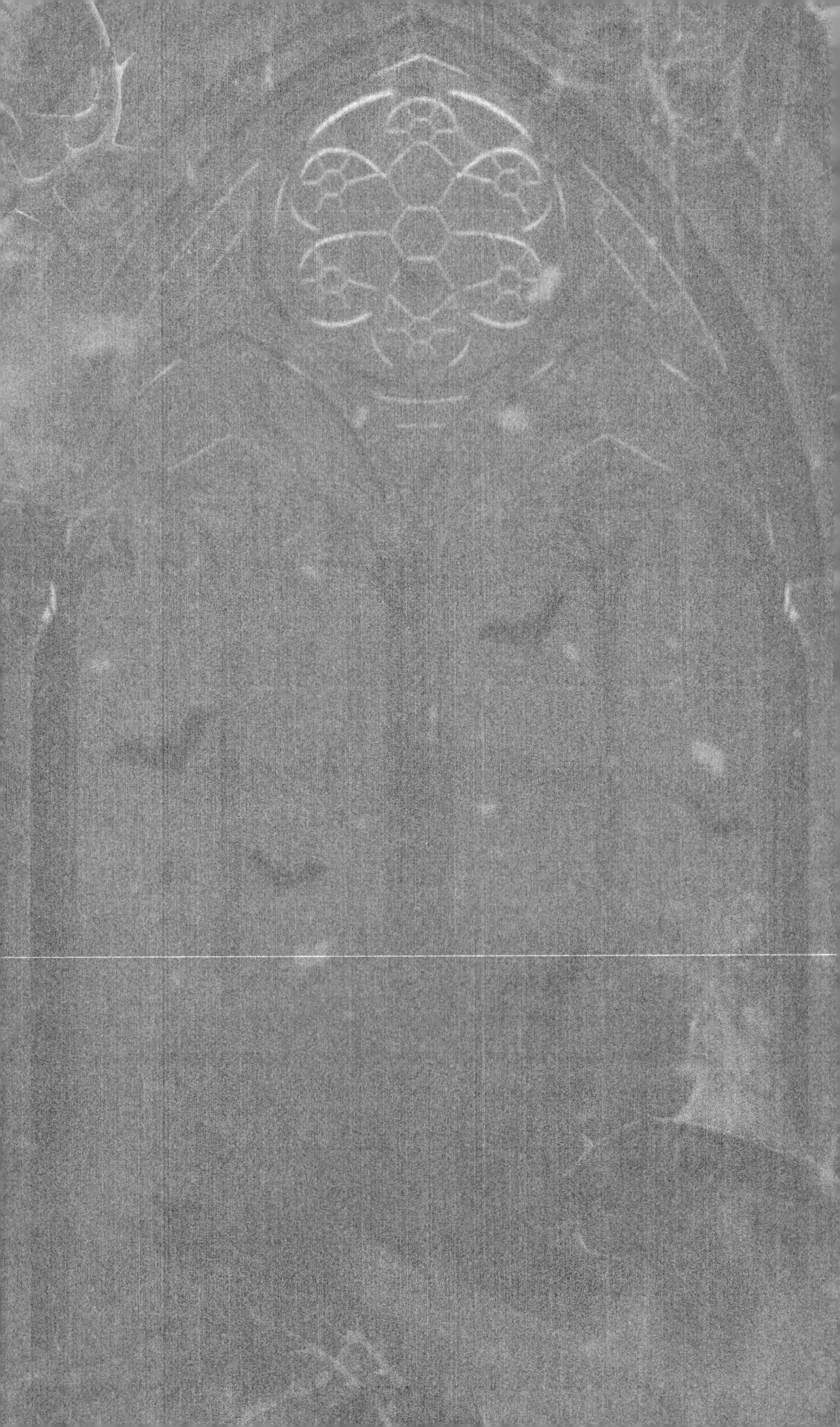

Twenty-Nine

MAYA

He'd given me an escape in more ways than one, with the books that took me away from this cruel, harsh world. But I was never quite sure what was going to happen in my real life from one day to the next.

Who was the real Damien Firethorne?

He'd started out as a devil, who seemed to revel in my misery. But now, he was slowly becoming something else. A saviour, maybe?

From the depravity of that night at the party, he was beginning to show me a different side to him. Dare I say, a thoughtful side. A side I never expected to see with a man like him.

His daily visits often surprised me. He would ask me about myself and my ideas, and he'd actually listen to my responses. Something my own father had never done. In fact, I don't think anyone had really taken the time to listen like he did.

But the nights were the worst.

I'd read *Emma* on the sofa until I could barely keep my eyes open, then I'd put it on the coffee table and padded silently through to the bedroom, hoping I'd sleep better in the bed. A lot of nights, I'd slept on the sofa, but sleep rarely found me. Tonight, I'd hoped it'd be different. But as the wind whistled through the trees and rain began to tap on the windows, I struggled to drift off.

I closed my eyes, lying still, hoping I could quieten my noisy mind for just a moment to allow sleep to creep over me. But quiet and silent meant time to think. Time to play over and over in my head every little thing that'd happened to me. Time to question, why me? Time I didn't want to have.

As I lay still, my mind started to play tricks on me. My ears hearing noises that my brain interpreted in the worst way.

Was that the creak of a floorboard outside the door?

Was someone out there trying to get in to hurt me?

To take me away?

Was it The Butcher?

I heard a rumble of thunder in the distance, and I jolted, sitting up in bed and staring around the room, watching the shadows of the trees dance on the walls. Taunting me. It didn't feel right to stay in here. I wanted to put my mind at rest that everything was okay, so I got up and walked across the carpet, heading for the door.

I creaked the door open slowly, and then stepped out, taking gentle, cautious footsteps as I made my way to the living room. My senses were alert, listening intently. More rumbles of thunder and a flash of light made my heart skip a beat, and

I reached out to hold the wall, to steady myself for a moment.

The rain was lashing the windows harder now as the storm picked up. And I came to the living room and peered around, trying to see if anything was out of place. That's when I noticed my copy of *Emma* lying open on the coffee table. I hadn't left it like that, and my heart hammered in my chest as my breaths came a little quicker now. I leant down to pick up the book, and a crack of lightning sparking up the night sky made my head shoot up. And there, reflected in the window, standing behind me was a dark figure.

I screamed, spinning around, ready to fight for my life, but there was no one there.

I scrambled for the light switch, switching it on and bathing the apartment in light. The storm was raging now, and even though I could see that there was no one here, that figure still haunted me.

Was I seeing things?

Did I imagine the whole thing?

Maybe it wasn't a figure, but something else?

The mind can do strange things to you when you're grieving, like I was. Acute stress and trauma can play with your senses and make you doubt your own existence. Perhaps I needed to give myself some grace and recognise that my mental state wasn't as strong as it used to be. That after everything, I needed time to heal, both mentally and physically.

I slammed the book shut and headed back to the bedroom. Then, once inside, I closed the door and pulled a chair across the carpet to place it under the door handle. I couldn't lock myself in, so this was the next best thing. I lay back down on the bed again, above the covers, and I tried to focus on the steady beat of the rain as the thunder began to subside. And eventually, I drifted off to sleep.

Firethorne

Crack.

A spark of lightning woke me with a start, bathing the room in light, and for a split second, I saw a dark figure looming over me at the end of the bed. I screamed and scrambled to sit up, kicking my legs as I crawled up the bed. But no sooner had I seen the figure, it disappeared.

I panted, staring at the spot where I'd seen that figure only moments ago. Maybe my mind had placed it there, like an image from my dreams projected into the real world. That had to be what I'd seen, because the windows were secured, no one could enter the apartment that way, and the chair I'd placed against the door hadn't been moved.

I was going insane.

I spent the rest of the night sitting on the bed with my knees tucked into my chest and my arms wrapped tightly around them, waiting for the sun to rise so I could drink way too much strong coffee to stay awake and count the minutes until the night came again. Until the nightmares and night terrors found me again.

Would they ever go away?

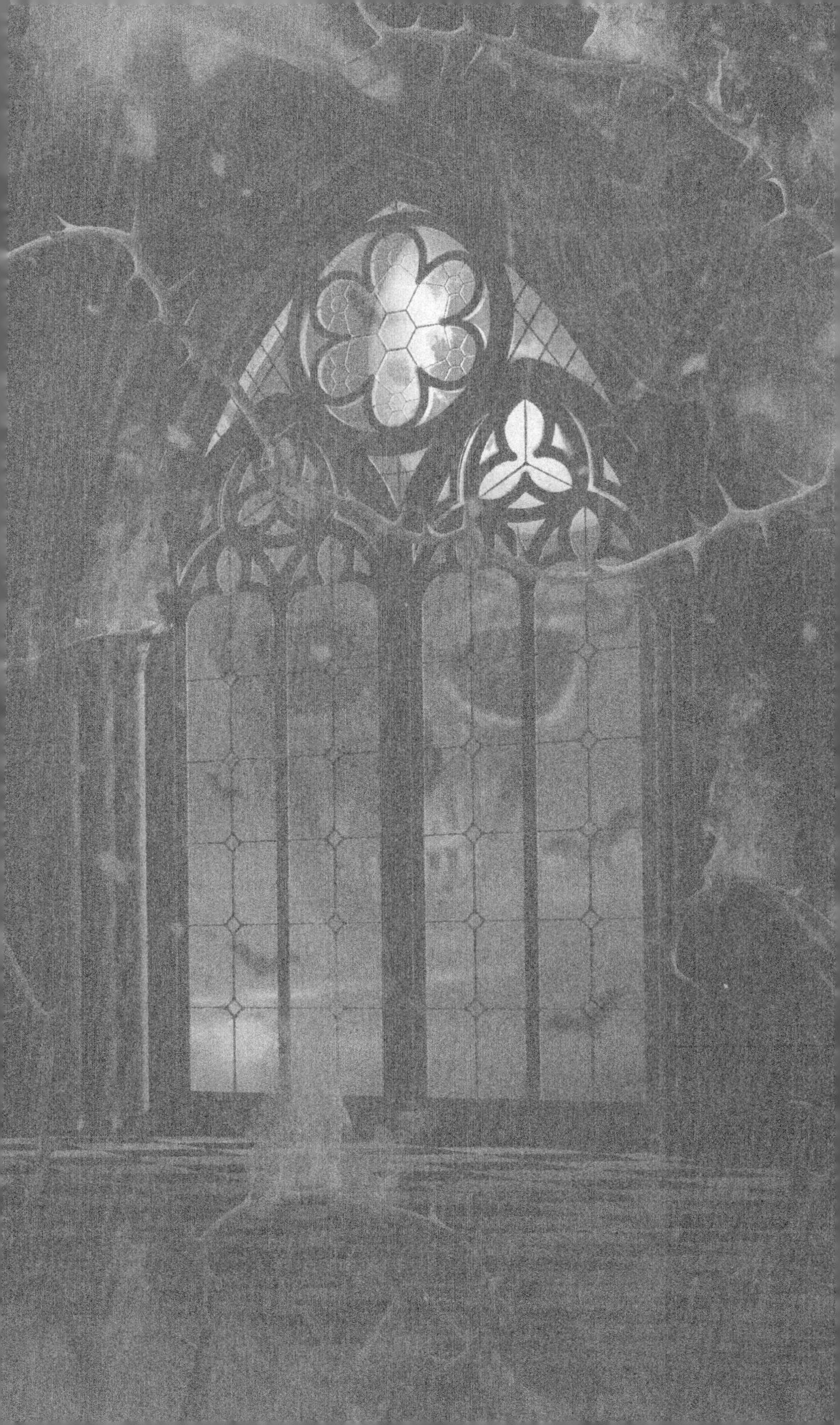

Chapter Thirty

DAMIEN

I walked into the apartment, holding my bags, expecting to see Maya on the sofas, but she wasn't there. So, I headed to the kitchen to put the food away and make a start on today's task to help Maya rehabilitate and heal, my way. When I walked through the door, I found her sitting at the kitchen island, sipping a black coffee and looking like she hadn't slept in a week. There were dark rings around her eyes, and she sat hunched over, her shoulders sagging and her eyes downcast.

When she saw me, she brightened up a little, sitting up on her stool and watching intently as I placed the bags on the counter and started to unpack everything.

"Good morning," she said, stifling a yawn. "What have you got there? The flesh of your enemies?"

"I wish." I smirked, taking a carving knife from the bag and stabbing it into one of the steaks. "Serving my enemies up as the main course sounds right up my alley."

The way she flinched at my stabbiness made me realise she actually believed me. God, I was good at this villain shit.

"So, what'll it be?" I asked her. "Rare, medium-rare, well done?"

"What?" she replied with an incredulous look on her face.

"How do you like your steak cooked?"

She didn't reply right away. Just stared at me like I'd spoken a foreign language.

"Why are you cooking me steak?" she asked, mistrust swimming in her eyes.

"Because you're looking pale, Maya," I replied plainly as I unpacked the rest of the groceries. "And I thought I could cook something healthier for you, build up your strength." And turning to give her a pointed stare, I added, "You'll need it."

She ignored me and shot back, "How am I supposed to eat a steak when there's no cutlery here? Everything is paper or plastic. Paper plates, plastic cups…"

"I have steak knives," I announced, pulling them from the bag and holding them up.

"And you trust me to use those to eat… and not to stab you and escape?"

The fact she was still fighting made me smile, and I slid a knife across the counter towards her and took slow steps over to her, holding my arms out. "If you want to stab me, I won't stop you." She picked up the knife, and I took a few more steps to stand directly in front of her. "You have to do what you feel is the right thing for you." She held the knife out in front of her, but from the resignation on her face, I knew she'd never do it. Not to me. "So go on then," I urged. "Fight me, if that's what you think you need to do." I reached forward and picked up her hand that was holding the knife, putting it against my chest as she gasped.

"I couldn't stab someone," she announced. "I could never hurt another person like that."

"And that's what makes you different to everyone else in my life," I replied. "Because you actually have a soul."

I spent the afternoon preparing the meal for her, occasionally stopping to check my emails and messages. She pretended she was reading, but I could see her out of the corner of my eye, watching me as I watched her sitting on the kitchen stool.

"Do you need any help with that?" she'd asked a few times.

And every time I'd replied, "It's all in hand. You don't need to do anything. I like cooking."

She always responded with a slight scowl that indicated she didn't believe me. There were a lot of things about me that she probably wouldn't believe.

Once the steaks were cooked to perfection, with the vegetables and accompanying sauces ready, I set up the small dining table in the corner of the living area and called her over to eat.

She sat down, sighing as she breathed in the scents and proclaimed, "This smells delicious." But she cut her meat up into tiny slices and nibbled like she thought I might've poisoned the damn thing.

I dropped my knife and fork onto the table a little too dramatically and stated, "I came here to feed you because you're looking pale, Maya." She stared at me, not saying a word as she chewed the smallest mouthful. "So stop eating like a fucking rabbit and dig in. The steak isn't gonna kill you."

"No," she said as she swallowed. "The steak might not kill me, but you might."

I paused, my fork in midair, holding a prime cut of steak. "If I was gonna kill you, don't you think I'd have done it by now?" I retorted, then ate the food from my fork as I glared back at her, chewing and savouring the taste as fire burned inside me.

"Then answer this," she asked, placing her cutlery on the plate, leaning her elbows on the table, and then resting her chin on her entwined fingers. "Why am I still here? Why are you keeping me locked up?" She leaned forward a little, darkness clouding her face as she whispered, "And who the fuck was in the apartment last night, trying to fuck with my head?"

I almost choked on my steak, and I dropped my own cutlery onto my plate as I replied, "What the fuck are you talking about?"

Her eyes narrowed as she gritted her teeth, seething, "You know exactly what I mean. Don't play with me."

I mirrored her stance, leaning across the table as I said, "Are you telling me you thought someone was in here last night?"

"That's exactly what I'm saying," she snapped. "I know what I saw."

I didn't want to tell her about the cameras. But I was damn sure I'd be checking them out as soon as I could. I'd watched a little of the footage from last night, but after she'd gone to bed, I'd stopped watching. But the windows and doors were alarmed. If anyone had even attempted to breach my security, I'd have been alerted to it. No one had been in here. But I kept cool, my expression unreadable as I asked her, "Then tell me exactly what it was that you saw."

She began explaining how she was having trouble sleeping, that she'd come into the living room during the storm and found her book had been moved. That was something I didn't read into. She could've easily left it like that herself and forgotten.

Then she told me about the dark figure behind her. A figure that disappeared when she'd turned around. And how she'd barricaded herself into her bedroom but woke to find a figure standing over her, despite the chair she'd placed in front of the door remaining unmoved. She was spooked, on edge, and once she'd offloaded it all to me and let out a deep breath, her body relaxed slightly as the weight of what she was carrying subsided a little.

I told her, "First, you are safe here. No one could've gotten into this apartment without setting off all sorts of alarms that would've alerted me and Trent. And if I find any breach when I assess it all in a moment, I will stop at nothing to put it right. But second, I believe you. You saw something last night, and you were right to be scared. I will look into it, but I think you need to remember how powerful the mind can be. Especially one that's been through the trauma you're going through. You're bound to be on edge. And under stress, you will see things, experience things that might upset you. I'm here to help you, Maya."

"Whether it's real or not, I can't sleep. I can't handle being locked up in here, not knowing what's happened to my father, or what could happen next. I feel like a sitting duck. You have to let me go."

I wasn't going to let her go. That was out of the question. But I'd do what I could to get her through this.

"I've already told you, it's not safe for you to leave now. I'm working on getting you out of here, but it takes time. To escape, you need a new passport, a new identity, cash and a place to run to. I can't put that into place overnight."

It was already in place, but I'd never let on about that.

"And my father?" she asked, the faintest glimmer of hope

still shining in her eyes.

"Is long gone," I replied. "He isn't coming to save you, Maya."

I had my suspicions that he wasn't here anymore, as in, my father had gotten to him and silenced him for eternity. And I didn't believe in an afterlife, but if I did, I'd think that maybe that was who she saw, standing behind her, watching over her. A shadow of retribution, trying to make right the sins of his mortal life.

"You're gonna be okay, you know," I assured her. "You're strong. You'll get through this."

She nodded but she didn't speak, just picked up her knife and fork and started to eat again.

And so, we ate the rest of the meal in silence. Maya consumed by thoughts of what her future looked like, and me, desperate to get online and check the CCTV, feeling like I wanted to take my steak knife and stab it into the nearest wall. She was hurting, and that made me feral.

My father's day of reckoning couldn't come soon enough.

After the meal had been eaten and everything was tidied away, I checked my cameras. I saw Maya in the living room, and I watched the flash of lightning illuminate the apartment as she spun around, but there was no one there. No dark figures. Only Maya.

I sat with her on the sofa as she spoke about her fears at night, how she struggled when she was alone. We tried to watch a movie, but her heart wasn't in it.

"You don't have to watch this," I told her. "I can put

something else on."

"I don't mind what's on the TV," she replied with no conviction, no enthusiasm. It worried me that she seemed to have lost some of her fight.

"What are you reading at the moment?" I asked, and instantly she brightened a little.

"*The Handmaid's Tale.* I've read it before," she replied, gesturing to where the book was on the table in front of us.

I reached forward and picked it up, opening to the place in the story that she'd bookmarked with a scrap of paper. And then I turned the TV off and sat back, and I started to read to her.

As I read, she seemed to settle more on the sofa, her eyes drifting closed as she imagined the world I was painting with my words. A dystopian world, not a million miles away from the kind of ideals my own father held, but a million miles away from mine.

I got lost in the story, too, reading chapter upon chapter until I stopped to ask her thoughts on something, and as I turned to face her, I saw that she was fast asleep next to me. I didn't know when she'd drifted off. Maybe it was a few seconds ago, maybe minutes, could be an hour. I had no idea. But the sight of her lying still, at peace, with her mouth slightly open, letting out short, gentle breaths made warmth bloom in my chest.

The book had soothed her.

My voice had soothed her.

And now, she was getting the rest she so desperately needed.

I stood slowly, careful not to wake her, and walked over to the corner of the room to fetch a throw to cover her and keep her warm. But as I draped it over her, I realised I wasn't going to be leaving her tonight. Even if my absence raised suspicion back at Firethorne, I didn't want to go. She'd fallen asleep with me here; I didn't want her to wake alone. I wanted to be here when she opened her eyes.

So, I sat back down on the sofa next to her, then I put my arm around her and pulled her towards me, resting her head on my chest as I leaned back, letting her lie down on me as I held her close.

I closed my eyes, breathing in the scent of vanilla and Maya. In many ways, having her close, in my arms, it soothed me, too. And as I listened to the sound of her gentle breathing and felt the rise and fall of her chest as she slept, I fell into a deep sleep, too.

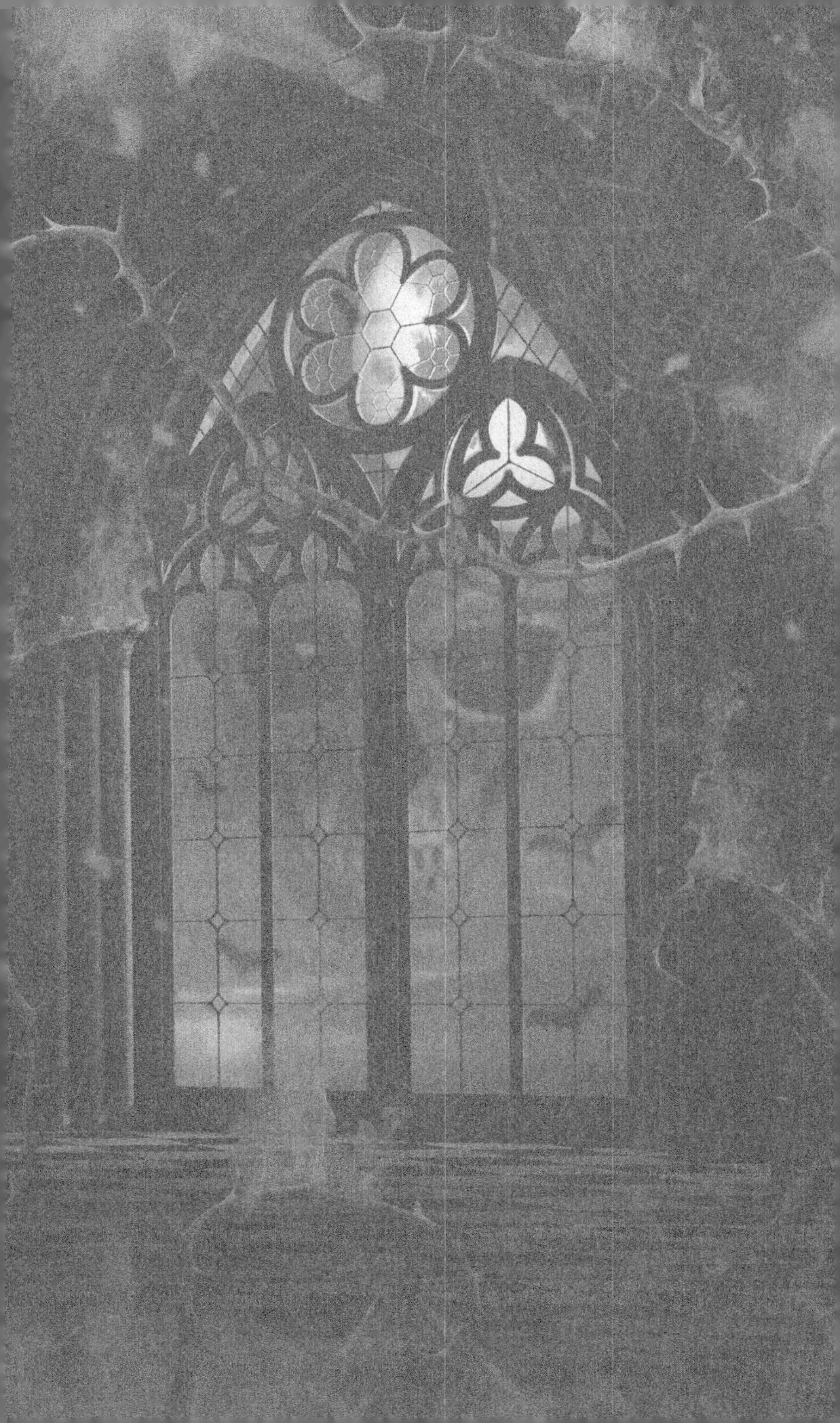

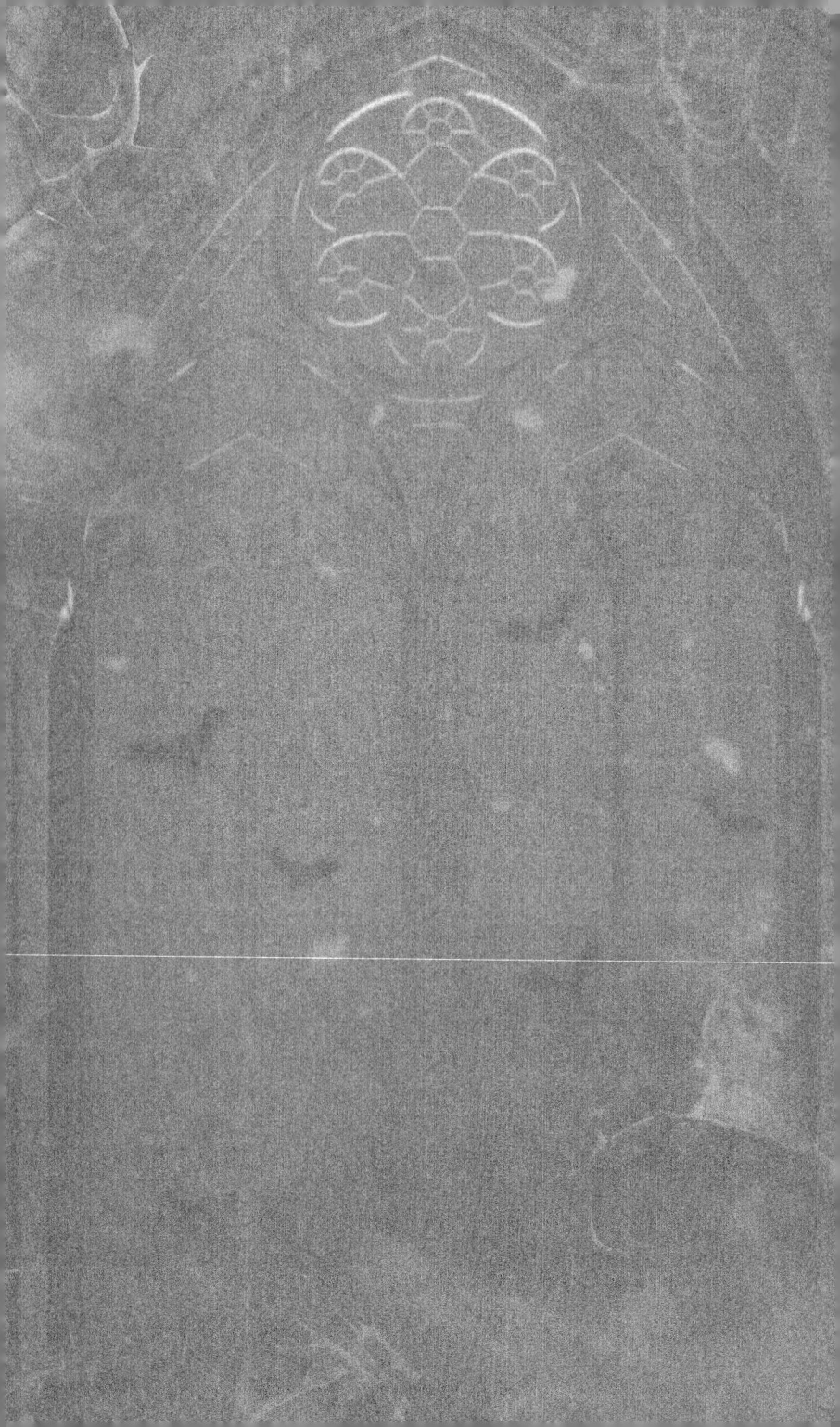

Thirty-One

MAYA

I woke up to a rhythmic beat resounding in my ears. The sun was up, but I didn't open my eyes right away. I let the brightness grace my eyelids as I listened to the sound of breathing, the feel of a chest rising and falling, and the warmth of the soft fabric against my cheek. But it was the distinctive scent of sandalwood that told me exactly where I was. The same scent that'd haunted my dreams since it'd enveloped me on the night of the devils and angels party, when the arms that held that scent had wrapped around me, and the body that exuded it had caged my own. Manly, powerful, almost… familiar. Like home.

It was Damien.

He'd stayed here last night, and I was currently lying on his chest as I roused from my sleep.

I could tell by the way he breathed, steady yet shallow, that he was asleep too. I didn't want to wake him, but I felt like I should move to my own space before he came around. But as I lifted my head slowly off him, he stirred and glanced down at me with hazy, sleep-misted eyes as I sat up.

"Good morning," he said, stretching his arms above his head, and then grinning back at me, he asked, "Did you sleep well?"

I didn't want to tell him it was the best sleep I'd had in weeks. Part of me felt a little embarrassed about falling asleep on him the way I had.

So, I shrugged and told him, "It was okay." Then added, "Won't they notice you're missing?" referring to his family and the fact that he'd stayed out all night to be here, with me.

"They don't care where I am, and I don't care enough to tell them. It's none of their fucking business. As long as I do my job, that's all my father expects from me. Lysander and Miriam will question it, but I'd never give them a proper answer."

He stood up and asked me, "Coffee?" but I shook my head. Everything felt a little too relaxed, too familiar, and I wasn't sure how to process how it made me feel.

I stayed sitting on the sofa, but my eyes tracked him as he stood up, casually walking over to the kitchen, and then I could hear him making himself a coffee and humming quietly.

He wasn't affected by any of this like I was.

He seemed to be able to switch off his emotions, or at least appear like he did.

For me, it wasn't that easy. Everything felt heightened. And as I gazed around the apartment, I had the feeling that I'd swapped the confines of the manor for an asylum. In fact, I was convinced I had. White walls, clinical cleanliness, nothing here that I could use to harm myself or others. Bolted windows and doors that others could unlock, but not me. But my straitjacket was metaphorical, invisible. It was the emotional trauma of being kept confined, the night terrors and inability to express myself. The constraints grew tighter with every day that I was kept here.

Some days, I wondered if I'd ever get out. But then most days, Damien was here to remind me that there was a world outside of these walls. A world I had to get back to. But I could only get to it through him. He held all the cards.

Eventually, Damien sauntered out of the kitchen, sipping his coffee. Then he told me, "I checked the CCTV last night. There was no one else here. But I'm going to show you something that might help you the next time you see something."

"How about you let me go? Then I won't need help," I barked back.

Damien huffed, and the look on his face told me he thought I was being ironic.

"You know I can't do that." He lowered his gaze. "Not yet, anyway."

"I can look after myself," I argued.

"Like you did back at Firethorne?" I gritted my teeth as he mocked me, playing it off as him being truthful. "We all know how that went, and it wasn't great, was it?" he chided.

I swallowed, wanting to snap back, as Damien placed his coffee on the table with an ease that made me want to pick the damn cup up and throw it at the wall or his head. Either would work for me.

"It isn't safe for you to leave," he added. "You just have to trust me." Then he turned his back on me and strolled over to the front door, clearly indicating that he was done with this conversation.

But I wasn't.

"Shouldn't I be the judge of what's safe or not? It is my life, after all. If I don't want to be here, you should let me leave."

He stopped in front of an abstract painting that hung next to the door, and I saw him shrug as he silently acknowledged what I'd said, then composed himself and totally ignored it.

Without a word, he pulled the frame of the painting forward, and it opened like it was on hinges.

How had I missed that?

I'd been over this whole apartment with a fine-toothed comb.

I sat forward and watched as he exposed the wall behind the frame, and I saw a red button on the white plaster hidden behind the painting.

"I should've shown you this earlier. That's on me," he said plainly, then he gestured to the button. "This is a panic button. If you ever get scared, need my help, or if anything happens, you need to press this. Someone will be here within minutes, seconds if we're already on site. But it'll alert us right away. Wherever we are."

"I don't need a panic button, I need a key to leave or for you to open the fucking door," I shot back.

He ignored me and closed the frame back over the button, reiterating, "You're safe here, Maya. I don't want you to have sleepless nights. Not if we can help it. But you need to accept that, for now, you're not going anywhere."

"You said *we*," I replied. "So, it might not be you answering the alarm or coming in here?"

He spun around to face me, his dark expression burning as he regarded me from across the room.

"It'll always be me," he stated firmly. "The others might see the alert, but I'll make sure they know to do nothing but observe you, to make sure you're not in any immediate danger. No one except me will ever enter this apartment. You have my word."

"I get the feeling I'll be your prisoner here for a lot longer than I want to, longer than is healthy. Not that being held prisoner is ever healthy."

"You're not a prisoner, Maya." His jaw ticked as he took a moment before saying his next words. "You're my guest. My responsibility. This won't be forever. But it is your reality... for now. You need to accept that."

I stared back at him. His words and actions were working against each other.

"I don't need to accept anything. But *you* need to accept that I can't stay here for much longer," I stated. "I need to get out." I faltered and almost didn't say the last part. But I added, "I need to find my father."

Damien charged across the room to stand over me, or rather, to leer over me in a threatening manner, his hands braced on the back of the sofa as he leaned down and glared with a fury he was trying to contain.

"No good can come from looking for him," he spat. "I've already told you, if you speak to him, my father will find you. I can't let that happen. This is why you can't leave yet, Maya. You're not ready."

"And I can't stay here forever," I shouted, jumping off the sofa and turning to face him, my fists clenched, and my breaths ragged as my heart beat frantically against my ribs.

But Damien just pushed himself off the sofa he was leaning on and stood taller, a grin spreading across his face as a calmness fell over him. He took a few steps forward, picked up his coffee cup from the table and took another sip, then announced, "I need to go. I have work to do today. But I'll be back later this evening." He put the cup back down and said, "We'll discuss this later."

"We'll discuss this now," I argued as he walked towards the door, but it was useless. Damien wasn't willing to engage in this conversation any longer.

"I got to chapter forty by the way," he called over his shoulder.

Firethorne

"Serena Joy told Offred to sleep with Nick so she could have a baby. Gilead sounds grim, like my father's perfect holiday destination. In fact, I think he'd stay there permanently."

"I couldn't give a rat's ass what chapter you got to," I hissed. "And I haven't finished talking about this."

"See you later." Damien gave me one last grin over his shoulder then disappeared through the door, leaving me to growl in frustration.

I grabbed his empty coffee cup from the table and threw it at the door, because in that moment, I felt so unbelievably mad at him. And yet, the fact that he'd held me all night tapped away at my brain. Reminding me he wasn't a total monster.

He'd read from my book, using his voice to soothe me to sleep. And not once, throughout the whole night, did I have a night terror or a bad dream. He'd been there, he'd fought the demons in my mind, and knowing that made me curse him, because I knew then that he had a power over me that even I couldn't fully comprehend.

I spent the rest of the day pressing that panic button and shouting into the void of the apartment that I needed to be let out.

And guess what?

No one answered.

Later that night, Damien walked back into the apartment with a bag of Chinese food in one hand and a box tucked under his other arm like nothing had happened.

And I just watched him, ignoring the voices in my head that told me to fly across the room and fight for my freedom.

"I figured we might be too busy to cook, seeing as I'm a little late this evening, and you might get distracted once I give you this."

"I pressed the alarm," I announced, ignoring his suggestion that I'd be distracted, and he smirked, placing the food and the box down on the coffee table.

"Yes. You gave that button quite a workout today," he replied. "But you do know what happened to the boy who cried wolf?" He turned to hold my gaze with his as he stated slowly, "Save the panic button for when you need it."

"When?" I tilted my head in question. "Not if?"

Damien started to pull out boxes of rice, noodles, and chopsticks, avoiding eye contact with me as he replied, "Slip of the tongue. Ignore that. Now eat."

I had no appetite, but I couldn't deny, I wanted to know now what he'd brought that he thought would distract me.

What did he possibly think could distract me from my freedom?

After a few minutes of Damien eating silently, as I sat still and stared at him, he pointed at the food and said, "Eat, Maya. Before it goes cold."

"I'm not hungry," I replied defiantly, putting my feet up on the sofa and sitting back.

"You're never hungry," he stated, putting chopsticks in front of me and then passing me the rice. "But you have to eat. Remember what I said. You need to keep your strength up."

I had no strength. None that I could feel, anyway. But I knew he was right. So, I huffed like a petulant child and took the chopsticks, then started to pick at the rice. After a few bites, I asked, "What's in the box?"

"Eat enough of this food and I'll show you." His eyebrows danced in delight at the prospect of surprising me, and controlling me, no doubt.

"I'm not that desperate to see what it is," I snapped, knowing

I sounded like a sulky teenager, but I didn't care.

"Then I'll just take it back home with me." He shrugged. "Can't miss what you never had."

He liked talking in riddles, teasing me. Pulling me in, like he did last night when he held me on the sofa in my sleep, then casting me aside, pushing me away as if he didn't remember it the next morning.

Or maybe it was me?

Maybe I was the one doing all the pushing. Pushing him aside, pushing everything aside.

Perhaps it was both of us.

Performing a weird, strange dance to torture ourselves. As if I needed any more excuses to bring more pain into my life.

Holy fuck, I was so confused. My mind was a twisted mess, like barbed wire was wound tightly around my brain, making every thought painful but there was no let up. The piercing, pounding pain only intensified the more I tried to fight it.

I took a few more mouthfuls, ignoring the screeching voices in my mind, and I heard Damien huff and mutter, "Fuck it," as he put his chopsticks down and reached forward to pull the box closer to him. "I've waited all day to bring this to you. I wanted to see your face when you saw what it was. I'll be damned if I let your appetite of a pigeon ruin that."

He wanted to see my face when I opened it.

There it was again.

He was pulling me right back in, and just like always, I was letting him.

He ripped the tape off the lid then pushed it towards me to open the box. I was too intrigued to argue further, so I leaned forward in my seat and opened it.

And inside was a laptop.

"Don't get too excited. You can't access the internet, so you won't be able to email anyone. But you can use it to type." I stared in wonder at the laptop as he spoke. "I thought you might be able to make a start on that book you said you'd always wanted to write, seeing as you have so much free time here. Or not. Whatever. I know your head is scrambled. Perhaps it's not the right time to do something like that. I don't know." He shrugged it off, going back to eating his noodles like nothing had happened. "It was just a thought."

"It was the best thought," I replied truthfully, because it was. I hated being locked up in here, but he'd just given me something else that could help. Something other than the books. Something to give me an outlet for my pent-up emotions.

I continued staring at the laptop in a daze, feeling my fingers itch, wanting to open it and start writing something, anything. It didn't matter what it was. This was a way I could express myself. A therapy of sorts.

How did this man, who presented himself as the devil when I first met him, continually surprise me with his thoughtfulness and kindness?

The push and pull between us really was a mindfuck.

"What are you gonna write about?" he asked, his voice anchoring my swimming thoughts and pulling me back to the here and now. "Are you gonna write about me?"

I opened the laptop and watched the screen glow to life, an empty Word document already open and ready to whisk me away to another world.

"My professor always told me to write what I know," I said, my fingers ghosting over the keyboard as I gathered my thoughts. "But I always thought that was ridiculous. If we only ever write what we know, we miss out on visiting worlds we can only ever dream of. Magical worlds. Fantasies to escape to. I won't write what I know, I'll write what I love, what excites me."

"That sounds like the perfect plan," he replied, watching me intently. "I can't wait to read it."

Firethorne

"What makes you think I'll let you read it?" I shot back, and he smiled.

"Because I know one day, you'll be a published author. And I'll go into any bookshop to buy your book."

"And what if I decide not to publish? To keep my thoughts and ideas just for me?"

"Then I'll imagine what you wrote. And I'll know, without even reading it, that it's a masterpiece."

"*Really?*" I narrowed my eyes in suspicion.

"Really," he replied sincerely. "Because it came from your mind. And no one else I've ever met thinks or expresses themselves the way you do, Maya. You're one of a kind."

I didn't respond.

What could I say to that?

The devil had pulled me under once again, and I didn't even want to come up for air. I was becoming more than happy to drown in his praise.

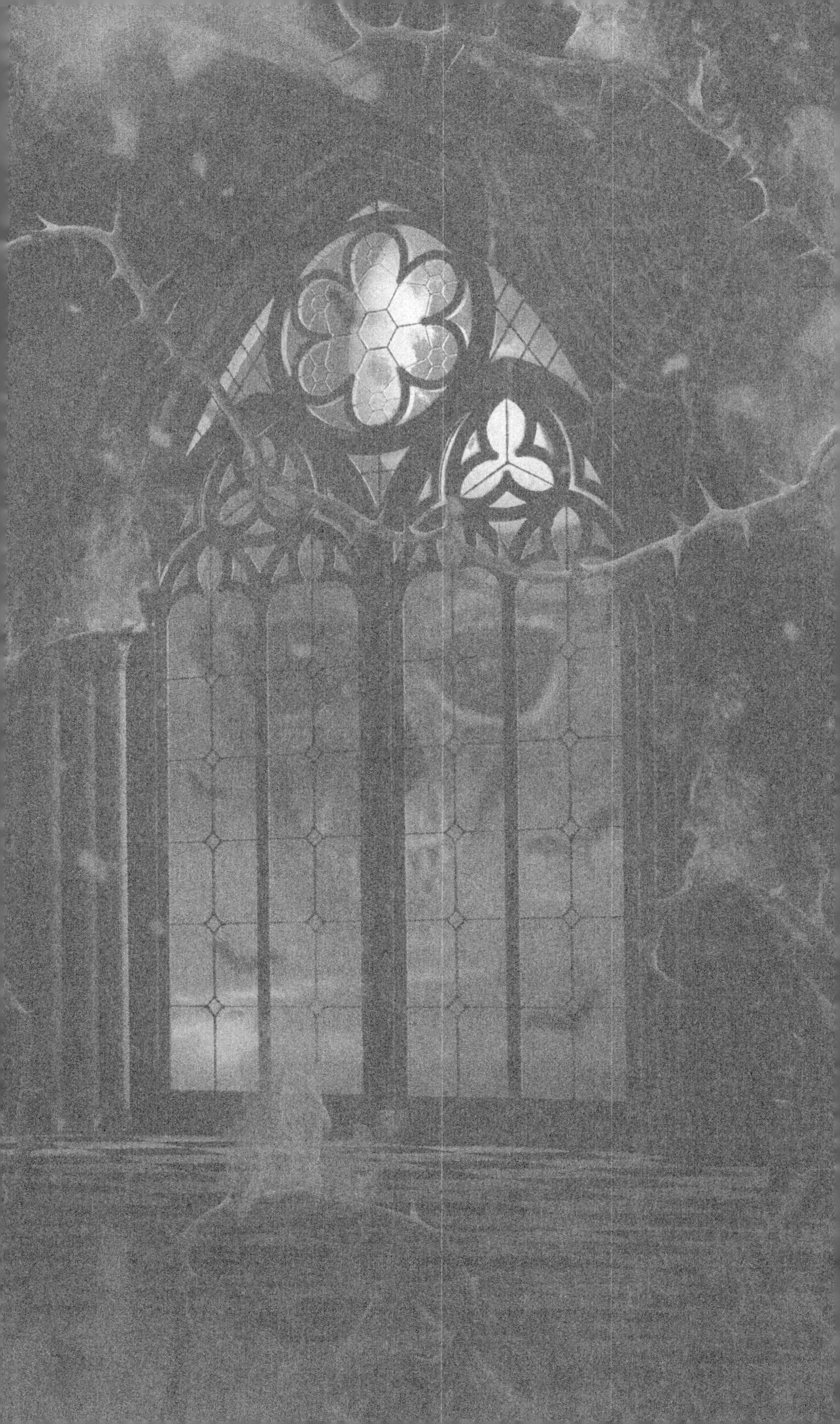

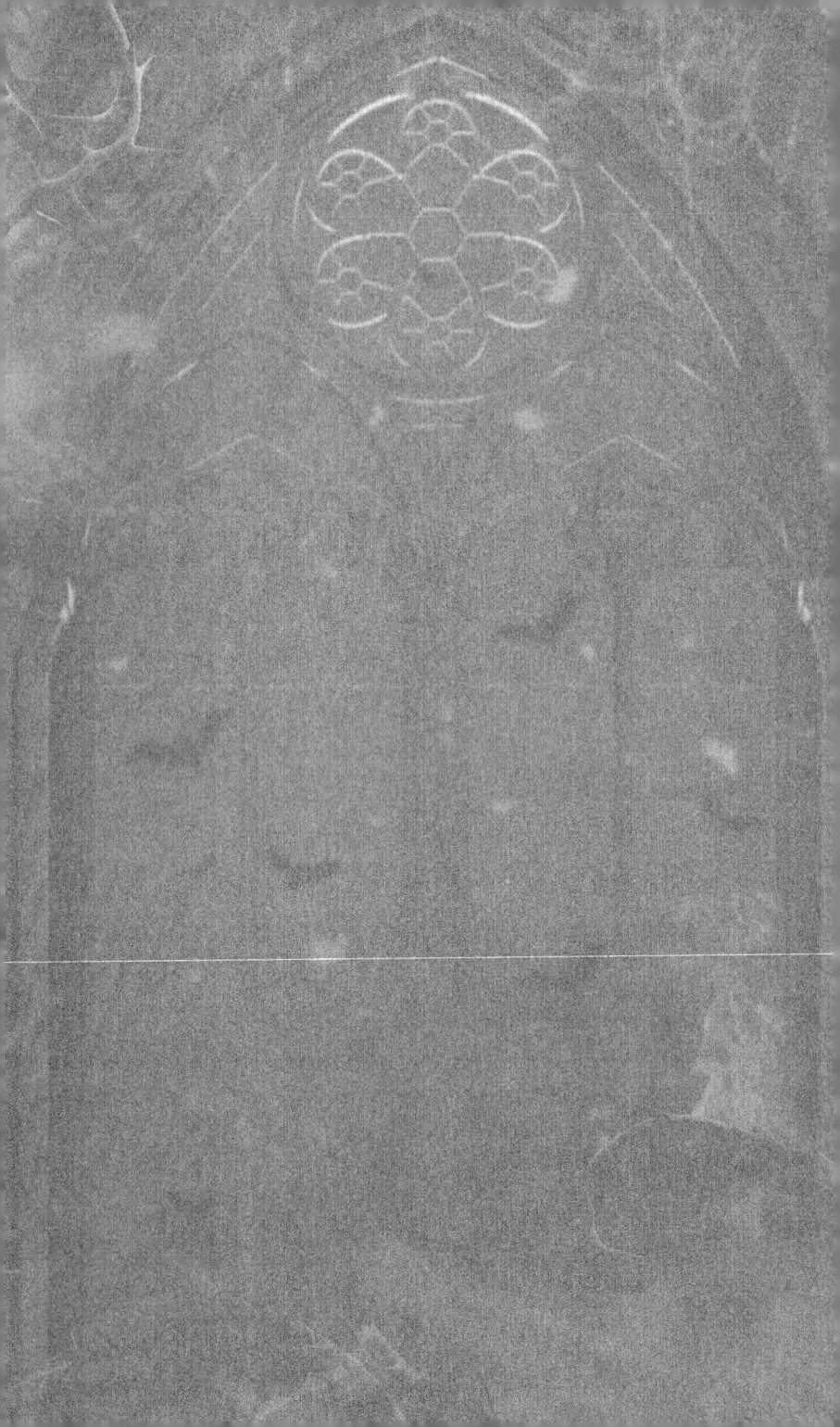

Thirty-Two

MAYA

Damien left soon after, and I sat for hours writing ideas, scenarios, thoughts, and dreams, anything that came into my mind. It didn't have to make sense, but to me, it felt like a purge. It was freeing. But as the night drew in and darkness loomed from the windows outside, I put the laptop to one side and picked up my book, ready to read a few chapters and give my fingers a rest from tapping on the keyboard.

As I opened the book, I noticed that the page had been marked by a piece of paper, with the words, 'You're not alone', written on it. A message that felt eerily like the ones I'd been given by Damien at Firethorne. I put the paper on the seat beside me and started to read, but as I sat reading, I became distracted, hearing every creak of the floorboards and whistle of the wind outside. It was a routine I was becoming tired of.

I glanced up, after what sounded like the groan of a footstep invaded my ears, distracting me from the story, and there, in the reflection of the blank TV screen in front of me, I saw a dark, shadowed figure standing behind me. I jumped from the sofa, letting the book fall to the floor as I spun around, screams dying on my lips when I saw that there was no one there.

But there had been someone.

I'd seen them.

I wasn't going insane.

Was I?

Instantly, I ran over to the picture frame, moved it to expose the panic button, and I pressed it over and over again.

But no one came.

I stood in the middle of the apartment and screamed out, "Whoever is watching this, you need to come and let me out! Now!"

But no one did.

And then, I noticed the scrap of paper that'd fallen to the floor as I'd shot off the sofa after seeing that reflection. The paper that told me I wasn't alone. And a cold shiver ran down my spine.

Maybe Damien hadn't left that message.

It could have a completely different meaning.

Not a 'You're safe' message.

No.

A 'Someone is watching you' warning.

That thought made my stomach lurch, my mouth grow dry, and my heart start to beat even faster than it was before.

Nothing felt right here. Not now. Not when I was on my own.

I kept pushing the button. It was all I had.

But after one night, it went unanswered.

And then one night turned into two, and still it went unanswered.

By the third night, with no response, and no visit from Damien, my panic turned into a sickness that threatened to drag me under.

Why wasn't Damien coming? He came here every day.

Something had gone wrong on the outside. I knew it.

Why wasn't anyone answering the panic button?

And how was I going to escape this water-tight asylum of an apartment, if all I had left now was me?

Thirty-Three

MAYA

After four days and nights of being alone, I felt deranged, paranoid, neurotic, and utterly delusional. I was a caged animal, ready to fight until my nails bled to get myself out of here. And I would get myself out of here.

I threw anything I could find at the windows, trying to break the glass, but it was impenetrable. I tried to prise them open, but they wouldn't budge. In desperation, I'd kicked the door, but only left scuffs and marks where my feet had been. I'd scoured the apartment for vents or anything I could crawl through to escape, but I was left with nothing but exhaustion and the feeling of total and utter hopelessness.

And what use was a panic button if no one answered it?

I guessed he'd been lying about that part. It was a button that did nothing. I was wasting my time pounding on the thing and screaming for someone to come and get me.

Because they never did.

As the fifth day dawned, it felt like I was becoming psychotic, fearing I'd never see another soul again. Imagining terrible, awful things that might happen. Slipping away from this world into one that was a padded cell of a nightmare.

One I could never escape.

And so, when I heard the click of the door unlocking, I sprang from the corner of the room I'd been sitting in, huddled on the floor like a lunatic in my asylum, charging towards whoever would appear from behind that door. My hair was as wild as I was, like something from a Japanese horror movie that'd crawled out of the TV, but I didn't care. I *was* feral. Ready to defend myself like a rabid creature.

I launched myself on the dark figure that entered, my teeth bared, ready to bite, fingers like claws to scratch, my body poised for attack.

Strong hands like steel closed around my wrists, holding me in place as I thrashed and hissed. A solid, male body clung to me, twisting me in their grasp and pushing me up against the wall, my back to their front as I huffed out a breath on impact and panted against the white plaster of the walls. I tried to break free, but they were stronger.

The hunter had caught his prey.

"There she is," a familiar, deep voice whispered in my ear. "I knew you still had some fight left in you. But you need to calm the fuck down, Maya. It's only me."

I didn't calm down.

I couldn't.

Not when I was being restrained like this, my mind

grappling for anything, any idea or ounce of power I could muster to break free of his hold.

"Breathe, Maya. Breathe with me." He started to pant in time with me, bringing my breathing back to a normal level as he pressed his hard chest against my back. His hips pushed forward, his legs encasing mine as I closed my eyes, seeing stars dancing in front of me as my head began to swim.

"You're gonna pass out if you don't calm down," Damien said, every inch of his body flush with mine.

And as the realisation filtered through my brain that it was Damien, he'd come back, my breathing slowed, but I couldn't stop the tension running rampant through my body. I couldn't halt the flow of adrenaline urging me to stay vigilant. My muscles were taut, ready, and as I struggled once again in his grasp, he moved against me, holding me closer, hissing, "Stop fucking fighting. I'm here now."

"The button is a fucking lie," I growled, my teeth clenched as my cheek grazed the wall. "I pressed it, and you didn't answer. No one did. It was a fucking lie to keep me here, subdued for as long as you wanted under the pretence that I was safe. I'm a fucking fool."

"I couldn't be here," he responded, not giving an inch as he held me tight. He wasn't about to let me go any time soon.

"I'm done with playing your games," I hissed.

"What fucking games?" His breath was warm against the shell of my ear, his body heat radiating into me, a reminder that he was in control.

"Why are you doing this to me?" I asked.

"Doing what? Saving you?"

"You're not saving me. Kidnapping me and keeping me here isn't saving me. I should've known..." I couldn't stop the words from tumbling out. "You're no better than your father."

Instantly, he pushed his face right next to mine and growled, "I'm nothing like my fucking father."

"Then prove it," I challenged.

"I already have." I felt the pressure from his body that was pressed up against mine ease a little as he said, "Haven't I made it clear yet? I'd do anything to help you, Maya. I'd fucking die to save you."

We stood together in silence as the words he'd spoken settled in the air around us. My body flush against the wall and him. His hands on my wrists, his face so close to mine I could feel his breath on my skin.

And then, as the seconds ticked by, I said, "You've done your job, now you need to let me go." But as I said the words, the thought of being out in the world on my own, alone, just like the last few days, filled me with dread and fear. Did I really want that? To cut the strings that bound us together? To walk away and never see him again? After everything?

He didn't reply right away, but when he whispered, "I'm sorry, I can't do that," I needed to know why.

"Why not?" I asked in a hushed tone.

"Because... you're different. Because this is different."

I paused, taking in what he'd said. Then I asked him, "Which one is it? *I'm* different or the situation? Because none of this is making sense, Damien." And I wanted him to make it make sense. I wanted to know what he was thinking, what he was feeling. What he felt about me.

He rested his cheek against mine and said in his deep, gravelly voice, "I love it when you say my name."

"Then I won't say it again. Not until you tell me what the fuck is going on," I snapped, goading him like I always did. But in the back of my mind, a gentle, hesitant voice asked, *is that all you love?*

He gave a gruff, low chuckle.

"My father sent me away for a few days on business. I couldn't get out of it. It would've looked too suspicious. But I had eyes on you. I've always got eyes on you. You're more than a fucking job to me, Maya."

And in that moment, I knew the strings that bound me to him, bound him to me just as tightly. In reality, there was no taming a man like Damien. He was still a Firethorne, after all. Like lightning in a bottle, you had to savour the magic that was uniquely him. And yet, despite being a Firethorne, he had moments of kindness, softness, a thoughtfulness that belied the brutal upbringing he'd endured.

And he had them with me.

"I was here for days, on my own. I thought I'd never get out of here. That I'd never see anyone again. I thought... that I'd never see you again." I spoke calmer now, even though a fire raged in my belly and my heart. "If something happens to you out there, what happens to me? Because I tried to get out of here, and I tried—"

"Nothing will ever happen to you." He let go of my right wrist and began stroking the hair from my face. "There's an escape plan in place if something happens to me. You'd be out of here and in another country, living a completely new life within a week. I've made arrangements."

I pressed my free hand against the wall and said, "Then let's go. If that's the arrangement, let's go now."

Another stroke of my hair and he said, "You know I can't do that."

"Damien." I spoke his name breathlessly, like a plea, and he smiled, twisting my hair as he hummed in response. "What is going to happen here? Tell me, how does this end?"

Tell me what you want.

His hand worked my hair, twisting and twirling it until he'd pulled it into a ponytail of sorts, gathered in his fist, and then he tugged, pulling my head back as he yanked hard.

"Is it so wrong that I want to keep you here for a while, and see where this could go?"

"What do you mean?" I asked, my voice barely a whisper.

Hope blossoming in my chest.

"I mean, that I can't ignore the fact that we're drawn together. Every time I see you, I feel these... urges. Like the night of the party. I could've walked you to that door, shown you who Lysander and Miriam really were, and walked away, but I couldn't. And deep down, I think you know yourself that you didn't want me to. I had to touch you, because I knew, that night I knew that you were mine. I touched you because I couldn't stop myself. But you wanted me to touch you, didn't you? We're like magnets, you and me. We fight, repel each other, but when we work together, when those fucking stars align, that magnetic forcefield is fucking unstoppable. Nothing can break it."

"But you won't leave with me."

"I have to see this through to the end. You know I do. But I'm not a fool, Maya. I know exactly what I want. And I saw you... that night, when I stood outside your bedroom window and watched you get yourself off, your fingers buried inside that tight little pussy. You were thinking of me that night, weren't you? You were imagining me, wanting me. And I wanted you so fucking badly it hurt."

I swallowed, barely able to breathe.

"I watched you make yourself come," he went on. "And it took every ounce of restraint I had not to smash that fucking window, climb through and take what I wanted. What was mine."

He was right. I had thought about him, but the spiteful part of me couldn't help but blurt out, "You didn't stay long enough to save me that night, though, did you? You stood and watched, but if you'd been there moments later, you could've stopped them when they came for me." I hated myself sometimes. I hated that my mouth sprang into action before my brain could engage.

Why was I blaming him?

He'd done everything for me.

"And there's not a minute goes by that I don't hate myself for that," he hissed as his body pressed closer to mine. "But life goes on. We won. And now, I've waited long enough. I want to claim what's mine."

"Which is?"

"You."

His words were like boulders crashing through my restraint. His body a wall of heat, warming my stone-cold heart. Damien had been an angel and demon to me. And it's hard to let go of the demons that haunt you when they're the ones who catch you when you fall. And he had, caught me, that is, each and every time. Even when I didn't know he was doing it. He was there. Always.

I could feel myself folding, softening, and as the whisps of anger inside me withered away, turning into something else, I whispered, "You're all I've got, Damien. I don't have anyone else. Only you. My whole world revolves around you."

The hold he had on me, on my hair as he pulled it a little tighter didn't ease up, but his voice was different when he whispered back, "Do you think it's different for me? Because it's not. It's exactly the same. You're all I have, Maya. All I think about. All I want."

"You have a family." I sighed, feeling the swell of tears I didn't want to shed gather in my eyes.

"I have people who share my last name. A name I despise. I have colleagues with a common goal. But the only thing that gets me out of bed every day, that spurs me on, that ignites anything inside me, is you. I wasn't fucking joking when I said I have a cold, black heart underneath it all. How else do you think I've survived in that house and that family for this long? But with you, everything is different. My life has gone from shades of grey to screaming colour. Do you really think I'm going to let that go? Let you walk away from me and take any chance I have at living a normal life with you? Because I won't. I can't."

I blinked, the tears falling down my cheeks now, and I tried to hide them as I whispered, "Why me?"

"Because it is you," he replied. "Why is the sky blue? Why do we need air to breathe? Why did it feel like I'd been hit by a train the minute I walked into the foyer of the house and saw you for the first time that night?

"I tried to hide it. I played the role of the bastard perfectly, like I always do. But I could barely breathe. I had to walk away and leave you with Lysander, all the time knowing how wrong it felt. Because I wanted you to be mine. You were mine. And yet, I knew why you were here. I wanted to scream it from the rooftops and run away with you. But I couldn't. I couldn't jeopardise our whole operation. It's been my life's work to bring this evil trafficking ring down. But you? You're my reason for everything now. Tell me, Maya," he begged. "Tell me you feel it too."

He was being vulnerable in a way I'd never expected him to be. In a way that made my own heart bleed. My raw and aching heart, that had been through so much, yearned for him, too. Needed him to make it better, make it all go away. Because every moment spent with Damien, was a moment when I felt free again. When I lived. I didn't want to give that up, but I was so confused. I didn't know how to navigate my way through this. The grief I felt over my father, the pain from what'd happened, it all became unbearable sometimes, but he was the only one who could numb it.

"Yes," I gasped. "I feel it too."

And instantly, he spun me around, pressing my back to the wall as he caged me in.

His hips were flush against mine, and his hands cupped my face as he said, "I can't fight this anymore. I won't. I was inside you, at that party. And there hasn't been a day since that I haven't craved to be inside you again. I need you, Maya. I've just spent four days with the worst fuckers in this world, pretending that I'm one of them. And now, I need to get lost in you. I need to remember how good you feel."

His words, his body, the way he was looking at me like he wanted to devour me made me crave him, too. Made me want all the things he was promising. And his face, so close to mine, his breath lacing my own, made me yearn for him to kiss me. So much so that I couldn't wait any longer, and I leaned forward, pressing my lips against his. Taking the first step for both of us.

I closed my eyes, wanting to block out the rest of the world as I drowned in the taste of him. And he kissed me back, sliding his fingers into my hair, gripping the nape of my neck as he tilted his head and opened his mouth to deepen the kiss. His tongue tangled with mine and I groaned, wanting more, wrapping my arms around him as I pulled him closer.

Damien tugged my hair, yanking my head back, making me gasp. With his lips a whisper away from mine, he growled, "If you're not ready for this, you need to say now. Because once I start, I won't be able to stop."

"I don't want you to stop."

I tried to edge forward, to put my lips back on his, but he held my hair tight, angling my head back as he said, "I'm serious, Maya. Consent is important to me. I need to know I have it."

"I get that. It's important to me, too," I gasped. "I want you..." Then I hesitated, and I saw a flicker of something in his eyes, uncertainty perhaps, or fear maybe? "I want you to make the pain go away."

I felt his body stiffen.

"I'm not a distraction, Maya." He watched me for a moment, contemplating his next words. "I don't want you to use me to forget. I can't—"

"Bad choice of words," I stated, knowing exactly how my words had made him feel, and regretting the way they'd come out. "You're not a distraction, Damien. But you do make me forget. I can't deny that. And being with you, I feel like I have a purpose, a future. I want to feel, I want you to make me feel. I want you."

I waited with bated breath, expecting him to launch himself on me, to carry on devouring me like I wanted him to. But he didn't. He just cocked his head and asked me the same question I'd asked him only moments ago.

"Why me?"

He released my hair, letting my head fall forward, but he stayed pressed against me, waiting for the answer he needed. Staring at me intently, his eyes flickering between my lips and my eyes, waiting.

"Because every time I'm around you, you affect me. You alter the chemistry in my brain, the air around me. Your presence makes my whole body spark to life. Because when you look at me, my insides do a thing that makes me feel like I'm on some kind of rollercoaster. Like that night, when you walked down the stairs for the first time at the party and I saw you. You took my breath away. You always take my breath away. And because..."

I paused, ready to open my heart.

"You knew what colour my eyes were when you made that sketch of me that you left in the dining room. The one I thought Lysander had drawn. But it wasn't. It was you who made my blue eyes shine. And even when you were playing the role of the bastard, you always looked out for me, protected me from the drugged drink at the party, sending me gifts to give me hope. And you saw me. The real me. You know what books I like, you think of ways to help me, cooking for me, encouraging me with my dreams. You're the first person to ever stop and listen. And when you talk, your voice echoes through me, it calls to me. At the end of every day, when you leave, I still hear it. I savour it. You're like the anchor that's kept me grounded and sane throughout this whole godforsaken mess. You're my person, Damien. No matter how much I argue with you or try to fight my feelings, I know it. You are my person."

I stood still and waited for him to respond but he said nothing. He just stared back at me.

"Say something," I urged, feeling self-conscious and worrying that maybe I'd said the wrong thing, but he shook his head.

"I don't know what to say," he replied quietly. "I think you just made every single dream I've ever had come true."

My heart swelled at his words, and I couldn't help but smile.

"And yet, you've barely touched me. I guess that proves the power of our words."

"And actions," he added.

"Actions speak louder." I leaned forward to press my lips to his again, and I whispered against them, "I think I'm ready for more of those actions now."

Damien reached down to lift me up by the backs of my thighs, and as he did, I wrapped my legs around his waist.

"As much as I want to bend you over that sofa and prove that you're mine, I'm not that much of a bastard, despite what people say," he said as he carried me across the living room.

I wrapped my arms around him, holding on tight as he added, "For your first time, you deserve a bed."

"I just want you," I told him, speaking my truth. "Not a watered-down version. Only you."

"Oh, I won't be watering anything down, don't you worry." He hummed. "I want to take my time, make us both comfortable, and then, I'll fuck you until you can't take anymore."

"Is that a promise?" I asked.

"Damn fucking right it is."

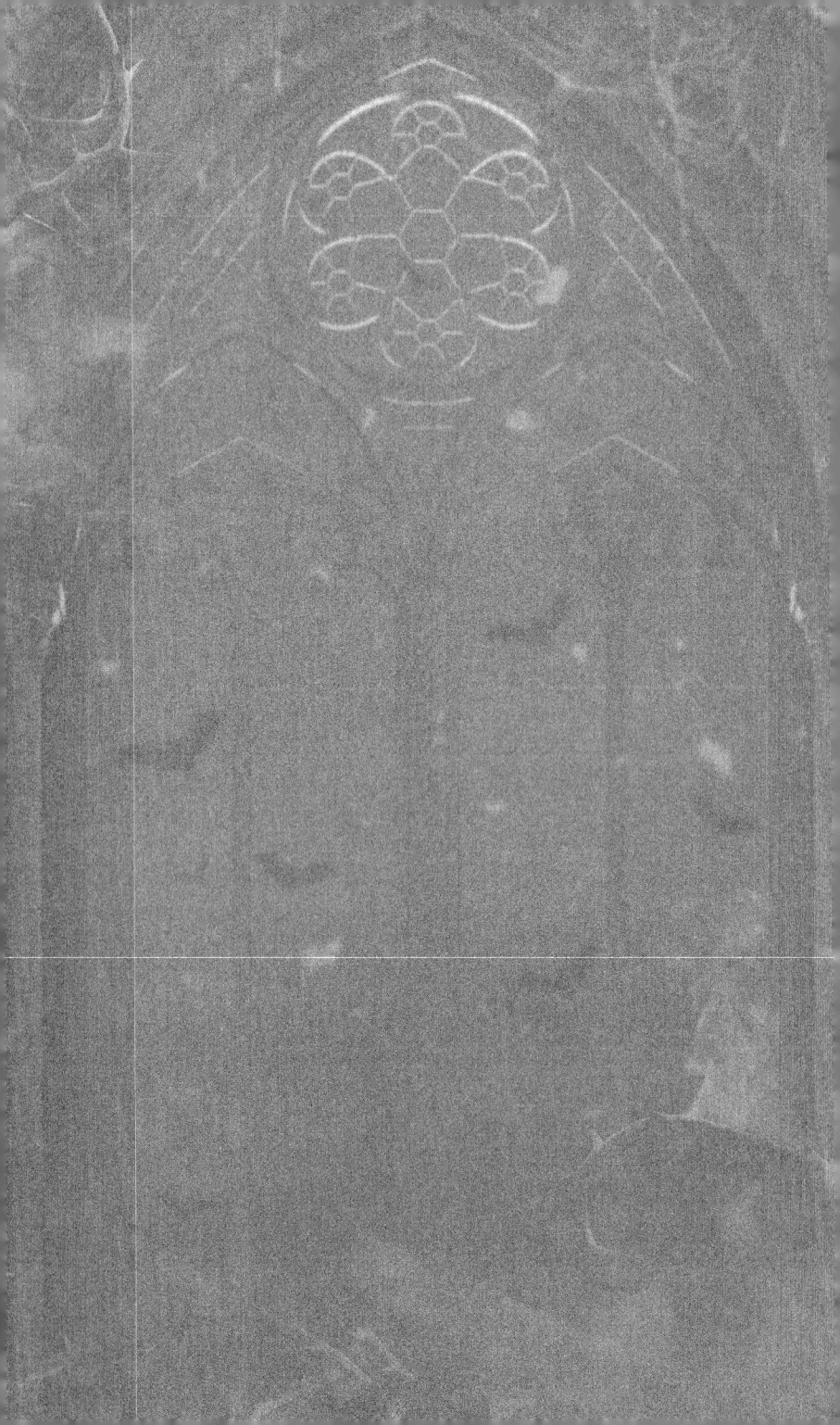

Thirty-Four

MAYA

He carried me through to the bedroom, and then, releasing my arms from around his neck, he threw me down onto the bed.

"I might've brought you in here so you'd be more comfortable, but don't think for a minute that I'm going to go easy on you," he growled as he stood at the side of the bed, staring down at me, lying there, waiting for him. "Now take your fucking clothes off. I want to see every inch of you."

The commanding way he spoke sent shivers down my spine and flutters through my belly.

Biting my lip, I watched as he reached backwards and

pulled his T-shirt over his head. Such a simple action, and yet, he looked so fucking sexy. Then, with his heated stare never wavering from me, penetrating right through me with its intensity, he unbuttoned his jeans and pulled them down, kicking them off.

There was a sly smirk on his face as he watched me tentatively pull down my leggings, slowly kicking them to the end of the bed. Then, I sat up and began to take my T-shirt off.

"That's it. Take it all off," he demanded, his voice deep and gritty, reverberating right through me.

The lustful way he looked at me, like he couldn't wait to devour me as he stared at my legs and then followed my hands as I lifted my T-shirt over my head, made me want to tease him more. To elongate the pleasure for both of us.

"I need to see you, Maya. All of you," he rasped.

"I need to see you, too," I replied, glancing provocatively at his boxers and the noticeable bulge I could see at the front.

He smirked and pushed them down his legs, then stood up, exposing his gorgeous body in all its glory. And glorious was exactly what he was. Strong, muscular, tanned, and so fucking perfect. Seeing him for the first time, how big he was, made my nerves flutter, and I tried to hold in my gasp. I couldn't stop staring at his long, hard, thick cock. And he wrapped his hand around it, giving himself a few slow pumps as he watched me watching him.

"I can't wait to be inside you." His eyes were hooded with desire as he spoke, devouring me as I unhooked my bra. "And I can't wait to fuck you, Maya. Your tight little pussy, your mouth, your ass," he said with a wicked grin, and then, when he saw my breasts for the first time as I sat on the bed, he sighed. "And those tits. Fuck, they're even better than I imagined."

"You're even better than I imagined," I replied, unable to shift my gaze from his hand stroking his cock. "And I imagined you... a lot."

He liked that I'd said that, and I felt the pride bristle from him as his shoulders fell back and his smirk grew more cocky and wicked.

He gave his cock a few more strokes, then climbed onto the bed and pushed me to lie backwards.

"No need to imagine any more," he growled. "You've got the real thing." And I felt his cock graze my thigh as he lay over me, kissing me brutally and hard.

His tongue plunged into my mouth, invading, tasting, taking what he wanted. Our teeth clashed, and our lips tangled in a punishing, almost bruising fight to claim each other.

He took my breast in his hand and squeezed hard, and I moaned through our kiss at the excruciatingly sensual touch. A touch that felt like he was branding me, claiming me as his. Every inch of me.

The gentle pulse between my thighs beat a little harder and a little faster in response to everything he was doing. My need for him growing stronger as he touched and kissed me like he wanted to fuse us together, body and soul.

I threaded my fingers through his hair, groaning into the kiss as he massaged and teased my breast, rolling my nipple between his thumb and forefinger. And when I arched my back, scraping my nails across his scalp as I groaned, he broke the kiss and said, "I love how fucking needy you are."

"And I love the way you touch me. So, please don't fucking stop," I urged.

"I love a woman who knows what she wants," he said as he started to kiss and lick his way down to my breast.

"Then give it to me," I demanded, and he took my nipple into his mouth and sucked hard, making me cry out. "Oh, fuck yes. That's it."

I fisted his hair in my hand and watched him feast on me. His tongue swirling and darting over my nipple, making my pussy throb with need.

He sucked hard, then pulled back, popping my nipple out of his mouth and blowing lightly on it. Then he moved to my other breast, giving it the same treatment, making me roll my hips forward, rubbing against him, trying to ease the yearning that I felt down there. I still had my panties on, and when he felt me brush against him, he popped the other nipple out of his mouth and said, "You're so fucking wet, Maya. I can feel you on my leg. But those panties need to go. Now."

He sat up and moved to the end of the bed, and told me, "Take them off, and then open wide for me."

I did as I was told, wriggling my panties from my hips and pulling them down my legs. Once I'd thrown them to the floor, I hesitated for a moment, feeling a little unsure.

"Do it," Damien commanded. "Open your legs and let me see you."

Slowly, I rested back on the pillows and opened my legs, feeling the wetness between my thighs. I stared at him, heat burning in my cheeks. But his eyes never strayed from my pussy, and he breathed heavily, his voice coarse as he said, "Wider."

I opened my legs wider, bending my knees so I could bare myself to him the way he wanted me to.

He nodded in approval and said, "Beautiful. Now use your fingers. Tease that pussy open for me. Show me every inch of you."

I wanted to please him, so I moved my hands, placing them between my legs, and with my fingers, I pulled myself open for him, exposing my clit.

"And your pussy too," he demanded.

I could barely breathe as I did what he said. I'd never been so turned on in my whole life.

His breathing was shallower now, a soft pant as he watched me graze my fingers over my pussy, touching and teasing myself.

"Fuck yourself," he commanded. "Like you did in the cabin that night."

I nodded and closed my eyes, letting my head fall back as I ran my fingertip over my clit, up and down then around in little circles, before I slid downwards and pushed a finger inside myself.

"More than one finger," he snapped, and I obeyed, pulling it out, and then pushing two back in as he groaned in appreciation.

"Faster," he commanded. "Rub your clit with your other hand while you fuck yourself."

"Yes," I sighed and began to rub my fingers over my clit as I pumped my hand faster. My hips arched off the bed in response, rocking furiously against my hands as I felt the familiar tingle bursting to life inside me.

"That's it. Be a good girl and make us both come."

I opened my eyes to find Damien stroking himself as he watched me. And the way his eyes glazed over, his mouth open as he thrust his cock into his hand, made the tingle grow into a spark and then an exquisite pulse, and I knew it wouldn't be long before I came.

"Don't stop," Damien pleaded, still pumping his cock as he knelt between my legs, watching me finger myself. And then he let out the sexiest moan I'd ever heard as he came in hot spurts of white cum all over my pussy and my hands.

"Fuck yes," he moaned. "Use my cum, Maya. Push it inside you."

I pulled my fingers out, smearing them in his cum before pushing them back inside my pussy.

"So fucking beautiful," he moaned, watching intently as I filled myself with his cum, and then he lay between my legs and pushed my hands aside, saying, "I need to taste this pretty pussy."

His cum was dripping all over me, but he didn't care. He

buried his face in my pussy, spearing his tongue inside me and lapping like he couldn't get enough. Groaning with each lick as he ate me. And all I could do was throw my head back on the pillow and scream at how fucking amazing it felt. He moved his lips, clamping them over my clit and sucking hard, and without warning, I came, my legs shivering as my hips bucked, and I cried out into the room, "Jesus fucking Christ."

He held my thighs as they shook, keeping his face buried between my legs as the orgasm tore through me. My clit pulsed, my pussy flooded and contracted, and I tensed, willing the sensation to go on forever. I never wanted it to end.

Damien wasn't giving up. His tongue flickered on my clit, rolling over and around in circles that drove me crazy, and before I knew it, another orgasm was sparking to life, only this time it was stronger, and I whimpered as my walls contracted violently, squeezing inside of me, warmth flooding my pussy. And the shivers I'd felt before became tremors, earth-shattering tremors, as pleasure ripped through me.

"More," Damien demanded before covering my pussy with his mouth again and eating me like he was a starving man. His tongue teased me to perfection. His lips kissed and sucked me so beautifully I lifted my hips, wanting more, harder. And as I did, he put his hands under my ass and tilted me into the position he wanted me. "That's it, fuck my face," he growled, and I did.

I put my hand behind his head and pushed him into me, rocking my hips and grinding my pussy on him, and when I came for the third time, I gritted my teeth and snarled, "Fuck yes. Fuck my pussy. Fill me up and fuck me good."

I didn't even know where those words came from. They just spilled out of me like I was a demon possessed. But I wasn't in control of my body, my mind, or my words. The only one in control here was Damien.

"Do you want that?" he asked, grinning up at me as his face

glistened with our cum. "Are you ready to get fucked?"

I nodded, but he cocked his head to the side and tutted.

"Words, Maya. You know I like to hear the words. Tell me you want my cock."

I reached forward to take his cock in my hand, but he edged away from me, and with another tut he said, "What are the magic words?"

I huffed.

"Please, Damien?"

He laughed.

"No. The magic words are, 'I want to feel your huge cock inside me, Damien, and I promise to come all over it, squeezing it until I make you scream'."

I smirked back at him.

"That too."

He grinned, reaching forward, using his finger to trace delicate little strokes along my pussy.

"And when I'm inside you," he said with a cocky smirk. "You'll realise how fucking perfect we are, that you were made for me. That this pussy is all mine. I'm the only one you'll ever want."

"I already know that," I replied breathlessly.

"Knowing and experiencing are two completely different things," he said, then he crawled over me, holding himself above me as he stared into my eyes. "Last chance, Maya. If you're not ready—"

"I'm ready," I snapped. "I'm so fucking ready that if you don't fuck me right now, I will go insane."

"That's my girl," he said, then he took his cock in his hand and started to stroke it through my swollen pussy, rubbing himself over my sensitive clit and teasing at my entrance. "I won't lie to you. This might hurt at first."

"I can deal with pain," I hissed. "Now stop playing around and fuck me the way I deserve to be fucked."

"Yes, ma'am."

He reared back and then lifted both my legs, putting them over his shoulders before settling forward again. I was bent out of shape, but I didn't care, I wanted to feel him. I wanted him so badly.

His arms were braced either side of my head, his cock against my pussy, and as his hips drove forward and he entered me, I screamed from the sharpness of the pain. He'd done what I asked and thrust into me hard and fast. And as his hips rested flush against mine, he stilled, his teeth gritted and his body shaking as he asked, "Are you okay?"

"I'm fine. No watering down. Remember?" I said, trying not to break the bubble he'd created. It did fucking hurt, but I knew the worst was over.

He huffed a smile, and the way his eyes darkened, I knew he was about to let go completely.

And boy, was I right about that.

He gripped the headboard above me, and leaning down, he whisper-growled in my ear, "Hold on tight."

Then he started to thrust into me at a punishing rate, his hips slamming into mine, his cock invading my pussy, stretching me, rutting into me, and making my body jolt and writhe as he pinned me to the mattress.

I clung to him like I might fall into an abyss if I didn't, and he pounded into me over and over again, groaning, "You're so fucking tight, Maya. You feel so fucking good."

The headboard was banging against the wall, my cries echoing around the room, mingled with his groans and the sounds of our sweaty bodies slamming against each other. It was beyond anything I'd ever felt before. It was more than euphoric. It was fucking mind-blowing. Life altering.

I could feel my orgasm building and I sunk my nails into his back, dragging them downwards until I reached his ass. Then I grabbed him hard, squeezing his ass as I begged him, "More.

I need more."

He pushed my legs up higher so he could slam deeper into me, and I let my head fall to the side, my eyes closed as I gripped his ass and moaned on every thrust.

"That's it, Maya," he growled. "Come for me."

I angled my hips, chasing the high, and then I felt my walls clamp down on his cock as I came hard.

"Holy fuck," he cried as he dropped his head onto the pillow next to me and continued to rut into me as I came over and over again. And then, with an almighty roar, he came too, his cock throbbing as he spilled everything he had inside me.

We both panted as we lay together, our bodies fused as our orgasms slowly subsided. Then Damien moved to sit up, letting my legs relax back down onto the bed as his cock slid out of me. I felt a warm trickle of cum slip from my pussy to my ass, and he used his finger to catch it and push it back inside. That was Damien's kink. He didn't want me to waste a single drop of his cum. It did something to him, knowing that it was inside me. It did something to me, too. It made me feel special. That he needed to claim me and own me in that way.

"You have the prettiest pussy," he said, stroking his fingers along my swollen, aching pussy, pushing his fingers gently into me each time a drop of his cum seeped out. "I'd die a happy man buried inside of you."

"Did I bleed?" I asked, and he shrugged in response.

"A little, but it's okay. Blood doesn't scare me."

And he winked and then took his cum soaked fingers and lifted them to his mouth, licking once, then pushing them towards me and saying, "I think we taste fucking delicious. Don't you?"

I felt my heart hammering in my chest, but I didn't want to deny him anything. So, I leaned my head forward and let him push his fingers into my mouth, sucking on them before letting him pull them free.

Firethorne

"Now you need to tell me which part of you you'd like me to fuck next," he asked. "Because we are only just getting started."

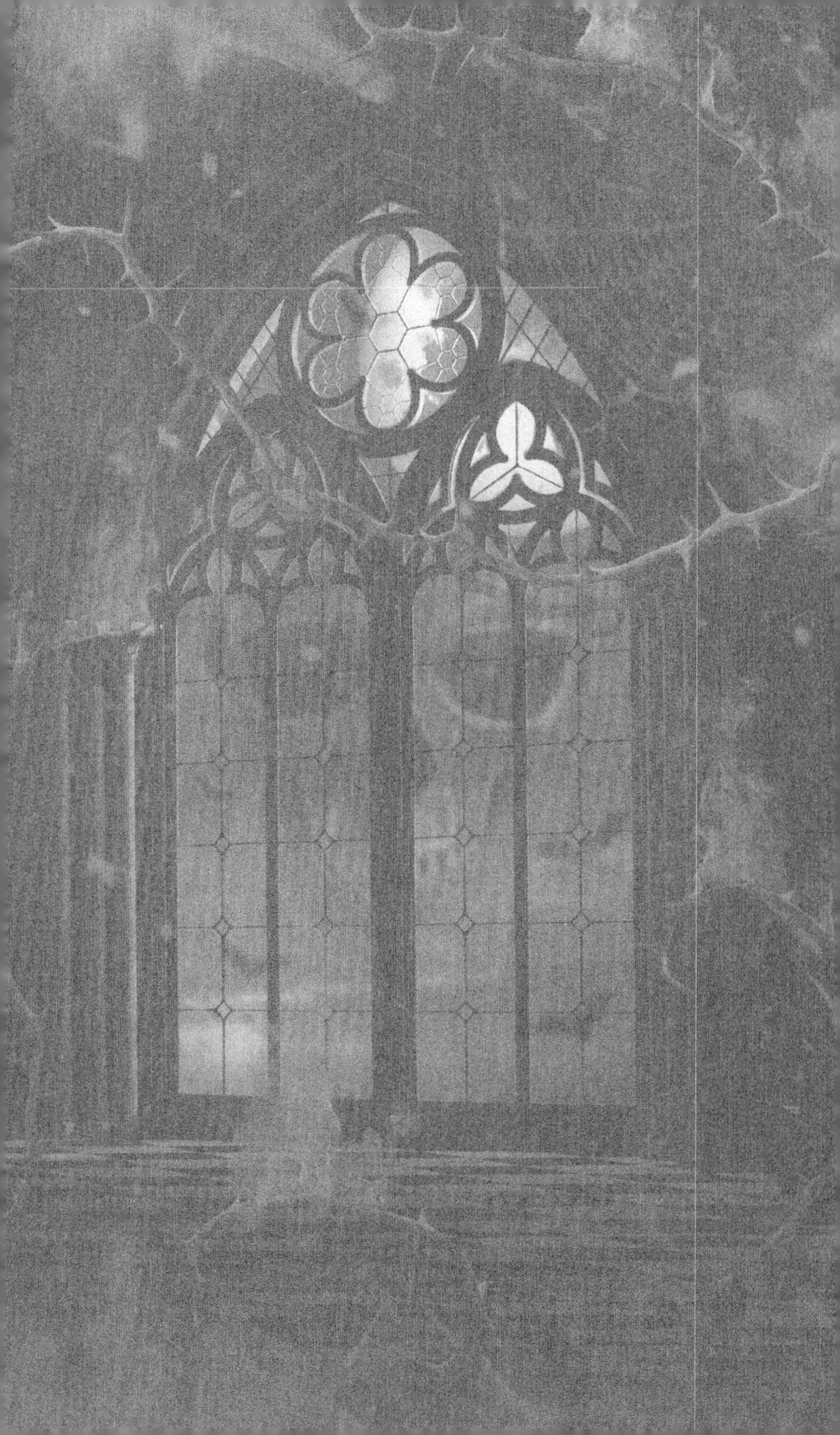

Thirty-Five

DAMIEN

She looked more beautiful than I'd ever seen, lying in front of me, thoroughly fucked. But I couldn't stop. I had to have more. In giving herself to me, she'd opened the fucking floodgates, and they were never going to close. I needed to consume her. She was like a fucking drug.

She smiled up at me, a lazy smile that told me she'd do whatever the fuck I asked of her, and then her smile turned wicked.

"You've had all the fun, tasting and teasing me. I think it's only fair I get to do the same."

"Do you want to suck my cock?" I asked, taking hold of my

cock and stroking myself, taunting her.

She nodded and sat up, edging closer towards me and opening her mouth, but I sat back and shook my head.

"Fingers and hands first, then lips and tongue, and then we go for the throat."

She stared back at me, wide-eyed, reminding me how naïve she was, how innocent. Perfect for corrupting in the best way. A toy, just taken out of her packaging and only ever to be played with by me.

"Lick your palm, then hold my cock," I told her, and she did as she was told, licking her hand and then reaching forward, wrapping her delicate fingers around me. "You can be firmer than that," I instructed, putting my hand over hers to show her how I liked it. "Now stroke, nice and slow, that's it."

She stroked my cock, and seeing the way she looked at her hand with such fascination, desperate to do it the best way she could, made me feral. I rocked my hips, fucking her hand, and groaned to show her she was doing it perfectly. But in truth, whatever she'd have done would feel amazing, because it was her. Her tiny, warm hand felt like the best thing ever. I knew her mouth would too, because it was Maya. And everything with her was just... *more*.

"Now use your tongue, just around the tip, on the edge," I told her. "And underneath, it feels more sensitive there."

She leaned forward, her hand still gripping the base of my cock as she used her tongue to lick the head of my cock, swirling around the rim and then stroking with the tip of her tongue underneath, and I felt my balls tighten and my spine tingle as she drew me closer to orgasm.

"Fucking perfect," I said, grabbing a handful of her hair and wrapping it around my fist. "Now use your other hand. Gently stroke my balls. Just here."

She put her free hand on my balls and started to gently stroke, and I opened my legs a little, using my hand to guide her to the space just behind my balls that I knew would feel fucking amazing when her addictive little touches hit that spot. She teased me there, and I threw my head back. "Fuck, that feels so fucking good."

She started to suck the head of my cock, her tongue flat against the underside as she moved her hand at the base to give me more slow pumps, and the combination of that and her stroking between my legs drove me wild.

"I need to fuck your face," I begged, becoming desperate for more, and I used both hands to grab the back of her head and angle her the way I needed to. "Breathe through your nose and tap my leg if it gets too much, okay?"

She nodded, and I pushed my cock into her mouth, then down her throat, and she took me so fucking well, tilting her head so I could deep throat her, not gagging at all. She was a fucking angel.

With a mouthful of cock, she grabbed my ass with both hands as I used her with slow thrusts that became more frantic as she swallowed around me and sucked harder.

"Fuck yes. That's feels so fucking good," I praised her. "Look at me."

She glanced up at me with her eyes watering, and seeing that made me fuck her harder. She looked fucking stunning with tears streaming down her face, and my cock rammed down her throat. "You know you're gonna swallow, don't you?" I stated, and she nodded as best she could. "I don't want you to waste a drop of my cum."

Another nod, and I drove home hard, thrusting into her mouth and moaning as my orgasm started to hit. My cock pulsed and throbbed as I came down her throat, and like the fucking goddess she was, she swallowed, just like I'd told her to, her eyes closed as she took everything I had to give her.

"That's a good girl," I told her, stroking her hair as she swallowed and sucked. "*My* good girl."

Firethorne

Once she'd taken every drop, I pulled out of her mouth and then reached down and rubbed my thumb over her swollen lips. Then I put my thumb in my mouth and sucked, humming in appreciation at the taste of her and me.

"Who knew?" I rasped, unable to keep the grin off my face. "That Maya Cole would become my dirty little cum slut." And then, grinning wider, I added, "I fucking love it."

Her wide-eyed gaze as she stared up at me made me want to flip her over and go again. And when she said, "Are you going to fuck me in the ass now?" I couldn't hold in my growl.

Where had this perfect angel come from?

Because right now, I felt like every damn prayer I'd ever made was coming true.

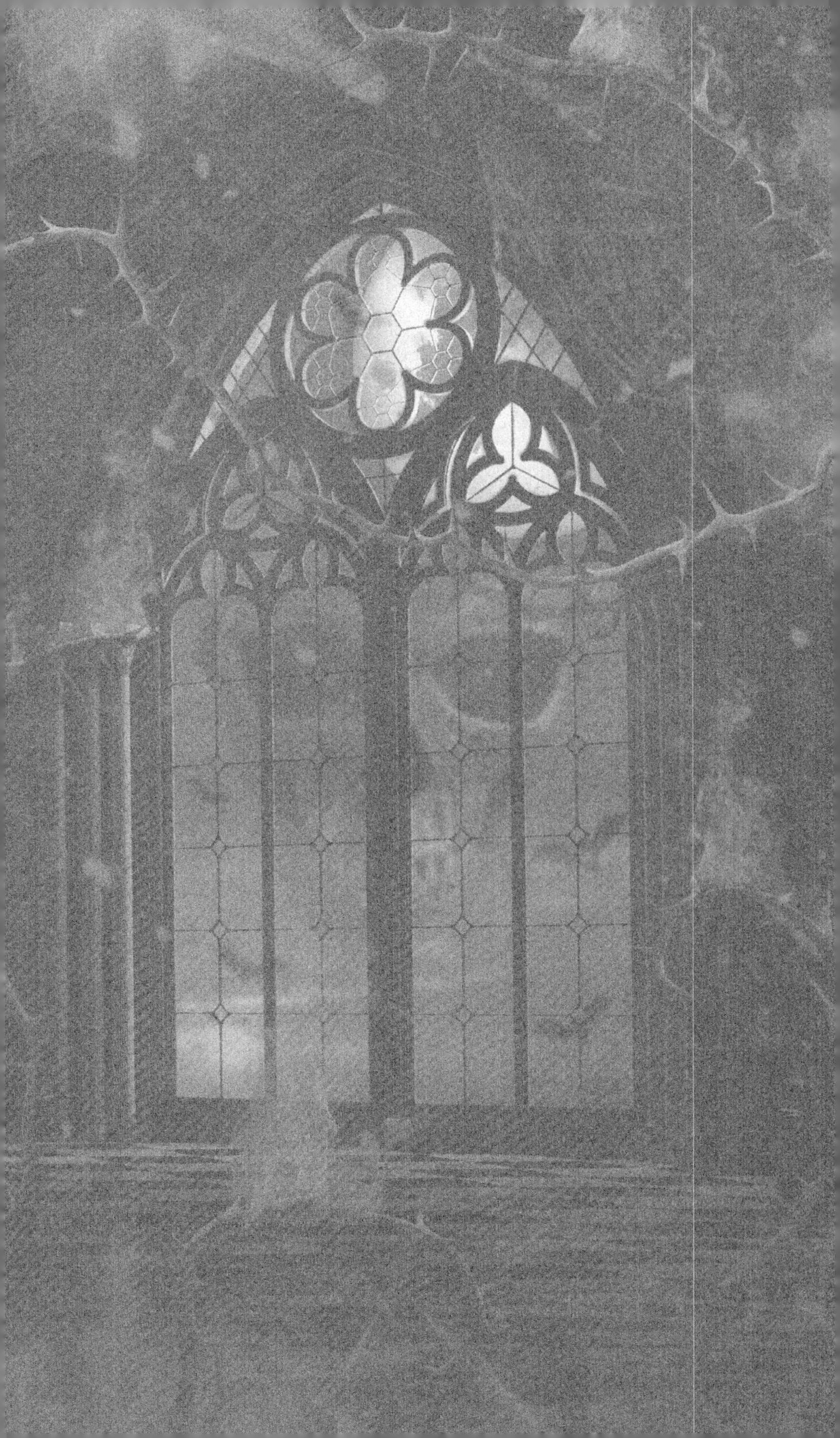

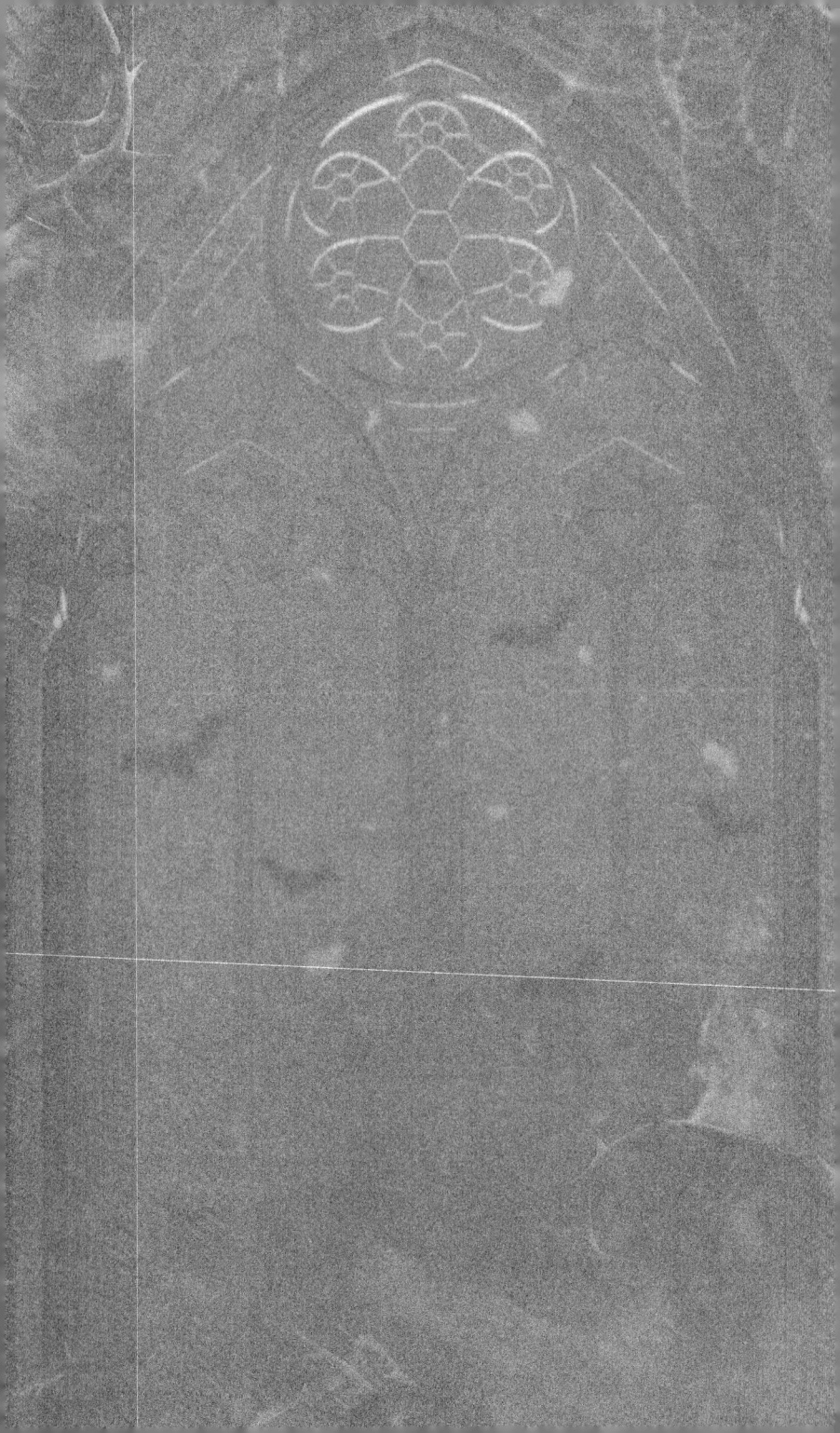

Thirty-Six

MAYA

He was insatiable, and I wanted to keep up with him. Show him that I was his equal in every way. So, I asked him, "Are you going to fuck me in the ass now?" and he growled. He fucking growled, showing that I'd said the right thing, and at the same time making me feel nervous.

I was getting a lot of firsts tonight. I wasn't sure I was ready for that one. But he sat back on the bed opposite me, and took my face in his hands, caressing my cheek, stroking with his thumb as he shook his head.

"I'm a bastard. You know I am. But even I think it'd be best for you if we left that first for another day. Unless you want me to totally ruin you?" He paused to see how I would respond, and when I didn't, he added, "Let's head to the shower and get you cleaned up. Let me look after you. And then after, we'll see where the night takes us."

I nodded, and he took my hand, climbed off the bed and led us through to the bathroom.

Once inside, he reached into the shower stall to turn the water on, waited for it to heat up and then walked us forward to stand underneath as the hot water cascaded over us.

I was sore, so the sensation of the hot water trickling over my skin helped to soothe some of the aches, and as I tilted my head back and ran my hands over my scalp to push the water through, he pushed himself against me and murmured, "You make everything so sexy," as he snuggled his face into my neck. "I don't think I'll ever want to take a shower again unless it's with you."

"I don't think we'd get much showering done, though, if that's the case," I replied with a hint of humour, and he moved his head to look at me.

"I can take care of you in a lot of ways in a shower like this."

"Is that so?" I teased, picking up the shower gel.

"Very much so." He winked as he took the bottle of gel from my hands, squeezed some out and started to lather it, rubbing his soapy hands slowly over my breasts.

"That's the part you think needs the most cleaning?" I quirked my brow, and he smirked back at me.

"It's the part I want to clean first. But you are a dirty girl. I think there's parts of you that are going to need very close attention."

"And those would be?" I continued to taunt him, pushing my chest forward and licking his wet cheek, catching the shower droplets on my tongue and then licking my lips.

"You're a fucking tease," he rasped. "Has anyone ever told

you that?"

"No. But I haven't wanted to tease anyone before. Not until you," I replied, and his reaction to what I'd said, that he was the only man to have me like this, ignited a fire inside him.

He grabbed my arm and spun me around, so my back was to him, and he whisper-growled in my ear, "See that handrail on the wall?"

I nodded.

"I need you to bend over and hold it."

I did as he asked, bending over a little and holding the rail with my hand, but I heard a tsk, and he added, "You can do better than that. Now hold on with both hands, Maya."

I grabbed the rail with my other hand and bent a little more, then felt the pressure of his hand pushing down on my back, showing me exactly where he wanted me.

"Now this," he said, reaching between my legs from behind. "Needs special attention. This pretty pussy is so swollen and full of cum, I need to make sure I clean you thoroughly down here."

I let out a little moan as he rubbed his soapy hand between my legs, his fingers stroking and delving between my folds, more probing than cleaning, but I didn't care. It felt so good, I pushed back against him, craving more.

"You like that, huh?" he asked, and I gave a breathy sigh in response. He pushed his fingers inside me, grunting as he said, "Fuck, Maya. Do you have any idea how good you feel? You're so fucking tight."

His fingers stroked my walls, stretching and rubbing, driving me insane. I hung my head as the water fell over us, and his fingers thrust slowly into me.

"Jesus, Maya," he groaned. "I need to be inside you again. I fucking crave this pussy. It feels too fucking good."

He pulled his fingers out, lined his cock up at my entrance and then thrust hard into me, grabbing hold of my hips tightly as I cried out.

I held the handrail as he set a punishing pace, rutting into me fast and hard. The water battered my back as he pounded my pussy, and I held onto the rail as best I could, almost letting go on each thrust with the power of his movements. Over and over, he thrust into me, his cock stretching me in the most sublime way. I wasn't sure I could take anymore, and yet, I couldn't get enough.

"You take my cock so fucking well," he growled. "It's the sexiest thing ever, watching my cock sink into your tight little pussy. My fucking pussy," he stated, and slammed harder into me to prove his point.

His fingers dug into my hips, his cock filled me at a brutalising pace, and I cried out, "More," as he slapped my ass hard and told me, "You'll get everything, baby. Don't you worry."

I could barely breathe, and I panted as his thrusts became more frantic, more punishing. Then he moved so he could reach around and stroke my clit as he fucked me, his front lying over my back as he moaned, "I need you to come for me, Maya. I'm so fucking close."

The touch of his hand on my clit set sparks flying, and my legs buckled as I started to come, gripping the handrail as my body began to spasm and my pussy contracted on his cock.

"That's it. Fuck, that's so good, Maya. You're such a good fucking girl." And he rested his head on my back as he hissed, "I'm coming. I'm fucking coming. You made me come, Maya."

And his cock throbbed as he came, his hips slowing but still thrusting as he emptied himself inside me.

"I don't think I'm ever gonna get enough of you," he sighed as he clung to me.

"I really fucking hope not," I whispered back quietly.

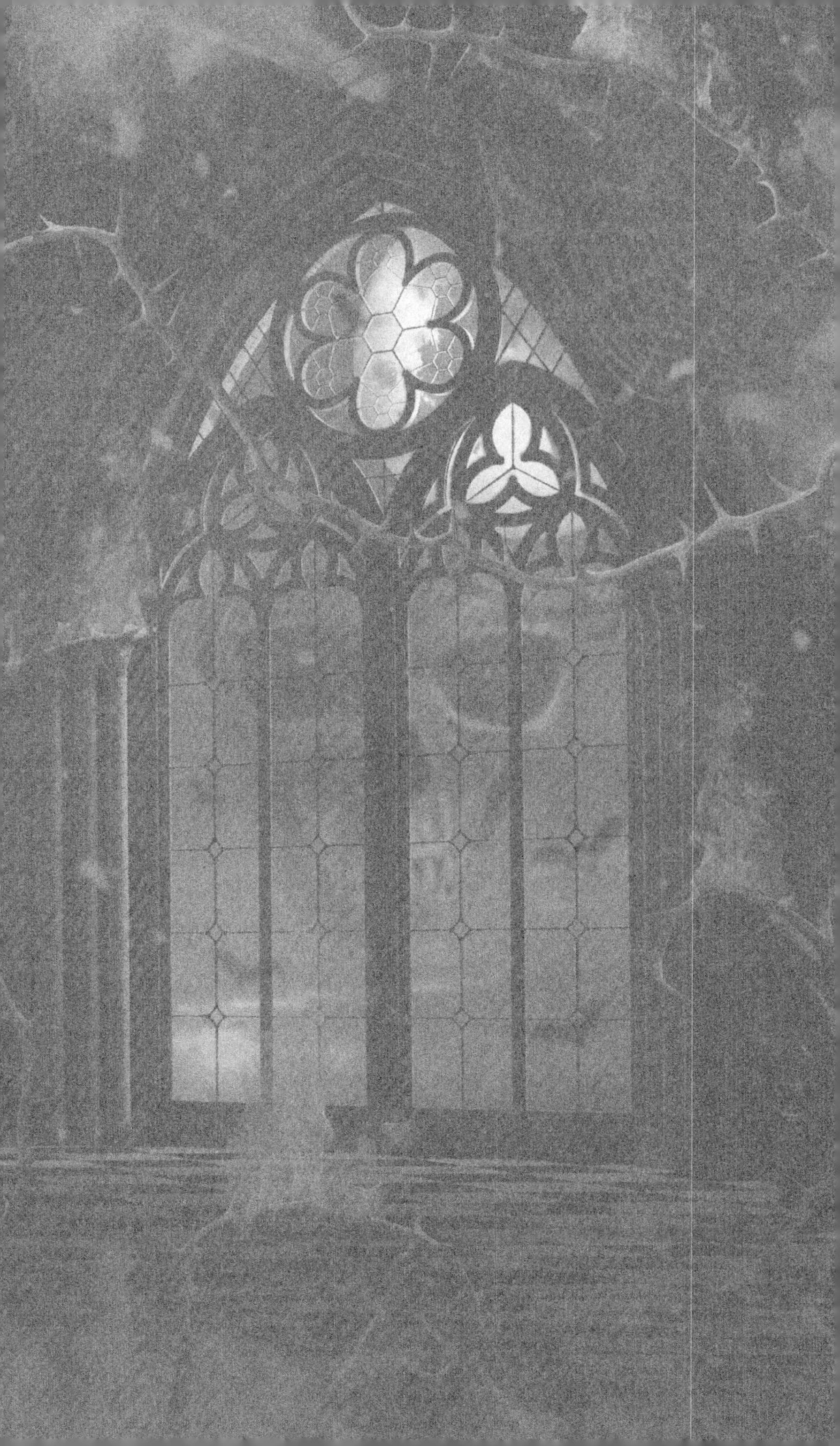

Thirty-Seven

MAYA

Damien didn't tell lies. I'd learned that from my time at Firethorne and since he'd moved me to this apartment. He certainly proved it last night, when he took me so many times, I'd lost count of all the orgasms I'd had—in the shower, after the shower. He'd claimed me in whatever way he could. In every way he could.

Eventually, we'd both fallen into an exhausted, sex-induced sleep in each other's arms. And when I woke the next morning, I kept my eyes closed for a few seconds longer to savour the warmth of his body next to mine and the sound of his gentle breaths as he lay sleeping.

Firethorne

When I eventually opened my eyes and turned my head to watch him, I couldn't believe how peaceful he looked as he slept. He breathed quietly with his mouth open slightly, and the lines he sometimes had on his brow were smoothed out now. He looked younger as he lay still. A man who, whilst dreaming, didn't seem to have a care in the world, but I knew, the second he woke up, the weight of the world would be back on his shoulders again, and evident on his beautiful face. The Firethorne guilt that dragged him down every day wasn't evident now. He was just... Damien.

My Damien.

My saviour.

At some point during the night, we'd gone from lying in each other's arms to lying beside one another, but I was still worried I might wake him when I moved. So, carefully, I lifted myself from the bed, swinging my legs onto the floor, and stood quietly. Luckily, he didn't wake, so I silently congratulated myself on my success, put a T-shirt on so I wouldn't get cold, and headed out the door.

Moments later, when I walked back in with a small tray, he was sitting up, yawning and watching the door, waiting for me.

"What's this?" he asked, frowning as I placed the tray on the bedside table.

"Breakfast," I replied.

"You made me breakfast? But that's my job. I'm supposed to take care of you."

I knew he'd say that.

Damien was the most thoughtful man I'd ever met. But at the same time, I wanted to do something for him. He'd done so much for me already.

"I wanted to spoil you a little." I picked up the coffee cup and handed it to him. "Black, no sugar. Is that okay?"

"Perfect." He smiled, taking a sip, then placed it on the table beside him and asked, "Are you feeling okay?"

"I feel fine, more than fine. I feel... alive."

"I didn't go too hard on you last night?" he asked, reaching out to grab me and pull me closer to him on the bed.

I lay next to him, with my head on his chest.

"You went hard, but I'd expect nothing less." I peered up at him. "It was what I asked for. What I wanted, remember?"

He leaned down to place a gentle kiss on my forehead, and then he sighed.

"You know I have to go back to the house today, don't you?"

"You go back every day. It's fine. You need to keep working. I wouldn't want you to stop on my account."

I wished he could stay, but I didn't want to pressurise him.

He wrapped his arms around me, giving me a gentle squeeze as he replied, "I know. But after what we did last night, I feel like I should spend the day with you."

"When I get out of here..." I glanced up at him with a knowing look. "Or when you let me out, we'll have all the time in the world."

"Will we?" he asked, his face suddenly turning solemn. "Because at the moment, I can't see how I can keep you close and still work on bringing my father's network down. I still have so much work to do, Maya."

I reached up and placed my hand on his cheek.

"Try not to think that far ahead. We'll find a way," I assured him. "There'll always be a way."

"Love will find a way," he said, without thinking about what he was saying, and I saw the way his eyes widened at his words. The meaning behind them hitting him just like they were hitting me.

"You'll stop your father's network," I said, taking the focus off our feelings. "I have faith in you. And until then, we'll take each day as it comes."

"Live for the moment," he added. "I like that."

Firethorne

He started to tickle me, making me giggle and roll around in his grasp as he teased me. My body wriggled and writhed against him, my bare legs kicking out on the bed, and my T-shirt rode up to expose my nakedness. He growled, and his playfulness became erotically charged.

"No panties. Now that's what I want to see first thing every morning. Your gorgeous wet pussy open and ready for me."

Damien was naked under the covers, and he threw them back, exposing his hard cock as he lifted himself to kneel in front of me. "On all fours, Maya," he commanded, becoming serious. "Head down and ass up."

I did as I was told, lifting my ass in the air and resting my head on the pillow.

"Fucking beautiful," he growled, running his fingers through my wet pussy, and then he moved them higher, rubbing the wetness over my asshole. "I know exactly what I want to eat for breakfast."

He leaned forward, his tongue licking through my pussy, flickering over my clit as I buried my head in the pillow and cried tears of fucking joy.

His warm mouth felt so fucking good, teasing and sucking, eating me and coaxing out my first orgasm of the day. The sensation of his tongue rubbing, swirling, and spearing inside me, made my hips rock backwards, begging for more.

He held my hips firmly as he ate me, his fingers digging into the flesh of my ass. Then he started to rub his thumb over my asshole, teasing me there, pushing the tip of his thumb in lightly and pulling it out, making me gasp. He was easing me into whatever was about to happen.

His mouth licked and sucked my pussy, and then I felt his tongue venturing upwards, heading towards my asshole. He moved his thumb away and started to lick over my ass, humming with pleasure as he flickered his tongue over my puckered hole. It felt dirty, taboo, and so freaking amazing.

I angled my hips, tilting my ass up higher, wanting to open myself up more to him. And as I did, he muttered, "Good girl," and then speared his tongue into my asshole.

The sensation was incredible.

Like nothing I'd ever felt before.

I never expected to feel so sensitive back there, and I never expected to want more and more of what he was doing.

"That's it," he praised as I let out a sound like a kitten mewling. "Relax for me. Let me take care of you back here."

His tongue was inside me, his fingers pulling at my ass cheeks, opening me up, and I couldn't stop my fingers from reaching for my clit and stroking, forcing the orgasm that was cresting to burst free. Within seconds my orgasm hit hard, tearing me apart as I came in my pussy and my ass.

Mind.

Fucking.

Blown.

"That's it," he rasped as he licked and sucked me. "Good girl. That feels fucking amazing, doesn't it?"

I couldn't respond, but I knew the animalistic noises I was making were answer enough.

He started to push his finger into my ass as I continued to orgasm, using the wetness from my pussy and his mouth to lubricate my asshole, and then he said, "Are you ready for a little more playtime in here?"

I grunted, nodding into the pillow, unable to form a sentence, and he huffed a gentle laugh.

"I'll take that as a yes."

I felt movement behind me, and then something cool and hard rubbed against my asshole. It wasn't his cock, it felt like metal, and I prised my eyes open, tilting my head to look behind me.

"If I'd have known this was going to happen, I'd have come better prepared," Damien said.

Firethorne

"What is that?" I asked through my sex-induced haze.

"It's my knife." He saw the panic on my face, and he quickly added, "I'm not gonna hurt you. I'm just gonna use the handle. The grooves in the metal and the shape are perfect for what I want to do to you. Do you trust me?" he asked, a pleading look in his eyes.

I nodded, because it was true. I did trust him.

"Good. Now let me fuck this tight little ass the way it needs to be fucked."

I put my trust in him one hundred percent and rested my head on the pillow.

He started by rubbing the knife handle over my asshole, gently prying me open as he pushed it in, just a little, then pulled it back out again. I felt myself tense and he switched to licking me with his tongue, and then blowing as he said, "Relax. I won't hurt you. I promise this'll feel good. Maybe push back onto it, and it'll go in easier."

He gave me a few more sensual, slow licks to help me loosen up and then he tried again, sliding the handle in and out of my ass, going a little deeper each time.

I did as he said, and pushed my hips backwards, taking what he was giving me, and as the handle filled my ass, I heard him moan as he watched what he was doing.

"So fucking hot," he gasped as he pushed the knife handle deeper, twisting it as he began to thrust harder.

The cool metal felt foreign, and it filled me so full it almost took my breath away, but I soon adjusted to the size and craved more. With each thrust, he had me rocking back onto the knife handle and moaning into the pillow.

He continued to slide the handle in and out, and then started to alternate between the handle and his fingers, stretching me and massaging my walls. Making me elicit sounds I didn't even know I was capable of making.

"I need lube," he suddenly rasped. "I can't go another minute without my cock in your ass. But I can't do it without lube."

He threw the knife down on the bed and reached forward, grabbing something off the tray I'd brought in, and then I heard him rip the lid off the plain yoghurt.

I turned my head to watch him scoop out the yoghurt and lather it over his cock, and then he rubbed it over my already soaked asshole, smearing and pushing it inside me. He was so desperate to have me, he was ready to use anything. And knowing that made me feral for him.

"Are you ready?" he asked, the urgency evident from the need in his voice.

"Yes," I whimpered, feeling so needy, so desperate, I was ready to beg for his cock.

He pushed himself into me just a little and stopped, letting me adjust to his size.

"You need to relax," he told me as I started to tense up again. "Play with your clit and focus on how good your body feels. Lean back into me. It'll help you open up."

I reached forward, stroking my pulsing clit and then pushed my hips back.

"Good girl," he moaned and pushed his cock in a little more, groaning as my muscles gripped him tightly.

I tilted my head so I could look at his face, and the expression of pure bliss as he stared down at where his cock was penetrating my asshole made my orgasm tingle and spark to life.

"Fuck my ass," I begged him, knowing that'd push him over the edge. "Let me feel every inch of you."

His fingers gripped my hips, and he pulled me back even more, sliding my ass onto his cock. Then he pushed in slowly, filling me until I could feel his hips resting against my ass.

"I'm gonna come so fucking hard," he moaned. "I'll fill your ass full of my cum. And you're gonna love every minute, aren't you?"

I whimpered, "Yes," and then he started to move. Slow thrusts at first, but once he knew I could take it, he worked me harder, pounding my ass and making my whole body shake with need. Fucking me like he'd die if he didn't thrust as hard as he fucking could.

I buckled; my arms unable to hold me up as my shoulders hit the mattress. Damien reached forward and grabbed some pillows, shoving them under my hips to keep me upright as he fucked me harder.

"Fucking come for me," he commanded, holding my hips firmly as he pumped into me. "Play with your pussy while I fuck your ass and come for me, Maya."

I didn't need to touch myself; his dirty words made me explode, my pussy and my ass contracting hard as I cried out, squeezing his cock as he thickened against my pulsing walls. And then he roared as he came too. Cries of pure pleasure as his cock throbbed inside me.

He held my hips tightly as he emptied himself, and then, slowly, he pulled his cock out of my ass, and I could feel his hot cum trickling out.

I knew he wouldn't like that.

He didn't like to waste a drop.

Suddenly, I felt cold metal against my ass, and the sensation of him scooping the yoghurt and cum. I turned my head to see him with a spoon, collecting what he could and putting it back into the yoghurt pot.

"What the fuck are you doing?" I whispered.

"It was this or my mouth cleaning it up," he replied, like both options were viable.

I was speechless.

Totally spent and satisfied, but utterly speechless.

"You could've used a towel," I shot back, and when he carried on regardless, I said, "Please tell me you're not going to eat that?"

"Why not?" He raised a brow. "Eating cum flavoured yoghurt out of your ass wouldn't be so bad, would it?"

"*Damien!*" I gave him a look, and he smirked back at me. This man was too much.

"Too soon for that?" He winked.

"Errr, yes!" I replied, and then I couldn't stop myself from giggling. I knew life with Damien was going to be one hell of a ride, and I was here for it.

We never did get around to eating a proper breakfast. By the time Damien had finished fucking me, we both collapsed on the bed and fell into a light sleep. And then he'd had to leave, telling me his father had called an urgent meeting and he needed to get back to the house, so he didn't arouse any suspicion.

I didn't argue, but watching him leave felt like a part of me was walking away with him. Here was another day where I had to lose myself in books, my writing, or daydreams about him. Anything to take my mind off the hopelessness of our situation. But at least now I had some new memories to replay in my mind, memories that made me yearn for him all over again.

Thinking about our night together made me realise how well I'd slept with Damien beside me. I hadn't encountered any dark shadows haunting me, or any night terrors. Not like I did most nights in this quiet, lonely apartment. Hopefully, now it wouldn't feel so lonely. Now I had him.

I read a few more chapters of *The Handmaid's Tale* to stop myself from falling down a Damien-shaped hole of need and pining for the rest of the day. Then I started to write, my mind choosing to go back in time to the days when my father first told me about his bankruptcy. I found writing about the fallout of what he'd done therapeutic, and before I knew it, daylight turned to dusk, casting shadows over the apartment.

I saved my work and closed the laptop, standing from the sofa, ready to turn the lights on. Butterflies fluttered in my stomach at the thought of what Damien would want to do tonight. But as I turned, I saw the door to the apartment was ajar and I gasped.

My pulse thrummed in my ears as I stared at the unlocked door, and adrenaline hit me hard, making me feel sick.

When had that happened?

The door had closed behind Damien when he left this morning, I was sure of that.

Had I been so engrossed in my laptop that it'd opened without me noticing or hearing it?

Was there someone here?

I whispered, "Hello?" Then, a little louder, "Hello? Is anyone there?" But no one answered.

If Damien was here, in this apartment, he'd have made his presence known. He wouldn't play with me like this.

So why was it open?

Was Damien standing on the other side, waiting for me to push the door open so he could surprise me with my freedom?

I took slow, trepid steps across the living room towards the door, nervous about what I'd find, but I had to know what was going on. I had to walk through that door.

My fingers trembled as I stood in front of it and reached forward to touch it, placing my hands on the reinforced steel that'd kept me locked up in here for so long.

I curled my fingers around the edge of the door and slowly, so slowly, I pulled it open to reveal a hallway.

I'd never seen this hallway before, but it looked exactly

like the apartment, with the same white walls and carpet. Tentatively, I peered around the doorway, expecting to see Damien waiting for me, but there was no one there.

"Hello?" I called down the hallway as I moved my head from left to right, but no one answered.

I took a step forward, taking myself from the apartment into the hallway, and I stood still for a moment, not sure if I was doing the right thing as I gazed down one side and then the other.

Maybe I should go back into the apartment and close the door? Wait for Damien to come back.

Maybe I should hit the panic button? Tell them I needed help. But past experience had told me that'd be pointless.

Or maybe, just maybe, I should do the right thing for me and walk the hell out of this apartment, out into a world that I hadn't seen in so long. Feel the breeze on my skin. Breathe fresh, clean air. Walk on something other than plush carpet and start living my life again. A life that had so much hope now that Damien was in it.

Yes, that's what I'd do. I'd walk down this corridor and leave. I had no idea where my feet would take me, but wasn't this what I'd wanted from the start? To be free to make my own choices. I smiled to myself, thinking that this was so Damien-coded. He loved to give me freedom in whatever way he could, and that's exactly what he was doing now. I knew it.

I decided to turn right and head that way down the corridor. Right had to be the right choice, after all. My heart beat faster as excitement stirred in my belly.

This was it.

This was the end.

Or the start, whichever way you looked at it.

My steps were slow but purposeful, my heartbeat pounding in my ears so loud, I didn't hear anyone come up behind me. But when something was thrown over my head, strong arms

Firethorne

grabbing me in a punishing grip, and a mean voice hissed viciously, "There you are, slut," I knew I'd made a big fucking mistake.

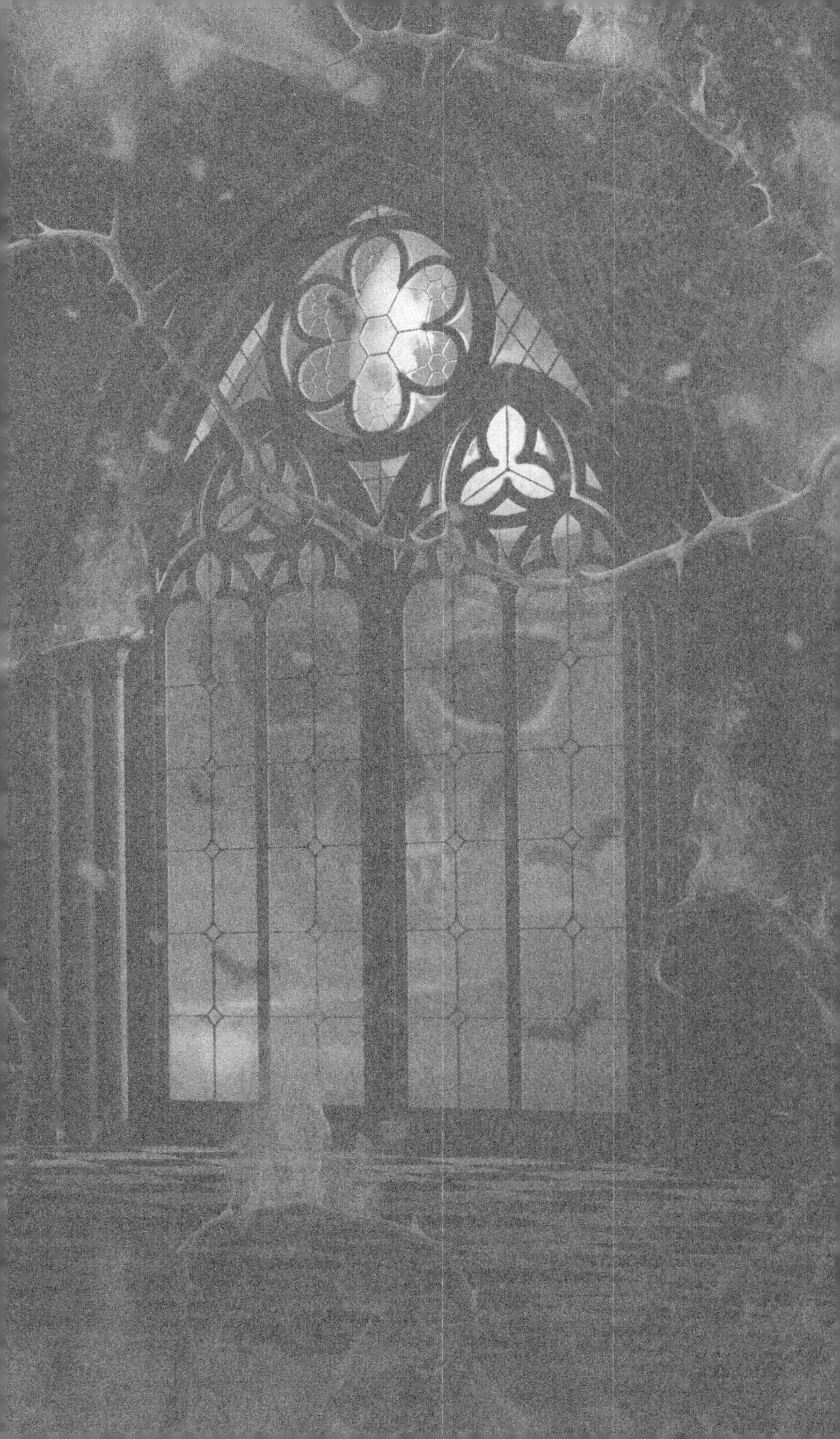

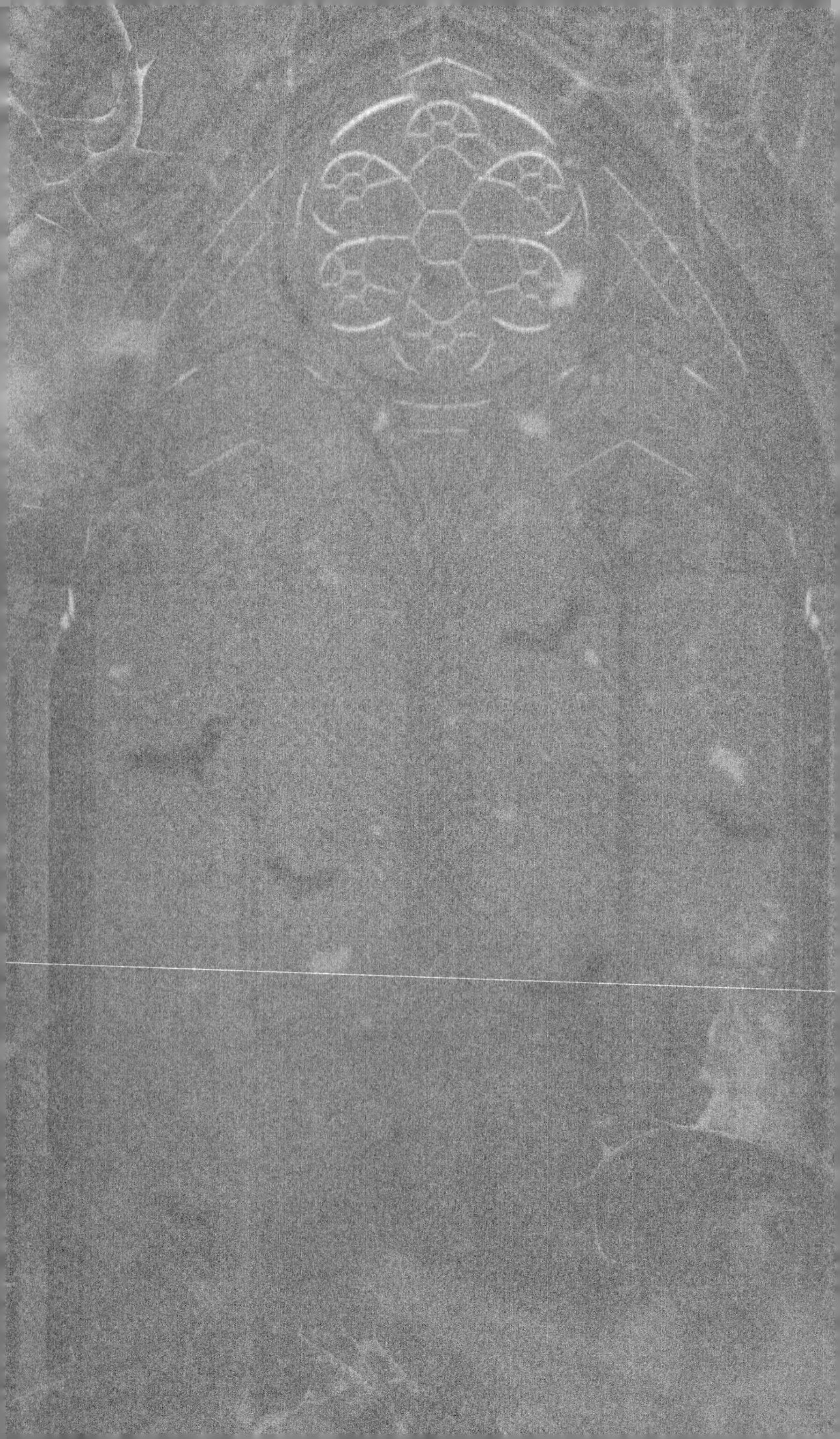

Thirty-Eight

MAYA

They didn't even bother to drug me this time. Whoever it was that'd jumped me and shoved the sack over my head put me in a headlock and squeezed my throat. I clawed and scratched at their arm, fighting for my life, my legs kicking out to try and take them down. But it became impossible to breathe, and as deadly stars danced in front of my eyes, I slipped away, falling unconscious into the arms of my captor.

I don't know how long I was out for, but when I came to, I was lying on the cold metal floor of what appeared to be some sort of van. It stank of oil and paint, and the engine roared as

Firethorne

it sped across uneven terrain, throwing my body around. I had to brace myself as best I could with my wrists and ankles bound together, and I could already feel the pain in my body from where I'd been knocked about while I was unconscious. My mouth was taped shut but I still cried out, using my muffled screams and banging my feet against the floor to fight back.

It was no use, though.

There didn't seem to be anyone else in the back of the van with me.

Whoever had taken me, and I had a pretty good idea who it was, they were up front, driving me back to the hell I thought I'd escaped.

I heard the whip and crack of branches against the side of the van as we drove at speed, twisting and turning, bumping along the roads. And then, the van began to slow down and eventually stopped. The engine continued to run as the driver opened his door then slammed it shut.

I didn't know whether to play dead or prepare to attack when the rear doors opened.

I couldn't decide how to play this.

I didn't know the best way.

Maybe there wasn't a best way.

I just had to do whatever I could to survive.

So, I opted for silence, lying still as the back door creaked open and cool air rushed in, gracing my skin with the kiss of death.

I kept my breaths shallow, barely moving as I braced myself for what was about to happen. I sensed the floor dipping as the driver climbed up into the back of the van. Then rough hands grabbed my arms as a vile, gruff voice rasped, "Don't pretend to be asleep. I heard you banging just now."

He pulled me into a sitting position and then ripped the sack from my head. I squinted as a bright torch was shone into my eyes.

"Welcome home, Maya," Firethorne said, and he moved the torch to shine it on the woodland floor, giving my eyes some relief.

He was standing outside the van, smiling at me like I was a long-lost relative who'd come back to the family fold. And beside me, Beresford kicked out at my legs, telling me, "I always knew you'd be trouble. You won't fuck us over again, though, will you?"

"She won't get the chance," Firethorne shot back. "She's about to find out what happens when you double-cross a Firethorne."

He stepped to the side and moved the torch to shine it into the dark woods, and as he did, the bottom dropped out of my world.

I felt sick.

I tried to turn my head, so I didn't have to look as tears began to flow down my cheeks, but Beresford knelt behind me and held my head, forcing me to see.

And there, in the trees, swinging from the noose Lysander had shown me, was my father. His face was swollen and blue, his eyes bulging, his neck was broken, and so was my heart.

I closed my eyes, sobbing with my whole chest, but that image was seared into my brain, reflecting back at me from behind my eyelids. An image that'd haunt me forever.

Beresford grabbed my face, trying to force my eyes open, scratching me as he did, but I refused to look for a second longer.

Firethorne's laugh cackled in my ears.

"If it makes you feel any better," Firethorne goaded. "He did try to save you. The fool thought he could take the money and the prize. Run away with you to somewhere safe. But that was never going to happen. So I gave him the ending he deserved, as a traitor to this family. And soon, there'll be another body taking his place for that same crime."

Firethorne

Beresford cackled in my ear as I tensed, knowing they meant me.

"Oh, not you," Firethorne announced, like he'd read my thoughts. "You'll get what's coming to you, but this won't be your final resting place, *sweetheart*. Oh no. I meant your little plaything. My bastard son. Damien."

The fear and visceral grief I was drowning in multiplied, and I slumped forward, feeling physical pain at the thought of what he was saying.

"That's right," he said, his voice brimming with scorn and revulsion. "He's here. Well, his body is. After the beatings and torture we've given him today, I doubt he's still alive."

Beresford huffed his pleasure as he stood up, then kicked out, knocking me back to the floor.

"Drive her back up to the house," Firethorne instructed. "We'll take it from there."

I watched through watery, heartbroken eyes as Beresford jumped back off the van and slammed the doors shut, locking me back into the darkest hell I'd ever known.

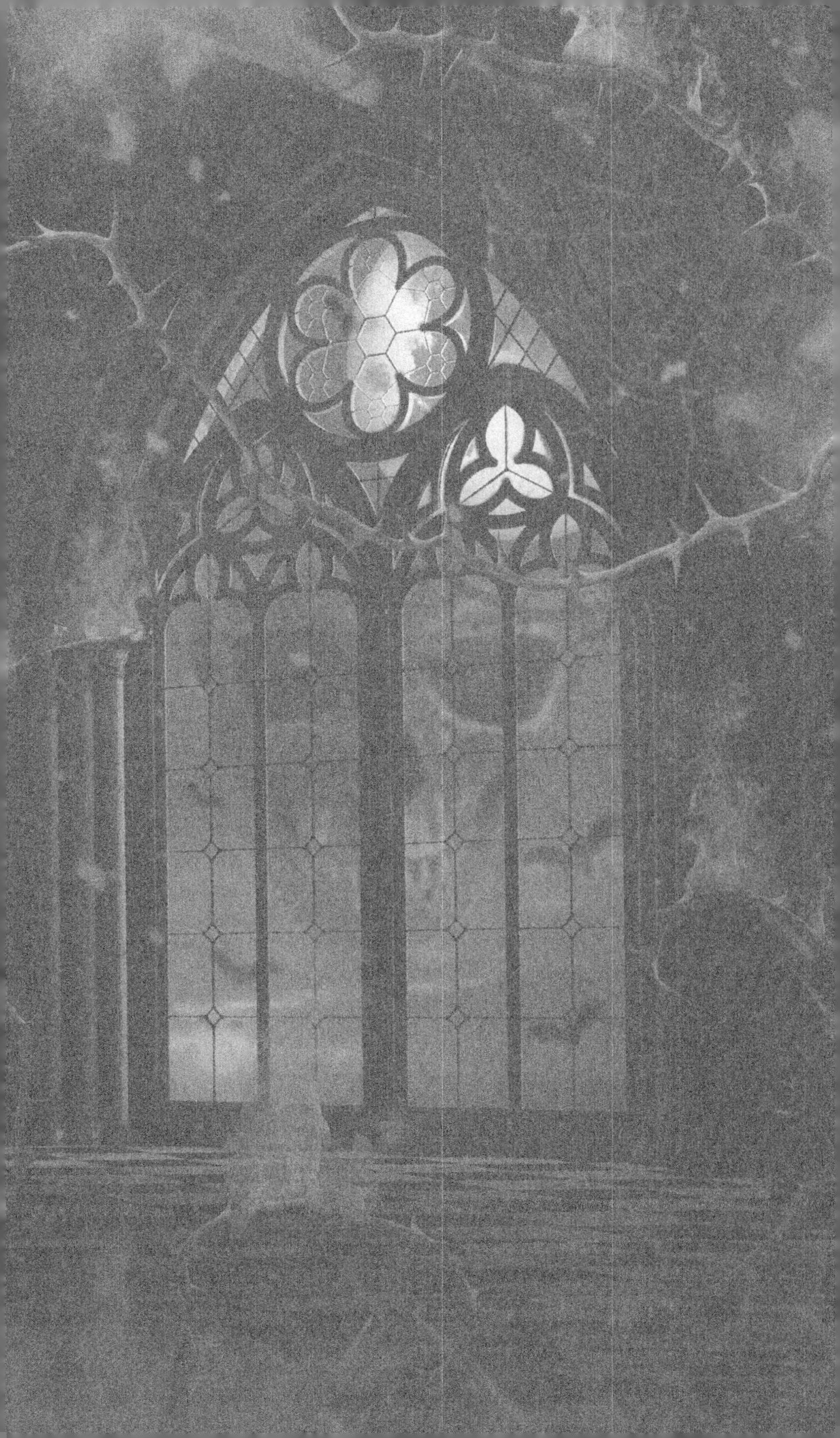

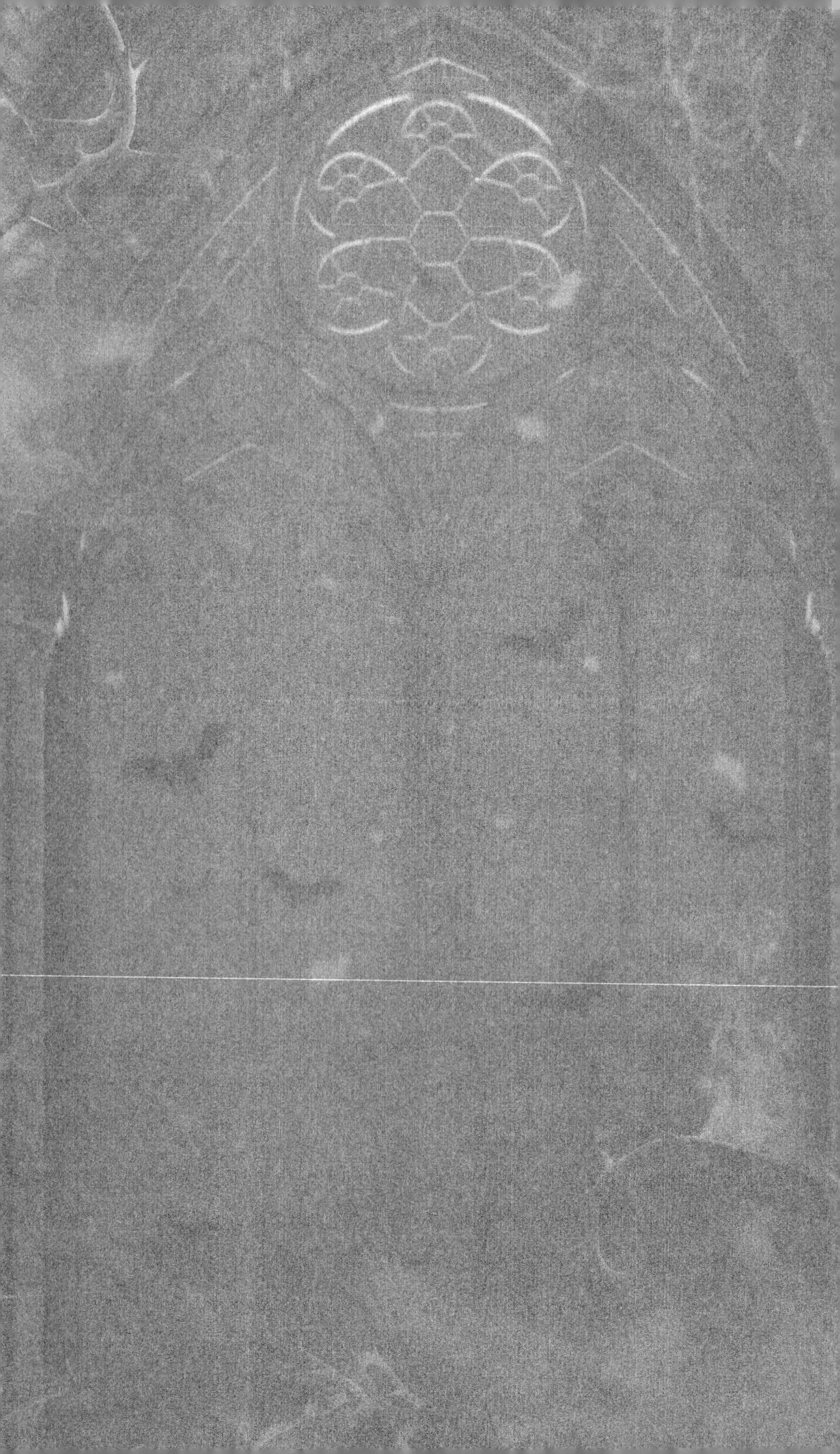

Thirty-Nine

MAYA

I was freefalling.

Lost in immeasurable grief for my father and the realisation that I'd never get the closure I needed. That I'd never see him again. I knew visions of his final hours would haunt me forever. That, and the sickening image of him in that tree.

Why was there so much evil in this world?

Tears streamed down my face, and my body ached, wracked with the sobs I couldn't hold in anymore. Losing him would always be an unbearable darkness, a weight that I'd feel inside my heart for the rest of my life.

Firethorne

And then there was Damien.

My warrior, my saviour.

It was all so unfair.

So fucking cruel.

We hadn't even had the chance to live. To get to know each other on a deeper level that I knew we would've, given the chance. Because he was just like me, a reader, a thinker, a dreamer. Fate had put someone so perfect in front of me, given me a glimpse of what happiness looked like, then cruelly ripped him away.

Actually, it wasn't fate that'd taken him. It was his bastard father. And I'd use my dying breath to make sure he paid for what he'd done.

When we reached Firethorne Manor, I was bundled out of the back of the van and carried into the house.

Beresford stalked up the stairs with me slung over his shoulder, veering towards Firethorne's office when he got to the second floor.

Once inside, he threw me down at Firethorne's feet, slamming me onto the ground without care. I hissed from the pain, curling myself into a ball, and then squeezed my eyes shut. I didn't want to look at them, these men that disgusted me, but when I heard a female voice, my eyes shot open.

"Why did you bring her back here?" Miriam sneered, wrinkling her nose as she stared down at me. "She doesn't belong here."

Miriam stood in front of the roaring fireplace, and next to her, with his head down, was Lysander.

"Not that it's any of your business," Firethorne snapped. "But I brought her here because she owes this family a debt, and tonight, she's going to pay."

"Make her pay how? She doesn't have any money," Miriam scolded. "Look at her. She's a mess."

I wanted to rip the cable ties from my wrists and pounce on

her like a tiger, with my claws ready to gouge her eyes out. She stood over me as if she was superior, when she was the worst kind of woman. A woman who stands by and lets the men around her hurt other women. Maybe she didn't know the full extent of Firethorne's business, but she wasn't innocent. She wouldn't do a damn thing to help me tonight.

And neither would Lysander.

He couldn't even look at me.

"There are other ways to pay a debt, you know that all too well, Miriam," Firethorne sneered. "And we don't need more money."

"Everyone needs more money," Miriam purred. "And the amount we'll get when she's moved on to her new owner will be payment enough."

My stomach rolled.

She knew.

That bitch fucking knew.

"Debts are about more than money," Firethorne snapped. "She tried to double-cross us. She needs to learn that actions have consequences. Fuck with a Firethorne, and they fuck you harder." He smiled at that last part, making my blood run cold.

And still, Lysander remained silent.

He had to know, too.

He had to have been a part of all this.

I wanted to scream at him. Ask him if he had anything to say after deceiving and betraying me the way he had. But I knew, even if I could speak to call him out, he wouldn't say anything. He really was as vapid as I thought he was when I first met him, only he was worse. He was spiteful and vindictive, too. Totally and utterly shameless. He had to be implicit in what his father was doing, because he was just standing there, not doing a thing to help me. He couldn't care less.

"Shall we get things started?" Firethorne asked, leaning across his desk to pick up a knife. But he put it back down when his son spoke up.

"I don't think we should stay for this part," Lysander announced, glancing nervously at Miriam. Ever the coward, he wanted to leave me to the mercy of his evil father.

Firethorne turned to face him with a look of disgust.

"On the contrary," Firethorne replied. "I think you should stay. She tricked you, too. You're owed a pound of flesh, or however much you want to take. It's open season tonight. At midnight, she'll be on her way to The Butcher, but until then, we get to have all the fun."

The Butcher.

That name sent a chill down my spine, and I grunted through the tape over my mouth, yanking on the ties at my wrists and kicking out with my feet.

"Ah." Firethorne smiled down at me, the kind of smile that would make a devil cry. "You're familiar with The Butcher then?" He leant down to stare right in my face. "You know what lies ahead for you."

I narrowed my eyes at him, wishing he'd self-combust and take the place reserved for him in hell.

"Remember what he is and how much worse it's going to get for you when you're paying our debt tonight," he went on. "It might help you survive to see the morning. Let that survival instinct kick in. Or not. I couldn't care either way."

There was a commotion outside in the hallway, and they all turned their attention to the door as it suddenly burst open. My heart shattered into a million pieces at what I saw, but I also felt the smallest glimmer of hope.

There, flanked by two huge men who were holding him in place as he kicked and fought against them, was Damien.

His face was badly swollen, blood running from his nose. His eyes were barely open, and blood poured from a cut above his eyebrow.

But I could tell he wasn't broken.

He was stronger than that.

Firethorne stiffened, clearly bothered by the fact that Damien was fighting so hard, and he stood tall as he announced proudly, "So glad you could finally join us, *son*,"

Damien turned to face him, and that's when he saw me.

Every muscle in his body tensed and he clenched his jaw, spitting and cursing as he thrashed even harder against the men restraining him.

"I thought you'd be dead by now," Firethorne went on. "But maybe this has worked in our favour. Now you get to see what happens when you fuck me over."

"Fuck you." Damien spat at him from across the room, but Firethorne just laughed.

"Did you really think you'd get away with it? That I wouldn't find out what you were doing?" He shook his head. "I might've acted like I trusted you, but I didn't. I don't trust anyone. I had multiple people tracing your online activity, *Damien*. I bugged every room you've ever been in, tracked your car, your phone, all of it. You thought you could outsmart me, destroy my whole business, but you were wrong. I told you, I'm always one step ahead. But in your case, it was a mile."

Damien hissed, spitting blood on the floor as he continued to try and break free of the men's grasps.

"I'll fucking kill you," he snarled at his father. And then he looked at me, and that fury exploded, evolving into a visceral, palpable force that engulfed the room. "You're a fucking dead man."

"I don't think you're in any position to be giving threats, do you?" Firethorne sneered. Then he reached down to run his rancid finger along my cheek, grinning as Damien spat and swore, bucking against his captors. "Maybe you should stay here and watch the fallout of your actions. It's going to be a good show." Evilness shrouded him as he added, "But let's make one thing clear... the only one doing any killing around here, will be me."

Damien thrashed in the men's hold as he shouted, "Get your fucking hands off her. I swear, if you fucking touch her again, I'll break your fucking neck."

"Oh, I'm going to do more than touch her," Firethorne threatened, taking the knife from the desk and holding it up to fuck with Damien and strike more fear into my heart. "I can't wait for you to see how creative I can get. Do you think The Butcher came up with those moves all on his own?" He shook his head and made a tsk sound. "No. He learnt from the best."

Damien let out a feral, animalistic scream that pierced my heart. And as the hopelessness of our reality hit him, his knees buckled, and he whispered pleas that went unheard as the men yanked him back up to stand.

Firethorne was cackling, and Miriam grinned wickedly as her fucked up uncle knelt beside me on the floor.

"Do you want me to pin her down?" Miriam asked. "Like I've done with the others, while you—"

She didn't get chance to finish.

"I don't want him here," Lysander butted in, cutting through the fear-laced atmosphere with his grave urgency. "Get rid of him. Now."

Firethorne stood back up and tilted his head as he regarded his eldest son curiously.

"*Why?*"

Lysander puffed his chest out, dominance radiating from him as he replied, "Don't you think you owe me this, at least, after all the times I've stood by you? You said I could have my pound of flesh, but I don't want him here while I take it. I don't want to see his face ever again."

Firethorne took a minute, and I was sure he'd tell Lysander to go to hell, but he didn't. He just nodded.

"Fine. I suppose I could video it and make him watch it after." And he gestured for the men to leave and take Damien with them.

Damien protested, fighting against them with everything he had as they dragged him out of the room, shouting and hollering threats that he knew he was powerless to act on.

But as I glanced back at Lysander, it wasn't hate and revenge I saw reflected back at me, but a sadness and resignation that seemed to say, 'I know I can't do much, but the least I could do was save you the degradation and shame of having to go through whatever you're about to go through without him seeing it.'

His weakly heroic act was too little, too late.

But it was something.

"Thank you," Lysander said to his father. But then he turned to Miriam, and they began to exchange strange glances, as if they were holding their own muted conversation. They knew what the other wanted to say without having to saying a word.

Mr Firethorne was oblivious to them, though, and he cleared his throat, stating, "Let's get this started then, shall we?" But Miriam interrupted him.

"Could Lysander and I be excused? For now. We'll be back, but we have some unfinished business we need to attend to first."

I could see the apprehension in her face. She didn't want to provoke Firethorne, but she wanted to support Lysander in whatever they'd agreed in their silent exchange.

"What unfinished business? What could be more important than this?" Firethorne bit back, and falling eloquently into her temptress mode, Miriam fluttered her eyelashes at him and purred, "Nothing is more important. I'd just like some alone time with Lysander. All this violence and talk of revenge has me feeling a certain way."

Firethorne's knowing grin made my stomach roll.

"You never change," he told her. "But come back here once you're done. You know how horny I get after a bit of torture."

Firethorne

I wanted to throw up.

This family were beyond fucked up.

They made me sick.

Miriam nodded sweetly, almost bowing to him, and without giving me a second glance, the two of them backed out of the room, leaving me alone with the devil in front of his roaring fire.

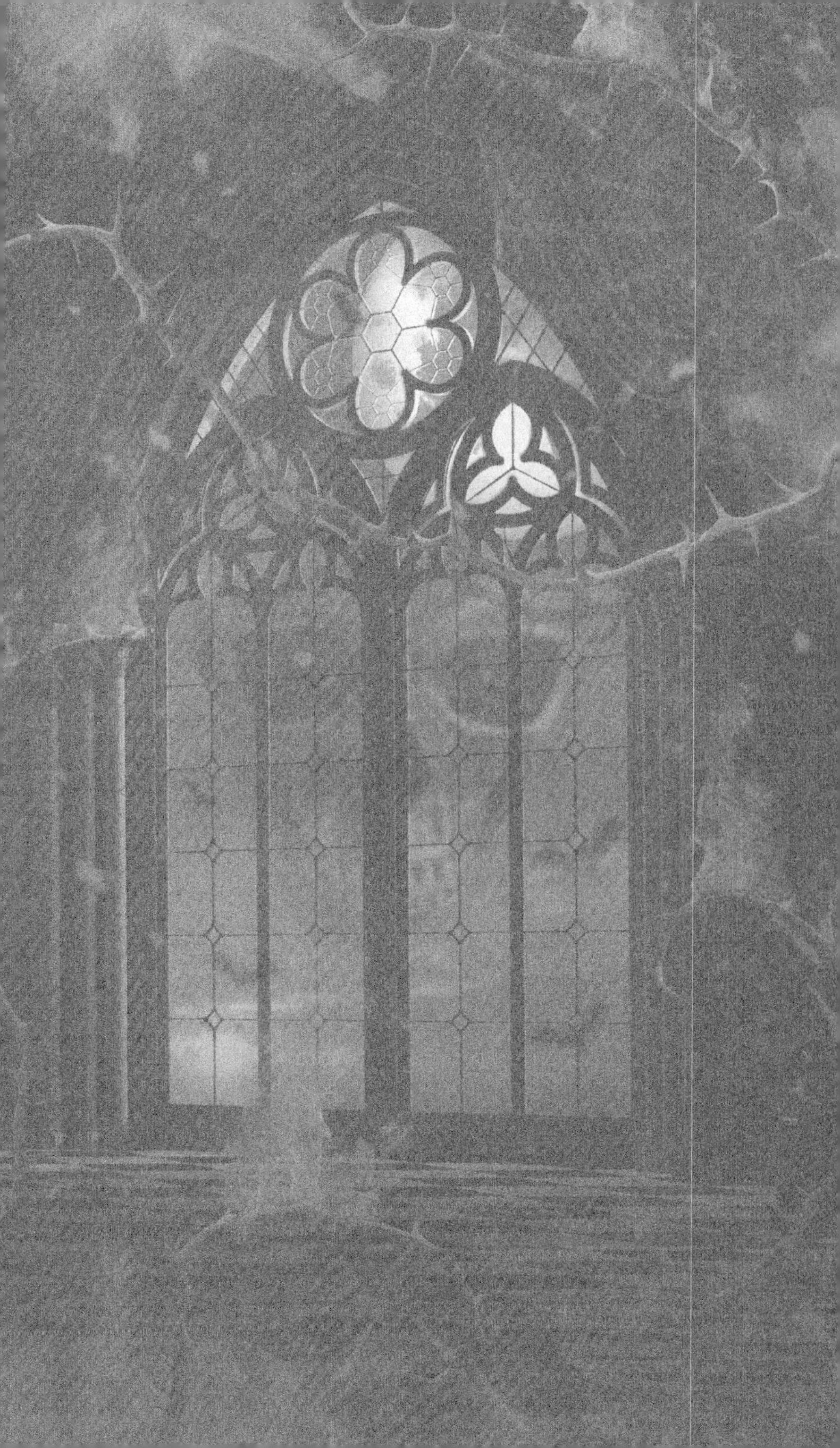

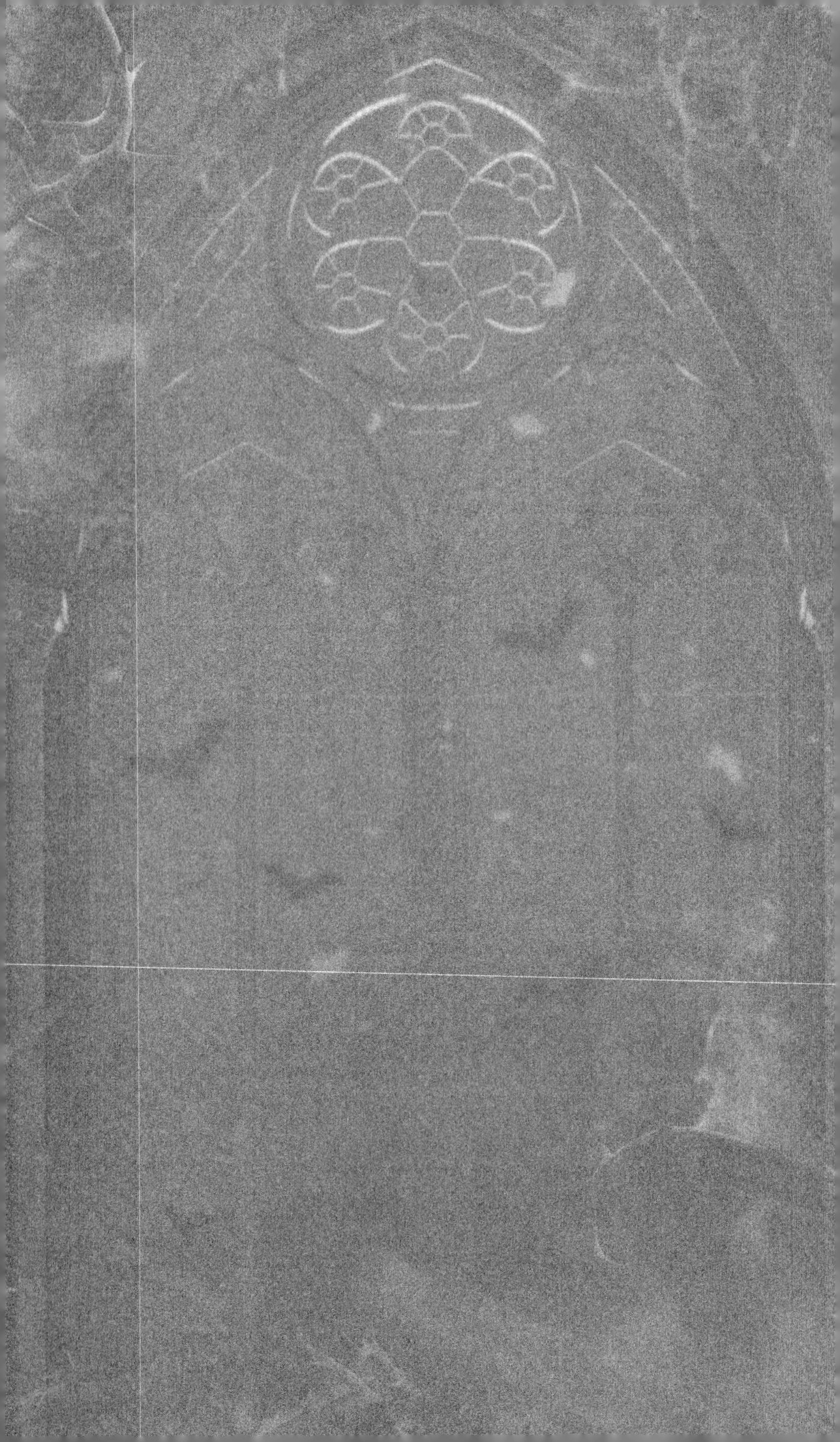

Forty

MAYA

Firethorne knelt down, moving his knife towards me, and I jerked backwards, scuttling away from him as best I could, but there was nowhere for me to go.

"Stay still, unless you want the knife to cut more than your ties," he hissed, running the blade under the tie at my ankles and cutting it loose. I stilled, and he did the same to the one on my wrists, freeing me. A move I didn't see coming.

"I'm full of surprises," he said, raising his brow at me, and then leaning into me, he ripped the tape from my mouth and threw it into the fire behind us, before whispering, "I like it better when they fight me. It turns me on."

Firethorne

He wanted me to fight.

It gave him pleasure.

And knowing that made me want to wretch.

I rubbed over the ache at my wrists and watched him stand up, throw the knife back onto his desk, then turn to face me, evil emanating from every pore.

"I won't go easy on you," he stated. "You cost me a hell of a lot of money. You cost me my reputation, too. Something I cherish more than anything in my line of business." He came to stand over me. "I'm the best at what I do, you see. People come to me because they know I can cater to every sick and twisted fantasy they've ever had." He cocked his head as he stared down at me. "And I'm about to show you what some of those fantasies are."

"Go to hell," I snarled, and he laughed.

"Sweetheart, I've lived in hell all my life." And grabbing the belt on his trousers, he pulled hard to open it, as he said, "It's my favourite place."

He whipped his belt from his trousers and wrapped it around my neck, and I clawed at the leather as he pushed the belt through the buckle and tightened it, creating a noose for my neck, making it difficult for me to breathe.

"I thought we'd do a little choking first; a bit of extreme breath play while you suck my dick." He shrugged. "Don't worry, I won't let you pass out, unless I really have to. I need to feel you sucking me, and if you do it well enough, you get to breathe. Anything else, and I'll choke the fucking life out of you. Think of it as a kinky game of Russian Roulette. If you perform, you live. Give me substandard head, and well... I don't think I need to tell you what the consequences will be. But just know, when you're unconscious, I will do the most fucked up shit to your body. So, trust me, staying conscious is the aim of the game."

I'd always said I hated Firethorne. But in this moment, I

despised him with every fibre of my being. I wanted to rain hell down on him. Make him bleed and feel every second of pain that he'd caused other people inflicted on him now.

If he wanted a game, I'd play. But I'd play by my rules.

He kept one hand on the belt and used the other to pop the button of his trousers open and pull the zip down. Then he pushed his trousers and boxers to his ankles and stood there, smirking at me, with his rancid cock standing to attention.

My heart broke as tears fell down my cheeks, and fear made my ears ring and my body shake.

No one was coming for me.

No one was going to save me.

I had to do this for myself.

He yanked my head forward by tugging on the belt and seethed, "Open your mouth, you fucking slut, and suck my fucking cock."

I didn't open at first.

I couldn't.

I didn't want to do this.

I squeezed my eyes shut, wishing myself away from this nightmare.

I felt the belt go slack, and I opened my eyes just in time to see his fist flying towards my face. A steel fist that hit my cheek hard and rattled my brain, knocking me onto my side from the force of the impact. Stars danced in front of my eyes, and the ringing in my ears turned to an ear-splitting screech that made me cry out in pain.

He leaned down, spit flying from his mouth as he screwed his face up and snarled, "I said suck my dick. Hesitate again and I'll use my knife to pry your fucking mouth open and then slice your face on every thrust. Do you understand?"

I nodded through my tears.

"Good. Now get on your knees and do your fucking job."

He took a hold of the belt again and jerked on it, forcing me to kneel. Then he took his dick in his free hand and pushed it against my lips.

"Open wide, slut. Let me in." And with a quieter, more menacing tone, he added, "I can't wait to split your fucking throat in two."

I breathed slowly through my nose, buying myself seconds before facing the inevitable.

"Remember," he teased. "Suck me good and you'll get through to the next stage."

I didn't want to get through to the next stage.

I wanted to die.

No.

Scrap that.

I wanted *him* to die.

Fighting against every instinct, I slowly opened my mouth, and he shoved himself inside me.

He used the belt for a while to lightly choke me as I sucked him and willed my mind to escape this room, to be anywhere but here. But eventually, he let go of it, getting lost in the way I was making him feel, holding the back of my head as he thrust hard into me and threw his head back, groaning into the room.

That's when I let my survival instincts kick in, and as he pushed his dick right down my throat, I didn't hesitate. I bared my teeth and bit down hard, as hard as I could, determined to never let go.

"Fucking Christ!" he screamed, as he fisted my hair and tried to pull me off him, but my teeth were clamped tight, and I wasn't going to let go.

He grabbed the belt and started to pull, but my teeth bit harder, forcing him to claw at my face, trying to force my jaw open as his blood coated my lips and filled my mouth, streaming down my throat. He lashed out, smacking and punching the side of my face, my head, any part of me he could hit, but this was the only chance I had. I wasn't going to let it go.

The knife was too far away for him to grab, and as I felt my teeth sinking through his flesh, I started to shake my head like a dog with a rag in its mouth. Within seconds, I'd bitten his dick off, blood pouring down my chin, and he slumped to the floor, passing out in front of me.

I wretched as I spat his dick out of my throat, puking all over the carpet as his blooded dick fell to the floor. And then, I shut my brain off, refusing to think about what I'd done as I lurched forward, grabbing the knife from the desk.

I knelt beside his body, holding the knife in both hands, and then I raised it over my head and plunged it into his chest.

"That's for my father," I hissed, and I yanked it back out again, then plunged it back in.

"And that's from me, you fucking piece of shit. Rot in hell," I snarled, as I pulled it out and then pushed myself to stand on quivering, boneless legs, holding the bloody knife in my hand in a death-like grip.

I stared at his lifeless body for a moment, then I spat at him, and turned my back, before darting across the room.

I had to get out of this hellhole, but before I did, I needed to find Damien.

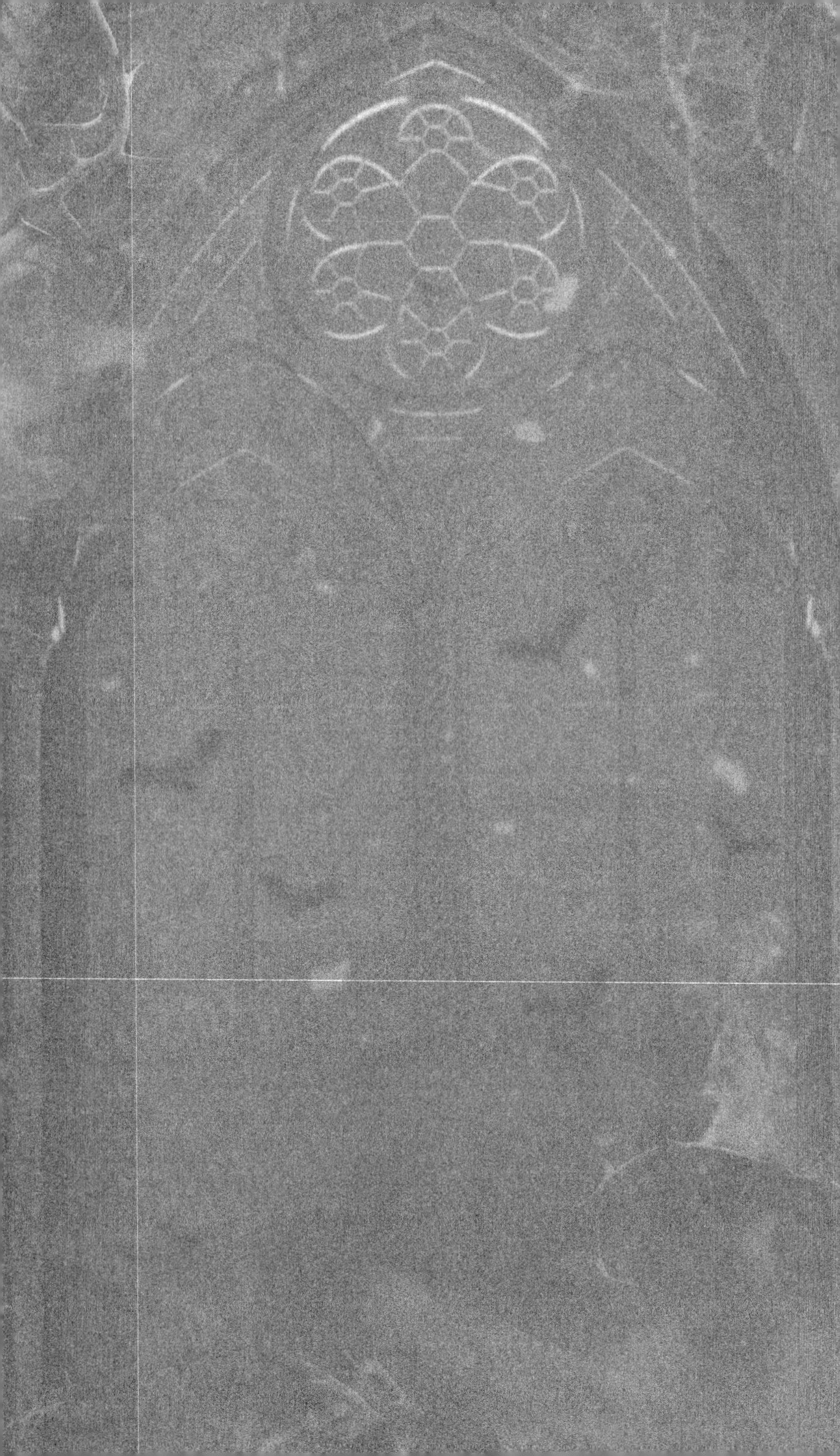

Forty-One

MAYA

I moved like I was on automatic pilot, my head swinging from left to right as I checked the hallways, but there was no one there. I headed for the staircase and ran down it as fast as I could, holding the rail to stop myself from tumbling as my feet scrambled to escape. And as I came to the bottom, I saw them, Miriam and Lysander, about to make their getaway through the front door.

They spun around and took one look at me, my breathing heavy, my face covered in blood, my eyes bulging and frantic, and the bloody knife still in my hand.

"Where is he?" I rasped.

Firethorne

Miriam looked shocked to see me. Then the shock turned to disdain as she sneered, "You can't save him. He's probably dead already."

I took a step closer, holding the knife up as I hissed, "I said, where is he?"

"It's pointless," Lysander interjected. "Just leave, Maya. Get out of here. You can't do anything to save him."

"Yes, I can." I gritted my teeth as I spoke. "Now tell me. Where the fuck is he?"

"Come on, let's get out of here," Miriam said to Lysander, trying to block me out. But I wouldn't let her.

"Try and leave, and I'll gut you like a fucking fish," I snarled.

"I'd like to see you try," Miriam goaded, but she had underestimated me.

I flew across the foyer, throwing my whole body at her, forcing her against the wall. Holding the knife to her throat, I glared at her, pinning her in place as I tilted my head and said, "Let's start again, shall we? Where. The fuck. Is he?"

She wasn't going to tell me. Her jaw was clamped shut and her eyes glared back at me with toxic venom.

Lysander stood in the doorway, making no effort to come between us, but quietly, he said, "He's in the cellar." And Miriam rolled her eyes, pissed that he'd given up so easily.

I didn't move, though. I didn't want to. I had Miriam right where I wanted her, and the urge to push on the knife and send her to hell to join her uncle was all-consuming. So much in fact, that I did push on the blade, pressing it into her skin and drawing blood, making her hiss from the pain.

But she didn't fight me.

She just kept her eyes on mine, that venom still burning within.

"Please, Maya," Lysander begged. "Just let us go."

He took a step closer, but I warned him, "Stay back," as I sliced a little deeper into Miriam's neck, drawing more blood to stop him from doing anything stupid.

"You're wasting time here, with us," he went on. "Time that could be used to save Damien, if he's still alive. Just let us go. Please."

"And let you run away like you always do?" I shot back. "You knew what was going on in this house. You knew what he was doing. You're as guilty as your father. You deserve to die. You both do."

I saw Lysander stiffen, but Miriam just laughed.

"Then you have a dilemma, *sweetheart*," she sneered. "Stay here and kill us or let us go and save him. You might be too late, already. But if you stay here and take us on, the sand in his timer will definitely have run out. So, what's it going to be?"

I hated that she was right.

I didn't have time for this.

"I will find you," I hissed, pushing the knife into her neck one last time. "And I will kill you. You won't get away with this."

Reluctantly, I took the knife off her neck and stepped back.

Instantly, Miriam raced over to the door, shouting to Lysander, "Let's get out of here."

Lysander followed her, but before he walked out of the door, he stopped and turned to look at me.

"I really am sorry, Maya. And you were right. I'd guessed what was happening here, but there was nothing I could do. Nothing at all."

"Save it for someone who gives a shit," I sneered and turned my back on him to run down the corridor, heading for the cellar.

Once I reached the kitchen, I shoved the doors open and they slammed off the walls. There was no one here. The kitchen was empty and quiet, except for the buzz of the electrical appliances.

The light of the moon shone over the pristine worktops.

Firethorne

Mrs Richardson wasn't in here, and I don't know why I'd expected her to be. But as I stood for a second, holding my breath and gazing around, I heard a scream, and I darted into action, hurtling across the room and through the door that'd lead me down to the depths of this place called hell.

I flew down the small staircase, thankful that I knew this part of the house after being down here myself for so many days, because it was pitch black, and all I had at my disposal were my wits, acute senses, and a knife that I gripped so tightly it felt like it'd become a part of me.

When I reached the bottom, I peered around. One of the rooms in the cellar was in darkness, the other was dimly lit. Then an almighty crack resounded off the walls, and Damien screamed in response. I bolted, charging into the dimly lit cellar, ready to rain hell.

And then I stopped, my already splintered heart bleeding freely when I saw what they'd done.

Damien's arms were above his head, and his wrists were shackled to the wall. He hung his head as blood dripped onto the dusty floor. But even though his body was broken and bleeding, and his bare chest was full of cuts from the lashes they'd inflicted on him, he hadn't given up. His muscles flexed, fighting the pain as he spat blood on the floor and growled through his clenched teeth.

The men stood in front of him, holding whips in their hands as they prepared to give him another lashing. A table of knives and weapons was waiting for them off to the side, but I wouldn't let them get to that stage.

"Get the fuck away from him," I growled, holding my knife out in front of me and bracing myself, as I took up a stance, ready to fight.

The two men turned around, and when they saw me, they started to laugh.

"I fucking mean it," I hissed, and I saw Damien lift his head to look at me, his eyes wide as he said, "No, Maya. Get out of here. Fucking go."

"Not without you," I stated, stepping back as the men moved closer to me.

"What are you gonna do with that, sweetheart?" one of them sneered as he pointed at my knife. "I'd be careful if I were you. You might hurt yourself."

The other one laughed at his partner and then cracked his whip in my direction, but I moved away just in time, faltering a little and praying they didn't notice.

This was my only chance.

I held my knife firmly, determined to show I could fight, but they weren't scared of me or the damage I could do. They were amused, and by the way they gave each other a wickedly sinful grin, they thought they'd just been gifted a new toy to play with.

"Get on the floor and put your hands behind your head," I commanded.

"Whatever you say, love," the other one said, mocking me and blowing me a kiss. Then he threw his whip to the floor and pulled out a flick knife from his back pocket and opened it. "Or we can play a little game." He cocked his head. "We like games."

"We really do," the first one bragged, and as he reached into his pocket and pulled out his weapon, gunshots rang out, and I dropped to the floor.

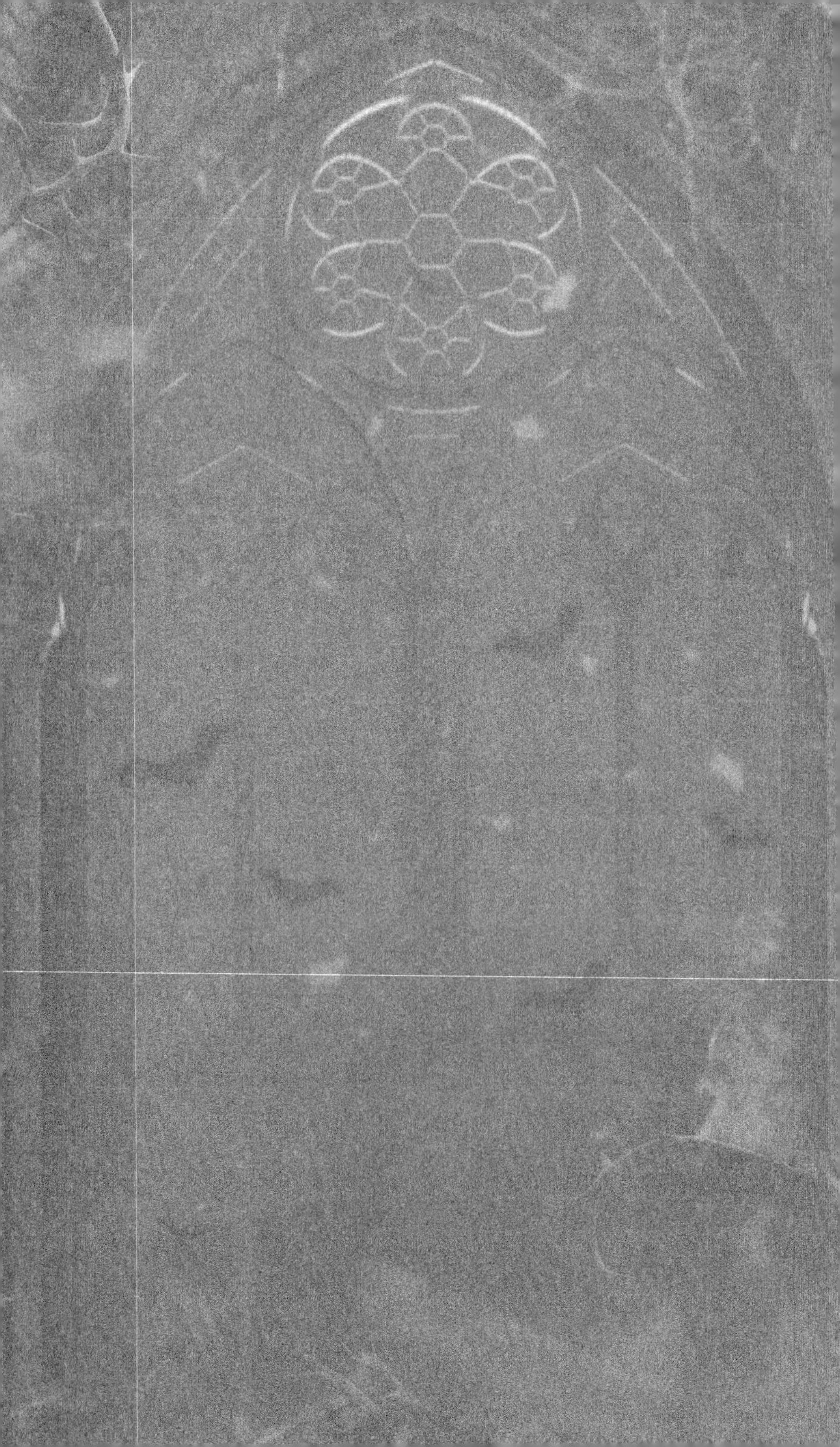

Forty-Two

MAYA

I cowered on the cold concrete, covering my head with my hands as the sound of the gunshots rang in my ears. I didn't want to open my eyes and see what'd happened. It was a reality I wasn't ready to face.

Had they shot Damien?

Were they about to shoot me?

I whimpered, scared out of my wits as I forced myself to open my eyes. And there, lying before me on the ground in pools of their own blood were the two men who'd tortured Damien.

Damien was still chained up, still breathing, but his eyes

weren't on me. He was looking at the doorway.

"I couldn't leave you here to die," a voice said from behind, and I glanced over my shoulder to see Lysander, standing there with a gun in his hand. "I've taken care of Beresford. And I'll do the same to anyone else I find on my way out, but I meant what I said earlier. You need to get out."

I swallowed through the razor blades embedded in my throat, trying to calm my racing heart as I blinked through my tears.

He took a moment, then nodded and turned around, leaving without uttering another word.

I was in shock.

I couldn't believe he'd come back to save us.

But fear soon eclipsed everything, and I sprang from the floor, running over to Damien.

I took his face in my hands as I asked frantically, "How do I get you out of these?" I reached up to grab the cuffs that he was enslaved in. "Where's the key?"

"His pocket," Damien rasped, coughing through the dryness in his throat. "The key is in his pocket."

He nodded to the dead guy to the left of him, and even though touching either of these men was the last thing I wanted to do, I stalked over to his body, knelt beside him, and pushed my hand into his pocket.

"He hasn't got it," I cried, after checking both pockets.

"Then that one'll have it," Damien said breathlessly, with urgency, and I scrambled over to the other guy, shoving my hands into his jeans in desperation.

And there, I found a key.

I jumped up, racing over to Damien, and I pushed the key into the lock. The cuffs clanked open, and Damien fell into my arms, relief at being free over-powering him in a rare moment of weakness. But he soon righted himself, strength flooding through him as he wrapped his arms around me and said, "I'm so sorry, Maya. I'm so fucking sorry."

"I'm fine," I told him, but he clenched his jaw and shook his head.

"I can see the blood and bruises on your face. You're not fine."

"I will be," I urged. "Once we get out of here. Can you walk?"

"Of course I can walk," he said, standing taller, but giving a quiet moan as the sting and ache of his wounds hit. But he was strong, and he knew what he had to do to survive, just like I did.

Damien took the knife out of my hand and put his arm around my shoulders as I wrapped mine tentatively around his waist. With fierce determination, we walked out of that cellar and headed towards the staircase that led back up to the house.

"Is he dead?" Damien asked, and I faltered.

"I stabbed him in the chest. Twice." I left out the other part. It wasn't something I wanted to admit out loud.

"But is he dead?" Damien repeated, urgency clear in his voice.

"I think so. He looked dead."

Damien's head fell back as he let out a frustrated breath.

"I need to see him," he demanded. "I have to make sure he's dead. I can't leave here without knowing that."

"But he is. I'm sure of it. And we don't have time for this, Damien. We have to go."

I didn't want him going up there and seeing what had happened.

"If he's dead, then there's no rush," he stated plainly. "He can't chase us if he's dead, can he?"

I couldn't argue with that logic, so I begged, "I don't want to be here for a second longer. Please, Damien. Come with me. Let me get you to a hospital."

"You can wait for me down here, or outside on the driveway," he told me. "But I can't let this go, Maya."

Firethorne

That was out of the question.

There wasn't a chance in hell that I was letting him out of my sight again, not after I'd just found him. But I didn't want him seeing what I'd had to do to escape, not without me being there.

"I go where you go," I said, placing my hand gently over his blood-soaked chest. "If you want to see his body, I'll go with you."

"No, Maya." Damien took my hand from his chest and placed a gentle kiss on the back. "I want you safe. That's what I've always wanted. That's what I live for. I'll be happier if you're out of this house."

"And I'll only be happy if I'm with you. I'm not leaving you again, Damien. I'm never leaving you."

He closed his eyes and rested his forehead against mine, and with the gentlest whisper, he said, "You know I love you, don't you?"

"I love you, too." I sighed. Wishing those words could've been spoken at a better time, and yet, the timing couldn't be more perfect if I really thought about it. Because we'd won. Love had kept us going and brought us to this place, where we were free. Nothing could hurt us now.

Or so I thought.

We held on to each other as we walked up the stairs that led to Firethorne's office. As we came to the top, we saw Beresford's dead body slumped against the wall. The bullet wound that Lysander had inflicted went straight through his forehead.

"Couldn't have happened to a nicer guy," Damien quipped as we passed him.

Then we came to the office door, and Damien pushed it open.

I expected to find Firethorne on the other side, lying on his back where I'd left him.

But he wasn't.

He was sitting up against his desk, his breaths short, sharp and laboured, as red stained the front of his shirt.

He had a blanket thrown over his lap to hide the mutilation I'd inflicted, and he looked ashen. But he wasn't dead, and that thought sickened me.

"And here... they are..." he managed to croak. "My beloved... son... and his... little... whore."

Even as he sat there, with no hope of fighting back, he still lashed his wicked tongue at us, thinking his words could hurt us.

"Father," Damien said, letting his arm drop from my shoulder as he stepped forward. He puffed his chest out as he pointed to his wounds with the knife in his hand and announced, "Is this the best you could do? A few lashings from two useless fuckers who wouldn't know how to torture a man if they tried."

Firethorne huffed.

"Looks like... I employed... the wrong... people," he stammered as his breaths became weaker. Then, pulling the blanket off his lap to expose his own wound, he added, "I should've... paid her... to do it. She really... knows... how to... get a job done." He glanced towards the fire, where his severed dick lay in a pool of watery vomit on the carpet in front of it.

Damien saw it, too.

And I almost threw up all over again.

Damien flew across the room and launched himself at his father, grabbing him around the neck, and dragging his limp body over to the fireplace where his dick lay.

The urge to finish what I'd started burned viciously inside me, and I ran over to them, taking the knife out of Damien's hand, desperate to use it again. But Damien blocked my attempts to fight, forcing me to move back so I didn't injure him.

Firethorne

"No, Maya," he said. "I need to do this." And then, addressing his father, he seethed, "I told you if you touched her, I'd break your fucking neck," he hissed in his ear as he added, "And now I'm going to prove to you that I'm a man of my word."

Holding his father's head in a vice-like grip, Damien yanked it to the side, breaking his neck with a snap that made me shudder. Then, Damien pushed his father's limp body head first into the roaring fire, giving Firethorne the ending he deserved, burning in his own hell.

"I'm not ready to hear about what happened here tonight," Damien said quietly. "But I will, eventually, and I want you to know I'll be there for you. I'll help you in whatever way I can. We will get through this."

"I know," I replied, dropping the knife and going to him. I wrapped both of my arms around him, burying my face in his neck as I let my tears flow freely. "I love you."

"I love you, too," he said, kissing the top of my head. "But we have to go. This place is going to go up in smoke."

Firethorne's body was on fire, and the flames were spreading to the carpet beneath him. There wasn't time to lose.

We bolted, racing out of the door and flying down the corridor.

When we came to the stairs, it suddenly hit me that Cora could be somewhere on the estate.

"Where's Cora?" I asked. "We need to make sure she's safe."

"She's not here," he told me as we took the stairs two at a time. "She's at her cottage in the town. She's safe, Maya. But we're not. We need to get away from here. Now."

When we reached the foyer, we ran to the front door.

"We need to run as far away from this place as we can," Damien said, pulling me by the hand, desperate to get us to safety.

And I agreed with him, to a point.

But the other half of me wanted to stay and watch this place burn. I wanted to see it razed to the ground like it should be. Like it deserved to be.

We raced down the front steps of the manor and then charged down the driveway, heading away from the chaos towards the wrought iron gates of the Firethorne estate. When they came into view, I slowed down, letting the other half of my brain take over.

"I want to see it burn," I told him, panting as we both came to a standstill. "I *need* to see it burn."

"You need to see it burn like I needed to check that he was dead," Damien replied, understanding right away where I was coming from.

I nodded, and he stood behind me, wrapping his arms around me as we stood facing the manor.

At first, the fire was just a glow in an upstairs window. But eventually, that glow spread from room to room, and then black smoke billowed into the starry night sky as the flames grew stronger.

It was surprising how quickly it spread, glass shattering as the building groaned from the pressure of the heat of the fire, all sounds we could hear, even from the distance we were standing. But even more surprising was the fact that no sirens were blaring in the distance. No one had called the fire brigade. Maybe no one cared. Perhaps, they wanted it to burn as much as we did. It wouldn't surprise me.

As time moved on, and the flames engulfed the manor house, Damien reminded me that emergency services, or worse still, The Butcher's people would be heading to the estate soon, and we needed to leave.

I thought how fitting it would be for The Butcher to find a pile of ashes. It was all he deserved. That, and the reception he'd receive from Damien's men.

You see, Damien told me, as we watched his childhood home burn to the ground, that *he* might've been exposed when his father tracked his movements, but by the grace of God, he'd managed to keep the identities of his associates secret.

It was one of the reasons his father had kept him alive for so long, torturing him to get those names.

But Damien didn't break.

And he was confident that Trent, Isaiah, and anyone else working with him would have intel on The Butcher's movements tonight.

Once he stepped foot on English soil, he was a dead man walking.

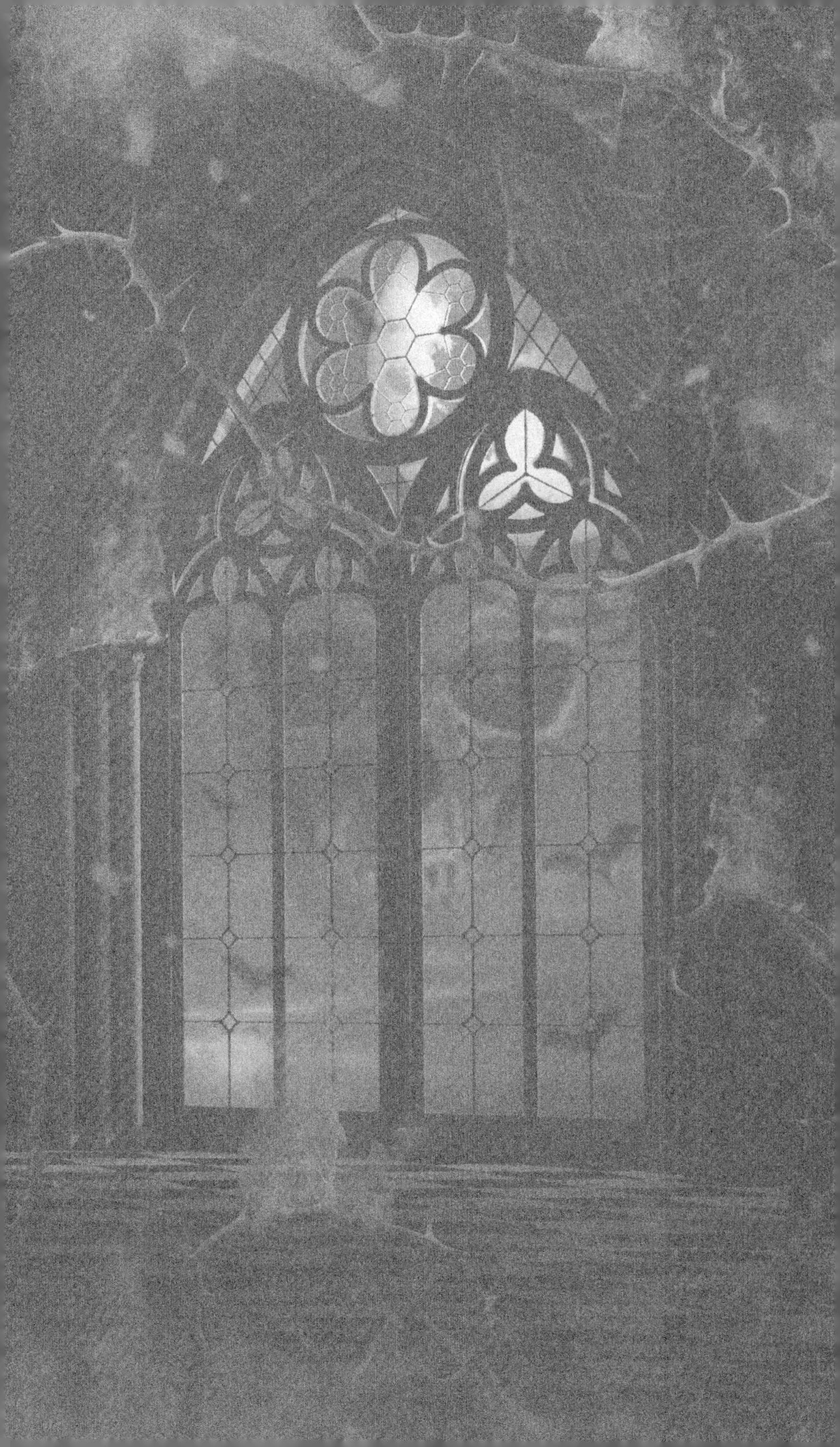

Forty-Three

MAYA

The fallout from the fire and the days that followed were some of the hardest we'd ever lived through.

I knew that for the time being, I'd have to live my life filled with unbearable anger, regret and inconsolable grief. My father had betrayed me, but I still loved him. I hated him, too, but I had to find a way to learn to live with that. After all, I hadn't fought so hard to survive, only to live a bitter half-life.

I wanted a full life.

The life I...

No...

We deserved.

Firethorne

I never found out why I kept seeing the shadowed figure behind me when I was at the apartment, being cared for by Damien. But I liked to think it was my father watching over me, making sure I knew that he was still there.

But I never saw it again.

Maybe my mind had been playing tricks on me, but it gave me comfort to think it was him.

That he wanted to make amends.

Wanted to put right what he'd done.

It helped me to think that was the case, anyway.

On the fateful night, when the fire engines eventually showed up, they battled throughout the night to put out the fire. By morning, all that remained was a shell of the mansion it'd been. Blackened ruins that Damien wanted to tear down with his bare hands.

As the firefighters had fought the blaze and the police began to scour the grounds, we managed to get to the woodland where my father was, before anyone else found him. Damien, Trent, and another man I'd never met before, who was introduced to me as Isaiah, worked together to cut my father down and then dispose of the noose. Damien begged me to stay in the van so I wouldn't have to witness it, and I agreed to do as he'd asked. I didn't want to see my father's body again.

Trent and Isaiah took my father, and a few weeks later, we were able to give him a proper burial in the cemetery in our old town.

The town I'd left behind.

We buried him next to my mother, and I felt some comfort, knowing that he was finally at peace.

The Butcher never did show up to the manor that night, but Damien assured me he'd been dealt with. I didn't need to know any more than that. Damien told me his men had their ways of dealing with things, and I was relieved to know that another sicko had been taken off the face of this earth.

As for Damien's father, the investigators found his charred remains in the wreckage, along with those of Beresford and the two other men, the ones who'd tortured Damien in the cellar. There was talk of a criminal investigation, that maybe it'd been arson or some other foul play. But the townspeople weren't forthcoming when questioned about the family and what went on at the estate. It was a blight on their town that they didn't want to acknowledge, a stain they were relieved to know had been snuffed out.

The police tried to track Lysander, Miriam, and Damien down to question them, but we all went to ground, hiding from the authorities. From the intelligence Damien received, Lysander and Miriam weren't in the country anymore. Apparently, they were living in France, as a couple, and partaking in the lifestyle they'd thrived on when they lived here with their exclusive 'parties'.

Their days were numbered, though.

We'd sent an elite group to France to join them at their next event. I don't think they were going to enjoy the toys I'd sent over that were specially engraved with my name and a 'fuck you' on them. But those bullets were nothing that they didn't deserve.

As time passed, and Damien's associates worked their magic, hacking into police files and altering the trajectory of the case, things began to die down. The deaths in the manor were reported as accidental, and to everyone's relief, the case was eventually closed.

Damien decided to adopt a whole new identity, discarding the name Firethorne and taking on a surname that didn't carry the shame that his real name had. Of course, this was all carried out by his people, hidden from the powers that be, so he could remain hidden. But there was one person he didn't hide from.

Cora.

The day after the fire, we secretly visited her in her cottage

Firethorne

in the town. She looked exhausted when she opened the door, but when she saw Damien, her face lit up.

She invited us in and put her kettle on to make drinks. And then, as she sat down at her little wooden table with us in her kitchen, she said, "I only ever stayed there because of you, son. I felt like it was my duty to watch over you, in a way." She paused, and then in a solemn voice, she added, "I saw what they did to your mother."

Damien tensed, and said, "I'm not sure I want to know what happened to her. Not yet."

"A story for another day, then." Cora nodded to herself. "I'll always be here, ready to talk, whenever you need closure."

I wasn't sure if Damien would want that closure. I think he'd blocked out whatever had happened. He knew it wasn't going to be a pleasant story. Nicholas Firethorne didn't have some sordid love affair with his mother, that much was true. The truth of what actually happened lay in the grey areas where Damien always told me he lived, and the secrets and lies that were buried at Firethorne.

Maybe Damien's mother was out there somewhere. Maybe she'd been one of the girls who'd survived.

Or maybe not.

But that was Damien's decision on whether he wanted to find out.

As if reading my mind, he straightened in his seat, and without looking up from the coffee cup he was staring at on the table, he asked, "Is she still alive?"

"No," Cora replied, sorrow on her face as she reached across the table to try and touch Damien's hand.

But he remained still, his hands in his lap as he replied, "I don't need to know any more then. She's at peace. That's enough for me."

"She is," Cora said, moving her hand away and sitting back in her chair. "She'd have been so proud of you, though. So, so proud of what you've done." Cora didn't elaborate further, which made me question how much she really knew about that family, but then, what did it matter now? The Firethorne branch of the business had been destroyed.

That chapter was over.

But the war raged on.

Damien had made it clear that once the heat died down, he'd be going back to work. Evil was still out there, and he'd worked too hard to walk away now. He still had targets he needed to take down.

We left Cora's cottage soon after and agreed to stay in touch. Cora whispered to Damien that she wouldn't tell a soul that we'd been there, and we believed her. We trusted her.

We gave her one last hug and then headed down her path, towards a new life that awaited us.

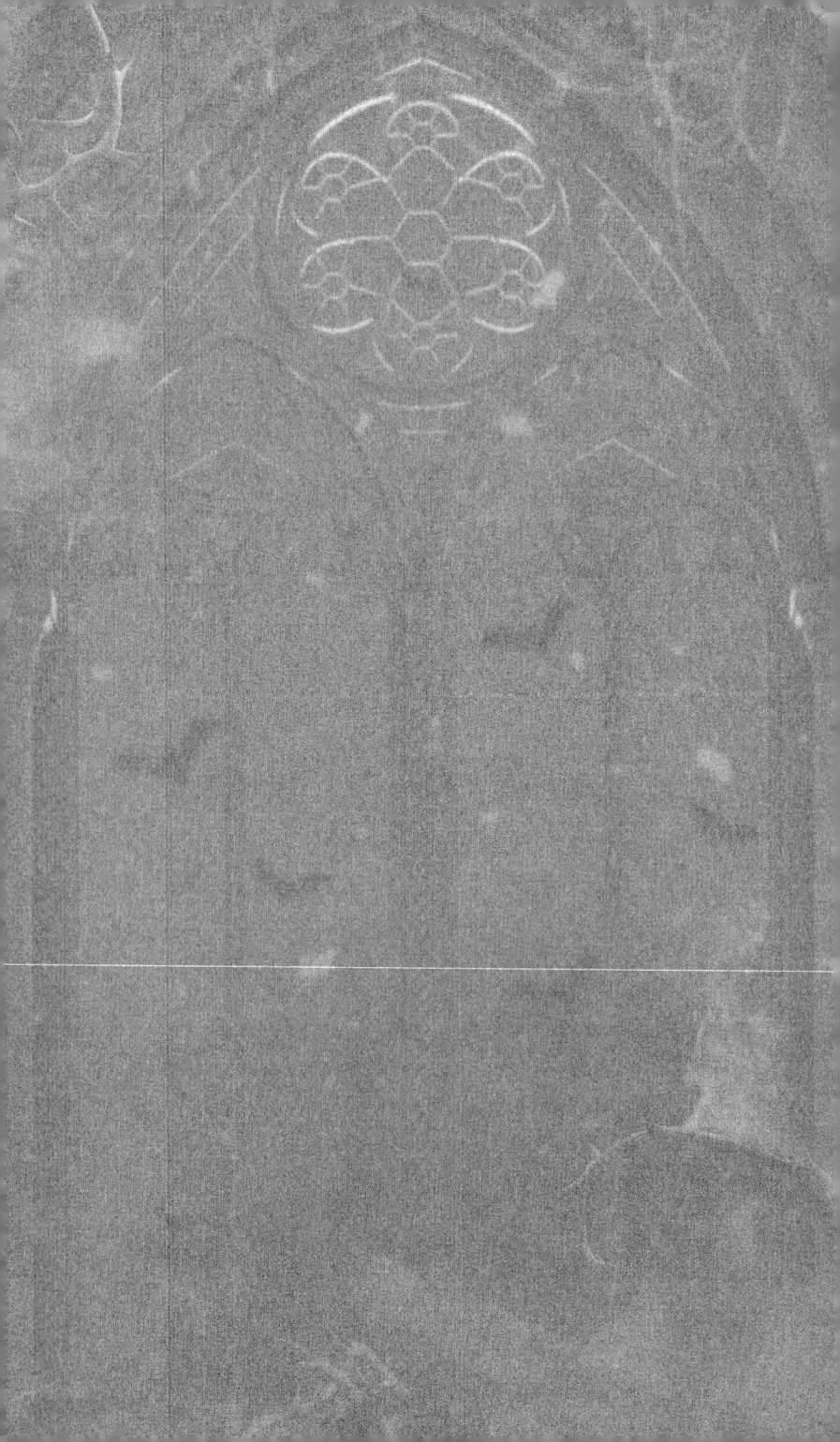

Epilogue

TWO YEARS LATER
MAYA

Damien had been standing in the window all morning, cursing the timekeeping of the delivery company and huffing as he peered up and down the lane outside.

"They're not going to appear any quicker because you're standing there," I told him.

But he refused to move, stating, "They're three minutes away, or at least, that's what the last text said fifty minutes ago."

"They probably got lost down the country lanes. This isn't the easiest cottage to get to," I reminded him, but he just scoffed, crossing his arms over his chest and glaring at the lane outside.

I knew he was excited. He kept telling me this was my day, but it was his as much as mine.

We heard the faint rumble of an engine, and then a white van ambled down the lane, stopping outside our gate.

"I'll get it." Damien sprang into action, heading for the front door before the driver had even gotten out of his van.

I took his place at the window, watching him stride down the drive and open the gate, greeting the driver as he jumped down from his cab and went to the back of his van to retrieve the boxes. Damien went to the back of the van, too, and took the first box off the delivery driver, turning to walk back down our path and into our cottage with a huge, shit-eating grin on his face.

As he came into the dining room and put the box on the table, I told him, "I'll come and help."

But he shook his head.

"We've got this." He pointed at the box and said, "Don't open this without me." Then he marched back out, heading to the van to help with more of the boxes.

Once the last box had been placed on the table, the delivery driver's paperwork signed, and the front door had been locked, we both stood over the table, staring at the boxes like two kids at Christmas, ready to open their presents.

"Go on then," Damien urged, gesturing to the box closest to me. "Open it. I want to see how it turned out."

I picked up the scissors I'd brought in from the kitchen, and used them to slice through the parcel tape across the top of the box. Then I pulled the box open and stared in wonder at the contents.

"That cover looks even better in real life. It's stunning," Damien said, lifting one of the books out and turning it over in his hand to see the blurb at the back.

"I love it," I said, lifting another copy out, unable to keep the grin off my face as I traced my fingers over the foil embossed title, *Firethorne, A Dark, Gothic Novel*. "I can't believe I wrote this. I'm a published author."

"I'm so fucking proud of you," Damien said, leaning in to place a kiss on my head.

"Do you think anyone will believe it's a true story?" I mused.

"Who cares?" Damien shrugged. "It's our story. That's all that matters."

After everything that'd happened at Firethorne, and with my father, Damien had suggested I see a counsellor, and she had suggested that my idea, to write about what had happened to us, was a good one. That it'd be cathartic. And it was. It was a form of therapy to get it all down in a book, every thought and feeling, every wild and wicked thing, the good, the bad, and the downright ugly. And when I'd finished, I'd shown Damien.

He read it and told me I should publish it. I didn't think it was good enough. I wasn't convinced people would want to read a story like ours. But he had more faith in me than I had in myself, and he sent my manuscript off to various publishers, until one of them came back to us, eager to take it on.

Which brought us to today, the two of us, standing in our idyllic cottage in the middle of the countryside, holding copies of my first book, *Firethorne*. A book that would enter the world on Damien's birthday, October thirtieth.

I thought that was a fitting touch, having the dates coincide, seeing as he was the inspiration behind the whole thing.

He'd encouraged me, been there when I felt like a failure, or when the dreaded imposter syndrome struck, and I questioned why I was even trying to become an author.

He believed in me, always.

"I'm so fucking proud of you," he said as he flicked through the book. "Can I keep this copy?"

"You can have as many copies as you like."

Firethorne

I laughed as he grabbed a pen and thrust it towards me.

"You need to sign it, then. I want my copy signed by the author. It could be worth a lot of money in the future. It's a first edition."

"It might be the only edition," I replied, and he tutted at me.

"I know for a fact our shelves will be full of Maya Cole bestsellers in the future. This book is only the start. You've got more stories inside you still to be written."

"I'm so glad you have faith in me," I replied as I opened his copy and signed my name with the message, 'Forever my muse. My love. My Damien.'

"I fucking love you," Damien growled as he took the book off me and grinned at the message I'd written. "And this," he went on, holding the book up. "Is the best birthday present I've ever had."

"I love you, too," I said, leaning in to kiss him on the cheek and wrap my arms around his waist. "So fucking much."

I closed my eyes, losing myself in the warmth of his body, the comforting smell of him, and the sound of his deep, velvety voice as he cleared his throat and started to read our story...

"I know we made the right decision," my father said, smiling absent-mindedly as we sat in the dimly lit carriage of the night train. "Leaving that town and taking this job, it's the best thing that could've happened to us. It'll be a fresh start. Just what we need."

The End
Copyright @ Nikki J Summers 2024

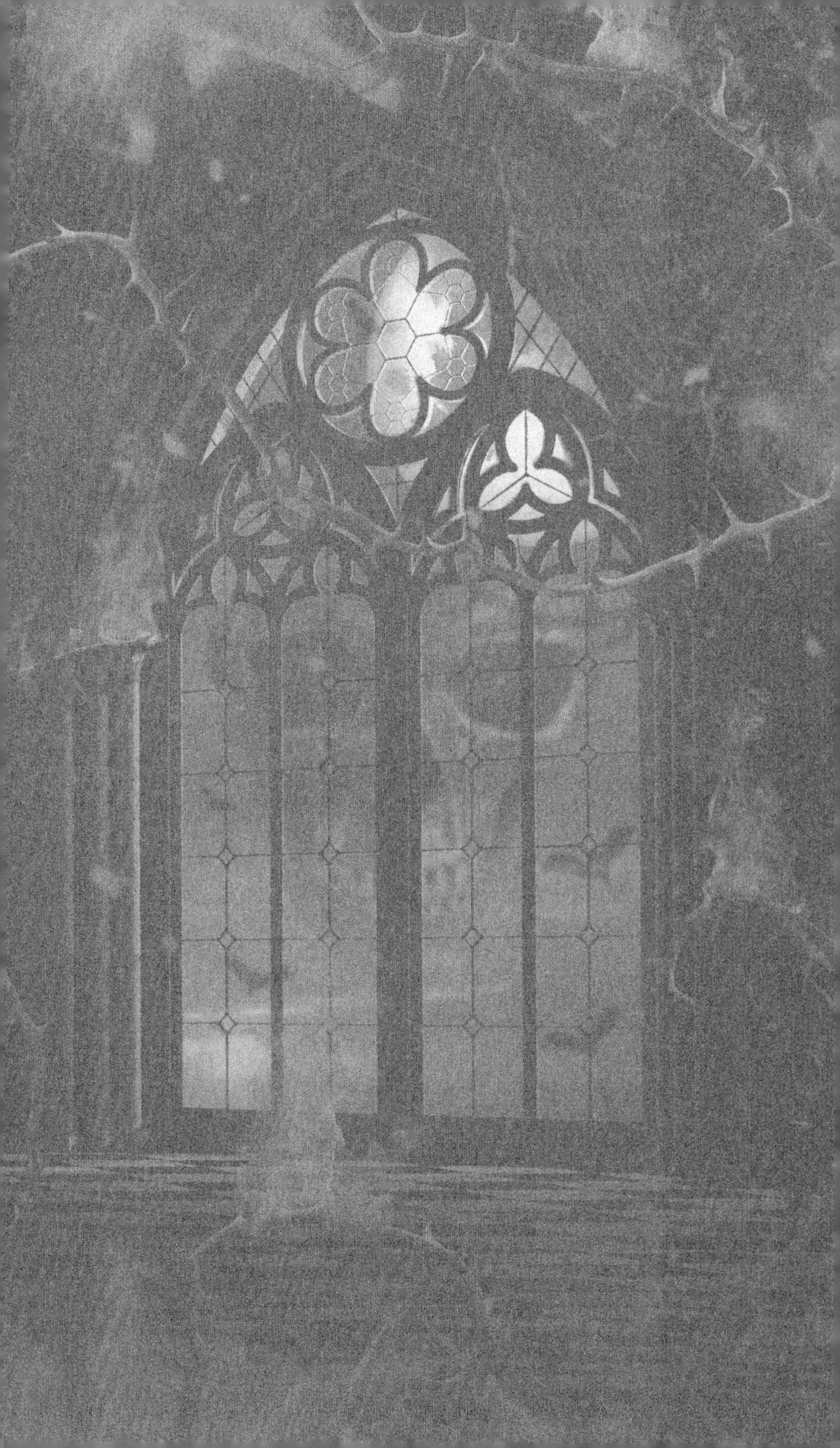

Coming Soon

THE TASKMASTER

NIKKI J SUMMERS

A Dark, Standalone Romance
*They took her from me.
Now, I'm going to send them all to hell.*
https://mybook.to/TheTaskmaster

Author Acknowledgments

Firethorne was a labour of love for me. Of all the characters I've ever written, these were some of my favourites, and yes, even Miriam is included in that statement. I have so many people I need to thank for helping me and making this book what it is today.

First of all, my family. Thank you for everything you do to help me, so I can concentrate on my writing. That includes all the cooking and cleaning. Haha. But seriously, you support me, listen to me when I'm feeling down, and you're always there. I couldn't do this without you. Thank you.

Next, I must thank SBR Media and my agent, LaSheera Lee, who has helped me so much since things got a little crazy. Thank you for all your help and guidance. Plus, I love your motivational Facebook posts!

This book wouldn't be what it is today without the magic touch of some amazing and truly talented people. Designs By Charly, thank you for creating the most amazing cover, internal formatting, and for designing gorgeous teasers that have blown my mind. You're incredible. I appreciate everything you've done. Also, Emily Wittig Designs, for producing the most stunning special edition for this book. I could not stop looking at that cover. It is awesome. Thank you. To Lou J Stock, thank you for formatting the special edition and always adding that special touch. You ladies are brilliant at what you do and I'm so thankful to have found you.

To Lindsey Powell, for being an amazing editor and an even more amazing friend. You always go above and beyond for me, and I would be lost without your friendship and support. I'm so grateful for all you do. Thank you, my lovely friend.

Caroline Stainburn, thank you for having the most

incredible eye for detail and helping me to polish this story. Your edits are always first class. Thank you for being there, listening to me, helping and guiding me through this whole process. You're amazing.

To Candi Kane PR, you're the best at what you do and I'm so grateful for all your help to spread the word about my book. Thank you for organising the cover reveal, release day, and all the promotion. You've made my life a million times easier.

I will forever be amazed and in awe of all the awesome, hardworking, and truly talented book bloggers, bookstagrammers, Tik Tokers and everyone on social media who take the time to read, promote, and spread the word about our books. Your work is amazing, and you always go above and beyond. I am truly grateful. Thank you for every single post, share, and comment. It means the world. I wish I could list everyone, but the acknowledgments would be longer than this story! You all do such a fantastic job. Thank you from the bottom of my heart.

To the indie author community, I love how supportive, encouraging, and utterly amazing you are. Strength comes from lifting each other up, and you do that with so much style. Thank you. I'm proud to be a part of such a fabulous community.

Last, but not least, to all the readers out there who have taken the time to download, read, and review Firethorne, thank you. Thank you for taking a chance on me. Thank you for making this all worthwhile. Thank you for being as enthusiastic about Firethorne as I am. Your messages and comments give me life. I'm so grateful for you. Thank you for sticking with me through this journey. Here's to many more in the future!

Lots of Love,
Nikki x

About the Author

Nikki J Summers is a British author who was born and raised in Birmingham, the home of the *Peaky Blinders*. She currently lives in Staffordshire with her husband, two children, and a cavapoo called Poppy.

Nikki writes U.K. based new adult, dark, and contemporary romance stories about morally grey heroes who would burn the world to save their heroine. Those heroines usually save themselves, but the heroes are always by their side, holding the matches.

When she's not writing, you'll find Nikki curled up with a good book, bingeing a Netflix box set, or out walking her dog.

She loves to hear from readers, so please feel free to reach out.

To receive updates on all things Nikki J Summers,
sign up for her newsletter.
https://nikki-j-summers.ck.page/de073fb83a

Printed in Great Britain
by Amazon